TRANSLATION OF THE ARAMAIC TEXT FROM THE COVER ILLUSTRATION:

Hear, O Israel! The Lord is our God, the Lord alone. You shall love the Lord your God with all your heart and with all your soul and with all your might. Take to heart these instructions with which I charge you this day. Impress them upon your children. Recite them when you stay at home and when you are away, when you lie down and when you get up. Bind them as a sign on your hand and let them serve as a symbol on your forehead; inscribe them on the doorposts of your house and on your gates.

You shall not take vengeance or bear a grudge against your countrymen. Love your neighbor as yourself. I am the Lord.

DEUTERONOMY 6:4-9
LEVITICUS 19:18
THE GOSPEL OF MARK 12:29-31

THE ALEXANDRIA LETTER

George Honig

GEORGE R. HONIG

Synergy Books

The Alexandria Letter
Published by Synergy Books
P.O. Box 80107
Austin, Texas 78758

For more information about our books, please write to us, call
512.478.2028, or visit our website at www.synergybooks.net.

Publisher's Cataloging-in-Publication
(Provided by Quality Books, Inc.)

Honig, George R., 1936-
    The Alexandria letter / by George R. Honig.
    p. cm.
    Includes bibliographical references.
    LCCN 2009933518
    ISBN-13: 978-0-9823140-8-1
    ISBN-10: 0-9823140-8-6

    1. Christianity--History--Sources--Fiction.
2. Bible. N.T.--Sources--Fiction. 3. John, the Baptist,
Saint--Sources--Fiction. 4. Paul, the Apostle, Saint--
Sources--Fiction. 5. Jesus Christ--Sources--Fiction.
6. Suspense fiction, American. 7. Detective and mystery
stories, American.   I. Title.

PS3608.O53A44 2010   813'.6
                    QBI09-600130

10 9 8 7 6 5 4 3 2 1

To my dear wife Olga,
With love and gratitude,

And in loving memory of Karen

1

Late one evening, in the spring of the year 362, the venerable Athanasios, Bishop of Alexandria, received a visit from one of his deacons.

"I am obliged to bring you disturbing news," the deacon said to him. "I learned today from one of our catechumens of a Jew in this city who has been disseminating scurrilous falsehoods about our religion and our holy scriptures. This man has discouraged others of the Jews from being baptized into our faith, and he has been telling the most vicious lies about our Gospels. He claims to have an old manuscript, a lengthy epistle of some sort, that contradicts, in a most evil fashion, the writings of our revered saints."

"That must be stopped immediately," the bishop replied. "Who is this man?"

"He is called Maimon…Maimon ben Levi."

The scribe's wooden desk was piled high with stacks and bundles of parchments, scrolls, and manuscripts. An adjacent wall shelf was filled with yet other documents, as well as a number of books. Two small oil lamps provided the dim illumination of the room that late night. From the bed, close by, Maimon could hear the soft, rhythmic sounds of his wife's breathing. She had gone to sleep a long while earlier, as he continued on to complete one final bill of sale. It was a contract for the transfer of several parcels of land, and Maimon had promised to deliver the completed document early the next morning. He had accepted more work that week than he could normally handle, and now he needed to give up his sleep to make good on his commitments.

As a scribe and a notary, Maimon followed the profession of his father and of his grandfather before him. In addition to his native Greek, he was proficient in Latin and the Coptic Egyptian language, as well as Hebrew and Aramaic, and his services were much in demand in Alexandria.

After finally completing his work for the night, Maimon extinguished one of the lamps, and then he roused his wife.

"Sara, you must be certain to wake me at dawn. I still need to review this contract before I deliver it."

In the morning, Maimon made several small additions to the bill of sale he had prepared, and then he went out to deliver the document to his client.

He met with the man, a wealthy Greek landowner, and together they made a careful review of the contract to be certain that everything was in order. Finally, Maimon presented the bill for his work.

"Twenty denarii—why, that's robbery!" his customer said. "The last contract you drew up for me was for only half that much."

"I suppose I was rather generous to you that time," Maimon replied. "But I will remind you that this one was much longer and more complicated, and besides, you needed it in only one day. It took me all of yesterday and most of last night to finish it. Any other scribe would have charged you far more.

"Thief," the man growled, as he threw the bronze coins onto the ground, obliging Maimon to pick them up.

Afterward, Maimon proceeded toward the marketplace of the Jewish quarter, to make contact with a client there. On his way, he encountered another of Alexandria's notaries, his own cousin Ezekiel.

"Ezekiel!" he said, "where have you been? I haven't seen you in weeks."

"I've been spending most of my evenings at the Christian catechetical school," Ezekiel replied. "I've been receiving instruction there. In fact, they tell me that I'm now ready for my baptism. That will take place at St. Mark's Basilica tomorrow morning."

"Those people despise us," Maimon said. "They spit on us and treat us like dogs. Why would you want to become a Christian? Oh, I'll wager that your Greek wife had something to do with that."

"Well, yes," Ezekiel said. "When we were first married, Philomena made an occasional visit to the Temple of Zeus, and one time she offered a sacrifice at the Temple of Athena. None of that seemed important to her, but when she converted to Christianity, she became quite religious, and she began to attend church every Sunday. When the baby was born, she gave me no peace until I consented for him to be baptized. So, all in all, I've come to believe that for harmony in my family, it would be best for me to convert also."

Maimon paused for a long while. "That might be a bad mistake, especially if the Emperor Julian carries out his plan to rebuild the Temple in Jerusalem. The Christians have been telling anyone who will listen that God has forsaken us Jews. They say that now they are God's chosen people. They claim that this is our punishment for not accepting their Jesus, and that the destruction of our Temple is proof that God abandoned us. Well, if the Temple is restored, who will believe anything they say?"

"I can't imagine the emperor would really do that," Ezekiel replied.

"There's something else," Maimon said. "I'm sure I told you about the old manuscript, a long letter, actually, that I got from my father, the one that's been in our family for so many years. Have I shown it to you?"

"No," Ezekiel replied.

"There is a great deal in those pages that you really should know about before you commit yourself to becoming a Christian. Come to my house after dinner, and I'll show it to you."

Ezekiel stared blankly for a moment, and then nodded before he took leave of his cousin.

Maimon's customer was nowhere to be found in the marketplace, so he returned home to resume his work.

Later that afternoon, a middle-aged man, a Greek whose accent made it clear that he was not a native Alexandrian, appeared at Maimon's door.

"My name is Andros," he said. "I need to have a will drawn up, and you have been recommended to me as a competent notary."

"Certainly, please come inside. I will be happy to prepare a will for you, but I must let you know that it will be at least a week before I'll be able to take on any new work," Maimon said. The two of them sat down together near Maimon's writing desk, and he explained to the man the specific information he would need in order to draw up the document.

"So then, I'll prepare everything you asked for, and return here in a week," the man replied.

That evening, Ezekiel arrived considerably later than Maimon had expected. Suffering from a lack of sleep, Maimon was barely able to remain alert, and he was rapidly approaching the point where he could no longer stay awake despite his best efforts to do so.

"Here is the manuscript," Maimon said as he reached up to a shelf near his bed, took down a cloth-covered bundle, and unfolded the heavy wool wrapper that protected a large sheaf of papyrus pages. "You should read this before you make any final decision about going for baptism. I promise it will give you a very different picture about Christianity than what they've been teaching you. I do wish you'd come earlier in the evening," he added, yawning. "I can't go any longer without some sleep."

"Well then, would you mind if I take the manuscript home with me?" Ezekiel asked. "I'll take good care of it and bring it back in the morning."

Maimon was all too happy to accede to his cousin's request.

That night, long past midnight, three men entered Maimon's house, slipping silently through a side window. Two of them moved directly to the bed where Maimon and his wife were sleeping. Each was armed with a razor-sharp stiletto. The men positioned themselves carefully on either side of the bed, and then, with deft synchrony, they plunged their blades deep into the hearts of their victims.

Paralyzed by searing pain, neither Maimon nor Sara uttered a sound. Within seconds, Maimon's chest filled with blood, and he and Sara, who had suffered the same fate, were soon dead.

"The deacon ordered us to find a manuscript and bring it back so he can destroy it," one of the men whispered, "but that fool Andros failed to tell us that there are piles of parchments and papers everywhere here. There's no way we can know which one he wants, and we can't possibly take all of them with us."

The men quickly revised their plan. They gathered up all of the scrolls, manuscripts, and books in the house, stacking them over the bodies of Maimon and his wife. Then, they emptied the contents of Sara's large jug of olive oil onto the bed, taking care to saturate the manuscripts with the thick, brownish liquid. Finally, they set the bed afire using the flame from the oil lamp that had remained burning on Maimon's writing desk. The fire was tentative and very smoky at first, but once the papyrus scrolls began to burn, the conflagration gained strength rapidly. The men made their escape only minutes before the entire house went up in flames.

Ezekiel ben Aaron had taken home with him the manuscript he had borrowed from his cousin Maimon. He spent the entire night reading its pages and reflecting on the meaning of its text. In the end, much to his wife's unhappiness, he elected not to present himself for baptism.

After the period of mourning for Maimon and his wife had ended, Ezekiel paid a visit to his uncle Levi, Maimon's bereaved father, bringing him the manuscript.

"Maimon lent this to me," Ezekiel said. "I am returning it to you."

The letter remained with Levi's family, passed on from father to son, from generation to generation.

2

To my dear grandson Joshua, with my kindest greetings,

As I write to you now, our holy city of Jerusalem is in turmoil. Roman soldiers in full battle armor with helmet, dagger, and sword, are everywhere to be seen, especially in the precincts near the Temple. It is their purpose to suppress disorder and rebellion and to capture those Jews who resist and fight against their occupation. The Romans try to enlist the help of informants who are willing to betray their countrymen for money, and sometimes they succeed. But more often, they arrest any Jews on the slightest suspicion of sedition.

On a recent day, their soldiers rounded up more than twenty young men. The most tragic of them was a boy of not more than eleven years. Thin and pale, dressed in scarcely more than rags, the lad had been sent out to find firewood. It was his misfortune to be nearby when the Romans made the arrest of two men. The soldiers beat the three of them severely, then put them in chains and dragged them away.

The boy, who had no understanding of what was happening, began to cry as the group of them were dragged along. The Romans showed no pity for the terrified child, but some of the other prisoners, in spite of their own fear and foreboding, tried to console him with kind words. One prisoner tried to explain to his Roman captors that the lad was not guilty of anything, and that it was a mistake to have arrested him. The reply he got was a blow to the side of his face from a heavy club.

The punishment inflicted on them, surely the cruelest that the Romans could devise, followed immediately: each in turn, the child among them, was bound to a post and flailed mercilessly with leather whips fitted with razor-sharp tips of lead. This savagery was continued until their flesh hung from their bones in bloody shreds. Then, the remains of their torn bodies were dragged to a place outside of the city, where they were nailed onto wooden crosses and left there, in plain view, writhing and screaming in pain. The more fortunate of them met their deaths quickly.

These atrocities by the Romans are intended to inflict terror in the hearts of those who would contemplate revolt against their occupation of our country. But I can tell you that the effect of their cruelty has only been to harden the resolve of those who witness these awful scenes.

Much of the strife and turmoil in Judea has come out of the oppression and greed of the men who have been sent by Rome to rule us. None of them has shown any willingness to govern justly, and they have tormented our people and pillaged our country most appallingly. Their only aim has been to amass great riches, and their avarice has known no bounds.

Not long ago, when the procurator was displeased because the collection of taxes that week had been insufficient to satisfy his greed, he brazenly stole a large quantity of gold from the Temple treasury. The Jews in Jerusalem were outraged, and many took to the streets in protest of this unwarranted action. Others mocked the procurator by taking up a collection in the marketplace to aid him in his financial need. In revenge for all of this, Roman soldiers were sent on a rampage through the city, invading homes, stealing, and killing at random. Hundreds of the protesters were arrested, and so many were crucified that day that the Romans ran short of wood to build their murderous crosses.

Several prominent Jews have appealed to Nero Caesar to relieve us of the tyranny of this procurator, but with all the turmoil in Rome, nothing has come of that. Now there are many in Jerusalem who speak of widespread revolt, and already there are some who have begun moving away from the city out of fear of what might happen here. The High Priest, who nowadays is scarcely more than a lackey of the Romans, has tried to dispel rumors of Rome's intention to destroy our city. But I have come to know that plans have been made to remove the scrolls of the Temple's library to a safe place away from Jerusalem in the event that conditions worsen. With all of this, I am happy that you and your family are safe, far away from here, in Alexandria.

Those of our small group who were disciples of Yehoshua, and also others who have joined us since that time, pray each day that the time will be close at hand when Yehoshua will return to us. Then, with God's miracles to sustain us, he will finally lead us in driving the Romans from our land and restoring Jerusalem as a holy city. And then, God's kingdom on earth will at last be established.

So this, my dear grandson, is what I promised you when you were here last year for the Passover festival. It is my account of the two magnificent men who were my teachers and my masters, and all that happened during the time I was with them. Though it seems like only yesterday, thirty-five years have now passed since that terrible day when Yehoshua was so cruelly nailed to the cross and left there to die in agony. And it is two years more since Herod, may his name forever be cursed, ordered that Johanan be killed.

In my old age, I sometimes become forgetful, but my memories of these beloved prophets will always remain with me. Yehoshua had many disciples when I was with him, sometimes more than thirty, and I surely was the least amongst them. But now I can honor his memory by making you aware of all that happened during those fateful days. So much has been written, and more still has been said about Yehoshua and about Johanan these many years, but most who have given these accounts knew neither of these men. And indeed, much of what they say now never happened, and their falsehoods only increase with each year that passes.

But before I tell you about my two great masters, I will relate to you some of my recollections of my family and of the early years of my life. I was born in Galilee, in the small town of Korazin. The house in which our family lived was built of the gray, almost black stone native to our area. Surrounding our home was the garden that my mother tended with care, and from it came some of the most cherished memories of my mother and of my childhood.

My father, Shimon ben Eliezar, was a pious and righteous man. The words of God were always upon his lips. At the rise of the sun, he bound tefillin, the small leather boxes containing words from the Torah, onto his hand and his head; and each morning and each night he prayed. He faithfully observed the Sabbath as a time for rest from his work, and he spent much of that day in our small synagogue, studying the law and the writings of the great prophets with the other men. Each year, he gave a half-shekel for the Temple, as the law commanded. And one-tenth of his wages he contributed to the sons of Aaron who serve in the Temple; another tenth he spent in Jerusalem, and shared with those in need.

My father's work in our town was as a scribe. It was he who prepared letters, bills of sale, wills, deeds, and other documents. In addition to Hebrew and Aramaic, he was literate in the Greek language. It was my father who taught me to read and to write.

When I reached my seventh year, my father declared that I was old enough to come with the family to Jerusalem, for the Festival of Booths. After the Day of Atonement ended, we set out on the long trip, together with three other families from our town.

The clear, cool days of autumn had arrived, and the hillsides we passed on our way were ripe with the golden grains of wheat, barley, and lentil. Walnuts and almonds were nearing the time for their harvest, and pomegranate, fig, and apricot trees were heavy with fruit. The journey to Jerusalem, to the place of God's holy Temple, brought unbounded joy to our hearts, and as we crossed through the hills and valleys of our beloved land, we rejoiced and sang verses from the Psalms of David.

We arrived at our destination on the fourth day, prior to the eve of the festival. Though so many years have passed, I will always remember my first visit to Jerusalem. Great numbers of pilgrims were streaming into the city then, from many different countries, and their often strange appearance was a remarkable sight for a young child. There were Jews from Phoenicia, their linen tunics lavishly embroidered with every kind of fruit, flower, and animal. Others, from Babylonia, had arranged their thick black hair and their beards into row upon row of tightly curled ringlets that overflowed their woolen mantles. There were men of great wealth and position, in fine silk and bejeweled with gold rings and chains. But in far greater numbers were the poor, the beggars, and the cripples, many of them in sackcloth.

The merchants' stalls in the city presented an astonishing array of goods. They displayed great bolts of textiles, and many of the fabrics had been dyed, something I had never before seen; they presented an amazing range of colors, from pale yellow to the darkest blue. There were fine silks and linens, some of them beautifully embellished in gold thread. Other stalls were filled with pots and vials of rare and exotic spices and oils; yet others displayed gold and silver jewelry. In more distant areas of the marketplace were purveyors of leather goods, pottery, and wine; others sold charms and amulets. The richness of the city's infinite treasures was everywhere to behold. Jugglers, street musicians, and moneyc hangers provided still more variety to an astonishing and colorful spectacle.

And to add to this feast for the senses, the marketplace presented us the savory aroma of roasting meat as well as the inviting smell of freshly baked bread, all intermixed with the earthy tang of the sheep and the other animals being brought into the city for the sacrifices that were soon to begin.

My father bought wood, tree branches, and rope, and with the help of the other men, built booths, with branches for their roofs, along the west wall of the Temple Mount; and there we dwelt for seven days.

My parents and the adults from the other families who were with us went together to the mikva, a specially consecrated pool that was filled only with rainwater. That, as my mother once told me, was water sent to us directly by God. In the mikva, each of them immersed themselves. This may have served to cleanse their bodies, but that was not its purpose. Rather, they did this so as to cleanse their souls, so that they would be pure before God and worthy to enter the courtyards of His holy Temple.

In the morning, I accompanied my father when he went to buy a lamb. Near the stairway to the Temple, as my father held the animal in his arms, a priest examined it to be certain that it was without blemish or disease, and he placed a mark on its head. Then we all joined the great assemblage of pilgrims gathered there, and we slowly ascended the broad marble staircase that brought us to the Temple's entrance. We first made our way into the enormous Court of Gentiles, and from there, we climbed the fourteen steps, and then five steps more, to bring us into the Court of Women, where my mother and my sister entered the women's gallery. I held my father's hand tightly as, together, we ascended the final fifteen steps that took us to the great bronze gate through which we entered the Court of the Israelites.

The courtyard was filled with a great gathering, yet the multitude remained silent in reverence of the place, and apart from the bleating of the animals, all that could be heard was the singing of the great chorus of the Levites and the sound of their trumpets, harps, and drums. The High Priest had sacrificed a bullock as a burnt offering, and the smells of incense and burnt flesh were everywhere in the air.

My father carried the lamb he had bought for an offering of thanksgiving. The animal was taken from him and brought into the Court of the Priests. A Levite confined the lamb against the low parapet that divided the court, near where my father stood. Then my father, reaching over the parapet, placed his hand on the animal's head; he gave thanks for all that God had given to him and to his family, and finally he took the knife, and with a quick stroke he sacrificed the animal. A priest collected the blood, and some of it he spilled onto the altar. The lamb was prepared in accordance with the law, and my father received his portions of it. My mother and the other women roasted the meat later that day, and all of us celebrated with a great feast.

On the seventh day of the festival, my father and the other men joined in the great procession around the high altar of the Temple. I was there, holding my father's hand. The men carried branches of palm tree with willow, myrtle, and a sweet-smelling fruit, the etrog. They waved their palm branches as the Levites chanted the psalms of the Great Hallel.

At the end, the High Priest ascended onto the dukhan, a high platform from which he could be seen by everyone. As he raised his hands, all fell silent, with bowed heads. Then the High Priest intoned the ancient benediction, the words that had been handed down to Aaron:

"God bless you and protect you! God make his face to shine upon you and be gracious to you! God bestow his favor upon you and grant you peace!"

And the great chorus of the Levites responded, "Blessed be the Lord God, the God of Israel, to all eternity."

Happy and fulfilled, we returned home to Korazin.

Next, I will tell you about a tragic change that happened in my young life, and then, how I first came to know Johanan.

3

When Sharon, my sister, was twelve years old, our father consented for her to be betrothed to Benjamin, a young sandal-maker from the nearby town of Magdala. Their wedding, which took place the following spring, was held in the garden of our house. It was a warm, clear day, and masses of the fragrant red roses that my mother so loved had just come into bloom. My sister wore a yellow linen dress that our mother had embroidered with red and violet flowers, and our grandmother wove a crown of tiny white lilies into the folds of Sharon's long black hair. All of our neighbors came to celebrate with our family and to share in the wine and the dancing, which continued far into the night. Afterward, Sharon was soon gone, to live with her husband's family in Magdala, and it was only seldom that we saw her.

Then, one day, while my mother was cutting flowers in her garden, she happened to pierce her finger from a thorn of a rose bush. At first, her *injury seemed of no consequence, but soon Mother's hand became swollen and painful to her. Then, red lines began to appear on her arm. The healer in our village, Ruth, the wife of Boaz, prepared a poultice from the leaves of a red-colored herb, and she applied that to the parts that were affected. And later, when my mother began burning with fever, Ruth used a sharp knife and made cuts into the swollen part of the hand, and from that a yellow, bad-smelling matter came out from the wound. My mother then seemed better, and it appeared she would regain her health.*

But that night she slept fitfully, and twice I was awakened when she screamed out. When I went to her, I could feel that her fever had returned, and that it was worse than before. She thrashed about in her bed, and spoke words that neither my father nor I could understand. My father applied a cool, wet cloth to her forehead, and she again fell asleep. But early the next morning we discovered, to our horror, that my dear mother had died.

Even after the thirty days of mourning had ended, no one could console my father in his grief. Much of the time he sat alone, his eyes filled with tears, and he ate very little. From his melancholy, he could not continue his work as a scribe. I cried often during that terrible time, and my father could give me little comfort. Our neighbors brought food for the two of us, but there was no one to provide the care I needed. Finally, my father realized that we could not continue as we were, and so we left our house and went to stay with the family of my mother's sister, who had two young children. I was happy to be with my cousins there, but they had little room for us, and we soon became too great a burden for them. It was then that my father sold our house and everything else he owned, and we departed from our town of Korazin.

The two of us went to live with a group of Zadokite Essene men, at their community on the edge of the Wilderness of Kadesh. It was the place where my father's uncle Asher had come, many years earlier, after his wife had died.

The Essenes were men of the most extreme piety. My father, who himself had always been devout in his religious observance, found great comfort living among them, and he was eventually able to overcome his melancholy. But for a young boy, life there was severe, and seldom pleasant. There were about one hundred men, and also fourteen or fifteen boys, but no women were permitted, as the Essenes believed that their presence would distract them from their religious duties. None of the men was permitted to have any possession of his own, and even the clothes they wore were lent to them by the community.

The place had three buildings, which were built out of stone. The largest of them, a long, low structure with a flat roof, was the synagogue; on weekdays, it was also the place where the scribes, including my father, did their work. The men slept, prepared their food, and ate in large tents.

The surrounding area was desolate and remote, a half-day's trip to the nearest village in Galilee. There was a small wooded area nearby, but the wilderness was mainly a rocky place where only an occasional plant or shrub grew. After the spring rains, however, the landscape came to life with a profusion of red and purple anemones. In summer, the bright sunlight in a cloudless sky gave us oppressive heat day after day.

All of the men there took great care to lead lives of righteousness and piety. Prior to their meals, they removed their work clothes, and wearing only loincloths, they immersed themselves fully in a mikva filled with rainwater. This was so that they would always be in a state of purity when they ate. They observed the Sabbath scrupulously and all of the laws. But they did not offer sacrifices in Jerusalem. That was because of their conviction that the Temple had been defiled by the high priests, whom they regarded as being little more than collaborators of the Romans. It was the belief of the Essenes that in the end of days, a new temple would be built in Jerusalem, with a just and righteous priesthood officiating over it.

The men spent nearly all their time at work, in prayer, and in studying the holy writings. It was my responsibility, with one of the other boys, to look after the goats, taking them out to pasture and returning them at night, and that was how I spent my time. I did not often see my father, and I was frequently alone. It was at such times that I so greatly missed my mother, and I often wondered what would become of my life.

At our meals, when we boys were all together, was when I first got to know Johanan. He was eleven years old then, three years older than I. Johanan had come to that place with his father, Zechariah ben Jonah, after his mother, Elesheva, had died. Johanan's work was to prune and care for the olive trees, harvest the fruit, and assist the men who operated the olive press. In spite of Johanan's young age, they allowed him to study with the men, and indeed, Johanan argued and discussed the law even with the oldest and most learned of them.

One Sabbath morning, I came into the synagogue with another boy. We sat at the back. That day, they were speaking about God's divine presence, and in the course of their discussion, a man rose and posed a question to the others:

"In one passage of the Torah, according to the words of Moses our Teacher, 'The presence of the Lord was there like a cloud, filling the Tabernacle.' But then it was King Solomon who said, 'Behold, even the heavens to their uttermost reaches cannot contain the Lord.' Is there not a contradiction between these?" None of the men was able to answer him. Then, for the first time, I noticed that Johanan was there among the men. We saw him stand and ask permission to speak.

"This," he said, "is like a cave near the shore of the ocean. Once the tide reaches its full height, water can fill the cave, yet the ocean remains as it was before. And so it was that God's presence filled the Tabernacle, yet His greatness was undiminished throughout the earth and the heavens." The men all agreed that Johanan had given a most excellent answer to the question.

My father and Johanan's father were given work as scribes, copying the holy texts. My father found this to be an agreeable occupation, and in time he seemed to recover his enjoyment of life.

One of the men served as the teacher for us boys, instructing us in reading, writing, and in the study of Torah. But it was Johanan from whom I learned the most, and in time he came to be like an older brother to me. In addition to offering me his friendship, Johanan taught me much about the holy writings of our people. And whenever loneliness or the lingering sadness from the loss of my mother overcame me, it was Johanan more than anyone else who gave me words of encouragement. His arm around my shoulder at such times was what sustained me most during that difficult period of my life.

Then, one day after we had lived with the Essenes for about a year, my father took to his bed complaining of pain beneath his ribs. He suffered greatly, so much so that his agony could only be relieved with large amounts of opium. He refused to eat anything, and he rapidly sickened. Two days later, he died. They buried my father before sundown that day, *and after everyone had left the grave, I sat there and cried for a long time. Never in my life had I felt so alone. But when I finally arose and turned to leave that place, I saw that I was not by myself. Johanan had remained there with me.*

"Your father was a kind man and a man of great learning," Johanan said to me. "He was deeply respected by everyone. The Essenes," he said, "are like a family, and you will always be well cared for by the men here. You need never be troubled by that." We remained there together well past nightfall, and I was greatly comforted then by talking with him.

And in the days and weeks that followed, Johanan spent much time with me and gave me many opportunities to speak about my father and my family. In spite of his young age, Johanan then truly became like a father to me.

Several months later, shortly after the festival of Shavuot, many of the men became sick with fevers and coughing, and it was then that Zechariah, Johanan's father, also sickened and died. So then Johanan was also without family. I endeavored to comfort him, as he had done for me. From this, the two of us formed an even closer bond of friendship.

Johanan was in his twelfth year by that time, and it appeared that life among the Essenes was entirely agreeable to him. So I was greatly surprised at what he told me, only a few weeks after his father's death: "Todah, I have made the decision to leave this place."

As a frightened nine-year-old, the thought of remaining there alone left me terrified, and I begged Johanan to allow me to go with him. Johanan did not tell me where he was planning to go, nor why he wanted to depart, but none of that mattered. My only wish was to be able to remain with Johanan. I was overjoyed when he told me I could come with him.

It was only much later that I came to understand why Johanan left there when he did; it was because of the oath.

"When a man reaches the age of thirteen, he must make a solemn pledge," Johanan told me. "He must swear he will follow all of the rules of the Essene community. He must take his meals only in a state of purity, to immerse in the mikva as they always do before eating, and to share food only with others in a state of purity. Because of that oath, any who commit to it are obliged to remain with the Essenes for the remainder of their lives," he said. "I am not now willing to take such a vow. But if I should

have a change of heart and decide to return there later," he said, "I believe they would accept me back among them."

So we departed and set out together into the wilderness, taking with us only a small quantity of food and water. Johanan also brought with him his father's tefillin.

Johanan, still not quite thirteen years old, was already quite tall, though unusually thin. But in spite of his youth, he already possessed the knowledge and wisdom of a mature man. I was still small, even for a nine-year-old, and in every respect I was a child.

At first we suffered greatly from the cold, especially during the night. We ate wild olives and figs, as well as almonds and walnuts that fell from the trees. I still remember what happened when we came upon a beehive and attempted to take some of its honey. Its inhabitants attacked us both without mercy, and it was a long while before we attempted to find honey again. But soon, we learned to build a fire to keep ourselves warm. And we found other fruits that were good to eat, as well as grasshoppers and roots that would satisfy our hunger.

All of this was a great adventure for a young boy, and never did I question Johanan as to the purpose or the destination of our travels in the wilderness. Johanan seemed to require very little sleep, and whenever I was awakened during the night, he always seemed to be fully alert. On one such occasion, Johanan had gone some distance from where I was sleeping, but I could still hear that he was praying. "Lord," he cried out, "we beg you for your mercy. We implore you, guide us so we may do as you wish of us. Show us the path we must follow to serve you. Our plea to you is for a sign of your will."

While Johanan waited for an answer, he devoted much time each day to prayer. I spent those times watching the birds that visited our area, climbing on rocks and on trees, and examining the behavior of the snakes and lizards that were our neighbors. I truly believe that Johanan did, in time, receive a sign from God.

Each night in the wilderness, Johanan told me stories from the Holy Scriptures—about God's creation of the world, the Great Flood and the story of Noah, the exodus from Egypt, and Moses receiving the Ten Commandments on Mt. Sinai. To a young boy, this was an unending and magnificent saga.

When I asked him questions about the stories he had told me, Johanan often had yet other tales that would provide me an answer. After he had explained to me how God revealed himself at Sinai and how He gave the Torah and its laws to Moses, I asked my young teacher how it happened that God had chosen our people to receive his Torah.

"God appeared not only to Israel," Johanan said, "but also to all of the other nations. At first, God spoke to the children of Esau, and He inquired of them, 'Will you accept my Torah and my laws?' 'What do they command?' they asked. 'You shall not commit murder,' God answered them. 'How can we live by such a law? Our very own father Esau was a murderer, and Isaac, his father, told him he would live by his sword. Your Torah is not for us.'

"So God went to the Ammonites and the Moabites. 'Will you accept my Torah?' God asked. 'What will it require of us?' they demanded. 'You shall not commit adultery,' God said. They replied, 'We owe our very existence to acts of incest. We could never live by your Torah.'

"And so God went to the desert people, and said to them, 'Will you accept my Torah and my laws?' 'If we accept them,' they asked, 'what will be required of us?' 'Among the laws is the commandment that you shall not steal,' God answered. 'Then we cannot accept your laws,' they said. 'Theft and robbery are our entire life and character.'

"And in time, God went to every nation, but none of them wanted God's Torah or His commandments. Finally, God came to Israel, who accepted God's laws, saying, 'All that the Lord has spoken we will faithfully do.'"

Another night, there was a spider spinning a web near where we sat. I asked Johanan what purpose God had for giving life to such creatures.

"All that God has created is part of His plan," he explained to me. "When David was hiding in a cave to escape from King Saul, God sent a spider to spin a web over the entrance to the cave. When Saul saw the spider's web, he said, 'There can be no one inside, as any who would enter would have broken the web.' Later, when David left the cave and saw the spider and its web, he spoke to the spider, saying, 'Blessed are you, and blessed is he who created you.'"

One very cold night, we built a large campfire and sat close to it to keep ourselves warm. Except for the occasional screech of an owl, all was *calm and quiet. But then we suddenly found that we were surrounded by a band of about a dozen men. Their leader, who carried a long sword, was a huge, muscular fellow who looked all the more frightful because of his red hair and beard. The others with him were armed with daggers, spears, and wooden clubs. Johanan and I were greatly in fear for our lives. We thought these men were robbers, but surely they could see that we had nothing of value to take from us. They made us go with them to their camp, deep within a nearby forest.*

There were about a hundred men there, each of them bearing at least a dagger or a sword. Their armory contained bows and arrows, clubs, spears, javelins, and even a supply of Roman helmets and armor. Their commander was a spirited man named Amos ben Isaac. We were surprised when we learned that these were not robbers, and that they were pious men who were zealous in their observance of God's laws. But we also learned that they often paid no heed to two of the commandments: "You shall not steal," and "You shall not commit murder."

Amos and his followers had a great passion for liberty, and they held bitter hatred against the Romans who occupy our land and who oppress our people so cruelly. So all of them refused to submit or to pay tribute to Rome. "No Lord but God" was their watchword. Their purpose was to bring harm to the Romans, as well as to any who gave the occupiers comfort and aid. These men attacked Roman outposts to steal arms and provisions. Killing Roman soldiers in these raids gave them no pause, and some of Amos' men lost their own lives on these missions. Those of our countrymen who welcomed the domination of our nation by the Romans also became enemies of these men, who plundered those Jews of their property and their livestock.

Johanan and I came to know that one of the most violent of their actions had been taken against a wealthy Jew from Jerusalem who at every opportunity had given aid to the cause of the Romans, and who sought shamelessly to curry favor with them. Amos intended to make an example of him. Two of the men loyal to Amos journeyed to Jerusalem at Passover. One of them was able to come close to this man, in the midst of a large crowd. Taking a dagger hidden under his cloak, he stabbed his victim without it being noticed. The assassin then dropped his weapon and managed to walk away without arousing suspicion. The man who committed that murder was named Simon. He was also known as Bariona, which in our Aramaic language carries the same meaning as your Greek word ζεαλοτ (zealot).

"Remain here with us," Amos said to Johanan and me. "We will provide you with food and shelter and also the company of many fine and righteous young men. The two of you are too young to bear arms, but there is much you can do here to assist us and to help our cause."

I was very much in fear of these men, and I did not wish to stay. But Johanan felt otherwise; it was Amos who persuaded him.

"Amos has studied with the great Pharisee sages in Jerusalem, and he is well schooled in the law," Johanan told me. "I have never before known a Pharisee, and I want to learn from a Pharisee teacher."

Who, I asked him, are the Pharisees? Do they have a different religion than ours?

"Oh, they indeed are Jews," Johanan said. "The Pharisees are known for their piety, and it is said that they know more of the law and of the holy writings than anyone else. They are highly respected as teachers. And because of their skill in interpreting the law, it is said that 'the Pharisees sit in Moses' seat.'

"The Pharisees also hold to a number of special beliefs," he explained to me. "One of these is that there is a second Torah, separate from the commandments in the books of Moses. It is not written, but rather it consists of oral laws, which the Pharisees say were given by God to Moses, and then were handed down from generation to generation by word of mouth. The Pharisees are firm in their belief that one who does not know the oral law does not really know the Law. And they patiently await the coming of the Messiah, who will become our king. When the Messiah comes, they believe that the righteous who have died will be resurrected from their graves."

I thought for a long while about what Johanan had said, and then I asked him, "Do you yourself not hold to those very same beliefs?"

"That is so," he replied. "However, there is much about the oral law that I still need to understand, and it is for that reason that I want to hear more of what this man has to teach us."

Amos, we soon found, was an able teacher indeed, and we learned much from him of the wisdom and the philosophy of the Pharisees. "King David," Amos said to us one evening, speaking in a tremulous voice and with tears welling up in his eyes, "was our great Messiah, the anointed one who overthrew his enemies in battle and established Jerusalem as a great and holy city. The sages tell us that again the Messiah, a great and mighty king anointed by God, will lead an army of Judea into a fearsome battle. This glorious king, who will be the greatest man among all of us and a descendant of King David, will be guided and protected by God's miracles and will drive the foreign enemies from our land. And all who are righteous will then enter God's kingdom, but those not worthy will be cut down and destroyed. This will then begin a time of peace and redemption for the whole world. War and tyranny will be gone forever, and God will be supreme over all. It will be the fulfillment of our longstanding hopes and wishes. And it has been said that the coming of the Messiah is not far off."

And then Amos recited words of the prophet Zechariah:

"Behold, a day of the Lord is coming. Then, the Lord will go forth and make war as when he fights in battle. On that day, his feet will stand on the Mount of Olives, which is before Jerusalem on the east. And the Lord my God, with all of the holy ones, will come. The Lord shall be king over all the earth, and in that day there shall be one Lord with one name. All those that have made war against Jerusalem, the Lord will smite them with his plague."

"You have told us that the Messiah will be of the house of David," one of the men said to Amos, "but how can we know who is David's descendent?"

Amos reflected for a long while before he gave his answer. "Many hundreds of years, perhaps even a thousand, have passed since David was King of Israel," he replied, "so no one can really be certain. But because King David had so many wives, and his son Solomon had even more still, I believe that all of us truly may be of his lineage." And with that, Amos laughed heartily.

We stayed with Amos and his men for nearly three months. During that time, many more men from Galilee joined Amos' army, and soon their group numbered more than three hundred.

Then, one fateful Sabbath morning, a detachment of about twenty Roman soldiers attacked our encampment. They appeared suddenly, when most of Amos' men were at prayer. The Romans were in full battle armor, each of them bearing a sword, a spear, and a dagger. Johanan and I hid ourselves behind a clump of trees, from where we witnessed all that happened.

In the initial onslaught, about fifteen of Amos' men were ruthlessly cut down. But the Romans had apparently not known of the large size of our group, and very soon, once Amos' fighters were able to arm themselves and engage the attackers, the advantage turned against the Romans. At the end of a terrible and bloody battle, Amos' men were able to kill all of the Roman soldiers. Twenty-six of our own men also lost their lives, and more than forty were injured. Amos ordered us to bury the dead and then to move our camp quickly before a larger force of Romans could return to find us. But Johanan strongly objected. "We must not dig graves today," he said. "This is the Sabbath, and the law forbids any such work on this day."

Amos answered him with a Pharisee saying that I later often heard repeated: 'The Sabbath was made for man, not man for the Sabbath.' And so all of us did as Amos had ordered, and we moved our camp deeper still into the forest.

Amos and his men continued their struggle against the occupiers of our land, but after witnessing the horrible battle with the Romans, Johanan did not want to stay with them any longer. So the two of us returned to the wilderness, and we lived there again as we had done before.

Some while later, we came upon two young men, who were brothers. Both of them appeared disheveled and fatigued from lack of sleep, and worry and dread showed on their faces. They told us that their uncle had become ill with fever, and that he was refusing to eat or drink. They led us to a shaded place where they had brought their uncle to rest. He was a tall man, with skin darkened from long exposure to the sun. He had not cut his hair or his beard for a long time, and his cloak was old and worn. His face was gaunt, with sunken eyes and dry, parched lips. At first, the man showed no response when we spoke to him, but then gradually and with much effort he opened his eyes. He acknowledged our presence with a barely audible moan, and then he closed his eyes again. I could appreciate that he was burning with fever.

"I fear he is near death," one of the young men told us, and with that, his brother began to weep. We stayed there with the three of them.

Johanan encouraged the man to take sips of water, and he also fed him small amounts of honey that we had brought with us. The two brothers told us that their uncle was called Simeon ha Nazir. They said they had been traveling together through Galilee when their uncle had taken ill, and for two days they had remained there with him.

We applied moistened cloths to Simeon's face to cool his fever, and we gave him more of the water and honey. Two days after that, his fever lessened, and he began to answer his nephews' questions more readily than before; after two more days, he started to eat again. Then, he gradually regained his health. His nephews rejoiced at Simeon's recovery. When his strength returned, Johanan and I accompanied the three of them as they traveled from town to town and village to village in Galilee. Each place they went, Simeon spoke to the Jews, in synagogues, in marketplaces, and anywhere else where people gathered.

In each of these places, he presented the same message: "Pay heed to what I say," he would begin, speaking barely above a whisper and at a slowly measured pace, pausing between each word. "The world will soon be destroyed. Everything that you can see about you, and also, I fear, many of our people, will be annihilated. A pitiless, raging storm of fire is about to descend upon us, and, listen to what I tell you—all of this will happen soon. It will begin with horrendous thunder and fearful bolts of lightning. Then great balls of flames will fall from the skies, and the conflagration will begin." Those last words he spoke at the top of his voice, nearly shouting, while punching his clenched fist into the air.

"The end of days will soon be upon us," he would repeat, "and all who have forsaken God's commandments will be struck down by God's hand. Prepare yourself—mend your evil ways! There is little time left."

Simeon almost always attracted large crowds when he spoke. And among the people of Galilee, we could see that he had gained a reputation as a learned teacher.

"Many here speak of Simeon as being a prophet," Johanan said to me one day. "I truly admire him, but I cannot yet understand why he believes as he does that the end of days is at hand."

For several months, we accompanied Simeon and his nephews on their travels, and during these times, Simeon taught us much about the law and the words of the great prophets of Israel. On one occasion, we were *with Simeon when he spoke to the people in a small synagogue in northern Galilee. After he had finished, two men drew Johanan and me aside. We had not recognized them at first, but we soon realized we had known them from the time we had spent at Amos' encampment.*

"We are here to recruit men to join our cause," one of them said to us. "Come back with us, I beg you. Amos now has more than four thousand fighters, and he is planning soon to attack the Roman garrison in Jerusalem."

"The day we have so long awaited is close at hand," the other man said, "and our people are elated that our holy city will at last be returned to us. Many are beginning to speak of Amos as the Messiah," he said, almost in a whisper, scarcely able to contain his excitement. "And after he succeeds in driving out the Romans, and restoring Jerusalem as a free and holy city, he will reign in triumph as our king."

I was amazed to hear all this, but I had no wish to return to Amos' camp. Johanan, however, was greatly taken by what these men had said. And in the end, we went, along with several other young men from that town in Galilee, to where Amos and his men had assembled. During our trip there, we learned that Amos had divided his army into three separate divisions, each of which was encamped in a separate area. The place where we were taken, which held the largest group of fighters, was in a rocky, desolate area to the west of Mount Hermon. We arrived there near twilight. Our approach was along a high, sloping ridge, and looking down upon the campsite, we could see many hundreds of tents, with bonfires interspersed among them. Men were moving about the campground, some carrying firewood, others in the midst of their evening meal, and yet others fabricating arrows and spears for the camp's armory. Shortly, most of the men, save for those who were serving on sentry duty, began gathering in a large clearing toward the middle of the campsite. Amos had come there to address them.

"My dear compatriots," he began, "it warms my heart to see you here and to know that you share my zeal for freedom. We began as a small group, committed to resisting the occupiers of our land. Now we have grown to become a magnificent force, and our numbers continue to increase. The day is close at hand when we can confront our enemy in battle."

And then Amos spoke further to his men, quoting and explaining passages from the writings of the prophets Isaiah and Zechariah. Afterward, he left the encampment, departing on horseback with three of his lieutenants to travel to another campsite.

And indeed, only a few weeks later, as Amos had forewarned, he ordered the three divisions of his army to assemble at a central point in the Jezreel Valley. Then, with Amos at their head, they advanced toward Jerusalem.

Johanan and I followed after them, and we saw all along the way crowds of Jews who came forward to cheer them and to wish them success. Some of them were in tears, overcome in their hope that we might soon be a free people again.

There were also those, especially among the Pharisees, who were in fear that the Romans would be too powerful for Amos' army. But we could see that their spirits were raised from seeing the new Messiah, and that they prayed fervently that he would fulfill his mission and liberate Jerusalem from the Roman oppressors.

Amos and his army progressed slowly, and ten days passed before the Temple first came into view as they approached Jerusalem from the east on their way to the Mount of Olives, where the great battle was to begin. But alas, the Romans had gotten word of the intentions of Amos and his men, and a large detachment of soldiers was waiting as they approached the city. The Romans mercilessly cut down the vanguard of Amos' army, and they took Amos and his captains as prisoners. Many of the others, Johanan and I among them, were able to flee from there and escape.

That very day, the Romans crucified Amos and all the others who were captured with him. But before they nailed Amos to the cross, as a final act of humiliation, they wrapped him in a purple cloak and placed a crown of thorns on his head. And on the cross above his head, they attached a placard on which it was written: "Amos ben Isaac, King of the Jews." The Roman authorities also spread word throughout the country that any others who sought to challenge their rule would meet the same end. There were heavy hearts everywhere among the Jews, and many of the Pharisees fasted and were in mourning that this new Messiah had failed to deliver us from the Romans.

Johanan and I remained in Jerusalem after that. Neither of us had been in that great city since we were young children. Both of us were able to read and write Aramaic and Hebrew—Johanan far better than

I—and because of that, we both soon succeeded in becoming apprenticed to the scribe Abraham ben Jonah; from him, we learned to compose letters, wills, and other legal papers, preparing ourselves to pursue our fathers' occupation.

We earned a small wage as apprentices, and from that we had the means to live in the city. We both worked from morning until nightfall each day, but in the evenings and on the Sabbath we had time to attend the public teachings of Jerusalem's great Pharisee sages. Hillel the Babylonian, who then was already very old, was surely the greatest of all of them.

In those days, Hillel, along with his grandson Gamaliel, and also Shammai and others of the famous Pharisee teachers, came from time to time to the courtyards of the great Temple with the disciples from their academies. There, these great sages spoke about the laws of the Torah and the writings of the great prophets, and they taught any who came there to learn from them. Whenever Hillel and Gamaliel appeared in the Temple, we endeavored to be there to hear them, and we both marveled at their brilliance and their unbounded wisdom.

The great Babylonian by then had become thin and frail. He walked slowly and with difficulty, and two of his disciples were always at his side to give him support. Hillel's flowing hair and his long white beard seemed to radiate from his face. He appeared like a supernatural spirit, a messenger sent directly from God. He sat in the midst of his students, who listened to his every word with rapt attention. He spoke softly, indeed with a voice that was barely audible. Although the Babylonian always maintained a serious demeanor in his teaching, whenever he was challenged with a particularly difficult question, or when he was presented with an interesting new idea, his face brightened like that of a child with a new toy. In his interpretations of the Law, the Babylonian followed a principle he was wont to repeat often: "The Law was made for man, not man for the Law."

But in spite of Hillel's benevolence, we later came to learn that both he and Gamaliel could be fiercely adversarial, especially when it came to the interpretation of Scripture.

4

September, 1978

A thinly veiled half-moon hung high in the late summer sky, its pale light suffusing the domes and spires of the ancient city with a dull, silvery glow. Off on the far horizon, a hint of redness behind a gathering of clouds served notice that daybreak was not far away.

Three men made their way separately to the airport that early morning, arriving at the Pan American ticket counter precisely at the appointed time. None of them had met before, but they were able to identify one other immediately as the participants for their carefully planned meeting. Once assembled, they turned into the already busy Alitalia concourse.

Vendors in the passageway were preparing their shops for the day's business, and the inviting aroma of freshly brewed espresso wafted from concessionaires' booths along the men's path. Passengers from early-arriving flights drifted past them in the direction of the baggage claim area. Others, on their way toward departure gates, formed a countercurrent of half awake, mostly self-absorbed travelers. The three men went unnoticed as they walked together in close formation through the long corridor. When they reached its end, they turned and retraced their steps without ever stopping, to insure against being overheard. They chose their words carefully, speaking in hushed tones.

Two of the men were Americans. The taller of them, well past seventy, displayed a full head of pure white hair, well-sculpted features, and a stately bearing. His dark suit was finely tailored and his silk necktie of elegant design, his entire appearance reflecting refinement and good taste. The other American, Rocco Conconi, thirty-four years old and from Chicago's west side, could hardly have been more different from his compatriot. Stocky and of muscular build, he wore a black silk suit and a dark polo shirt sans tie. He smoked, compulsively and continuously, consuming four of his Lucky Strike cigarettes in the course of their brief meeting.

Father Carlo Delvecchio, the youngest of the three men, carried a large paper shopping bag from Supermercato Di Meglio in which he had stored his carefully folded clerical garb. That early morning, he wore a blue-checkered shirt, open at the collar, and dark cotton slacks. A baseball-style cap covered his closely cropped black hair, with its brim pulled downward to reduce any likelihood that he might be recognized.

During the course of their discussion, the older of the two Americans produced a thick brown envelope, which Father Delvecchio quickly sequestered in his shopping bag. Later, the other man gave him a small package that had been carefully wrapped in silver foil. The priest slipped that into his pants pocket.

"It has to be stored in a cool place," he told Father Delvecchio. "It's best to keep it refrigerated," he added, "but make sure it doesn't freeze." Their brief conversation focused entirely on the smaller of the two parcels; nothing needed to be said about the large envelope, which had been filled with bundles of 100,000-lire bank notes.

Forty minutes later, Father Delvecchio's taxi delivered him to the tiny Santa Catarina church, hidden away on a quiet street less than three kilometers from the Vatican. The Santa Catarina, an ornate gem dating from the early seventeenth century, was continuing to serve its small congregation, but in recent years the church had also come to be a popular destination of tours of the art treasures of Rome.

That was because of the singular masterpiece that adorned the west wall of its sanctuary, a strikingly luminous life-size painting of its patron saint portrayed in lush pastoral surroundings. The finely sculpted features of the woman's face, and the emotion projected in her radiant smile, were invariably what first attracted the attention of her viewers. In one of her hands, she held a red leather-bound book, and in the other a single pure-white lily. Along the top of the panel, in a cloud-filled lacuna, the haloed Father and Son sat side by side on golden thrones, the Father in a pensive pose, and Jesus, projecting a placid countenance while holding a long, gilded shaft with its very top ending in the form of a crucifix. Above the two of them, there hovered a pure white dove, from which waves of beneficence emanated in every direction. And at the very bottom, depicted deep in shadow, dwelt the otherworldly creatures that populated the Saint's vision of hell: unspeakably hideous beasts, each more vile than the next, tearing apart the flesh of hapless sinners with their dagger-like teeth. The unsigned painting had been pronounced by a prominent Rome art historian to be the work of Caravaggio, but others of them would only concede that it was a work of Caravaggio's school.

The early morning Mass had ended, and except for two elderly women seated near the front, the church was deserted. Father Delvecchio installed himself in a pew in a dark corner at the back of the sanctuary, and a short while later he was joined by Giovanni Arpino, a portly, balding, sixty-year-old man. Arpino, like himself, was an employee of the Vatican. Father Delvecchio carefully transferred to the older man the small package he had acquired that morning.

"There are two vials," he whispered, "both with droppers. One dropperful with each meal will be enough. The drug has a slightly bitter taste, so best use it with foods that are more strongly flavored. He might develop stomach pain, but I doubt he would complain about that. And even if he should, the doctor they have for him is so incompetent, he wouldn't do anything to look into it anyway."

Signor Arpino pocketed the foil-wrapped package and immediately left the church, departing on foot. Father Delvecchio remained seated for several more minutes. Then, when he was confident no one was watching him, he moved quickly to the rear of the sanctuary. There, he drew back a heavy black curtain, immediately behind the pew where he had been sitting, to reveal the entrance to a narrow, curving stairway.

Descending to the basement, he entered a dimly lit storage room where he quickly changed into his clerical apparel. He cautiously returned to the main chapel of the church and then exited the building through a side door, making his way back to his small office adjacent to the Vatican Library. His position there was Assistant Research Librarian, but in reality a variety of assignments, many having little or no connection to the Library, occupied the greater part of his time.

That night, the priest carefully counted the bundles of banknotes he had received at the airport. Setting aside his own portion and that for Signor Arpino, he transferred the rest to a leather courier bag, which was picked up the following morning for transfer to a bank in Naples. The account in which it was deposited was under the control of a Vatican official with responsibility for "special projects."

The following day, Father Delvecchio placed a call to a man in London. "I need you to bid for me at the Sotheby's auction on the eighteenth. It's lot number 318-21N, a Roman gold solidus showing the Emperor Hadrian. It's a very rare coin, and it's in beautiful condition. It ought to sell for about £1,500, but if the big museums are interested, it could go for twice that much. My absolute maximum is £3,500."

The new pope had been elected only two weeks earlier. In the initial stages of the papal election, three leading contenders had had the support of approximately equal numbers of their fellow cardinals. But in spite of enthusiastic campaigning efforts on behalf of each of the men, it eventually became clear that none of them could garner enough votes to be elected, and so a new candidate needed to be found. Albino Cardinal Luciani, the Archbishop of Venice, ultimately became the successful compromise choice. In notable contrast to the other candidates, Cardinal Luciani had never been a Vatican insider, and he viewed his calling as being more pastoral than administrative. He certainly had no enemies, he was well liked by everyone who knew him, and his humble, kindly manner appealed to many of his fellow cardinals. But he also had written very little and had expressed no strong opinions, so none of the electors really knew much about him, nor about any plans he might have had for the future of the Church.

During his very first week as pope, Vatican insiders were shocked at a revelation that emerged about him, dating from the time when he had been the Archbishop of Venice. They learned that he had accepted an invitation to meet with representatives of a United Nations commission, to discuss their concerns about overpopulation in developing countries. Following that meeting, the cardinal had sent a letter to then Pope Paul VI, expressing the view that Church policy on contraception needed to be reconsidered. When that letter by the new pope mysteriously came to light, members of the Curia and other conservatives within the Church became outraged, feeling they had been deceived and betrayed, and seeing such a radical view as a first step toward undermining traditional Church doctrine. That left the pope under a heavy cloud of suspicion, evidenced by a palpable coolness toward him by many within the Vatican hierarchy.

Even more apprehension arose as the result of an article that appeared only days later in a widely read Italian news journal, *L'Osservatore Politico*. The paper identified a long list of prominent Catholics, several of them high-ranking Vatican officials, who it claimed were members of a secret Masonic order with criminal connections, known as "Propaganda Due," or "P2." The pope, incredulous that his most trusted senior aides could have been culpable of such an unforgivable offence, immediately launched an investigation to check the veracity of the damning report. To his horror, he learned that several members of the Curia, including the Vatican's secretary of state, were indeed guilty as charged. Church policy made it unmistakably clear that membership in any such organization was grounds for excommunication, and would perforce result in immediate dismissal from the service of the Holy See. Word quickly spread through the Vatican that a major purge of the Curial hierarchy would soon take place.

And if all of that were not enough, the new pope was also soon faced with the disturbing repercussions of a seemingly routine report that was presented to him in the third week of his papacy. Archbishop Paul Marcinkus, the director of the Church's Institute of Religious Works, better known as the Vatican Bank, was the bearer of that report. The purpose of their meeting was to familiarize the pope with the functions and activities of the Bank. What Archbishop Marcinkus presented to him that morning included a summarization of the Vatican Bank's major accounts and of its principal financial disbursements.

A gregarious, cigar-smoking American and a giant hulk of a man, the archbishop was known to be as much at home on the golf course as he was in his high position of Vatican influence and power. He was also a prominent member of P2. This savvy and strong-willed Goliath made a striking contrast against the diminutive and self-effacing pontiff who had summoned him for their meeting.

But the pope was not to be cowed by the self-assured visitor who sat across from his desk that morning. Indeed, the archbishop was taken quite by surprise when the pope demonstrated to him that he possessed considerable astuteness in the interpretation of financial reports, a skill he developed during the time he had had responsibility for budgetary matters as archbishop of Venice. Moreover, the new pope raised several pointed questions about the financial statements that had been presented to him.

"Holy Father," the archbishop responded, "this brief report was only intended to present you a very general summary of the Bank's activities. I will, of course, be happy to provide you more complete information if you wish it."

"Very well," the pope replied, "then please prepare a detailed financial report and let us meet again to review it tomorrow afternoon."

But their subsequent meeting only raised more questions, and their meeting following that one led the pope to wonder aloud if the

Bank was being properly managed. Moreover, he adamantly demanded additional information to dispel his increasingly strong feeling that large and unjustified disbursements were being made from the Vatican Bank. The two of them held several additional meetings, but the pope's questions and concerns were never addressed to his satisfaction. By then, the pontiff had already ordered an independent audit of the financial activities of the Vatican Bank.

On one occasion during that time, the pope shared his concerns about the Bank with his personal secretary, Father John Magee.

"Yes," the younger man commented, "the Vatican Bank may not always be run with the efficiency of other banks, but as everyone knows, managing money is hardly the highest priority of the Church. Such irregularities have always turned out to be the result of carelessness rather that anything improper. On the other hand, enemies of the Church have leveled all sorts of outrageous fabrications against us. You are of course aware of the scurrilous rumors that have tried to implicate Vatican banking activities in the workings of criminal elements, here in Italy and also in America. All of those are terrible lies, obviously intended to discredit the Church."

One day the following week, the pope told his secretary that he was not feeling well, and he asked to have his afternoon meetings cancelled. That evening he ate almost none of his dinner, and later that night, he complained of nausea and abdominal pain. The Vatican physician was called to examine him. He immediately recognized that his patient's pulse was slow and irregular; however, that finding did not seem to concern him.

"Holy father, what you have is probably nothing more than indigestion," the doctor told him. "Or if not that, perhaps a touch of the influenza."

Early the following morning, on Thursday, September 28, Pope John Paul I was found dead in his bedroom. The Vatican Information Office quickly issued a succession of reports of the pope's death, several of which were remarkably inconsistent. No medical examination or autopsy was allowed, and arrangements were made to embalm the pope's body only hours after it became known that he had died. The death certificate indicated a heart attack as the cause of death;

however, his personal physician later stated that the pope had never shown any indication of having heart disease. John Paul I was sixty-five years old. He had been pope for only thirty-three days.

5

October, 1981

As they always did whenever the opportunity presented itself, the two churchmen, the closest of friends ever since their seminary days, spent a long and pleasant evening together. That autumn was unusually cool in Rome, but they still chose to dine *alfresco,* at a small trattoria only a short taxi ride away from the Vatican.

Gianfranco Coglieri consumed far more than his share of the plate of antipasti they had ordered for the two of them, followed by a heaping bowl of linguini, and then *spezzatino di vitello con piselli,* the hearty veal signature dish of the house; afterward, he indulged his affection for rich, sweet cannoli accompanied by fragrant espresso. Coglieri's stocky limbs were oddly short in relation to the rest of his body, and his round face served further to accentuate his ample corpulence. His warm smile, his agreeable disposition, and his patient and kindly manner invariably served to endear him to everyone who came to know him. Ordained only months earlier as the Bishop of Guastalla, at the early age of forty-three, Coglieri was the firstborn son of an aristocratic Italian family that traced its ancestry to the sixteenth-century Duke of Modena.

The other man, Carlo Delvecchio, one of eight children of a postal clerk from a small town in northern Sicily, had been a gifted and ambitious student. With the patronage of the influential Archbishop of Palermo, he had been admitted to the Almo Collegio Capranica, Rome's oldest ecclesiastical academy, and one of its most distinguished. Following his ordination as a priest, Father Delvecchio entered the Pontifica Università Gregoriana, whose faculty awarded him a doctoral degree in church history and literature after a brilliant defense of his dissertation, "The Evolution of Two Heretical Movements in Germany in the Early Fifteenth Century."

Father Delvecchio ate little of his dinner. By the time they finished their meal, the other patrons of the establishment had departed, and the two men lingered for a long while over brandy.

"I often wonder," Coglieri reflected, "if I was too hasty in agreeing to take on the responsibilities of a bishop. My previous vocation as a parish priest was a great joy to me, but now I need to spend too much of my time fussing over budgets and other dreary administrative details. And you, Carlo? Are you still cloistered away in the Vatican library with your musty old books and manuscripts?"

"Yes," Delvecchio replied, "but lately I've also been spending a good deal of time as part of a rather secretive 'special projects' strategy group. And I should tell you that several of its participants are quite senior members of the Roman Curia. The primary mission of the group is to monitor individuals and organizations that are suspected of working to undermine the Church, and especially Church doctrine."

"Ah, a return of the Inquisition?" Coglieri asked, after taking a gulp of brandy.

"Hardly that," Delvecchio said. "But I must tell you there's concern at the very highest levels that certain organizations out there are bent on driving a wedge between the Catholic faithful and the Church."

"What organizations? Communists? Jews?"

"No," Delvecchio replied. His face brightened with a broad smile, but then only seconds later, his expression turned dark. With his lips pressed tightly together and his gaze focused on the flickering candle on their table, he sat silently for a few moments before continuing. "Lately," he said, "we've been keeping a close watch on the so-called New Age movement. Have you heard of it?"

"No, not really."

"Those people seem to have plenty of money at their disposal, and also a good deal of influence in many places. One of their main objectives is the development of a religion that will subsume and replace all of the other religions in the world."

"Now that doesn't sound like such a bad idea—in fact it's just what we've always wanted," the bishop interjected, his face contorted into a wry grin.

"Yeah, sure, Franco," Delvecchio replied, "but unfortunately Catholicism isn't what they have in mind. These people have come up with their own Christ figure—a strange character they call 'Lord Maitreya'—who they claim is the new messiah. They're trying to persuade Catholics, especially young people, that bringing in practices from Buddhism, neo-paganism, astrology, and even Satanism can add meaning to their religious experience. If they succeed in connecting with the Catholic faithful, that could be an important first step in their establishing a foothold in the Church. Some of those high up in the Curia are immensely concerned."

"It does sound like the work of the devil, but it's hard to believe nowadays that any of that could pose a serious threat to the Church."

"Yes, it's quite bizarre, but the movement is gaining considerable momentum, and a good many Catholics are apparently being taken in by it. So, we've been keeping close surveillance on their activities, and recently we've also begun to mount some resistance. We commissioned several Catholic writers to produce books and magazine articles that will help to counteract the movement, and we're providing subsidies to publishing houses to make sure that they get out to the public. And lately, we also started to indemnify some of the larger publishers so they'll stop putting out any more New Age propaganda. That last part, I'll tell you, is a very expensive undertaking.

"So what is your role in all of this?"

"Well, one of the senior prelates in the group refers to me as '*Il primo difensore della fede*,' but actually, I—"

"Defender of the faith? That sounds to me like Head of the Inquisition."

"No! I mainly act as a kind of coordinator for the group. I keep track of the various ongoing projects, I help raise money, and it's also my responsibility to evaluate everything we do, to make certain that nothing's unethical or illegal. That's always been very important to everyone."

"Hmm…interesting. Tell me something else, Carlo. Are you still spending all of your money on that coin collection of yours?"

"My Roman coins are my great passion," Delvecchio replied. "And let me show you one of my favorites—I acquired it only a few months ago." He removed from his pocket a small Lucite container that encased a coin only slightly larger than a dime. "I always carry this one with me now as a lucky charm. It's a silver denarius that was minted approximately in the year 20 AD."

"TI. CAESAR AUGUSTUS," the bishop read, as he examined the coin.

"That's Tiberius Caesar. And do you know why this is so special? Well, it's come to be accepted by historians that when Jesus said 'Render to Caesar the things that are Caesar's,' the coin he was pointing to was exactly the same as this one—or perhaps, as I like to believe, it was this very one!"

"Most interesting," Coglieri replied. "Carlo, I asked you about your coin collection for a specific reason. In Guastalla, we recently became the happy recipients of a magnificent bequest. It was from a man who died with no heirs and left us a wonderful collection of art works—about a dozen Renaissance paintings and a large number of very fine bronze pieces. Among the items, there also were two gold Roman coins, and I'd like you to look at them," he said, as he produced a small box containing the two objects.

"These are exquisite!" Delvecchio exclaimed, after examining the coins. "Both of them are in superb condition—indeed they're museum-quality pieces. This smaller one was struck during the reign of Gaius Iulius—Julius Caesar. It's very rare. The other coin depicts Diocletian and Maximian. From its size, it probably is a five-aureus piece. I can assure you that these are very valuable."

"I expect," Coglieri said, "that the art collection we received will bring us an excellent price when it goes to auction, and Lord knows we can use the money. But I got to thinking that even without these coins, we'll come out very well, and so do you know what I did? I arranged to have them removed from the inventory of the collection. So now, they belong to me, or rather, they belong to you, because I want you to have them."

"Franco, that's a magnificent present. I'm really overwhelmed. I can't thank you enough."

"I'm very happy to know that my little gift will bring you so much pleasure," the bishop replied, reaching across the table to pat his old friend's hand.

6

September, 2002

Nathan Tobin sat alone in a massive underground cavern formed of roughly hewn, jagged-edged rock. A single candle dimly illuminated the crypt-like chamber. The air was sodden and heavy, and a frigid draft emanating from a narrow joining passageway kept him in a state of bone-chilling misery. And each new numbing blast posed an added threat of extinguishing the flickering candle. Water from an invisible source high in the ceiling dripped onto the floor nearby, and Nathan shivered from the cold and the dampness of the place. He was seated on a low wooden stool, next to an enormous table overflowing with stacks of ancient, yellowing parchment scrolls and manuscripts. He had been sifting endlessly through the piles of documents, one after the other, but he had not been able to locate the object of his search. And above him a giant clock ticked loudly, as a constant reminder that his time was rapidly running out.

A powerful mid-Atlantic downdraft slammed the giant Boeing jet into a lower altitude, and Nathan was jolted awake. This was not the first time he had had that dream. The cause for his unremitting anxiety was no mystery to him. The sobering counsel of Professor Felix Mandelbaum, his former dissertation advisor at Johns Hopkins University, had summed it up all too well.

"All of you are well on your way toward distinguished academic careers," he had told Nathan and a group of his fellow graduate students. "Completing your PhD at a prestigious university program is, of course, the first crucial step. But equally important is what you accomplish in your postdoctoral work. You're going to have to do that at a first-rate institution, and in the short time that'll be available to you, you'll have to be highly productive—meaning that you'll need to publish some really impressive research, and in respected scholarly journals. You'll have to work harder than you ever have before and, I should add, a generous measure of good luck will help. Just keep in mind that for every good university position that opens in our field, there are ten or twelve, maybe even twenty, well-qualified people ready to compete for it."

Nathan often reflected on the odds he faced, but his fierce determination to be one of the successful ones only intensified when such thoughts occupied his mind.

He had inherited his father's sandy brown hair, his generous nature, his reflective temperament, and the extreme myopia for which both of them required thick corrective lenses. The resulting bookish appearance they shared seemed to presage the choice they had both made to pursue careers in academia. But whereas Arthur Tobin, his father, was a professor in a junior college, Nathan's aspiration was for a tenured faculty position at one of the top-tier research universities.

"You really look like a professor," he had been told by his fellow graduate student, Jennifer Allen, who had shared his apartment and his bed for almost a year before their relationship ended. But that small bit of encouragement had done little to bolster Nathan's optimism.

There was another driving force that more directly sustained Nathan's discomfort and fueled his foreboding, recurrent dream. That related to the research on medieval poetry he was about to begin in his new postdoctoral fellowship position. It had started with an e-mail message he received during the summer from Professor Chaim Elstein, Director of the Taylor-Schechter Genizah Research Unit of the Cambridge University Library, the man who would be Nathan's supervisor for the work he would soon be starting. The director had informed him that among the nearly 140,000 *genizah* manuscripts that were available for study, nearly one-third of them represented works of poetry. That left Nathan with the uneasy feeling that he might be faced with an overwhelming barrage of documents that would be impossible to organize or study in any useful fashion.

A subsequent e-mail from Professor Elstein made it clear that over the hundred or so years since the genizah collection had been brought to Cambridge, virtually all of the manuscripts, including those held by other libraries throughout the world, had been microfilmed and thoroughly catalogued. The director also pointed out that most of the documents had been restored and preserved in protective Mylar covers, and that considerable progress had also been made toward digitizing them, so that the most significant manuscripts and fragments could be accessed with a computer. And, most important of all, Nathan learned that a research associate at the library would be assembling a list of the available works by the more notable medieval Hebrew poets represented in the *genizah* collection. That compilation, he was assured, would be completed by the time he arrived in Cambridge. But the anxiety his dream so vividly depicted always remained with him.

Much to the annoyance of the man in the adjoining seat on the airplane, Nathan, now very much awake, switched on his reading light. He retrieved the folder of information he had received about the Genizah Research Unit, and he began to reread some of the sections he had previously highlighted with a yellow marker.

"The Cambridge University Library serves as the primary repository for the remarkable collection of medieval manuscripts that were recovered from the *genizah* (storage facility) of the ancient Ben Ezra

Synagogue in Cairo, Egypt. Both religious and secular writings, some now more than a thousand years old, had been placed there for safekeeping, following the traditional Jewish practice that forbids the destruction of any writing that contains the name of God. Solomon Schechter, a distinguished Cambridge scholar, arranged to have these writings brought to England during the 1890s, and subsequently a specialized unit was established at the Cambridge University Library for research and for the study of these documents."

Nathan then spent several minutes reading a tenth-century Hebrew poem that had been found among the Cairo *genizah* documents. He had received it only a week before he left on his trip to Cambridge, from Sarah Jackson, the research associate who was organizing the *genizah* poetry collection information for him. She had included with it her English translation of the poem.

"It was written by a woman," Ms. Jackson had said in her letter, "the wife of the renowned tenth-century Spanish rabbi, linguist, and poet Dunash ibn Labrat. She had written this poem as a farewell to her husband as he was about to leave Spain in exile."

היזכור יעלת החן ידידה	Will her love remember his graceful fawn
ביום פירוד ובזרועה יחידה	As they parted with her son in her arms?
ושם חותם ימינו על שמאלה	While he put his right ring on her hand,
ובזרועו הלא שמה צמידה	Did she not place upon his wrist her band?
ביום לקחה לזכרון רדידו	And then she took his mantle as a seal,
והוא לקח לזכרון רדידה	And for a keepsake did he take her veil.
הישאר בכל ארץ ספרד	But if he would half her lord's kingdom gain
ולו לקח חצי מלכות נגידה	Would he not remain in the Land of Spain?

Nathan was taken by the poet's masterly use of rhyme and meter and by the simple beauty of her writing.

"A fragment of a poem her husband had written in reply to these verses was also discovered among the documents in the *genizah* collection," Ms. Jackson had added in her letter.

Nathan turned off his reading light and covered himself with a blanket, and soon he was asleep.

His flight arrived at Heathrow Airport shortly before noon. A ride through the London Tube brought him to the King's Cross station, and from there he boarded a train for the short final leg of his trip to Cambridge.

A gregarious young man, sporting a blue tweed coat and a bright yellow necktie, took the seat next to Nathan on the train. He introduced himself immediately.

"Chris Hopkins," he said, extending his hand. "I'm in graduate school at Cambridge—mechanical engineering."

Nathan explained that this was his first time there, and that he was about to begin his postdoc at the Cambridge University Library.

"It's really a fabulous place. I guarantee you'll love it," Chris said. "The University Library is quite close to the railroad station, perhaps a mile or so. If you don't have too much to carry, it's a nice walk. And it'll give you a chance to see a bit of the university. If you'd like, I'll write out a good route for you to follow. I'll make sure it takes you past Emmanuel College, the 'Emma,' they call it here. That's where I spent my undergraduate years. Do you know who was one of the most famous graduates of Emmanuel? An American, a chap named John Harvard. After his graduation here, back in the 1600s, they say he went home to Boston and founded some sort of university there. And from what I'm told, they named the place after him."

Arriving at the Cambridge station, Nathan set off on foot as Chris Hopkins had recommended, following his suggested route. As it turned out, the distance to the University Library was actually more than three miles, but Nathan nevertheless enjoyed the opportunity to do some walking after his long flight.

His itinerary took Nathan up St. Andrew's Street, right past the spacious campus of Emmanuel College, providing him a close view of its famous chapel from 1677, designed by Christopher Wren. From there, a turn onto Trumpington Street brought him to the fifteenth-century Gothic buildings of King's College. Nathan's route then took him past the ornate domed gate of Gonville and Caius College, and then to the Great Court of Trinity College with its colonnaded fountain and its legendary sixteenth-century gatehouse, overseen by a life-sized statue of King Henry VIII, Trinity's sponsor and benefactor. From there, he crossed the Cam River, pausing briefly for a view of the graceful stone structure of the seventeenth-century Clare College Bridge.

The day was unusually warm for mid-September, and by afternoon, the sky was becoming increasingly overcast. As Nathan approached Queen's Road, he was engulfed in a sudden downpour. He had no umbrella, and with the suitcase and the backpack he was carrying, that would have been of little use to him anyway. He was drenched by the time he was able to take cover in the courtyard of a nearby building. When he finally reached the University Library, he was thoroughly bedraggled.

Cynthia Beckman, the secretary for the Taylor-Schechter Research Unit, was summoned when Nathan arrived, and she escorted him to the third floor of the building, to the Research Unit's office area. She was barely able to suppress a smile at the young scholar's disheveled appearance, but she managed to maintain a properly serious countenance.

"Dr. Elstein is expecting you," Ms. Beckman informed him as they rode up on the lift. "You might want to take a few moments in the lavatory for a change of clothes to make yourself a bit more presentable. I can get you a plastic bag for your wet clothing if you'd like."

Nathan was grateful for that opportunity, and he quickly substituted dry clothing from his suitcase for the thoroughly soaked outfit he had been wearing.

"Well, I'm sure that's more comfortable." Ms. Beckman said, when he returned. "Now, let's see if we can find Dr. Elstein."

The door to the Director's office was partly open, and it became immediately apparent to Nathan that a loud and contentious argument was in progress.

"That is absurd," one man bellowed in a voice that bespoke both anger and ridicule. "If you include an unsubstantiated statement like that in the paper, first of all they won't publish it, and on top of that, they'll assume we are two first-class idiots."

"Well, I realize it's a bit speculative, but if we throw that out, then the whole conclusion doesn't really amount to much," another man replied in a considerably softer and more controlled voice. "Then what will we be left with? Nothing very worthwhile, I would say."

"That is utter nonsense," growled the first man, carefully articulating each syllable and pausing menacingly between every word for extra emphasis. "The conclusion is perfectly fine without that."

For Nathan, the ill-tempered exchange provoked feelings of both anxiety and dread. From the telephone and e-mail correspondence he had had with Prof. Elstein, there had seemed to be every indication that the director was a kindly and supportive man with whom he could expect to have an amicable and collegial relationship. But now a very different impression flashed through his mind, conveying the prospect of his spending two unpleasant years being yelled at and humiliated by an insufferable tyrant.

Ms. Beckman tapped on the door, and she and Nathan entered the office. Professor Elstein, clearly the antagonist in the unsettling discussion that had been in progress, was seated at a small wooden table with a younger man who, Nathan surmised, must have been relieved that their meeting was being brought to an end. The director recognized Nathan immediately, and in spite of the unpleasantness he had provoked only seconds earlier, he seemed surprisingly gracious.

"So, you are here. Welcome! I hope you had a good trip," he said. "Nathan, let me introduce you to one of our very important people. This is Thomas Gans, one of our Senior Research Associates. His area is Semitic languages, and he's our premier specialist in ancient and medieval manuscripts."

Dr. Gans added his welcome to Nathan, then he quickly gathered up the pages of the research report that covered the table and took leave of them.

Short, stocky, and highly animated, the director wore a natty gray sport coat, which, Nathan thought, nicely complemented his massive beard. His small embroidered *kippah* had been carefully attached at the very center of the bald spot on the crown of his head. The unmistakable halo that this created struck Nathan as being notably out of character in light of the ferocity of his verbal assault on Dr. Gans.

"So come," the director said to him with a wave of his hand. "Let me show you around here, then we can get some tea and chat a bit."

The brief tour included the other offices, the conference room, and the computer and media room of the Research Unit. Finally, the director showed Nathan a small windowless office that contained two desks and a tall bookshelf.

"This will be your office," he said, "but you'll need to share it with another visiting associate who'll be joining us later this week."

In the Library's Tea Room, Dr. Elstein introduced Nathan to some of the other staff members of the Research Unit.

The first of them was Sarah Jackson, with whom Nathan had been in correspondence over the summer. Miss Jackson, whose main responsibilities were as the archivist and curator of the *genizah* collection, was someone he had especially looked forward to meeting. Her compilation of the works of medieval Hebrew poetry would be instrumental to his research. He later learned that Sarah Jackson was the granddaughter of a prominent Anglican bishop, and that it was her grandfather who had guided her in the study of Hebrew, Latin, and Greek. But what struck him most of all on meeting her was that she was considerably younger than he had expected; in spite of her impressive accomplishments, she was scarcely beyond her mid-thirties. Taller than Nathan by at least two inches, with a pleasant though restrained smile, she was hardly the stodgy figure that he had imagined an archivist would be.

"I'm very happy to meet you," Nathan said, "and I really want to thank you for the poem by Mrs. Dunash. It's a wonderful piece. I hope there are lots more like it in the *genizah* collection."

"I'm pleased to meet you, Dr. Tobin, and I'm glad you enjoyed the poem. It's a special favorite of mine."

"Please call me Nathan—everybody does."

"I'm quite confident you'll be very happy with the works of poetry we have here," she said. "I suspect the biggest challenge for you will be deciding which of them you'll want to work on. But I do need to tell you that I've been having more difficulty than I anticipated in compiling the information for your research. The system we use to catalog the collection isn't actually well suited for that sort of search. And as I'm sure you know, we have more than forty thousand works of poetry. But I do assure you I'll keep at it."

Nathan suddenly felt a tightness in his chest, and as a twinge of anxiety enveloped him, he held his breath. Maybe, he thought, that disturbing recurrent dream he had been having wasn't such a fantasy at all.

"Here's someone else I want you to meet," the director said, as they stopped at the door of a small, dimly lit office. "Fergus Wylie here has been with us for almost two years. He's a computer whiz—spends most of his time developing the digitized library of the manuscript collection."

"A great pleasure to make your acquaintance," said the skeletally thin young man, whose straw-blond hair was gathered into a long ponytail. He extended Nathan a warm handshake. "If you ever need help with your computer, I'll be happy to lend a hand," he added.

Back in the director's office, Nathan and Professor Elstein spoke for a long while about Nathan's plans for his research.

"I'm rather concerned about the problems Miss Jackson has been having…about compiling the information on the works of poetry in the collection," Nathan said.

"I'll talk with her later today," he replied. "In any case, I don't really think that will hold up your work," he reassured the young scholar. Then their discussion turned to practical matters.

"Ms. Beckman informed me that she completed the arrangements for a place for you to live here," Elstein said. "Did she send you the information about that?" Nathan nodded. "It's a flat in one of the buildings the university owns. Housing here is hard to come by, and it took her a good bit of effort to get that for you. Let's see now," Elstein continued, taking a note from his coat pocket, "it's off to the North a bit, near Chesterton. It's not too far, and if you ride a bicycle it should be no more than ten minutes. The building manager is a Mrs. Hastings. Did you know it will be £580 a month? Quite a bit, I should say, but that's about average for here. By the way, I'll be driving home in a half hour, and if you like I'll be happy to take you over there."

Professor Elstein carried Nathan's suitcase as they left the library. "My wife and I had hoped to have you come for dinner, but, we need to attend a reception this evening for some new faculty. So when the other new visiting associate gets here later this week, we'd like to have you both join us then."

"That's very kind," Nathan replied. "So who is the person who'll be sharing the office with me?"

"Oh, yes," Elstein answered, "a sociologist, an Israeli named Bassat."

"I'll look forward to meeting him," Nathan replied.

"That's Zippora Bassat, a young woman." As they neared the apartment building, Elstein pointed out a small storefront restaurant. "Middle-Eastern," he said, "rather good food and not very expensive."

The flat was one of twenty-four, on the third floor of an ivy-covered red brick building dating from the 1920s. Mrs. Hastings, a widow well into her sixties, lived on the first floor near the entrance to the building. When Nathan and Elstein arrived at her door, she had already begun preparing dinner, and she made no effort to hide her displeasure at the interruption. She left them waiting in the hallway, and several minutes later she returned with the key.

With two large windows facing eastward, the living room and bedroom in the flat were usually sunny in the morning, but on that rainy day, it struck Nathan as being rather gloomy.

"I'll expect your check for the first month's rent by tomorrow morning," Mrs. Hastings informed him sternly, "and if there's any-thing here that needs attention, you can let me know." With that, she left, and after a few minutes, Professor Elstein also hurried off.

After unpacking his clothes, Nathan took advantage of the remaining time before sunset to explore the surrounding area. Consulting a guidebook, he identified two architectural treasures nearby that dated from the 1300s: he spent a long while admiring the Chesterton Tower, a superbly restored stone building resplendent with two silo-like towers and a very medieval-appearing turret; he also had enough daylight for a good view of the magnificent St. Andrew's Church. Nathan finally made his way to the Lebanese restaurant Chaim Elstein had recommended.

He found it to be a lively place, its cubicles occupied mainly by an animated crowd of students, whose noisy chatter and laughter nearly drowned out a languorous Arabic song that played in the background. Nathan had missed lunch that day, and all he had eaten since breakfast on the airplane was the small biscuit he had had with his afternoon tea. The inviting smell of freshly baked khoubiz bread mingled with the aroma of sizzling lamb sausages added to his already acute craving for a full meal. He was happy to spot the only unoccupied table, in a back corner of the room. He eagerly devoured his first course, a plate of tangy baba ghanouj, and he followed that with a creamy and pungent shanklish. For his main course, he had musakhan chicken, which effectively satisfied his remaining appetite. He nevertheless finished the meal with an oversized portion of baklava dripping with honey, and strong, sweet coffee.

Nathan was weary from the long trip and the excitement of the afternoon, so the quiet dinner alone gave him an opportunity to unwind and to reflect on his experiences that day. Elstein's research unit seemed to be a promising place to do his research, though the director himself, with his temper, seemed more of an unknown than he had anticipated. Miss Jackson's failure to finish her review of the poetry works from the *genizah* collection also left him with an uneasy feeling.

He was happy with his new flat, although it had cost more than he had anticipated. Most of his fellowship grant would need to go toward the rent.

His musings took him to thoughts about the Israeli woman who would be sharing the small office with him. At Johns Hopkins, Nathan had worked for a short while with Chava Melzer, a visiting graduate student from Tel Aviv, a woman whose incessant complaining and unpleasant smoking habit inspired him to avoid her whenever possible. He hoped never to have to repeat that kind of experience. As he was about to leave the restaurant, Nathan noticed that the Internet terminal was not being used, and he took the opportunity to send an e-mail to his parents in Cleveland, to let them know he had arrived in Cambridge.

Nathan spent part of the next morning with Sara Jackson. He was relieved to learn that she actually had made a good deal of progress in her compilation of the medieval Hebrew poetry in the library's collection. Shortly before noon, the two of them met with Professor Elstein to review what she had accomplished. As Nathan was leaving Elstein's office, Thomas Gans intercepted him.

"Any plans for lunch?" he asked. Nathan shook his head to indicate that he had none, and they left together for a pub down the street from the library. The autumn Michaelmas term was about to begin at Cambridge, and the campus was coming alive with activity. The cloudiness and drizzle of the previous day had given way to a clear and sunny afternoon, and the two of them passed groups of animated students, and a few of their professors, milling about the byways and the stately halls of learning of the distinguished and venerable academy.

Gans's favorite pub was a noisy place, filled nearly to capacity, and the two of them were obliged to share their table and their wooden benches with a high-spirited quartet of undergraduates.

"I'm sure you know how pleased we all are now that the poetry collection will be getting some serious attention," Gans said. "By the way, I read your paper, the one you published last year on love poems from Mesopotamia. That really was an excellent piece of work. Was it part of your dissertation research?"

"Yes it was, but only a small part. Most of my research involved an analysis of the biblical Song of Songs, though along the way I did some comparisons with other examples of Near-Eastern love poetry. Actually, I had two very different dissertation subjects in graduate school. I started out to do a textual analysis of the book of Daniel, with the late Felix Mandelbaum. That was a difficult project. I spent almost a year learning Aramaic, but after all that, Professor Mandelbaum came down with Hodgkin's disease. When he got sick, he felt it would be best for me to find a new faculty advisor, and that's when I began to work on my analysis of the Song of Songs."

"I knew Felix Mandelbaum," Gans said. "I first met him at a symposium in Jerusalem. It was a pity he died so young. To change the subject, I want to be sure you realize that Elstein is hardly the ogre he must have seemed when you first met him. When he gets excited about something, he can become a raving maniac. But most of the time he's really very decent. He sets a high standard for all of us, but he's harder on himself than on anybody else in the research unit."

Afterward, Nathan went back to his new office, to see if the computer Ms. Beckman ordered for him had arrived. But as he approached the doorway of the small office, what immediately drew his attention was the young woman seated at the other desk. She was petite and slim, with dark, wide-set eyes and long, black hair.

"Hello, good afternoon," she said to Nathan, in distinctly British-accented English. After his reflection the previous night about his unpleasant interactions with Chava Melzer, Nathan was unprepared to imagine that this comely and demure young woman could be Zippora Bassat.

"I…I thought you were Israeli," Nathan said.

"Oh, yes," she answered, smiling at his ungraceful reply, "but I was born in London. My family moved to Israel when I was twelve years old." Nathan also learned that Zippora had returned to the University of London for her undergraduate years, and that she had recently gotten her PhD degree from the University of Chicago, the same university where he had been an undergraduate student some years earlier.

"So how long have you been here?" Nathan asked.

"I arrived about an hour ago," she replied. "Apparently not a very convenient time. Ms. Beckman was away for lunch, and Dr. Elstein is in meetings until three o'clock. So, one of the other people directed me to this place, and here I am."

"If you haven't had lunch," Nathan said, "I would be happy to join you. I've already eaten, but I wouldn't mind another cup of coffee."

"That is an offer I cannot refuse," Zippora replied happily.

"I understand that you're a poet," Zippora said, as she looked up from studying the menu.

"I'm not really much of a poet, though I did have two of my poems published in a literary journal when I was an undergraduate," Nathan answered. "My research here will be on medieval Hebrew poetry from the *genizah* collection. And you, I'm told, are a sociologist. What is your research interest?"

"My work deals with population dynamics," Zippora replied, "from a historical perspective. I'm here on a rather meager fellowship grant from the Ginsberg Fund, at Hebrew University. The foundation primarily supports studies of Jewish communities. They felt it was a bit of a stretch, but they agreed to let me have a one-year grant for research on Jewish-Muslim relations in medieval Cairo."

"So how did your family happen to move to Israel?"

"It was my father. He's a scholar—a poor scholar I should say," Zippora replied, then she laughed. "That wasn't a comment about the quality of the scholarship, only about his financial situation. He's a Talmudist, very religious. Not a good way to become rich, or, for that matter, even to earn a living. My mother's family in England were relatively well off, so money was never much of a problem. But then, my mother invested almost everything in a business venture with my uncle. It ended up a disaster, a total loss for both of them. A short while later, my father was offered a position in a religious academy in Jerusalem, and so off we went. My father, of course, is very happy, but my mother had an awful time adjusting to living in Israel. She still misses England terribly."

"So I assume you must be very religious," Nathan said.

"No, and my mother really isn't either," she answered, "but as long as everything is properly kosher at home, my father doesn't seem to mind it, or maybe he never really noticed."

Later that afternoon, Nathan was in the midst of setting up his new computer when Zippora returned from her meeting with Professor Elstein.

"He's pleasant enough, and he certainly is full of energy," she said in reply to Nathan's question about their meeting. "Also," she added, "Ms. Beckman told me the flat she secured for me is in the same building as yours. So, it appears that we're about to be neighbors."

"That's a nice surprise," he answered. "Did she tell you about Mrs. Hastings, the building manager?"

"She mentioned her."

"Well, I can offer you a bit of advice from my experience yesterday. Mrs. Hastings is none too pleasant when you call on her while she's preparing dinner."

"Well, it's almost tea time."

"Then this might be a good time to see her. Maybe after her tea Mrs. Hastings will be in a better mood. If you'd like, I would be happy to go with you. It's about a twenty-minute walk."

Zippora was happy to accept his offer. "How do you like your new flat?" she asked him as they turned onto Adams Road.

"It's fine. It's nicely furnished, though the bedroom is small. The kitchen is in good condition, and there's a comfortable living room."

"I'll be getting a very small flat, I'm sure not as nice as that," Zippora said.

Nathan's predictions about Mrs. Hastings's disposition turned out to be correct. She greeted them pleasantly, and she not only invited them to come inside, but she also offered them tea. Nathan politely declined her offer.

"I'm upstairs in 308," he told Zippora as he turned to leave. "Stop by once you're settled in."

Twenty minutes later, Nathan heard a knock on his door, but what followed was not at all what he had expected. There in the doorway was Zippora; she had her suitcase with her, and she was crying uncontrollably.

"Come in," Nathan said to her. "What happened? Are you all right?"

"Apparently there was some sort of mix-up," she said between sobs. "Ms. Beckman told me that they had a small flat for me that would cost £375. That was a lot of money for me to begin with, but now Mrs. Hastings says that the only one available here goes for more than £600. There's no possible way I could handle that. So now what am I to do?"

"You'll need to check into a hotel until it gets straightened out," he suggested.

"I don't think I can afford that either," Zippora answered.

"Look, why don't you leave your bags here for now? We can go for something to eat, and then I'll call Dr. Elstein for advice."

After some falafel and hummus, Zippora became more composed, but she continued to be visibly upset.

"I'm sure this isn't the first time they've had such a problem," Nathan said, in an effort to comfort her. "There must be something available for you until they can find you a more affordable place."

Zippora remained unhappy in spite of Nathan's attempts to cheer her up. As they were having coffee, her face suddenly brightened.

"Nathan," she said, "you have a large sofa in your flat. Would you mind if I stayed at your place tonight?"

The suggestion came as a surprise to Nathan, who had no interest in having an overnight guest. "I…I don't really think that would be such a good idea," he protested.

"I can promise you that I won't be any trouble," Zippora responded, "and it would only be for tonight."

Realizing that Dr. Elstein might not be able to offer anything helpful, Nathan gave in to Zippora's request. Once that decision was made, Zippora became notably cheery.

"Why don't we stop at the grocery on the way back, and I'll get some things for a nice English breakfast tomorrow?" she offered.

"Well, all right," he answered, with an obvious lack of enthusiasm.

And so, in spite of Nathan's reluctance, Zippora spent the night on his sofa. He had offered her the bedroom, but she refused it. The sumptuous breakfast she prepared the next day did raise his spirits, and he was greatly relieved later that morning when Ms. Beckman informed Zippora that she had found a nice furnished room she could have for only £300. Later that day, Zippora returned to their office with a bouquet of red chrysanthemums in a glass vase, which she placed on Nathan's desk, next to his computer.

"It's a little thank-you, for putting me up and for putting up with me, and especially for being so nice," she said. "Having an hysterical woman to deal with is probably the last thing you needed on your second day here." Then she kissed him on the cheek. With that, Nathan felt amply rewarded.

Several days later, Sarah Jackson finally presented Nathan with her compilation of the medieval Hebrew poets represented in the *genizah* collection. He was soon able to identify three important but largely unrecognized Spanish poets from the twelfth and thirteenth centuries.

Over the following weeks, as Nathan began his preliminary reviews of the poems he had chosen, Thomas Gans proved to be an invaluable resource, especially in helping him understand obscure and unusual

Hebrew words and phrases that appeared in the medieval texts. With Professor Elstein's generous help, Nathan began a comparative analysis of the poems he had identified, and he made rapid progress in organizing his work on the project.

But among Nathan's colleagues in the Taylor-Schechter research unit, the most supportive and helpful of all turned out to be Zippora. She was never too busy to listen to his ideas and to learn what his research had uncovered, and her critical judgment and intellectual rigor impressed Nathan immensely. Although she had made it clear that poetry had never been of particular interest to her, she proved to have a remarkable grasp of the subtlety and nuance that gave special meaning and beauty to the verses that Nathan had selected for his analysis.

In her own research, Zippora encountered an unexpected problem. Although she had had a good working knowledge of Arabic, the medieval Judeo-Arabic in which many of the most critical documents were written posed considerable difficulty for her. Fortunately, that was one of Professor Elstein's special areas of expertise, and he was able to devote a number of hours to help her get started. At Professor Elstein's suggestion, Zippora enrolled in a seminar in Semitic Philology given by the Faculty of Oriental Studies. That gave her the background knowledge and the confidence she needed to move forward with her work.

In the weeks that followed, Nathan made substantial strides in his study of the Spanish-Hebrew poetry texts. Zippora, having overcome her difficulties with Judeo-Arabic manuscripts, also began to make solid progress in her research. She soon was well along with a manuscript that she hoped to submit for publication before the end of the year.

Nathan, always an early riser, made it a habit to be at his desk each day by 7:00 a.m. But each Thursday morning, he instead rode the 7:45 train into London, and continued on the Underground until he reached the Municipal Children's Hospital. There, he donned a bright yellow jacket and took up his post in the spacious waiting area of the General Paediatrics Clinic.

"The program is called Reading for Kids," he explained to Zippora. "We read to the children while they're waiting to be seen by the doctor, and when they're finished, we give them books to take home.

Children love to have someone read to them, even somebody who 'talks funny,' as some of these British kids say about me."

As serious and deeply committed scholars, Nathan and Zippora each focused their thoughts and their considerable energy on the research they were pursuing. Their personal relationship was one of collegial support and cooperation, which contributed to their scholarly productivity and to their satisfaction with their work. They often lunched together, and they frequently attended lectures and seminars of common interest. Over time, they also shared occasional evenings, attending plays, musical performances, and films. It was an enjoyable and fulfilling time for both of them.

The closeness of their working relationship also provided Nathan ample opportunity to appreciate Zippora's wit and charm, her warm and easygoing manner, and inevitably, her considerable attractiveness. He enjoyed being with her, but in light of the intensity and seriousness of their scholarly pursuits, it seemed inappropriate for him to entertain any thoughts of a romantic relationship. Nevertheless, from time to time, he indulged himself in pleasant fantasies of lovemaking with Zippora. And at such times, he often wondered if she was in any way attracted to him.

One morning in early November, Zippora was boiling water in her electric teakettle as Nathan entered the office.

"You're just in time for tea," she said. "It'll be ready in just a few minutes. By the way," Zippora asked, "you are aware, aren't you, that the Michaelmas term here ends in early December? Then, I'm told, everything really quiets down. Apparently most people find it to be a good time for a holiday. I'll be visiting my family in Israel," she said as she poured hot water into her teapot. "My brother's getting married in December, and so that works out rather nicely."

"I don't think you ever spoke of your brother."

"Oh, well he's a carbon copy of my father, very religious and all of that. He'll be marrying a young girl, hardly out of high school, and she'll be a good little wife for him and have lots of babies," she added, with more than a touch of derision.

"In light of your family background, I'm surprised that you escaped such a fate yourself."

"Well, I'm sure that's what my father had in mind, but my mum wouldn't stand for any such thing. That, really, is why I came to London for college—it was a scheme carefully hatched by my mother. Have you made holiday plans?"

"I'm not planning on going home just yet. At first I thought I might stay here and work, but the idea of some time off is rather appealing. Especially if I could go somewhere that's warm. One thought I've been toying with is Cairo," he said, between sips of tea.

"Cairo?" Zippora replied with an incredulous frown. "Why would you possibly want to go there?"

Nathan laughed. "Why, to visit Fustat and the Ben Ezra *genizah*."

"Oh, yes," Zippora answered. "I suppose that might be interesting to see. Well, if you do go there, my advice is to be careful."

"Have you been to Egypt?"

"Yes," she replied, "on a school trip. We visited the very impressive Egyptian Museum, as well as the pyramids and The Sphinx. From what I saw of it, I would have to say that Cairo is not a terribly nice city."

As Nathan began searching the Internet to look into travel and hotel accommodations in Cairo, he was happy to learn that in December the off-season rates there were at their lowest. He found a direct round-trip flight from London for less than £300. On the advice of Chaim Elstein, he also paid a visit to Dr. Mohammed Sajid in the Faculty of Oriental Studies. Sajid, a specialist in Arabic literature and a native of Cairo, was able to provide Nathan with very useful information about his hometown.

"I always recommend the Horus House Hotel," he told Nathan. "It's inexpensive, and it's really quite decent. The hotel is also well located, on Gazirah Island in the middle of the Nile River. And it's not far from a Metro station. Be sure to mention my name if you go there."

7

April, 2003

At 10:40 a.m., Myron Geller made ready to execute an order to buy $400,000 of U.S. Treasury bonds. In the dimly lit trading room office where Myron spent most of his waking hours, a massive bank of eighty computers, terminal screens, and monitors formed a luminescent semicircle surrounding his desk. The terminals along the bottom row provided stock and bond prices from exchanges throughout the world. Others displayed quotation service data from New York, London, Geneva, and Hong Kong. And a large group of television screens, fed by a phalanx of satellite dishes on the roof of the building, supplied him with the latest newswire bulletins from every corner of the globe.

Those few individuals who had had the opportunity to discuss securities trading with the reclusive Mr. Geller almost always

came away with the impression that he had developed an ingenious strategy.

The underlying premise of his trading system was that news-
worthy events would inevitably have an almost immediate, albeit
often subtle effect on stock and bond prices. Geller's technique, he
explained, depended upon his ability to analyze news items and assess
their impact on the securities markets. His trading approach involved
buying securities that were ready to increase in value, and then quickly
selling them hours or occasionally even minutes later, to capture their
realized gains.

In his hands, that strategy, he was proud to tell anyone who would
listen, consistently produced profits of at least 20 to 30 percent per
year. And moreover, he kept his investors' dollars in cash accounts
most of the time, thereby protecting their capital against the perils of
the marketplace.

The imposing twelve-room mansion that doubled as Myron's
home and business headquarters in Greenwich, Connecticut, was hidden among the trees of its heavily wooded four-acre lot, barely visible
from the street. The residents of that exclusive neighborhood were
among the wealthiest and most powerful of New York's business and
financial leaders.

It was early spring, and the flowering shrubs and fruit trees on the
grounds were at their colorful and fragrant peak. Squirrels in a fren-
zied chase leaped from branch to branch among the stately oak trees,
and birds searched about for building materials for their nests. A flock
of geese had taken up residence in the pond behind the house. But
Myron saw none of that; his window curtains were all drawn closed,
to preserve the subdued illumination of his trading room. And Myron
never had had much interest in his surroundings anyway.

Lanky and six feet tall, with thick glasses and a bedraggled appearance, he seldom bothered to shave. Poorly fitting blue jeans and a
sport shirt comprised his usual working wardrobe, and he frequently
went about without shoes. Most people who met him concluded that
he was very strange, genius though he might have been.

Myron had grand plans for his future: he saw himself moving
into the league of such luminaries as Warren Buffet and Bill Gates.

The goal he set for himself was to become the manager of ten billion dollars of assets. He had begun his career as an investment broker, managing mostly small individual accounts, but he soon began to search for opportunities to trade on a larger scale.

His first big step in that direction came when he succeeded in buying a small insurance company that held nearly twenty million dollars in its cash reserves. The purchase price of the company was 3.7 million dollars. To buy it, Myron submitted a false affidavit of his net worth, and then he "borrowed" virtually all of the purchase price from investors' accounts that had been entrusted to him. After taking possession of the firm, he promptly extracted sufficient funds from its reserves to cover what he had taken from his investment clients. In the years that followed, Myron added six more insurance companies to his holdings. For the purchase of each of these new firms, Myron followed the same routine: he plundered enough from the cash reserves of the other firms he controlled to cover the purchase price of the new company.

With his empire by then having assets of nearly two hundred million dollars, Myron appeared to be well on his way toward becoming a major figure in the insurance industry. And with his ingenious trading strategy, he confidently expected to generate enormous profits for his companies and for himself.

But most of all, Myron dreamed of the day when he could join the ranks of America's foremost philanthropists. He spoke often with his employees about his deep commitment to charitable causes.

"For the poor, the sick, and the elderly, so much needs to be done to relieve their suffering. And for what better causes can money be used?"

As he fixated on his data monitors and newswire screens, Myron began to sense a tightening in his chest; imperceptibly, his breathing gradually became more rapid and then more labored, he became light-headed, and his vision became blurred. Then his headache began. At first he had the sensation of a constricting band around his head that, as it intensified, was accompanied by a succession of searing, shooting pains radiating toward the base of his skull and the back of his neck. His face became flushed and beads of moisture formed over his brow. He tore at the collar of his shirt to cool himself. The muscles in his arms began to tighten and his hands trembled so severely that he was barely able to execute the purchase order.

Having completed the transaction, Myron sprang from his chair and began pacing the room along a circular path that within seconds brought him back to the monitor that was transmitting the minute-by-minute progress of the bond issue he had just purchased. His headache worsened and aspirin gave him no relief. He tried to calm himself by lying on the couch in his office, but seconds later he returned to his pacing. By eleven fifteen, as feelings of terror and panic increasingly enveloped him, Myron could no longer bear the stress and, with his hands shaking uncontrollably, he was able only with the greatest effort to execute an order to sell the entire bond purchase he had made. He realized no profit from the transaction, but he was relieved to see that he had not taken a loss.

Myron explained his problem, which even some of his closest associates had not been aware of, as a "trading block," suggesting something akin to the difficulty writers occasionally encounter. But for Myron, this was an unremitting condition, and as a result, he was almost never able to put his trading skill into practice. The psychiatrist who treated him, in spite of many months of therapy, had made no progress in lessening the panic attacks Myron experienced whenever he attempted to initiate a transaction. But Myron never doubted that in time he would be able to put all of that behind him so he could work effectively as a trader.

In the meantime, Myron was faced with the costs of his extensive financial enterprise. He had hundreds of employees, there were the expenses of the mansion that housed his organization, and also of the limousines and chartered airplanes he hired. He needed security personnel, and numerous consultants and lawyers were required for his business operations. Moreover, Myron's irrepressible support of a host of charitable causes required substantial funding as well.

His solution, invariably, was to transfer assets of the insurance companies he owned into his private Swiss bank account, and then to use those funds to cover his expenses. To conceal all this, he fabricated reports that showed magnificent returns on the supposedly invested funds. To sustain this fraudulent operation, Myron made certain that insurance claims to his companies were always paid out promptly, and he continually shifted dollars from one company to another to keep state insurance regulators from becoming suspicious. He eventually created an extensive network of shell corporations and offshore accounts, and he conducted his business under a number of different aliases. Money laundering and outright embezzlement had become the two towers of Myron's castle in the sky.

After systematically looting his seven insurance firms for several years, Myron began planning for the next big step in the expansion of his financial empire. He was particularly anxious to develop an arrangement that would allow him to operate and manipulate the companies outside the scrutiny of annoying insurance regulators. The plan he devised was ingenious. Moreover, it provided Myron a new opportunity to direct money to worthy charitable causes.

The cover for his new operation would be provided by the Catholic Church; in fact, as Myron planned it, he would be in direct partnership with the Vatican. After extensive research and lavish payments to make the necessary connections, Myron arranged to be represented by Thomas O'Morrow, a devout Catholic who had been a well-regarded New York prosecutor and a former advisor to President Ronald Reagan.

Prior to the first meeting with his new envoy, Myron read extensively about the Catholic Church and especially about its saints, with particular attention to the life and works of St. Francis of Assisi.

"Mr. O'Morrow," Myron said as they sat together in Myron's spacious but cluttered office, "I've been fortunate as a businessman, and I've succeeded in amassing a considerable fortune. I'm now at the point where I'm ready to give back part of what was given to me, and I've come to believe that the Catholic Church will be best able to use the money to help those in need. I can make a sizeable contribution immediately, and eventually I expect to raise billions of dollars more for the Church's charitable works."

Arriving at the Vatican, O'Morrow first made contact with Monsignor Vittorio Sangiovanni, an emeritus judge of an important Vatican tribunal and a respected Church official. The monsignor was closely associated with the most powerful Vatican dignitaries, including the secretary of state, and soon afterward he arranged for Myron's emissary to meet with two other key individuals within the Vatican hierarchy: Bishop Antonio Gambo, the Secretary of the Supreme Court and of the prefecture of economic affairs for the Holy See; and Monsignor Domenico Pasquini, an official of the office of the Vatican Secretary of State.

"I represent a very wealthy Jewish philanthropist," O'Morrow told the three of them. "He wants to establish a Vatican foundation that will bring enormous resources to support the Church's work on behalf of the poor and the oppressed." What Myron Geller was planning, of course, was for the Vatican to become a money-laundering machine for the many millions of dollars he planned to loot from the growing number of insurance companies he intended to bring under his control.

"Initially," O'Morrow continued, "my client is prepared to donate fifty-five million dollars to the new foundation. Five million of that will become available immediately. The remainder will be transferred into a brokerage account. Over time, as the enterprise grows, much larger sums will be directed to the Church's programs."

O'Morrow also made it clear that under this arrangement, the Vatican would need to be prepared to certify, if needed, that all of the funds controlled by the new foundation had come directly from Vatican sources.

Two weeks later, Myron received a telephone call from Thomas O'Morrow.

"Mr. Geller, great news. I just received word from Monsignor Sangiovanni. He informed me that the Holy Father has given his approval for the new foundation. And there's something else you'll also be happy to hear about, especially since I know how important it is for you to maintain privacy in operating your business. You've been approved to have a personal account with the Vatican Bank. That's a privilege very few people are given, and it's probably the most confidential banking arrangement anywhere in the world. Only the Pope himself can disclose the details of these accounts."

And so the St. Francis Foundation was established as a charitable organization, registered in the Cayman Islands. With these new arrangements in place, Myron promptly transferred the ownership of the seven insurance companies under his control to the new foundation. Then he redoubled his efforts to purchase additional American insurance companies. His search turned to companies that were larger than those he had previously acquired, so as to provide correspondingly greater cash reserves for him to exploit. And as part of that process, the Vatican officials held true to the commitment they had made to Thomas O'Morrow, whenever inquiries were made about the sources of the funds of the St. Francis of Assisi Foundation.

So, when an attorney representing the Western Life Insurance Company contacted Monsignor Sangiovanni to ascertain how the foundation was being supported, the monsignor assured her that its funding had been provided by the Holy Father. On another such occasion, Sangiovanni stated that the foundation had been the recipient of more that a billion dollars from various Roman Catholic tribunals and charities. However, in truth, every dollar of the money that was being funneled through the shell foundation had been looted from the reserves of Myron's various insurance companies.

In the midst of this flurry of activity, the lawyer who represented Myron's company in Mississippi flew to Connecticut for an urgent conference.

"Mr. Geller," he said, "I had a long meeting yesterday with the Mississippi Insurance Commissioner. There's no way we can hold him off any longer. Not only that, but he's been in touch with his counterpart in Tennessee. Both of them are demanding that all funds belonging to the insurance companies in their jurisdictions be removed from brokerage accounts and deposited in banks within their states. I tried everything I could to get them to back away from that decision, but they won't take 'no' for an answer. That's where we are. They're giving us three days. No more."

Myron sprang up from his chair, his face scarlet with anger, his hands shaking. He grabbed the lawyer's necktie, pulling him out of his chair and bringing the man's face within inches of his own.

"I've paid you and your political hack cronies a goddamn fortune to take care of the insurance commissioners. Now you come and give me this kind of shit. Get the hell out of here and get those guys off my back!"

"There's nothing else to do," the lawyer said. "You have three days to transfer the money and that's it."

Myron had managed for more than eight years to escape serious scrutiny by state regulatory officials, but now they had caught up with him. His problem was that there was not enough ready money among all of his insurance companies to make good on their demand. He had not moved quickly enough to take control of additional insurance companies, which would have given him new cash reserves to exploit. Myron's house of cards was collapsing.

He quickly set about making plans to flee the country. At first, he thought Israel would be a suitable destination, but eventually he settled on Italy. He frantically transferred funds among his many accounts, and he then ordered his staff to begin shredding the massive files and records there in the mansion. Finally, he made contact with Ernesto Lanzi, a business consultant in Rome with whom he had invested in the past, and pleaded with him to arrange for an apartment there where he could stay.

The next afternoon, Myron and two of his employees, Susan Jenkins and Carolyn Hall, who had agreed to go into exile with him, departed from the White Plains airport in a chartered jet to Italy. Myron's baggage included two suitcases stuffed with cash. A smaller bag contained diamonds worth more than eight million dollars, which he had purchased a month earlier from a gem dealer in California. Myron also brought with him several high-quality false passports, each with a different fictitious name.

8

Our apprenticeship master, Abraham ben Jonah, was a fair and decent man, but he was also demanding and not easily satisfied. Whenever he detected an error, or even when he was unhappy with the appearance of my writing on a document I had prepared, he insisted that I completely redo it. Abraham treated Johanan and me as equals, but to me, Johanan continued to be my esteemed teacher and mentor.

At last, after two long years, Johanan and I completed our period of apprenticeship. I was eager to begin as an independent public scribe in Jerusalem, and I soon had all of the work I needed.

At first, Johanan also seemed to find his occupation rewarding, but later I could see that his enthusiasm was waning. By the time a year had passed, Johanan appeared to have lost all interest in our profession, and he increasingly devoted his time to study of the law and the Holy Scriptures. Then, Johanan told me of a decision he had made:

"I have become ever more taken by the teachings of the great Pharisee sages," he said, "and I intend to seek entrance into the academy of Hillel and Gamaliel, as one of their disciples."

The students of these esteemed teachers were very few in number, and they were carefully chosen from amongst only the most learned of the young men. There were many who sought to become disciples in Hillel's academy, and each of them was submitted to an examination that continued over many weeks. The questioning of the candidates was held in public for all to see, and there was much interest in these proceedings.

I recall all of this very clearly: at the start, about twenty men, Johanan among them, appeared on the appointed day to be examined by Hillel and Gamaliel. This took place in the Temple, in the spacious Court of the Gentiles. The two great sages presided, with Hillel seated on a high-backed chair, their disciples at their sides. Those who were there to be examined sat together as a group, facing their questioners. The considerable crowd of onlookers stood around them. Most of the candidates were young, although a few of them seemed well past their youth, and one, whose hair and beard had turned quite gray, must have been older still. From the fine clothing worn by some of the candidates, it was apparent that they were men of wealth. Others, attired in clothing of simple homespun, clearly were of limited means. But what they all shared was their considerable learning and their great passion for the holy writings.

The first challenges to the candidates were to quote from the books of Psalms and Proverbs, and to elucidate the passages assigned to them. Johanan was asked by Hillel to recite the Twenty-fifth Psalm, and I well recall what transpired. Johanan rose to his feet, and in a clear voice that could be heard by everyone there, he began:

"Of David.

Unto You, Lord, I lift up my soul.

My God, in You I trust.

Let me not be put to shame,

nor my enemies triumph over me."

But as he continued with the majestic poetry of that moving, acrostic psalm, Johanan's voice softened to the point of becoming almost inaudible.

At the same time, the large crowd of onlookers, captured by the beauty and emotion of Johanan's recitation, fell silent. By the time he came to the lines

"The distress of my heart increases;
Deliver me from my straits.
See my affliction and my suffering,
and forgive all my sins,"

Johanan had tears running down his face. His voice had diminished to a whisper. Hillel, too, seemed to recognize how deeply these words affected Johanan, and the great sage rose from his chair as a sign of his empathy and compassion.

Johanan's second challenge that day, from Gamaliel, was the Fiftieth Psalm. As before, Johanan began his recitation confidently and flawlessly, so much so that when he reached its midpoint, Gamaliel asked him to stop, apparently recognizing that continuing further would serve no purpose in demonstrating Johanan's knowledge of the psalm. Instead, he raised a question. "What does God tell us in this psalm concerning the making of sacrifices in the Temple? We prefer to believe that sacrifices are pleasing to God, but can we know that that indeed is so?"

"The psalm reminds us," Johanan replied, "that every beast, and indeed all that is in the world, is God's possession, and hence there is nothing we can truly give to God. It was said that King Solomon had a thousand wives, and that every day each of them prepared a great banquet, in the hope that the king would dine with her. And yet God's dominion is surely far greater than that of Solomon. God does not censure us for our sacrifices, but He does reprove us when we devote our mouths to evil and harness our tongues to deceit. And we also know, from the fifty-first Psalm, that what is most pleasing to God is prayer and a contrite heart. Moreover, a proverb of King Solomon reminds us that 'To do what is right and just is more desired by the Lord than sacrifice.'"

By the time this part of the questioning was completed, Hillel and Gamaliel had already rejected more than half of the young men there, but Johanan remained among the candidates.

The following part of their examination dealt with the laws of the Torah. In the course of this, I recollect one question that Gamaliel directed to Johanan, relating to the Ten Commandments: "For what reason," he asked, "were the commandments 'Remember the Sabbath day and keep it holy,' and 'Honor your father and your mother' placed consecutive to one another in the tablet that Moses received from God on Mt. Sinai?"

"It is said," Johanan replied, "that he who honors his parents honors God and affirms His holiness. And in the Torah, God said to his people, 'Honor your father and your mother that you may long endure on the land that the Lord your God is giving you.'"

The next part of the examination tested their knowledge of the Oral Law. Most of the questions that were asked I have long forgotten, but there is one that I recall well. It was Hillel who asked Johanan, "Under what circumstances does the Law permit healing to be done on the Sabbath?"

"Some acts of healing," Johanan replied, "are not only permitted on the Sabbath, but we are commanded by the Law to carry them out. That would apply when someone is gravely ill and his life is in danger. In such an event, everything possible must be done to heal that person. But if the illness is longstanding, and no additional harm would come from delaying the healing until after the Sabbath, then it would be forbidden."

With that answer, Hillel smiled and nodded his head in approval. And then he recited an often-repeated Pharisee saying: "The Sabbath, given to us by God, was made for man, not man for the Sabbath."

By that point in the examination, only Johanan and one other candidate were judged worthy by Hillel and Gamaliel to continue with the questioning. That other young man, Ezra ben David, was the eldest son from a distinguished priestly family of Jerusalem. Ezra, we learned, had been taught since childhood by the most able and sought-after tutors, and it was expected by everyone that he was destined to become one of the great learned sages.

The crowd of people listening to the candidates continued to grow as the examination approached its end, and from the brilliance of their answers to the questions they were given, most of the people there came to believe that both of these men would be accepted into Hillel's academy. Some were also making wagers, and from these it seemed to be Ezra who was considered to be the better qualified of the two remaining candidates.

The final part of the examination was concerned with the wisdom and the traditions of the Pharisee sages, and especially with the ability of the candidates to interpret the Oral Law. This, we came to learn, was regarded by great Pharisee sages to be among the most crucial areas of questioning. And it was because this would demonstrate their suitability to make the important judgments that would later be required of them as rabbinic authorities.

The questions that were asked of the two men were exceedingly complex and difficult, and many of them dealt with subtle points of the law. Indeed, most of the bystanders in the crowd could not even comprehend what was being discussed. The answers from each of the candidates showed that they were remarkably learned men. And as the questioning went on, day after day, more and larger wagers were being made by those in the ever-growing crowd of bystanders.

When the examination was finally completed, it was Gamaliel who announced the decision: only one of the candidates would be chosen to enter their academy. And that man, to the surprise and disappointment of many in the crowd, was to be Johanan.

For several years that followed, I saw Johanan only seldom, on occasions when he accompanied the great Pharisee masters to the Temple courtyards where their public teaching was done. But even then, I was rarely able to speak with him.

During that time, there were many people in the city who sought me out as a scribe, and I never lacked for work. They were happy years for me, living in Jerusalem.

One day, when I was walking through a marketplace, I came upon Johanan, and we talked together there for a long while. By then, Johanan had gained a great reputation in Jerusalem for his knowledge of the law. He had become a respected teacher in Hillel's academy, and his future as a leader of the Pharisees seemed assured. So what Johanan told me next came as a great surprise.

"I no longer believe that Jerusalem is where I belong," he said to me, "and I have made the decision to return to Galilee."

"But Johanan," I said to him, "you are well on your way to becoming one of the truly great religious authorities here. What better future could you possibly have?"

"I want to bring my teaching directly to my own people in Galilee," he said. "There are more than enough teachers of the law here in Jerusalem, but in Galilee there are few. I have come to believe that great changes are at hand, and that word of them needs to be brought to the people of Galilee."

I was even more surprised when Johanan asked me then if I wished to go with him in his return to the north. Although I might have been willing to join him, my circumstances had changed. Most importantly, I had taken a wife; it was not Sarah, your grandmother, for I married her only later. This was Shoshanna, a kind and beautiful young woman, who brought me much happiness. Moreover, Shoshanna was expecting our first child, and I could not consider leaving Jerusalem. And so when Johanan departed for Galilee, he went alone.

Later, when it was time for Shoshanna to be delivered, the midwife came, and she informed me that the delivery would soon take place. But the next morning, she sent word that the birth was not proceeding as it should, and that Shoshanna was growing ever more weak. That night they brought me the terrible news that my wife was dead. The midwife had tried to save the life of the baby, but she too had died.

I bought a plot of land, and I buried Shoshanna. I was overwhelmed with grief. I of course needed to continue with my work, and that in time helped me overcome my melancholy. And later, I again began to attend the teachings of the great Pharisee sages, whose words of wisdom were a source of comfort to me.

9

One Sabbath day, while I was in the Temple courtyard to hear Hillel and Gamaliel, I chanced to meet a young man there, a Greek named Paulos, who had only recently come from a city in the North. His linen tunic, his well-cut mantle of dark blue-dyed wool, and his finely-tooled sandals identified him as a man of means. I eventually came to know that he possessed sufficient wealth so that he had no need to work. Although Greek was his mother tongue, he had excellent command of Aramaic, which he told me was widely spoken in his home country. I later also learned that Paulos possessed his own scrolls of our Holy Scriptures, which surely must have cost him a considerable sum. He told me that they were in Greek translation, and that he had begun to study them with the greatest of attention.

On first meeting Paulos, I could appreciate his endless store of restless energy. He was scarcely able to remain seated for long, springing suddenly to his feet and pacing about. And he invariably had much to say about any subject we had occasion to discuss. His endless flow of ideas ranged from the political to the philosophic, and inevitably to the religious. He was not a Jew, at least not then, but the religion of the Jews was what interested him most of all. His greatest pleasure was to engage in conversation, often while consuming cup after cup of wine. As I needed to remain alert during the daytime to pursue my profession, I seldom wished to indulge this habit of his after the hour became late. But as I was continuing to suffer greatly from loneliness, I appreciated the company of this active and energetic young man. We came to spend many of our evenings together, and over time he gave me an extensive account of his life and his family.

"I am from Cilicia," he told me, "from Tarsus, which I tell you is no mean city. Tarsus is justly famous for its school of rhetoric, and it is only Athens that has the equal of our distinguished teachers and sages, among whom is the venerable Athenodorus, the greatest of all of the Stoic philosophers. And our city's wealth of scrolls, books, and manuscripts surpasses even that of the great Library of Alexandria.

"My father," he said, "was an important government official. His occupation brought him prestige and also opportunities to amass considerable wealth. But to maintain his position, he needed to stay in the good graces of our Roman governor. That required frequent and generous gifts and also substantial bribes, which consumed a goodly part of my father's income. Nevertheless, he enjoyed a comfortable life that brought him everything he desired, or at least nearly so. There was one thing my father dearly wished to have, but could never quite afford—that was Roman citizenship.

"My mother was, in her younger years, a priestess of the Mysteries of Attis. In our city, the majestic Temple of Jupiter, with its great marble columns and its awe-inspiring statue of the god, was built upon the highest hill. The Temple of Attis, nearly as tall, stands next to it. Both of these magnificent shrines can be seen from great distances, even from tall-masted ships that sail close to the harbor of our city.

"Though both my father and my mother took great pride in her having served in the Temple of Attis, they strongly discouraged me from taking any interest in the mysteries of that god.

"'The rites are terrible, involving awful pain and deprivation,' they told me, and also, 'some of those who sought to become mystae were driven to madness, a few even losing their lives in the process.'

"In my youth, I studied astronomy, rhetoric, geometry, and the works of the great Greek writers, but more than all of these, it was philosophy that held my greatest interest. I learned much of the wisdom of the Stoics, and also of the writings of Plato and of various others of the philosophers who followed in his footsteps.

"I should also make you aware that many of my teachers there took every possible opportunity to speak of their contempt for the Jews. 'They are people of the devil. The Jews have been duped to believe in a flawed and trivial god,' they said. They taught us that the God of Israel, the creator of the world, is an inferior and evil god, a demiurge. I now know that those who said such things are fools.

"It was always my father, whom I much admired, who guided me in my education and in all of the important decisions I made about my life. When he died, after a short illness, I became like a rudderless ship, unable to chart a course for myself, and also much in need of direction for my troubled soul. It was early spring then, the time when initiates were accepted into the mysteries of Attis, and in my yearning to calm my spiritual turmoil, I presented myself to their temple.

"As a mystes, I was first obliged to take a solemn oath that I would never divulge any of their secrets to the uninitiated. But since I now have forsaken any allegiance to their foolishness, I no longer feel bound by that oath, and I speak as freely as I wish about them.

"We began our initiation into the mysteries by assembling together outside of their temple. The Galli, their priests, all of them eunuchs, then led us in a parade which marched through the city accompanied by a loud clamor of drums, bells, cymbals, gongs, and horns. We proceeded to a wooded area some distance away, and it was there that we remained for four days.

"That was the time for our purification, to prepare us to be worthy to receive the mysteries, and there they tested us severely. Scarcely anything was given to us to eat, and we were exposed to the elements without protection against the cold and rain. We were allowed hardly any sleep, and we were awakened throughout the night to chant long verses that extolled *the greatness of Attis. Each morning we were obliged to immerse ourselves in the frigid waters of a river. After all of this, we returned to the temple, again in a noisy parade.*

"It was then that we began to become acquainted with the mysteries. For the following two days, we mystae were kept as naked as the day we were born, except that our eyes were covered by blindfolds. In this helpless state, our senses were greatly heightened to the myriad sounds, smells, tastes, and feelings that we experienced. Incense of various varieties burned much of the time, and the pleasant fragrances of many different flowers and perfumes were also presented to us. There were, as well, far less agreeable smells that greeted our nostrils: surely the most oppressive of them was the stench of putrefying flesh, to remind us of the grim reality of death and decomposition. As we contemplated these unpleasant thoughts, the head priest introduced us to secrets from the mysteries: 'Attis, the Most High and Bond of the Universe, he who was born of a virgin woman, died,' he said, 'but his body did not decay. He died so that you might be saved. And with the resurrection of our god, those who have learned of the mysteries will be reborn in triumph with Attis. He will redeem us; he will protect us; in him, we need no longer fear death.'

"In our blinded nakedness, we heard the melodic sounds of the flute and the lyre, but also, when we least expected them, there were terrifying screams, mournful sobbing, the fearful screeching of wild animals, and also angry shouts of words that disparaged and humiliated us. Honey and sweet elixirs were placed in our mouths, but also the bitterest tasting of potions. We were doused with scalding hot water, and at other times with cold. We were flogged most fiercely, made all the worse because we were incapable of anticipating the blows inflicted on us on account of our blindness. Finally, with our hands bound behind us, we were led through fire that brought us close enough to the flames that the hair on our heads and on our limbs became burnt.

"Afterward came the Day of Blood. On that morning, a pine tree was cut down in the forest, to commemorate the hallowed evergreen that sheltered the holy Attis as he castrated himself and then died in a pool of blood. The sacred tree, bedecked with violets and purple ribbons, was then solemnly carried into the temple at the head of a column of priests and priestesses, all of them attired in black, followed by those already initiated

into the fellowship of the mysteries of Attis, and finally, by us, the mystae. A great statue of the god, as well as baskets containing objects associated with his mysteries, and yet others filled with white roses, completed the august procession. And with that began a day of tearful wailing in lamentation, with fasting and tearing out of hair by the faithful, in mourning the death of Attis. Many slashed themselves in their grief, causing a profusion of bloodshed. And some men, it has been said, have taken this occasion to castrate themselves, in emulation of the passion of the holy Attis.

"All of this continued for two days. The third day was the Day of Resurrection, when grief and lamentation turned to joy. Early, long before sunrise, we were brought to an open grave where we stood as the Galli, now in white robes, chanted hymns extolling the greatness of Attis, followed by others that spoke of the supreme happiness that comes with his rebirth.

"Then, with great solemnity, the priests led us back into the temple. There, on a high platform, had been restrained a bull of fearful size and disposition. The animal had been anointed with fragrant oil so that its coat shined, and its horns were bedecked with ornaments of gold and silver, including tiny bells that were heard whenever the beast moved its head. A wreath of white lilies had been placed around the bull's neck, and a gold crown upon its head. They positioned us beneath the platform, and the priestesses began a loud clatter with the sound of the tympanon. Then they performed a wild dance, punctuated with shouts and screams. Finally, the head priest sacrificed the animal, slitting its throat with a long silver knife. We were bathed in the blood that poured down from the bull, as the priests intoned a psalm proclaiming that in Attis we are born again into eternity.

"That night, we mystae, clothed all in white, were again brought to the temple. The chief priest, also in white and wearing a huge mask of a bull, addressed us with these words:

'I am Attis, resurrected from death. In me, fear of the grave will no longer torment you, and through me you will have eternal life. This is my flesh and my strength,' he said, giving us meat from the bull. 'Eat this. And this is my blood,' he said, holding up a cup of blood from the sacrificed animal. 'Drink it. Do these things and salvation will be given to you.'

"Later, in the evening, I was given a strong-tasting potion of dark green color to drink, and soon my vision became clouded, and I could no longer stand without help. I saw great flashes of light; first it was of many different colors, but later the light was pure white. And then I had a vision of god. It was Attis, who held me tenderly in his arms, and he said to me, 'Keep faith with me and eternal life shall be yours.' When I awoke, a feeling of warmth, comfort, and great happiness overcame me. And in the end, they crowned me with a wreath of yellow carnations and solemnly welcomed me into the fellowship of Attis.

"Ah, and yes, there was one final act in this great drama. It was the communion with the god Attis, in what was spoken of as the 'mystery of the ecstasy.' To prepare me for this, my skin was anointed with scented oil, my hair was combed and braided as is done for a bridegroom, and then I was clothed in a white toga that had been stitched from the finest of linen. After these things were done, a young woman, whom I had not seen before, entered the room and she poured from a silver ewer a fragrant elixir, which she gave me to drink. Her hair was bedecked with blossoms of many colors, whose subtle fragrance combined with that of her perfume to produce a quickening of my senses. Her lips, colored ruby red, seemed like luscious fruit, and her shimmering, diaphanous gown revealed the considerable beauty of her form. She smiled, and then she took me by the hand and led me forward.

'Let us enter the chamber,' she said. And when we were there, she spoke to me thusly:

'I am Kybele, wife of the holy god Attis. Together, we will consummate your communion in ecstasy with our god.'

"Never before then had I been with a woman. And I will tell you that this girl possessed innumerable wiles, charms, and devices by which she brought me unbounded joy and delight, such as I had never experienced. I left the Temple of Attis in a state of happiness and fulfillment, with the firm belief that the god would protect me in my life, and that I needed no longer have fear of death.

"In the days and weeks that followed, my thoughts were often directed to all that had happened to me. Then, one day, I happened to come upon one of the men who had been initiated with me into the mysteries, and we talked together for a long while. In the course of our conversation, I spoke with him about the young woman with whom I had had my communion of ecstasy.

'She is the youngest and the most beautiful of all of the priestesses there,' he told me, and with those words, for the first time, I immediately came to a horrible realization. It subsequently dominated all my thoughts and left me confused and upset, and, more than anything else, I became furiously angry. I could not eat or sleep, and I neglected my studies at the School of Rhetoric that then were my only responsibility. Why had my parents, and especially my mother, discouraged me so strongly against the mysteries of Attis? I asked myself. The answer should have been obvious to me much sooner; it was because she had been a priestess of that despicable cult.

"In my ever-growing rage, I sought out my younger brother, Roufon. Our mother, I shouted at him, was a whore, and I explained my reason for making so rash a statement. And also, I told my brother something else; perhaps, I said, I can now understand why I so little resemble our father, or at least the man I always believed was my father.

"From that day, out of my disgust and anger, I have never gone again to see my mother. Moreover, I have completely forsaken those fools who deceive young men with their falsehoods about mysteries and their pagan gods.

"For many weeks afterward, I spent my time wandering aimlessly through the city, seeking to calm my unsettled spirit. Then, one day, as I came to the central square near the marketplace, I encountered a crowd of people who had gathered to listen to a speaker who had come from afar. The simple cloak of this tall and very thin man was of ordinary homespun wool, and his hair and his long beard had turned to white. But in spite of his advanced age, he possessed considerable vigor. He was speaking about the God of the Jews. I later learned that this man was a Pharisee. There were of course Jews living in our city, a hundred or more, and they had built two synagogues, but none of these Jews counted themselves among the Pharisees.

"I stopped to listen to what this man was saying. His first words were about Jerusalem and about the magnificence and grandeur of the great Temple there. Then he spoke of the eternal God, the Creator of the universe, and how the God of Israel was a god of great compassion. This man spoke engagingly, and with deep emotion, and I continued to listen to him.

"Then, he read from several of the Psalms and also from writings of the Hebrew prophets. These moved me greatly. And finally, he spoke of the philosophy of the Pharisees concerning justice, charity, and righteousness. I was considerably taken by all of that, and afterward I sought out others of the Jews from our city to learn more from them. And on the Jewish Sabbath, I began to go to the synagogues in our city, to listen to those who spoke about the Law, and also to hear their readings from the Hebrew Scriptures.

"Over time, I became more and more captivated by what I was learning, and eventually I resolved to come to Jerusalem, to witness for myself the Temple and its rituals, and to learn from the great Pharisee sages."

A saying often repeated by the Pharisees is that "none is more zealous than the proselyte," and for Paulos that was certainly the case. The alacrity he showed in his new religious pursuit amazed me, and for a long while I could not comprehend why he was so greatly driven. Shortly after his arrival in Jerusalem, I soon found out, Paulos had hired learned men, most of them Pharisees, to serve as his teachers. And, with their help, he worked tirelessly to advance his knowledge. Whenever any of the great Pharisee sages appeared for their public teachings of the law, Paulos was always there, giving close attention to everything that was said. So I continued to see him often, and I maintained my friendship with him.

One evening, several months later, Paulos appeared in the outer court of the Temple, on a day when the great Pharisee sage Shammai and his disciples had come there to teach. The color was gone from Paulos's face; he walked slowly and with great difficulty. "Paulos," I said to him, "you seem not to be in good health."

"I am well, very well indeed," he answered. Then he smiled. "I am no longer Paulos," he said to me. "I have been given a new name, a Hebrew name. Now I am Saul. Two weeks ago, I had my circumcision, but soon afterward, a problem arose: I had a great deal of bleeding, and that continued for three days before finally stopping. By then, I was so weak that I could rise from my bed only with help from my servant." And then he laughed for a long while.

"In the midst of my troubles I had a dream. I dreamt that I was Attis, about to bleed to death!" And with that, he laughed again. "Is that not most amusing? But now, my strength has finally begun to return."

After several weeks, the newly named Saul seemed fully to have recovered his health, and with that he redoubled his efforts to become learned in the Law, the scriptures, and the writings of the prophets. I asked him why it was that he pursued all of this so seriously. His answer came as a great surprise to me.

"It is my intention to become a Pharisee, and indeed a leader among the Pharisees. And so now, I am preparing myself to become a disciple in the academy of one of the great Pharisee teachers."

I felt it was my obligation to impress upon him that very few are accepted into the Pharisee academies, and that those who are chosen are only the most learned of men. But he was not to be deterred from his lofty ambitions, and he continued on with his studies. Some months later, when Hillel and Gamaliel examined a new group of candidates for their academy, Saul and I witnessed the questioning that was directed to the young men.

"Do you now see how difficult an examination they give to those who seek to become disciples of these great men?" I asked him.

"I will tell you this," he said. "I learned from one of my tutors that the questioning is indeed always difficult, but it is also true that Hillel and Gamaliel pose many of the same questions to their candidates year after year. That tutor promised to prepare me to answer any question they might ask of me."

A long time passed after that, more than a year. Then, one evening in the late spring, after Passover had ended, Hillel and Gamaliel once again began the questioning of candidates for their academy. About twenty-five young men appeared that day, and there among them, to my surprise, was Saul. At first I did not recognize Saul, and that was because of the manner of his dress. In place of the fine, well-fashioned clothing he usually wore, that day his simple tunic and his goat-hair cloak were of the quality worn by men of the most modest of means. And his sandals, always of well-tooled leather, were nowhere to be seen; instead, he came barefooted. All of that, he later told me, had been recommended by of one of his tutors, who had advised him to effect a humble appearance. But in spite of the austereness of his clothing, Saul displayed the confidence, and indeed the arrogance, I had by then come to expect from him.

I was especially impressed with how Saul, who had possessed hardly any knowledge of our Holy Scriptures when he first came to Jerusalem, had achieved such mastery of these texts. I still recollect some of the questions that were directed to him.

First, as was their usual practice, the great Pharisee sages began the testing of the candidates for their knowledge of the Psalms and the Proverbs. They directed several of their questions to Saul, and for all of them, he quoted the designated verses in flawless Hebrew, and he then provided lucid and erudite explanations of their meaning. I well recall one that was assigned to him that day; Hillel asked him to recite the One Hundred and Tenth Psalm.

After Saul spoke the words of the psalm, every part of it correct, he turned and bowed low to the great Babylonian, in an exaggerated fashion, it seemed to me, and then after a long pause, he began his interpretation of its verses.

"It has been said by some of the sages that this is not a psalm by David, but rather one that speaks to him. Its principal message is that David will rule at God's right hand, and that he will have God's help in overcoming his enemies. And moreover, the psalm directs that David must also be as a priest to his people. However, because this psalm speaks of Melchizedek, who some believe was Shem, the son of Noah, it has been said by others of the sages that this was indeed a psalm by David, and that its message relates to Abraham, and to his victory over Chedorlaomer and the other kings."

Hillel immediately indicated his satisfaction with his explanation of the psalm. From his smug but restrained smile, it was clear to me that Saul was pleased.

And later in the examination, when the candidates were challenged to speak about the writings of the Law, Gamaliel addressed a question to Saul related to the Bereshit (Creation) section. This seemed at first to be the most minor of considerations, but it was one that I still remember.

"The words that God spoke as he made ready to create man were in an unusual form," Gamaliel began. "It was here that God said, 'Let us make man with our image and likeness.' Were there others beside God himself who took part in the creation of man?"

Saul again bowed low to his questioner, but this time he began imme-diately to present his reply. "God's words were also spoken in that form in the Book of Noah. But concerning this passage in the Bereshit, it is indeed possible that others, besides God, were there," he said, "or else God might have employed the manner of speech used by great monarchs, especially at that momentous occasion of God's creation of man in His own image. As for the others that might have been given a part in the creation of man, they could well have been the host of God's angels."

"If that is to be proposed, then how might we know if the host of angels was already present at the time that God created man?" Gamaliel asked.

"It was surely so," Saul replied with great confidence. "We know it was thus from the Book of Job."

"And what then are the words to which you refer?" Gamaliel inquired.

Saul answered him without hesitation:

"'Then the Lord replied to Job:
Were you there when I laid the earth's foundations?
When the morning stars sang together,
And the angels of God shouted for joy?'"

He had answered the question flawlessly, and the great Gamaliel acknowledged that it was so. I did take notice, however, that in answering this question, Saul made use of his Greek translation rather than the original Hebrew texts, and I wondered if this practice might eventually cause him difficulties. Yet it also impressed me that Saul, who had learned so much about the Holy Scriptures, was able to demonstrate such skill in the exami-nation in spite of his still limited knowledge of the Hebrew language.

By the time the questioning of the candidates by Hillel and Gamaliel reached the part that dealt with the Oral Law, all but four of those in the competition had been eliminated. Saul remained among that small group of learned young men. I well remember the next question that Saul was asked: "How," Gamaliel challenged him, "is the appropriate punishment to be determined for one who causes harm against his fellow man?"

Saul rose, turned to his questioner, and bowed, as was his wont. The expression on his face was a gravely serious one, but beneath that mask, I could recognize a slight curling at the corners of his mouth, and from that, I knew he felt supremely confident of his ability to respond correctly to the question.

"The punishment follows a straightforward principle of the Law," he said. "An eye for an eye and a tooth for a tooth, meaning that the penalty should equal the harm caused by the perpetrator."

"So, then, what will the judgment be against one who by his actions causes another man to lose the sight of his eye?" Gamaliel asked him. "Should the guilty man have his own eye put out?"

"That," Saul replied, clearly pleased to demonstrate his newly acquired knowledge, "would be needlessly cruel, and might also be unjust."

"Do you suggest that the Law is cruel and unjust?" Gamaliel asked him.

"Surely not!" Saul answered. "What I have spoken of thus far concerns only the written Law." Then Saul repeated a saying often quoted by the Pharisees: "'He who knows only the written Law does not truly know the Law.' Now," he continued, "I will explain what I meant concerning justice under the Law. If we consider the case of a man who by his actions causes another to lose his eye, if the one who made this happen were himself blind, would justice be served by having that man forfeit one of his useless eyes? And if one loses his eye due to the actions of another, what good would come to the injured man by having the perpetrator lose one of his eyes?"

"Those are wise questions you raise," Gamaliel said. "So how, then, might a more just punishment be determined for the guilty person in such circumstances?"

"The Oral Law prescribes the appropriate judgment for the injured person," Saul replied, and as he spoke these words, he held his hand over his heart in dramatic fashion, to emphasize his passion for justice under the law. "The perpetrator must pay just compensation to the man he injured," he said. "He must pay firstly for the loss of the eye, and also for the pain his victim endured, then for the cost to heal him, for the loss of his time, and also for the shame from his lacking an eye."

"And how should this compensation be determined?" Gamaliel asked him.

"For the loss of the eye," Saul replied, his voice projecting an air of great confidence, "the cost can be determined in the slave market. First, appraise the value of a slave who has lost an eye, and also how much he

was worth when his eye was intact. That will provide the answer. For suffering and pain, the compensation is more difficult to ascertain. Here it must be determined how much a man of equal standing would require to be paid if he were to tolerate such pain. The cost of the services of the physician who attended the injured person will be the usual amount for such care. For the loss of time, how much in wages did the victim forego? It will be that amount that needs to be paid. For his shame, the amount of compensation will be determined from the status of the injured person and also that of the offender, and in particular whether the perpetrator caused the injury intentionally or by accident."

By the time Saul completed his answers to these questions, a considerable crowd had gathered to hear him, and when he finished, the onlookers cheered and applauded. I could see that Hillel was smiling, and it was apparent that he shared the good feelings shown by the crowd.

I spent many hours with Saul that night. He was in his usual state of restless agitation, but I could also recognize that his conversation had taken a new turn.

"I now have come to conclude that the Pharisees lack effective leaders," he said to me, "and more important still, their movement is in need of better organization, and also of principles that are easier to comprehend, if they are to attract larger numbers of adherents."

From those comments, I came to realize that Saul was already making plans to become a leader of the Pharisee movement!

"Saul," I said to him, "I am truly astounded at all you have accomplished, and in so short a time. The answers you gave to the questions today showed that you have an amazing depth of knowledge, and both Hillel and Gamaliel seemed greatly impressed." And I informed him that the wagers being made by those in attendance had turned strongly in his favor. Saul seemed very happy, and he was clearly pleased to acknowledge his considerable achievements.

I will always remember what transpired the following evening when the examination of the two remaining candidates resumed. A question was directed to Saul by Gamaliel, concerning what seemed to be a relatively minor point of the Law:

"What," he asked, "does the Law direct for a man who is found guilty of a crime for which the penalty is death?"

Saul bowed to his questioner, as he always did, and after pausing for only a brief moment, he gave his reply. "After the execution, his body is to be hanged from a stake for all to see. But the law requires that he be buried before nightfall."

"And the reason that must be done?" Gamaliel asked him.

For his answer, Saul recited a line from the Torah. "It is because 'he that is hanged is accursed by God.'"

Saul's reply to that question affirmed my greatest concern on his behalf. The passage he had quoted was one of those that in the Greek translation conveyed a very different meaning from the original Hebrew text, and it was his Greek version of the holy writings that Saul had used to prepare himself for his examination.

After Saul gave his answer, Gamaliel rose slowly from where he was seated, and he turned to face Saul directly. Speaking in a noticeably solemn manner, he delivered his verdict:

"Once a condemned man has been put to death, he has paid his debt, and he no longer carries guilt. He therefore is not accursed by man or by God. It must also be said that the righteous of our people who have been crucified by those who occupy and torment our country surely received God's blessing. This passage from the Torah tells us that a hanged body is an affront to God; and that is because He made man in His own image. Therefore, to leave the body unburied is truly a curse against God, and it is they who fail to perform this duty who bring a curse on themselves."

Later, I came to wonder if Hillel and Gamaliel had raised that specific question as a test of Saul's understanding of the Hebrew Scriptures. In any case, Gamaliel regarded Saul's answer as incorrect, and sufficiently so that he summarily dismissed Saul as a candidate for their academy.

After that, I did not see Saul again for many weeks. But then one day I chanced to encounter him in the marketplace, though I could scarcely recognize him. His proud bearing, his lips pressed together in an imperious smile, his confident stride, the extra care he gave to attire himself in the most elegant fashion, all of that had vanished; he was much thinner than before, with a dejected appearance that bespoke both melancholy and defeat. Yet when he talked with me, it was mainly anger that he expressed.

"They treated me worse than a beggar," he said, "and they cheated me out of what I justly deserved." And with that, he hit his fist against the

table of a nearby vendor, causing many of the man's cucumbers and figs to fall onto the ground.

"Saul," I said to him, "the answers you gave in the examination showed that you have amazing intelligence and knowledge. You were brilliant, and moreover you far surpassed many others who had studied their entire lives for this." I reminded him that almost all the candidates, even the most able of them, needed to submit themselves to be examined more than once before they were accepted into the academies of the great Pharisee teachers. With that, Saul seemed to recover some of his composure, but it was only after several months that he gradually returned to his studies to prepare for the next opportunity to be examined by Hillel and Gamaliel. That, as it happened, was long in coming, and it was well more than a year, in the autumn following the Festival of Booths, that their next examination of candidates for their academy took place. By then, Saul's confidence appeared to be fully restored.

Of that fateful second examination of Saul by the great Pharisee teachers, I will only tell you this: in spite of the brilliance and erudition of Saul's responses to their questions, neither Hillel nor Gamaliel seemed to be fully satisfied with the answers he gave them. And early in the second week of the examination, they again dismissed Saul as a candidate for their academy.

That time, Saul's fury could not be assuaged, and his anger transformed into an unending diatribe against the Pharisees.

"They are pious fools, all of them," he would say. "They waste their time fussing over meaningless minutiae of the laws, yet they are heartless, lacking even the slightest kindness toward their fellow men. They are all hypocrites," he concluded. So the Pharisees, who for so long had had Saul's enduring respect and affection, those with whom he had so ardently wished to commit his life's work, had become the object of his contempt, and indeed they were now his most inveterate enemies.

Never again did I see Saul at the public teachings of the great Pharisee teachers, but I encountered him from time to time in chance meetings in Jerusalem. His fierce anger had not abated, and whenever I spoke with him, he never failed to shower words of disdain and hatred against the Pharisees, accusing them of small-mindedness and deceitfulness, and spinning bizarre accounts of their vanity and their vindictiveness.

Saul, as before, continued always to be in a state of high agitation, springing up from his chair with the slightest provocation and pacing about like a caged animal. It was not clear to me then how he was spending his time, and when I finally learned about the new occupation he had assumed, it came as a great surprise to me.

Who, I would ask you, was the greatest detractor of the Pharisees, yea their most committed opponent? That, of course, was the High Priest of the Temple. Saul, I finally came to know, had gotten an important position in the employ of the High Priest. I learned very little about this from Saul, with whom I continued to maintain a distant friendship, but it was others who informed me that Saul's work dealt with matters of special concern to the High Priest. Foremost among these was keeping close watch over any in our country whom they believed might be fomenting unrest, especially those with inclinations toward rebellion against the Romans who rule our land.

I eventually came to know that Saul, with the assistance of a large cadre of well-paid informants, had been assigned the responsibility of investigating such agitators. For any who were found to be provoking unrest, he had been granted authority to direct the Temple Guard to arrest and detain them. Saul's work frequently brought him to other cities, and because of that, I seldom saw him anymore. In was only many years later when I came in contact with him again.

10

Nathan's five-hour flight was scheduled for arrival in Cairo at 11:00 p.m., but because of a delayed departure from Heathrow, the giant Boeing 744 touched down well past midnight. By the time he emerged from the airport into the chill and drizzle of the early Egyptian winter, it was nearly 2:00 a.m. He made an immediate decision not to test his limited skill in spoken Arabic, and so he searched for a taxi driver who could speak English. After three tries, he succeeded.

"The Horus House Hotel? I take you there for £100 Egyptian." After further negotiation, they agreed on a fare of £60, about $12. "This is your first visit to Cairo? If you want a tour of the city, I get you a private guide who will show you everything—very good price." After driving for a few kilometers, the driver asked, "Now, it was the Windsor Hotel you want?"

"No, no, the Horus House."

"The Horus House Hotel? Surely they must have told you. That place has been closed down for quite a while—they had some kind of electrical problem, I believe. But no need to worry. I take you to another hotel, much nicer than Horus House, and also for less money. In fact, already I am taking you there."

"Either you take me to Horus House or else to someplace near here where I can get another taxi," Nathan said in a firm voice.

"What a surprise," the driver exclaimed when they finally arrived at the hotel. "They seem to be back in business again."

Nathan spent his first day in Cairo exploring on foot and taking in the ambience of the city. The Zamalek district of Gazirah Island, where his hotel was situated, provided him a dramatic view of the Nile River, as well as of elegant residences and foreign embassies on wide streets lined by rows of stately palm trees. Its main thoroughfare, Shari 26 Yulyu, presented a panorama of cafés and shops and of the commercial life of the city. After lunch at a tiny shish kabob establishment, Nathan ventured across the river, and he soon found himself in sight of the Egyptian Museum, which he planned to visit later that week.

The following morning, Nathan set out early for Misr al-Qadima, the "Old Cairo" district, with its ancient buildings and artifacts. Arriving at the Mari Girgis metro station, he immediately caught sight of the imposing dome of the Greek Orthodox Church of St. George. Passing between the church and the remains of an enormous second-century Roman fortress tower, he entered a small square. To his right was the entrance to the Coptic Museum. The agent in the museum's ticket office directed Nathan to a stairway that led downward from the museum garden, past the sixth-century Church of St. Sergius. A second stairway took him below the street level to the medieval Church of St. Barbara and then, a short distance farther, to the Ben Ezra Synagogue.

Nathan was aware that the synagogue and its adjacent buildings had been extensively restored in the early 1990s, but their appearance nevertheless took him by surprise. In contrast to the thousand-year-old church buildings that surrounded it, the Ben Ezra, with its freshly applied gypsum coating, seemed remarkably contemporary. But there could be no doubt that the rectangular, flat-roofed structure of the small building, its narrow peaked windows, and the distinctive cornice-work decorating the periphery of its roof were features clearly representative of medieval Egypt.

The ornate iron gate that opened into the Ben Ezra compound had been left open, and a second gateway on the right brought Nathan to the synagogue's entrance porch. The dimly lit interior of the sanctuary reflected the architecture typical of a Middle Eastern synagogue, but with distinctively Coptic features. The interior was finished in white marble. The Torah ark, on the eastern wall, was elaborately ornamented in geometric designs, highly reminiscent of Islamic art forms. The walls and ceilings were resplendent with even more complex and intricate decoration. The *bimah*, the readers' pulpit, was placed near the center of the floor, with rows of columns on either side separating the nave from the aisles, and supporting the women's gallery that wrapped around three sides of the second story of the building. As Nathan moved past the *bimah*, with his gaze directed upward toward the ceiling, he nearly collided with an elderly man who was replacing a broken tile on the floor. Neither of them had heard or seen the other until then.

"Oh, excuse me," Nathan exclaimed.

"Shalom," the older man replied, then continuing in Arabic, "I am Ibrahim, the caretaker of the synagogue." Ibrahim wore work clothes, and his callused hands reflected a lifetime of manual labor. Though he was beardless, his skullcap and the fringed *tallit katan* he wore identified him as a religious Jew.

"I would like to see the synagogue and the *genizah*," Nathan said in the best Arabic he could produce.

"I will call Mr. Kahn," Ibrahim replied.

Moments later, a tall bearded man appeared. Well past eighty, he was attired in a worn and slightly mismatched suit coat and trousers, with a necktie. He, too, wore a *kippah* on his head.

"Welcome to the Ben Ezra Synagogue," he said, in British-accented English, extending his hand to Nathan. "I am Jacob Kahn. I serve as President of the Jewish Community Council of Cairo. I am also the unofficial tour guide here."

Nathan introduced himself, and he explained the research he was doing in England using medieval works from the Ben Ezra *genizah*.

"So you are here to see where your manuscripts came from?" Nathan smiled and nodded. "First, let me tell you some of the history of this place. This is a nice warm day, so why don't we start outside." Standing near the entrance of the synagogue, Jacob Kahn pointed southeastward.

"Over there, close to the back of the building, you can see part of the remaining stone wall from the fortress the Romans built in the second century to protect shipping on the Nile River. In the year 641, when the Arabs came, their commander, Amr ibn al-As, drove out the Roman army and took over the country. They set up their base just beyond this place. They called the town al-Fustat, and it became the capital of Muslim Egypt.

"When the Arabs arrived here, there were already churches and synagogues in the fortress, and they were allowed to remain. The Ben Ezra Synagogue goes back at least to the year 950. Some records suggest that the building was originally a church. Over the centuries, the synagogue was destroyed and rebuilt several times. The last time was in 1892, when they put a new structure on the original foundation. Then, in 1992, the buildings were completely restored."

Continuing his tour of the synagogue, Jacob Kahn described in considerable detail the changes that had been made in the most recent restoration project. Finally, he asked Nathan, "Is there anything else I can show you?"

"Well…yes," Nathan answered, "Could I see the *genizah*?"

"Oh, of course," Mr. Kahn replied, "the reason you came here. That's not so easy to do—you'll need to use a ladder. At my age, that is difficult." After looking at his watch, he said, "My son will be coming here quite soon. He'll be able to show it to you."

David Kahn arrived a short while later, and it was immediately apparent to Nathan that David had not chosen to follow in his father's footsteps. Clean-shaven and dressed in a well-tailored suit, his appearance was that of a successful executive.

"The only way to get to the *genizah* is through the women's gallery," David explained, "and the stairway to the gallery is outside of the building."

With stepladder in hand, the two of them left the synagogue. The stairway to the second floor gallery, located some distance from the synagogue itself, led to a bridge that crossed over a small courtyard, ending at an entranceway in the south corridor of the women's gallery. The doorway into the *genizah* chamber was on the far wall, with its opening several meters above the level of the floor. Nathan climbed up the ladder, pulled open the door, and with illumination from a flashlight that Ibrahim had provided, he gazed into the spacious chamber.

So there it is, Nathan reflected: the treasure chest that held the amazing trove of documents that spanned a thousand years of history—the precious writings that had restored to life a nearly forgotten era—now only an empty garret, devoid of its literary wealth.

David returned the ladder to Ibrahim, and Nathan thanked them both.

"I'm glad I could be of help," David replied. "Have you seen much of Cairo?" he asked Nathan.

"This is only my second day here," he said. I'm especially looking forward to the Egyptian Museum. I'm going there tomorrow."

"My advice is to get there early, just when it opens, and plan to spend the whole day. Do you have plans for lunch today? The reason I came here was to pick up my father. Every Tuesday we get together for our midday meal, but now he tells me he can't come. Would you like to join me?"

Nathan was pleased to accept the invitation, and David drove them to a small restaurant in the Garden City district, on a quiet street not far from the Nile River.

"The lentil soup here is especially good," David suggested, and they each ordered that for their first course. While waiting for the rest of their meal to be served, Nathan commented on David's, and also his father's, excellent command of English.

"Actually, most educated Egyptians speak English reasonably well," David replied. "My father, though, has an amazing ear for languages, and he speaks several quite fluently."

"Did you inherit that ability, too?" Nathan asked him.

"Quite the opposite. Until I went to college in New York, Arabic was really the only language I spoke well."

"New York?" Nathan asked.

"Yes, I was a student at Baruch College. We have a family business here, textile import and export, and my college education in America gave me a valuable background, especially in the area of international commerce. I also improved my English a lot during those four years. My Uncle Saul, my father's brother, was in charge of our company. He died last year, and now my cousin and I are running it. The business continues to be quite successful. If it weren't for that, neither my cousin nor I would've stayed in Egypt. As you no doubt know, there are hardly any Jews left in this country. It's not an easy place for us to live. We keep a very low profile, and so far we haven't had any major problems."

For his entrée, David recommended the meloukhia. "They prepare it with rabbit or chicken. I prefer rabbit," he added. Nathan opted for chicken. "For my father," David commented, "living in Egypt now poses certain difficulties. He will only eat kosher food, of course, and there are no longer any sources of kosher meat here. He finally came to accept that Muslim halal meat is similar enough to kosher so that he can eat it—however, now he mainly stays with vegetarian.

"So what is the research you're doing with the documents from the *genizah*?" David asked him. "I would've thought that by now everything worth studying would have been finished."

"I'm mainly interested in the works of medieval Hebrew poets. In fact, there are still a good many manuscripts in the collection at Cambridge University, especially poetry, that haven't yet been well studied."

As they were having coffee at the end of their meal, David asked Nathan, "Were you aware that a good many old Hebrew manuscripts, a lot of them undoubtedly from the *genizah* here, still remain in private hands in Egypt?"

"I was told that there are documents from the *genizah* that have never been catalogued."

"My late uncle Saul was an avid collector of old Hebrew manuscripts, and he invested a huge amount of money in them. His widow, my Aunt Amira still has his collection."

After a momentary pause, David said, "Perhaps you'd be interested in seeing what Amira has. She's rather isolated and lonely, and I think she'd enjoy having a visitor. And I know she would be happy to show you my uncle's collection."

"Why, yes. That would be wonderful," Nathan replied.

"Let me give her a call," David said, taking a cell phone from his pocket. "*Allo Amidi Amira. Izzáyik?—Kwayyis.* Amidi Amira, there is a scholar from Cambridge University who's visiting us…Yes. He would like to see Uncle Saul's Hebrew manuscripts…Yes, that's right. So I'm calling to see if we could come for a visit. Oh, really? Tomorrow? Well, I certainly hope that goes well. I'll call you in the evening to see how you are. Yes, of course, maybe in a few days. *Ma' as-salaama.*"

"Amira is having eye surgery tomorrow morning, for a cataract," David said. "She expects to be back home by afternoon. She told me she would be happy to have you come, but with her surgery, she probably won't be able to have visitors for a few days. When will you be returning to England?"

"My flight leaves Sunday morning."

"Well, that would probably work out all right. I'll keep in touch with my aunt, and I can call you or leave a message at your hotel."

Early the next morning, Nathan made his way to the Egyptian Museum, arriving a short while before its opening time. At least fifty others who had preceded him were already waiting in the queue outside of its massive, classically styled stone edifice. Dotting the broad expanse of lawn that surrounded the museum were myriad examples of ancient statuary, stone sarcophagi, reliefs, stelae, and engraved marble plaques commemorating the exploits and victories of the great kings of that ancient land. Those archaeological treasures gave Nathan, and the others who waited outside with him that morning, a foretaste of the vast abundance of historical riches that lay within the museum's walls.

Once inside, Nathan made his way directly to the Tutankhamen gallery on the second floor, having been warned that this was by far the museum's most popular exhibit. He had seen pictures of the solid-gold death mask of the famous boy king, but now he could gaze directly upon that more than three-thousand-year-old work of art, with its inlaid quartz, lapis lazuli, and richly colored glass. Golden statuettes, superbly crafted wooden furniture, and jewel-encrusted ornamental objects all seemed as if they were of modern origin.

Other exhibits in the museum displayed enormous quantities of ancient papyrus art and metalwork. The extensive exhibits of gold and silver jewelry led Nathan to wonder if any real progress in jewelry making had been made since the time those precious objects had been created.

As the closing time of the museum drew near, even after spending the entire day there, Nathan realized that he had seen only a small fraction of the enormous collection on display. How so vast a quantity of extraordinary art could have been created by this long-ago civilization amazed him.

The final exhibit Nathan examined before leaving the museum displayed the Rosetta Stone, the extraordinary discovery that had been the key to the modern understanding of the hieroglyphic and demotic forms of ancient Egyptian writing. Only after reading the printed label of the exhibit did Nathan come to realize that what he was viewing was only a copy of the original, which resided in the British Museum in London.

The following day, he took a guided bus tour that brought him to the ancient city of Memphis, to Saqqara with its magnificent tombs and pyramids, and finally to the Great Pyramids and the Sphinx at Giza.

That evening, David Kahn telephoned Nathan at his hotel.

"I spoke with my aunt this afternoon, and she's recovering well from her surgery. She invited us both for lunch at noon on Saturday. I told her I would let her know once I had spoken with you. Would that be okay?"

Nathan readily agreed.

"Fine, then, I'll pick you up at about eleven forty-five. My Aunt Amira lives in Zamalek, not far from the hotel where you're staying."

On Friday, Nathan visited the Darb al-Ahmar quarter, with its historic mosques and exquisite Islamic architecture. He ended the day in the Khan al-Khalili district, where he bought a hand-painted teapot as a present for Zippora.

When Nathan emerged from his hotel shortly after eleven thirty Saturday morning, David Kahn's Mercedes-Benz was already parked in the driveway. David waved to him.

"Climb aboard," he said. "We're a bit early, and we're only about five minutes away from my aunt's house, so why don't we take a short drive around the island. Auntie is a rather proper lady, and I don't think she would be very happy if we surprised her by getting there early. I should also tell you," he said as they drove away from the hotel, "that Aunt Amira isn't Jewish. In fact, she comes from one of the most prominent Muslim Arab families of Cairo. My uncle Saul was never religious, in contrast to my father, but it was an unusual situation nevertheless."

"How did they happen to marry?"

"Well, they met while they were in college—New York, again. Uncle Saul was majoring in anthropology at Columbia University. Amira, as it happened, was studying, I think it was history, at Barnard. They took a course together. Anyway, as you might imagine, my aunt's family disowned her when she married my uncle. Now that he's gone, there's hardly anyone for her to talk to. It's really a sad situation."

The route that David took gave Nathan the opportunity to view Zamalek Island's elegant opera house, its extensive Khedival botanical gardens, and a number of foreign embassies.

From the street, Amira Kahn's Italianate residence was largely hidden behind the pairs of stately sycamore trees that flanked its main entranceway. Acacia and locust branches, extending over the top of the stone and wrought iron wall that surrounded the property, served further to insulate it from the outside. David entered an access code on the keypad near the entrance and the tall iron gate swung open, revealing a broad expanse of meticulously manicured lawn. Two giant Madagascar cacti near the driveway were shedding their leaves with the approach of winter, and pomegranate, peach, and fig trees along the periphery of the grounds were in early hibernation.

David parked his car near the entrance to the three-story building, near one of the groupings of tall palm trees that formed a canopy over the walkway. Mrs. Kahn answered his knock on the imposing wooden door, and she greeted her nephew and Nathan warmly.

Amira Kahn's fashionable hairstyle and her elegant brocade dress were Western in inspiration and design. She was past the age of eighty, but with the help of Cairo's most skilled plastic surgeons, she retained the appearance of a much younger woman. Nathan surmised that she must have been exceedingly beautiful in her youth, and that conjecture was amply confirmed when Amira later showed him a photograph of her husband and herself, taken at the time of their wedding. She expressed great interest in the research that Nathan was pursuing, and from the questions she asked, it was clear that her interest was genuine.

"Saul would have so much enjoyed meeting you," she said. "His manuscript collection was a joy to him, but he had few opportunities to discuss them with anyone who was a real scholar."

On their way to the dining room, it became apparent to Nathan that Saul Kahn's collection was by no means limited to documents and manuscripts. Shelves and cabinets filled with some of the finest examples of Jewish ritual objects and archaeological artifacts occupied each room that they passed, giving the exquisitely appointed interior of the house an ambiance much in common with many of the finer small European museums.

Amira's chef placed a dish of freshly baked pita bread on the table, followed by a warm soup with a base of watercress and lime. Its smooth, creamy texture and its subtle flavoring provided a thoroughly delicious start to the meal. He poured a light, dry Chenin Blanc, but Nathan accepted only half of a glass. The salad that followed, which, Amira explained, was traditionally Egyptian, consisted of a mélange of prunes, Turkish apricots, figs, raisins, and hazelnuts. The main course included baked eggplant, a delicately seasoned spinach soufflé, and couscous prepared with currants and pistachio nuts. For Nathan, the entire meal was a magnificent experience, but even without having had wine, the heaviness of the food left him drowsy as well as sated.

As an effective antidote to Nathan's impending sleepiness, Amira Kahn proved to be a lively and spirited hostess. Their conversation during the meal, invariably flowing from topics of Amira's choosing, was wide-ranging, though seldom profound. With her limited opportunities for social interaction, she took advantage of this visit to engage her guests as fully as possible. Their dessert, "also a traditional Egyptian specialty," Amira announced, was Om Ali, a warm, creamy custard made with a mixture of raisins, almonds, pistachios, and coconut on a baked phyllo base. Nathan, struggling to remain alert, limited his intake to a few small bites, concentrating instead on the fragrant and full-bodied coffee that was served with the dessert.

Afterward, Amira brought Nathan and David to a large windowless room near the back of the house. A sealed doorway and a temperature and humidity control system had been installed to maintain optimal conditions for document preservation. Specially filtered illumination served to minimize light-induced damage to the fragile manuscripts. The room was furnished with a library table and comfortable chairs. Large wooden cabinets, fitted with stacks of drawers, provided ample storage capacity for the extensive document collection.

"I've brought some paperwork, and I'll have to deal with that while you look at the manuscripts," David said to Nathan as he opened a briefcase and moved to the far end of the table.

"Perhaps you would first like to see some of the manuscripts that my husband always enjoyed showing to visitors," Amira began. "Once we've done that, you could browse through the inventory list on the computer, and I'll take out any of the documents you'd like to see. There also are some manuscripts here that Saul bought shortly before he died that are not included in the inventory. For some of them, there's not much information, but perhaps you'd like to look at them, too."

Amira placed two sets of vellum manuscripts on the table.

"First of all, Saul collected a large number of bibles and prayer books, many of them quite old."

"You—you might want to put on gloves before you handle those," Nathan interjected.

"Oh, of course, I forgot," Amira said as she turned to open a wall cupboard and took out a box of white cotton gloves. "Thank you, I have to remember never to do that again. So," she continued, "this manuscript is part of a Karaite bible from Fustat." The decorated "carpet page" frontispiece of the book was brightly illuminated in a floral design, in vivid gold, green, red, and blue. The other set of manuscript pages she showed Nathan, from a thirteenth-century Yemenite bible, was also elegantly decorated. Its intricate geometric design was formed entirely from micrographic Hebrew writing that could be read only with the aid of a magnifying lens.

"This set of books is by Moses Maimonides. He lived here, in Fustat, for a good many years," Amira said as she showed Nathan a remarkably well-preserved copy of Maimonides's monumental work, the *Mishneh Torah*. The first pages of each of the fourteen volumes of the book were magnificently illustrated, and Nathan marveled at their beauty.

"Saul also collected a large number of Hebrew marriage contracts, more than fifty," Amira continued. "Most of them are from Cairo. These are Egyptian, both from the nineteenth century," she said, displaying two intricately decorated parchment documents. "This next one is Italian, from the fifteenth century."

"Would it be all right for me to snap a photograph?" Nathan asked.

"Yes," Amira answered, "but Saul would never allow a flash picture to be taken of any of the old manuscripts. There's a specially lighted enclosure you can use for your picture."

Nathan, following her instructions, took a snapshot of the parchment page, using his digital pocket camera.

After viewing others of the documents, he made a rapid perusal of the extensive listing in the computerized inventory of the collection. He was delighted to discover an entry of a manuscript by Isaac ibn Yannai, one of the eleventh-century Spanish poets whose work he had been studying at Cambridge. When Amira brought out the yellowed parchment document, Nathan at once recognized the by-then familiar Hebrew script of the medieval poet. He could scarcely control his happiness when he realized that this was a work of poetry that was unquestionably different from any of the others he had seen.

"It's called הגן באביב, 'The Garden in Springtime,' evidently one of his secular poems," Nathan said excitedly. For the next several minutes, he sat totally fixated on this marvelous new discovery. Amira recognized how important this work would be to the young scholar's research, and without hesitation she graciously offered to lend him the manuscript for his research.

Nathan was exhilarated from this new find, but he was also growing weary from the long afternoon of examining the documents in this remarkable collection. Amira, however, showed no indication of fatigue. She was clearly happy to have this opportunity to spend time with the young scholar.

"As I mentioned before," she said, "my husband bought about a dozen manuscripts the year before he died, most of them from a dealer in Paris. They were quite costly, and Saul was very excited about them. But he became ill soon afterward, and he never had an opportunity to do anything with them. These," she said, as she placed three of the documents on the table, "were said to be legal papers, originally from the Ben Ezra *genizah.*"

"I won't be able to help you with those," Nathan replied, after examining the manuscripts. "They're written in Judeo-Arabic, which I don't understand. We do have people at Cambridge who could read these. With some photographs, I might be able to get you a translation." Amira readily agreed to that, and Nathan made a set of snapshots.

"I don't have any information at all about this one," Amira said, showing him a lengthy document written on deeply yellowed parchment. Its beautiful Hebrew calligraphy drew Nathan's immediate attention, but when he read its first lines, he paused for a long while. After scrutinizing the manuscript, he finally read aloud the familiar words with which it began:

שיר השירים אשר לשלמה:
ישקני מנשיקות פיהו
בי טובים דדיך מיין

It was the Song of Songs, the magnificent love poem that had occupied fully three years of Nathan's life when he was a graduate student.

"There was no information available about this manuscript?"

"Apparently none," she replied.

"This was one of the most widely copied sections of the Bible, but for me it's especially interesting," he said, with a hint of excitement in his voice. "Two really ancient fragments of the Song of Songs were found among the Dead Sea documents, and there are a number of later versions. If this one is as old as it appears to be, it would be wonderful to compare it with the others. May I photograph this manuscript? And some tiny bits of its parchment would be enough to do a radiocarbon dating, and that could provide very useful information about the age of the document." Amira was readily agreeable to both of these requests, and she provided Nathan a Mylar envelope to transport the parchment samples.

Amira displayed another group of Hebrew manuscripts, some of them beautifully illuminated. They all contained biblical passages, including several of the psalms, the book of Ruth, and sections from Jeremiah. Finally, she placed on the table a large sheaf of pages, encased in a threadbare and heavily stained wool wrapper.

"Saul was really excited about this large manuscript. There unfortunately wasn't any information that came with it," Amira added. Folding back the tattered cloth covering brought forth a cloud of fine dust, redolent of mildew with a hint of decay. Hebrew lettering was readily visible on its deeply discolored papyrus.

Nathan lifted a corner of the first page of the manuscript to examine the page beneath it. Its brittleness became immediately apparent as the corner broke away from the sheet. He also discovered two other such fragments nestled within the cloth wrapper.

"This is fascinating," Nathan commented, "and it's unfortunate there's no information about it. Radiocarbon dating might well be useful. I'd also like to photograph some of the pages to see what we can find out from the text."

By the time David Kahn drove Nathan back to his hotel, the young scholar was exhausted, but the wonderful Isaac ibn Yannai poem that Amira had lent him sustained his state of euphoria.

A large orange and three squares of chocolate remained on his dresser top, and that served as his dinner for that evening. He fell asleep early, in anticipation of his flight to England the next morning. That night, he dreamt of being happily with Zippora again, and of showing her the manuscript of the poem from Amira Kahn's collection.

11

When Nathan returned to the Genizah Research Unit the following day, hardly any of the staff were there. Professor Elstein had gone to New York to meet with a group of donors, Fergus Wiley was back home in Glasgow, spending Christmas with his family, and Zippora was still in Israel, not due to return for another week.

Nathan now found himself with several potentially important documents to deal with, including the Isaac ibn Yannai poem that Amira Kahn had lent him. That manuscript was his first order of business, and he carefully placed the parchment document, already in its protective Mylar pouch, in a heavy brown envelope to protect it from light exposure. Then he downloaded the photographs from his camera onto his computer. However, when he examined the images on the screen, he immediately discovered that most of the texts he had photographed had not reproduced clearly, and he regretted that his camera did not have a better lens. Finally, he made certain that the manuscript samples he had taken for radiocarbon dating were properly and securely stored. He spent almost two hours with the Isaac ibn Yannai poem that morning, making a preliminary translation of the first section of its text:

The Garden in Springtime

The hillsides awake from their slumber,
rejoicing refreshed in the fragrant [??] of dawn.
The chill of winter has vanished,
gone are its [?? obscure word].
The [tree or shrub name] are ablaze with color,
their intoxicating fragrance like a spicy incense.
The garden wears a mantle of many hues,
a wondrous sight to behold.

Thomas Gans was one of the few people at the Research Unit that day, and his search for a lunch companion brought him to Nathan's office. Gans's favorite campus pub was eerily quiet that afternoon, with most of the students still away on holiday. No one hurried them to vacate their table, and Nathan had ample time to tell his colleague what he had seen of Amira Kahn's remarkable manuscript collection.

"Chaim will most certainly be interested to hear about that," Gans told him. "His first question, of course, will be whether the lady might be interested in donating some of her collection to us. In due time, I suspect, he may want to contact her and maybe even pay her a visit."

Afterward, Gans came back to Nathan's office with him, to look at what he had brought back from Cairo.

"This is the Isaac ibn Yannai poem," Nathan said, showing him the manuscript. "I've made a first stab at translating it, and I already know that I'll need your help, but I want to work with it a bit more before I go over it with you. And here you can see the rather blurry images from the photographs I took."

"Actually the text of the Song of Songs manuscript isn't bad at all," Gans commented. "The three Judeo-Arabic manuscripts are not too terrific, but I think I can still make out what's there.

"These are all judgments from the Fustat Jewish religious court, the *bet din,*" he said, after looking over the images on the computer printout. "This first one concerns a widow. Apparently her husband wrote a will in which he left some land to her. But when the husband died, their son contested the will. In his petition to the court, he claimed that his mother was not eligible to inherit the land, and that instead it should go to him. The *bet din* evidently didn't see it that way, and this indicates that they ruled in favor of the wife, according to the terms of the will. Good for them," he said. "The second of these deals with the use of tax monies for the support of religious schools, and the third one has to do with procedures for slaughtering animals for kosher meat. If you'd like, I'll be happy to write out the translations for you."

"I'm sure Mrs. Kahn would appreciate that, and maybe her gratitude will inspire her to be more generous when Dr. Elstein calls upon her," Nathan said, smiling. "And these are the parchment samples I took for the radiocarbon dating," he added, showing Gans the tiny, yellowed fragments.

"There should be no problem getting that done," Gans said. "We have a contract with the Radiocarbon Accelerator Unit at Oxford University, which I think is the best laboratory of its kind in this part of the world. They're very good, and they give special priority to our samples. Do you also have pictures from the papyrus manuscript you told me about?"

"Oh, yes, here they are. I haven't gone over that set very carefully, but I believe the text is from the book of Isaiah."

"If you'd like," Gans said, "I'll be happy to look over those, too."

Nathan spent most of the afternoon reviewing the Isaac ibn Yannai poem, and before leaving for dinner, he began a transcription of the Song of Songs manuscript. The next morning, Gans stopped by Nathan's office to give him the translations of the Judeo-Arabic *bet din* documents.

"I also examined your pictures from the papyrus document," he said. "Yes, the text is from Isaiah all right, but it's very, very sloppy."

"Sloppy?" Nathan asked.

"Yes. The lettering was obviously done hurriedly, for one thing. There are misspellings, even whole words missing, and at least one instance of a word written twice."

"So, what do you make of that?"

"Well, first of all, that no self-respecting scribe would ever have turned out such a monstrosity. It's not only a fake, it's a very crude one."

"A fake?" Nathan asked. "I'm really surprised."

"In this business," Gans replied, "phony documents are everywhere. Sometimes they can fool you for a long time. But this one was so badly done that it was no trouble at all to spot."

Nathan found it difficult to believe that Amira's manuscript was a modern fabrication. He was well aware that documents could be treated in various ways to simulate aging, but this one had struck him as being truly old.

When Ms. Beckman returned from her vacation, Nathan gave her the two sets of samples to send for radiocarbon dating. Then he telephoned Amira Kahn in Egypt. First, he let her know that her Judeo-Arabic *bet din* documents had been translated and that she would be receiving their English texts.

"That very large manuscript, the one in the cloth wrapper—well, there's suspicion by our document expert that it's a forgery, and a rather crude one at that."

After a long pause, Amira replied, "My husband paid a small fortune for that manuscript. And the dealer who sold it to him was supposed to be among the most reputable of them. Well, Saul used to say that none of the antiquarian dealers are entirely trustworthy. Anyway, thank you for letting me know. I'll contact the dealer as soon as I can. I'll let you know what he says."

It was still dark outside when Nathan arrived in the office early the following Monday morning. He was surprised to see that the office door was open and that Zippora, not ordinarily an early riser, was there at her desk, sorting through her mail. Her face brightened when she saw him.

"Hi. It's great to see you back," Nathan said. "It was lonely here last week."

"Nathan, I missed you," she said, and with that, she stood, drew herself close to him, and kissed him on the lips.

"I…I missed you, too," he responded, surprised by her unexpected show of affection. "Well, um…it's rather early for you to be here."

"I just couldn't sleep, so I decided to come in to the office."

"I hope everything's all right."

"Oh, yes, everything's fine," she answered cheerfully.

"How was the visit with your family?"

"Very nice."

"And the wedding?"

"Oh, it was delightful. The things that I told you about my brother's bride were really rather unkind. She's a lovely young woman. The two of them are a great couple, and I'm sure they'll have a wonderful marriage. And your visit to Cairo?"

"It was an amazing trip. I saw a lot of the city, and of course I went to the Ben Ezra Synagogue. But I also was able to visit a woman there who has a fantastic collection. Her Hebrew manuscripts must be among the finest anywhere. When we have more time, I have a lot to tell you about it. And by the way, I brought you a little souvenir from Egypt," he said as he presented her the painted teapot.

"It's lovely," Zippora responded, and she kissed him again. "I have something for you from Jerusalem." Her gift was a volume of twentieth-century Israeli poets. "A bit more modern that what you've been reading lately." Nathan returned her kiss, and from her smile, he was glad that he had done so.

"Nathan, I really want to hear more about your trip to Cairo. Perhaps we could have dinner together in a nice quiet restaurant."

"Well, sure."

"It was my invitation, so let me make a reservation for say, seven o'clock?"

"Okay, terrific!"

In the afternoon, Nathan had a meeting with Chaim Elstein, who had returned from New York the previous morning.

"That document is a superb find," he said after Nathan showed him the Isaac ibn Yannai poem be had brought back from Egypt. "I thought I knew all of the major collections of Hebrew manuscripts. But from what you've told me, this woman in Cairo has a considerable number of very important documents. And yet I've never heard of her or of her husband. I certainly hope I'll have the opportunity to meet her. Perhaps she'd be willing to lend us other manuscripts from her collection."

Shortly before seven, Nathan arrived to pick up Zippora for dinner. Her landlady invited him to wait in the parlor. When Zippora appeared a few moments later, Nathan could scarcely recognize her. In place of the sweater and skirt that was her usual working outfit, she wore a fitted blue dress that beautifully emphasized her slim figure. Her dark hair, which normally fell down to her shoulders, was done up in a chignon, accentuating her clear, glowing complexion and the beauty of her face. As she kissed Nathan, the fragrance of her perfume, a sensual fusion of rose oil, sandalwood, civet, and musk, completed the picture of her now very alluring persona.

"Zippora, you look lovely," Nathan said to her. "Perhaps 'radiant' would be a better word."

"Oh, thank goodness, I was afraid you might not have noticed," she said, smiling happily. Then she kissed him again.

A short taxi ride brought them to a restaurant known to be one of Cambridge's finest. On that chilly Monday night, the place was nearly empty, and the two of them were seated at a table in a quiet corner, close to a fireplace with a blazing fire. They both enjoyed the dinner and the wine, and afterward they talked for a long while. Nathan described his experiences in Cairo, and Zippora spoke more about her visit with her family.

"I told everyone at home about you," she said. "My mother is looking forward to meeting you." Zippora smiled. "I should warn you that she plans to come here for a visit sometime in the next few weeks. When I told my father that you're a scholar, he also expressed an interest in meeting you. But then I thought it was only fair to tell him that you're not a religious scholar," she said, and she laughed.

"Nathan," she said hesitantly, "I thought about you quite a lot while I was away." He could see that she was trembling, and he reached over the table and held her hands.

"I thought about you also," he said, and with that, he could feel the tension in Zippora's hands abate.

"Did you really miss me?" she asked, looking directly into his eyes.

"I missed you very much," Nathan replied.

After a long pause, Zippora continued, "Nathan, do you remember the day I first got here, when you let me spend the night on your sofa?"

"I certainly do," he replied, smiling.

"Well, I…I think about it often," she said. "You were very kind." Before he could say anything more, Zippora squeezed his hands tightly. "Wouldn't it be nice to do that again?"

"You want to sleep on my sofa?" he asked her.

"Well, not exactly on your sofa. I've packed a little overnight bag, and we could stop by my room and pick it up." Nathan was astonished and altogether delighted at what he was hearing, and he lost no time in agreeing to her proposal.

After collecting Zippora's suitcase, they began the short walk to Nathan's flat.

"I suppose we should first stop at the pharmacy."

"Oh, there's no need to bother," Zippora replied, smiling and pointing to her bag.

For that night, Zippora had brought a low-cut, lacy, black nightgown.

"Do you like it?" she asked, turning around in front of him.

"It's beautiful. You look wonderful, really wonderful." Nathan took both of her hands in his, and then he drew her close to him. He kissed her lips, her shoulders, and then her breasts. Zippora pulled him toward the bed, and soon their professional and collegial relationship became transformed into one of impassioned intimacy. Exhausted, they fell asleep in each other's arms. But soon Zippora was awake again, and, blissfully happy, she lay there in the dark for a long while. Then, holding Nathan's face in her hands, she gave him a long, passionate kiss, and he too was awake.

"Nathan, do you love me?" After a brief moment, he replied to her question, paraphrasing the Hebrew lines that began the love poem he knew so well:

"Kiss me with the kisses of your mouth, for your love is better than wine."

Then he kissed her tenderly.

"I've been awake all this time," Zippora said. "Maybe you could help me fall asleep."

"I could warm up some milk for you," he answered her in mock seriousness.

"I don't really like warm milk," she replied, in a solemn voice.

"Would you like me to sing you a lullaby?"

"Do you sing well?"

"Well, no, actually I usually sing way off-key." Zippora gave him a long, deep kiss, and then she disappeared under the covers. When she reemerged minutes later, Nathan had a happy smile on his face.

"Have you come up with any other ideas?" she asked.

"I'm sure we'll think of something."

When Nathan awoke Zippora, it was well past nine o'clock. Although they were very late, Zippora insisted on preparing an elaborate breakfast. Tired but still exhilarated, their meal together served as a celebration of their newfound intimacy.

"Nathan, before we leave for the office, I want you to give me a serious answer. Do...do you think I'm attractive?"

He kissed her, and holding both of her hands, he answered her with more verses from the Song of Songs:

"'How fair you are, my love, how beautiful;
Your eyes are like doves.
Your hair like a flock of goats,

streaming down Mount Gilead.
Your teeth are like a flock of ewes,
climbing up from the washing pool.
Your lips are like a crimson thread.
Your mouth is lovely.
Your breasts are like two fawns—'"

"Nathan," she interrupted, pressing her finger to his lips. "That's very poetic, but frankly I was hoping for the short answer."

"Oh, well, okay then, yes!"

In the weeks that followed, Zippora spent many nights with Nathan. A month later, she moved into his flat.

12

The three-bedroom apartment that Ernesto Lanzi rented in Rome for Myron Geller and his two companions occupied the second floor of a small but attractive building on Via della Camilluccia, north of the center of the city. Its furnishings were predominantly in a rococo, eighteenth-century style, with intricately carved wood, velvet upholstery, and heavy, ornamented draperies. The elegant, rather formal appearance of the appointments impressed Myron. It was a comfortable place with easy access to shops and restaurants and to the cyber cafés where he kept abreast of the news.

He and the two women, Susan and Carolyn, in spite of their concern about being discovered, made numerous telephone calls each day, both to members of their families in the United States, and, in Myron's case, to many of his business associates. But by using prepaid telephone cards for their calls, they managed to evade inept police investigators, who remained in the dark as to where they had gone.

Myron had not yet been indicted for any crime, but within two days after their arrival in Rome, he learned from an Internet news item that the FBI had been actively seeking information about his whereabouts. But with a large amount of cash at their disposal, the three of them enjoyed themselves, taking in the sights of the city and sampling some of its better restaurants.

On the morning of their fourth day in Italy, as Myron and the two women were watching CNN, they heard their doorbell ring. Susan, without making any effort to identify their visitor, immediately opened the door. Realizing what was happening, Myron made a dash for the nearest bedroom, where he hid himself among the hanging clothes in a large armoire. The tall, middle-aged man who stood in the doorway, dressed in a black suit with a Roman collar, smiled and presented Susan with his calling card.

"Ernesto Lanzi suggested that I pay a visit to Mr. Geller. Would this be a convenient time for me to speak with him?" he asked.

"Please come in," Susan replied, "and I'll check with Mr. Geller." As she entered the bedroom, Carolyn, who was standing near the window, pointed toward the armoire.

"There's a man here to see you," Susan said in a loud voice, without opening the door to Myron's hiding place. "He's a priest."

"Why would a priest want to see me?" Myron asked, peering out from the slightly opened armoire. Susan handed him the calling card their visitor had given her.

"The Vatican Library?" Myron asked. "What the hell is that all about?" Then, looking even more bedraggled than usual as a result of his hasty retreat amongst the clothes, he extracted himself from the armoire and returned to the living room to greet his guest.

"Father Carlo Delvecchio," the priest said, extending his hand. "I'm a friend of the Lanzi family." Myron made no response. "I believe it would be best if I could speak with you alone now, if that would be all right." Myron waved the two women into a bedroom and closed the door.

"We consider you to be a good and generous friend of the Church," the priest began. "We understand that you're facing difficult circumstances, and we'd like to do what we can to help you. First of all, I want you to know that we can arrange safe sanctuary for you, in Rome or elsewhere Also, we can secure a Vatican passport that will be honored almost everywhere. And, if you wish, we can facilitate the transfer of funds into your personal account with the Vatican Bank, to assure that they remain protected."

Myron was pleased to hear the first of these offers, but it was the last one that he saw as a particularly appealing solution to his most pressing immediate need. He had spoken earlier that morning with his personal banker in Geneva. Nearly twelve million dollars remained in his account, all of which was still available to him; but he was also well aware that it was only a matter of time before his access to the money would be blocked.

After the priest departed, Myron made another lengthy call to his Swiss banker. The following morning at precisely nine o'clock, two men, who identified themselves only by the code numbers Myron had provided, arrived at the Geneva bank. In accordance with Myron's instructions, the men were given a pair of suitcases filled with cash, ten million dollars in all, to be transported to the offices of the Vatican Bank.

Myron and his two companions remained in Rome for three more weeks. During that time, the FBI made no headway toward discovering the location of their hiding place. Their investigation got its first big break when Susan Jenkins finally lost interest in sharing Myron's increasingly precarious existence, and she returned home to New York.

Susan had been on the FBI's wanted list. Customs officials at the Kennedy Airport notified the FBI when she arrived, and she was promptly apprehended. Fortunately for the fugitives, Susan never knew the precise location of their apartment, but now the authorities were aware that Myron's hiding place was in Rome.

The following day, Myron received a call from Ernesto Lanzi.

"I just got word from a friend in the *Polizia di Stato* that Interpol is on the lookout for you. They're concentrating now on the hotels in

Rome, so you're probably safe in your apartment, but you must be careful."

Myron had been keeping abreast with news about the worldwide search to find him, but after receiving Ernesto's telephone call, he panicked. He had not given much thought about other places where he could hide, but faced with the need to make an immediate decision, he chose to flee to Germany.

"Hire a car and a driver that can take us to Munich," he told Carolyn.

"Why don't you get in touch with that priest?" she asked him. "He said he could provide you a safe place to hide."

But Myron had only one thought then, which was to get out of Italy as fast as he could. And as it turned out, that idea was a timely one. Only two days later, Ernesto betrayed Myron's hiding place to Interpol, to deflect any suspicions that he himself might have been an accomplice in Myron's flight from the authorities.

When Myron and his companion checked into a small hotel in Munich, he used a false British passport. It was the same one he had presented to the immigration officer when they entered Germany. It bore the name Robert Ellington. The following day, they moved to a different hotel, and three days later, they left Munich, traveling to Hamburg.

There, the fugitives checked into a small inn overlooking scenic Lake Alster. Myron paid in cash, several weeks in advance, for a tiny suite. They remained there for a month, spending most of their time in the room, venturing out only for an occasional meal or to buy newspapers and snack foods. Myron became increasingly morose, hardly ever speaking to Carolyn.

"Myron, I know this is a terrible situation for you," she said, "but we can't go on like this. It's only a matter of time before they're going to catch up with us."

"Yeah, you're right," he answered. "It's just been a big disappointment, that's all. If I only could have gotten over my damn trading block, everything would have turned out fine. You know why I did all of this, don't you? Well, I'll tell you. It wasn't so I could make a lot of money. No, it was because I saw a chance to become a real philanthropist—to help people in need. And in spite of everything that went wrong, I did manage to give a lot of money to worthy causes. I gave five million to Father Sangiovanni for his projects. And more millions to other charities—a lot of money, a whole lot. I really wanted to do good. I'll tell you what my real mistake was—I never should have gotten involved with trading in the first place. I should have become a social worker. If only I'd done that, everything would have turned out fine."

That evening, Carolyn left their apartment alone, to pick up a newspaper and some food. On her way back, she called her lawyer in New York from a pay phone. She gave him their address in Hamburg and the number of their hotel room.

The following morning, as they were having coffee and croissants in front of the television, three German policemen arrived at their door with a warrant for Myron's arrest. Carolyn allowed them to enter the apartment, and Myron made no attempt to evade them or to put up any resistance. He felt numb and detached. He saw himself as being the main actor at center stage in a Greek tragedy, but there was no Greek god descending from the ceiling to rescue him.

Once the FBI knew of Myron's arrest, government prosecutors initiated extradition proceedings for his return to the United States. But before he could be repatriated, Myron needed to face the German criminal indictments that were being brought against him: he had entered the country with a false passport, and he had failed to declare and to pay taxes on the approximately eight million dollars worth of diamonds he had brought with him. Myron continued to be in dire fear of extradition. To delay returning to the United States as long as possible, he entered a guilty plea in the German court to both of the charges against him. He was sentenced to three years' imprisonment.

A week after Myron was committed to a Hamburg penitentiary, a tall man dressed in black, an Italian priest, appeared at the jail.

"I would like to see the prisoner Myron Geller," he said. After a brief wait, he was taken to the visitors' room, and a guard directed him to a small booth with a chair and a telephone. The priest could see Myron on the other side of the thick glass window. But throughout their brief encounter, Myron directed his gaze downward, refusing to make eye contact with him.

"How are you?" the priest asked, speaking through the telephone handset, but he received no answer.

"Is there some way I could talk with this man without that terrible window between us?" Father Delvecchio asked the guard, addressing him in fluent German.

"For what you are asking, you would need to talk with the superintendent. He is the only one who can authorize that." He directed the priest to the superintendent's office.

"*Guten Tag, Herr Oberaufseher,*" Father Delvecchio said. "I am here to ask a special favor of you." His request was for the opportunity to meet face-to-face with Myron.

"I will be happy to authorize that, Father, but I must say that I am surprised you are here to see him. You no doubt are aware that this man is not a Catholic, and in fact he is a Jew."

"Yes," the priest answered, "but it is clear to me that he has a deep spiritual hunger, and I believe he will soon be prepared to accept Christ. Perhaps more important for now, he seems very depressed, and without help, I fear he may even seek to take his own life."

"I agree with your assessment," the superintendent replied. "We already have him under continuous observation for that very reason. You certainly may visit him."

Father Delvecchio was escorted to a small room that had been arranged for his meeting. Myron was seated there on a wooden bench, his bowed head buried in his hands.

"Guard," the priest said, "would you please leave us alone for a few minutes? We want to pray together."

"Father, I am not permitted to do that," he answered, "but…as long as you are with him, I suppose no one would object."

The priest got down on his knees, and he motioned to Myron to do the same. With that, Myron suddenly came to life.

"The money," he asked, "is it still safe?"

"Why, yes, of course it's safe, and I'm sure it's continuing to earn interest," the priest replied, unable to suppress a smile at the audacity of Myron's question. But in fact, a truthful answer would have been that Myron's personal account in the Vatican Bank had been closed out some weeks earlier. And in candor, Father Delvecchio might also have told him that the large amount of cash that had been removed from his Swiss account had never actually made its way to the Vatican Bank in the first place. Instead, the money had been brought to a bank in Milan, and was deposited in an account under the control of a Vatican official with responsibility for "special projects." And later, three million dollars had been transferred to Father Delvecchio's personal account in a different Swiss bank.

"I'm really sorry it all came to this," the priest said to him. "We wanted to help you, but you disappeared before we could complete the arrangements."

"I know. It's not your fault," Myron answered.

"How do you feel?" the priest asked him. "You don't look very well, and the people here think you may be planning to kill yourself."

"No, not now anyway," Myron said. "They treat me okay here. But sooner or later I'll get sent back to the U.S. I talked with an American lawyer, and he told me I could get fifty or sixty years. Well, hell, that's no different from a death sentence."

"I understand," Father Delvecchio said. "I'll see what I can do to help you. I've got to leave now, but I'll be back to visit you again soon."

A week later, the priest again appeared in the superintendent's office, this time accompanied by Rocco Conconi, an obese sixty-one-year-old American with a noticeably nervous manner and heavily tobacco-stained fingers.

Herr Oberaufseher," Father Delvecchio said, "we are here to see Mr. Geller, and again, we ask your permission to meet with him face-to-face."

"I will be happy to authorize that for you," he replied, "but the other gentleman will need to wait outside."

"I would appreciate it very much," the priest added, "if Mr. Cohen could also visit with Mr. Geller. He is a convert to our faith, and I believe it would be helpful if he could join us now." Reluctantly, the superintendent gave his approval.

Once they were inside Myron Geller's cell, Father Delvecchio again persuaded the guard to leave them alone. And as before, they were on their knees as they held their brief meeting.

"Mr. Cohen is from Chicago," the priest said to Myron. "Now, you know that the Church is strongly opposed to suicide." Myron nodded. "We do understand the torment you've been going through, about the prospect of jail in America. So, with great reluctance, we're willing to help you if there is no alternative. This *bateau* is constructed of a plastic material that can't be detected by x-rays or metal detectors, and it contains three cyanide tablets in a waterproof pouch." And with that, the priest showed him a smooth, white plastic tube-like object, about the size of a man's index finger.

"I have no idea what that is," Myron replied.

"It's a French invention, a hollow chamber that's threaded in the middle, so that its two halves can be screwed together. It was designed for concealing money or other small objects. When it's placed in the rectum, it can remain there, undetected, for a very long time. Rocco, uh, Mr. Cohen here, will help insert it for you right now so that none of your guards will know you have it."

Myron instantly turned red, and he could barely hold back his tears. He turned his face toward the wall to hide his embarrassment, but then he allowed the man, who had put on rubber gloves, to insert the bateau.

After the two of them left the prison, Father Delvecchio told his accomplice, "I suspect he'll take the cyanide quite soon. And certainly before they send him back to the U.S." But although Myron kept the tablets, he never reached the point of swallowing them.

After two years of incarceration in Hamburg, and in spite of his considerable efforts to be allowed to remain in Germany, Myron was finally extradited to the United States. He faced twenty-one federal charges, including wire fraud, racketeering, and securities fraud. In a plea bargain with the prosecutors, Myron agreed to provide information that would help convict others who were involved in his illegal operations. He also agreed to cooperate in locating money that he had embezzled.

In all, eleven defendants in the case, most of them financial officers of Myron's insurance operations who had enriched themselves at the companies' expense, were eventually convicted of fraud. Monsignor Sangiovanni, his main Vatican collaborator, pleaded guilty of conspiracy to commit wire fraud and money laundering. The federal lawsuit also implicated the Vatican as a party to Myron's schemes, but their attorneys vigorously denied that the Holy See was in any way involved, and in the end no official charges were made.

Myron Geller was sentenced to sixteen years in a federal prison. He had cooperated with the prosecution, and moreover he had aided the authorities in locating some of the looted money. But, he had never made any mention to them about the ten million dollars that he still believed remained in his account in the Vatican Bank. Myron's Swiss banker, sworn to secrecy, also offered no information to federal investigators about the large cash withdrawal. There had been no apparent reason to interrogate Father Delvecchio about the case, and even if an attempt had been made to do so, the priest would not have been available for questioning. He had taken leave of the Vatican, for an indefinite period of spiritual renewal in a secluded monastery at an undisclosed location.

13

The following spring, during Shavuout, the Festival of Weeks, Jerusalem was filled with thousands of pilgrims who had come to present their first fruits of the year and to offer sacrifice in the Temple. As was his usual practice, the Roman procurator had dispatched a cohort of soldiers from Cæsarea to maintain order in the city during the festival. That day, a group of Romans were standing guard on the roof of the Temple portico from where they could observe the crowd below them.

As it happened, I was passing near the Temple Mount when the terrible commotion began. It all started when one of the soldiers on the roof, apparently bored by the tedium of his guard duties, turned and lifted his toga, exposing his naked backside to the Jews below him. Then, he stooped in indecent fashion and made a loud noise in keeping with his posture. Many of the Jews who saw this became outraged, and their response was to pelt the Roman soldier with stones. A riot ensued, and the Romans quickly dispatched additional soldiers to the scene. I left the area immediately, escaping along one of the city's narrow alleyways, and it was good that I did, because the uprising had terrible consequences. By the time it ended, hundreds of Jews had been killed.

In the aftermath of this tragedy, the streets and the marketplace remained nearly empty for a long time, because of fear of further reprisals by the Romans. It was then that I received a letter from my sister Sharon, who lived in the town of Magdala in Galilee. The news she sent was deplorable—her husband Benjamin had taken ill, and soon afterward, he had died. Sharon and her two children were left alone then, without means to support themselves.

I immediately wrote back to Sharon and sent her money. Then, especially in light of the unpleasant conditions that prevailed in Jerusalem, I resolved to take leave of the city for a while, to make a visit to my sister and her family. I had intended to depart without delay, but I soon learned that the trip to Galilee was hazardous then because of the large numbers of robbers and brigands along the way, particularly near the always-dangerous Samaritan town of Schechem. It was late summer by the time I was able to arrange to travel with a group of merchants, who had hired armed guards to accompany and protect them.

The benefit of this precaution became apparent the very first evening of our journey, a short distance after we had passed the town of Bethel. As the sky was beginning to darken with the approach of sunset, three men suddenly appeared from behind a clump of trees, quite close to the path we were following. Each man wore a scarf that covered his face, and at least one of them brandished a long dagger. But before they could assail us, our guards, who immediately made their presence known to the attackers, drew their swords. Seeing that, the three men ran back into the forest as quickly as they had come. For the remainder of our trip, I am happy to say, no one bothered us.

It had been eighteen years since I first arrived in Jerusalem with Johanan, and this was my first trip outside of the city during all that time. I had forgotten the beauty and peacefulness of our countryside in late summer. Our five-day journey brought us through its rolling green hills and along fields bursting with grain, trees heavily laden with olives and fruit, and vineyards with great masses of plump purple grapes nearing the time of harvest. The sight of young boys watching over herds of goats brought back memories of my childhood, from the time when I had lived with my father among the Essenes, where I had spent so many long days as a goatherd myself.

I had visited Magdala when I was a boy, but on returning there, it was not as I remembered it. Its crudely built stone houses; its dusty, unpaved streets; the three rather run-down wooden buildings that served as its synagogues; and its modest marketplace—all, of course, typical of any of Galilee's small villages—struck me then as being terribly rustic after my many years in Jerusalem.

My sister was thirty-two years old then, but from her already furrowed face and her graying hair, she appeared considerably older. I learned then that her husband Benjamin had been ill and unable to work for many months before he died. The hardship Sharon endured during that time left her nearly emaciated, with a pervasive sadness that showed on her face. But her children showed little indication of any deprivation. Her son Aaron, then in his fourteenth year, was already a strapping, vigorous young man, highly spirited and of a warm, friendly demeanor. And his sister Rebecca, ten years old then, was a girl of exceptional intelligence and sweet disposition.

Sharon and her children were without any other relatives in Magdala. Her husband's parents had both died, and his two sisters had moved away many years earlier. I had not had the enjoyment of family life since I was a child, and my stay with them gave me the greatest of pleasure. And there was much there to engage me. When we were children, our father taught Sharon and me to read and write, and she, in turn, taught her own children. But their lessons had been neglected for a long while, and I was happy to be able to guide the two of them in their studies. Other work had also been left undone: the roof of the house needed to be repaired, and the garden had become overgrown with weeds. But all of this was a pleasant diversion for me from the city life to which I had become so accustomed.

It had been my intention to return to Jerusalem after a visit of a few weeks, but the most unexpected of circumstances prolonged my stay there for a considerably longer time. It began when one of my sister's neighbors, who, having come to know that I had worked as a scribe, asked me if I would draw up a bill of sale for him, for a parcel of land he was selling. There had been two scribes in the village of Magdala, but as it happened, one of them had moved to another town and the other, a very old man, became ill and could no longer continue his work. So, I prepared the document he requested of me, and a while later I also wrote several letters for him.

"I am very pleased with all of the work you have done," the man said to me. And apparently his compliments were sincere, because only a short while later, many others in the village, and also people from other nearby towns, came to request that I prepare letters and other documents for them.

So I remained in Magdala, where my demand as a scribe soon increased to the point of filling nearly all my available time. Those months were among the happiest of my life, and I greatly enjoyed living with my sister and her family; moreover, the money I was able to earn lifted a considerable burden from Sharon's shoulders. So I stayed there, with no definite plans for my return to Jerusalem.

What caused me to leave Magdala began one day in the early spring I had occasion then to speak with a man from the village who had sought my services to prepare a will. I completed what he asked of me, and afterward he made mention of a great Pharisee sage who was coming to speak to the people of Magdala.

"He has been in our village twice before," he told me. "He is renowned in Galilee as a teacher, and there are many who regard him as a prophet. He will be here tomorrow, and you may be sure that everyone will come to hear what he has to say."

I was intrigued, and I asked the name of this great teacher.

"His name is Joel. No, that is wrong. Joseph? Not that either. I am not certain now. But I know he will be here tomorrow. I also am confident that you will be interested in what he has to say."

14

Amira Kahn telephoned Nathan from Cairo a few weeks later. "The dealer in Paris who sold my husband that old manuscript was out of the country when I first tried to contact him," Amira said. "Finally, I got a telephone call from him last week. He seemed surprised when I told him that the manuscript appeared to be a forgery. He called me again, a few days later, after he had contacted the collector in Istanbul who had sold him the document. The Turkish man evidently insisted that he too had understood the manuscript to be authentic. The dealer in Paris is investigating further. He promised he would send me a full report."

"Well," Nathan replied, "for now I suppose it would be reasonable to let him finish his investigation. If you'd like, once you get his report, you could forward me a copy. I'm sure that one of the manuscript experts here would be willing to review it."

"That would be helpful," Amira answered.

The following week, Nathan received a telephone call from the Oxford Radiocarbon Accelerator Unit.

"We've completed our analysis of the parchment fragments from the Song of Songs manuscript. We got excellent agreement from the three samples we ran. We can tell you now, with considerable confidence, that the document dates from between the late ninth and the mid tenth centuries," he said.

"That's really fabulous," Nathan replied. "By the way, do you have anything yet from the other set of samples I sent you, from the manuscript I labeled 'papyrus'?"

"That one," the technician told him, "needs additional work to be sure we get an accurate result. We'll probably need another two weeks."

In early February, Nathan received a copy of the letter that had been sent to Amira Kahn by the antiquarian dealer in Paris:

Dear Mme. Kahn:

This will summarize what I was able to learn concerning the papyrus document your late husband purchased from me.

As I related to you previously, the Turkish gentleman from whom I acquired the manuscript is a well-established dealer and collector. I can assure you he is a man of the highest integrity. When I enquired of him for more information about the document's provenance, he explained that he had purchased the work some years earlier from a well known, though, he confessed, not highly reputable dealer from Israel. He indicated that he was not successful in his recent attempts to contact the Israeli dealer, but he was able to speak with one of his business associates.

The man spoke with him at length about a large papyrus sheaf, similar to the one I had sold to your husband, which first had come to light in Alexandria sometime in the 1850s. What was most remarkable was that its pages were entirely blank; no trace of writing could be seen on any of them. He indicated that much later, during the 1960s, the document was examined more fully, including an analysis by infrared photography, which also failed to show any evidence of latent text.

This man claimed no further knowledge about the papyrus pages, but he offered the suggestion that a forger might have transcribed biblical text onto it so as to command a higher price in the manuscript market.

That is as much as I was able to discover. I want to deal with this matter honorably, and I will await your further instructions as to how we should proceed.

Dear Madame, please accept my most gracious sentiments,

Jacques Delacroix

Nathan reread the letter, perplexed by its strange story. Zippora also found it puzzling. When Nathan brought the letter to Dr. Elstein's office, the director was meeting with Thomas Gans.

"I think you can go in," Ms. Beckman told him. "The business part of their meeting ended some while ago. They're having tea now."

The director looked up and motioned to Nathan to come in. Thomas Gans removed a stack of books from the one unoccupied chair. Then Nathan read the letter to the two of them.

"That last part is certainly believable," Gans commented.

"Yes," Elstein added, "such mischief is well known in the antiquarian business."

"But what about the blank pages of papyrus?" Nathan asked. "Could this have been a palimpsest?"

"No," Elstein answered, "not when you're dealing with papyrus. Writing can be scraped away from animal skins, but not from paper. Soot-based inks have proven to be remarkably durable, but when inks were formulated from vegetable pigments, they often decomposed over time. That could provide a very plausible explanation for what this man describes in the letter. Infrared photography can sometimes reveal the latent images, but not always."

For the next two days, Nathan reflected at length on the perplexing swirl of ideas the letter had raised. Then, at Zippora's suggestion, he pursued the one loose end that remained. He telephoned the Oxford Radiocarbon Accelerator Unit. When he identified himself to the technician who answered the call, she asked him to wait. A few moments later, the director of the Unit came on the line.

"We were planning to contact you later this week," he said, "but there's really no reason to delay discussing this with you. When we got the first set of data from our analyses of the papyrus fragments, we felt obliged to reexamine our calculations. But the data all show consistent values, with remarkably good precision. This papyrus dates from the middle to the end of the first century, AD. We'll be sending you a full written report."

"Would you...did you really say *first* century?" Nathan asked him.

"That's right!" the director answered. "We were also very surprised to see that."

After hanging up the telephone, Nathan bounded down the stairs to the second floor to share the news with Zippora in the reference library. Then he ran back up the stairs, two at a time, to Chaim Elstein's office.

"He's on the phone," Ms. Beckman informed him.

"I'll wait," he said.

"He's talking with our biggest donor, and it may take quite a while."

"I'll wait as long as it takes." Thirty minutes later, Nathan was finally able to meet with Dr. Elstein.

"That really is astounding," the director said after hearing the news. "Why don't we meet over lunch to discuss this?"

"Okay, but, oh, I promised Zippora I'd have lunch with her today."

"We can all get together if the two of you don't mind, and let's see if Tom Gans would like to join us."

"I would start by doing carbon dating of other samples from the manuscript," Gans suggested, as they waited for their lunch to be served.

"Quite right," Elstein agreed. "Some infrared photographs would also be in order."

"But according to the letter from the dealer in Paris, that was already done," Nathan said.

"That's according to the dealer in Israel," Thomas Gans pointed out. "There's no way to know what they actually did. Or about the quality of their work."

"Do you think the woman in Egypt would be willing to send the manuscript here for the additional studies?" Zippora asked.

"That would require a great deal of paperwork and probably a long time," Elstein replied. "And the Egyptian government might raise objections about valuable antiquities leaving the country. Then there's the issue of insurance. That could be an enormous problem. I suspect that the most efficient approach would be for us to go there, if Ms. Kahn would have no objection."

That afternoon, Nathan telephoned Amira Kahn and explained the exciting new information he had received. When he inquired if he and Professor Elstein could visit her to study the manuscript, she was not only agreeable, but very enthusiastic.

"I have lots of room in my house," she said, "and I would be happy to have both of you as my guests here."

The next day, Dr. Elstein informed Nathan that Ms. Beckman was making travel arrangements for them for early the following week.

"How will we be able to do the infrared photography?" Nathan asked him.

"Well, we do have the equipment here, but I suspect that someone named Chaim showing up in Cairo with a big camera might be assumed to be a spy. I think it would be a good idea to make other arrangements. So, I spoke with Professor Sajid in the Faculty of Oriental Studies. He referred me to a photographic laboratory in Cairo that does high quality work. We're trying to contact them today."

"We'll be leaving Monday afternoon," Nathan told Zippora.

"I wish I could go with you," she said. "It'll be very lonely here without you."

"I'll miss you, too," he said, "but the whole trip will be only four days."

Nathan managed to maintain an appearance of optimism about their upcoming visit to Cairo, but beneath it all, he was unremittingly anxious about the prospects for its success.

15

My work as a scribe kept me engaged most of the next afternoon with one of my regular clients in Magdala, a man who had summoned me to write several letters for him. Afterward, as I was making my way back to my sister's house through the narrow, winding streets of the town, I was taken by surprise by a considerable crowd of people in the town's small marketplace. It appeared to me that everyone from Magdala was there, and many from other towns as well. I asked an old man to explain what was happening.

"Don't you know?" he asked me in return, "it's the Pharisee from Jerusalem. Whenever he's here, there's always a big crowd."

Although I had encountered most of these people before, seeing them together impressed me in a different way than before. They virtually all wore the simple homespun of working people everywhere. Their calloused hands, their deeply lined faces—even among the younger men—and their slow, deliberate movements, all bespoke lives of unremitting labor and longstanding fatigue. With few exceptions, these people were painfully poor. But in spite of their deprivation and the backbreaking work that dominated their lives, the mood in the crowd that afternoon was one of joy, indeed of elation.

Whole families were there, including many children, and a feeling of eager anticipation was apparent from their excited chatter.

Only moments after I arrived, the crowd turned silent. Everyone's attention became fixed on the far side of the marketplace, toward the elevated stone bimah alongside the synagogue.

Standing there was a tall man, very thin, whose skin was deeply bronzed and coarsened from having long been bared to the elements. His matted hair and beard, which clearly had not been cut or combed for a long time, were so thick and tousled as to form a mask that obscured much of his face. But his eyes, reddened from exposure to the sunlight, shown like a blazing fire. His simple cloak of goat's hair was thin and worn. Three young men, who, I later learned, were disciples of the Pharisee, sat along the edge of the bimah. When I saw all of this, my thoughts immediately turned to Simeon, the itinerant preacher whom I had known so many years earlier.

As the speaker paced back and forth on the platform, gesturing with his hands, I could see that as he spoke, he gazed directly into the faces of those within his range of vision, conveying that his words were meant for each one of them.

Once I was near enough to hear the speaker's voice, I immediately recognized, to my astonishment, that this Pharisee teacher was none other than my dear friend and mentor, Johanan. But the words he spoke that day showed little of Johanan's prodigious understanding of the Holy Scriptures, nor of his finely honed knowledge of the Law. Rather, his message was a plea to his listeners, and indeed it was a most alarming one.

"The signs and the portents are now unmistakable," I heard him say, in a soft voice, quivering with emotion. Then, speaking slowly and pausing between each of his words, and raising his voice so that he was nearly shouting at his audience, he delivered his main point: "The end of days is now rapidly approaching." And then he ceased, for a long while, so that everyone could reflect on what he had said.

"The whole world will be engulfed in flames—it will be the time of God's wrath. A grievous tempest of fire will be felt everywhere, and it will spread rapidly throughout the earth. And in its aftermath, all that is evil will be destroyed. And know this also—every one of you will witness these terrible events, for they will happen very soon." Again he paused before continuing, "But also hear this good news: all who have followed the path of righteousness, who have obeyed God's laws, will be saved. And afterward, in Jerusalem, God's Kingdom will be established, and all of the world will then live in peace and in harmony.

"Now, listen to me. This is what God requires of you," he pleaded. "Turn away from your evil inclinations, make amends for your sins, repent. Then you will be saved. But only little time remains." And again, he followed these words with a long period of silence.

But then, a man near to where Johanan was standing spoke out in alarm; driven to tears, the man could barely make himself understood: "What you ask of us is a hopeless task, one that can only torment us. There are hundreds of laws and commandments in the Torah. To obey all of them faithfully we would need to spend all of our time worrying about them. How can we do this? It is impossible."

"In truth," Johanan replied, "God's commandments in the Torah do number in the hundreds. But before I answer your question, let me relate an old Pharisee saying: 'The 613 laws God gave to Israel were reduced by King David to eleven, as it is told in the Fifteenth Psalm; the prophet Isaiah further diminished them to six; and then Micah reduced the number to three, which are: 'Do justly, love goodness, and walk humbly with your God.' We were given the commandments not to afflict us, but so that we can follow God's path of righteousness," Johanan continued. "Perhaps only the holiest of men can fulfill all of the laws. But you need not live in fear of this, because for offences against God, He will always grant forgiveness to you when you make atonement and offer sacrifice in the Temple.

"But you must know this also—for offences against your fellow man, God will grant you His forgiveness only after you have first made amends with those you have offended. Remember that among the most important commandments in the Torah is this: 'Love your neighbor as yourself.' And how can you do that? First, if you possess two cloaks, give one of them to someone who has none, and then do the same with your food." Then

Johanan ended his speech with a plea. "Do what God requires of you and turn away from your evil ways. Atone. Make amends. And when you have done that, come with me to the Jordan River, to confess your sins, to pray for forgiveness, and to immerse yourself so that you will be pure before God when the end of days is finally upon us."

A few who were there in the crowd cheered when Johanan stepped down from the bimah, but most stood in silence, in awe and in dread of the terrifying news he had given them.

I made my way quickly through the crowd to greet Johanan, whom I had not seen for several years, and to embrace him. He was surprised to see me in Magdala, and I explained to him the circumstances that had brought me there. Then, Johanan and his three disciples accompanied me to the house of my sister, where Sharon offered them food and drink, as well as a place to stay for the night. I saw that neither Johanan nor any of the young men who were with him partook of the wine or the grapes, and they accepted only little of the bread, olives, and dates she set before them.

That night, after all of the others had gone to sleep, Johanan and I walked together through the deserted streets of Magdala. We talked at length, about all that had transpired since we had last seen one another. I told Johanan I could see how greatly he had changed since the time he left Jerusalem.

"I have taken the vows of a nazir," he told me. "I avoid all vanity, and I don't drink wine or eat grapes. Otherwise, I subsist only on what God provides for me. That has brought me much closer to Him."

That night the face of my beloved friend and mentor showed unmistakable signs of longstanding fatigue.

"There is so much that I need to accomplish that I have little time for sleep," he explained, when I spoke of my concern about him. "But this I will tell you," he said, "nothing has ever brought me so much joy as seeing the great numbers of people who have made atonement and repentance and have turned to God. But there still are so many I need to reach before it is too late. The end of days is surely close at hand, yet there are a great number of people in Galilee who are unprepared for the fury of God's judgment."

Johanan was certain that the end of the world was imminent. But how he had come to know that, he never explained, either to me or to any of his disciples. But quite some while later, he did tell me what may well have been the answer to my question: "God has never failed our people," Johanan said, "and now the Jews of Israel are suffering mightily under the yoke of the Romans. God surely will bring a speedy end to the agony of the Jews and to the desecration of His holy city."

Then, as the first light of dawn appeared in the sky, Johanan made an impassioned plea. "Come with me and my disciples," he said to me. "I implore you, help us spread the word to our people so that they may be saved."

And I did. The following morning, I bade farewell to my sister and her children, and I departed from Magdala with Johanan and his disciples for the Jordan River.

"We first will stop at a place near K'far Hananya," Johanan said to us. "A relative of mine, a cousin of my mother, a woman whom I have not seen in many years, will be coming there so that we can meet. Afterward, we will go on to the river."

It was a warm spring day, and the verdant hills and valleys of northern Galilee were ablaze with red anemones; the almond trees were covered with masses of white blossoms.

As the five of us traveled together, I had my first opportunity to come to know Johanan's disciples. The eldest of them, Isaac, a tall, strapping young man of eighteen years, was utterly devoted to his master, staying always at his side and assisting him in any way he could. Isaac was a man of few words, and unless Johanan, or others of us addressed him directly, he preferred to remain silent. The other two disciples, Netzer and Nakkai, were brothers, indeed they were twins, scarcely past the age of fifteen. But whereas twins often bear a close resemblance one to the other, that was not so for them. Netzer was of a stocky build with a fair complexion and light brown hair; his brother, by contrast, was remarkably thin, with darker skin; the hair on his head was black. Those two always had much to say, and at times Johanan needed to chide them about their endless chatter.

When we reached a partly wooded plain to the west of K'far Hananya, we stopped to await the arrival of Johanan's cousin, and also to fill our water jugs from a nearby spring. A short while later, Netzer sighted a group of people coming in our direction. Soon we could see that there were three of them, one of whom was a woman covered all in black, obviously a widow. With her were two men. Johanan arose from where he was sitting, and when he recognized that the woman was his cousin, he rushed forward and embraced her warmly.

"Miriam," he said to her, "I am so thankful that you made the long trip to come here. I received word that your husband had died, and I hope you have been all right."

"It has been nearly two years that Yosef has been gone," she said. "Life has been difficult for me without him, but my family have been a great comfort. And especially my wonderful grandson. Little Naphtali is such a beautiful boy, like a little angel. And he is so intelligent! He is not yet four years old, and already he can read Hebrew like a grown man! He is truly the joy of my life. Now, if only my son-in-law would work a little harder to support his family, everything would be wonderful, but it is their little boy who brings me more happiness than I can begin to tell you."

Miriam was a small woman, but she was vigorous in her stride and of sturdy constitution. Her deep-set brown eyes, her aquiline nose, and her ever-present smile were her most striking features. Her face also reflected a lifetime of untiring devotion to the needs of her husband and her children.

Miriam stood back and looked carefully at her cousin. "Johanan," she said, "you're so thin. You must not be eating enough. Here, see what we brought. We have olives and dates, also fresh bread, and pomegranates, honey, dried fish, and some beautiful grapes. Please eat. Come, all of you," she said, motioning to the rest of us. "Johanan, do have some of these grapes."

"Thank you," Johanan replied, taking a date from the basket Miriam had opened.

Finally, she introduced the two men who had come with her.

"These are my sons," she said, holding her arms around the two of them who stood on either side of her. Yehoshua, the older of them was, I later learned, exactly the same age as I. He was of stocky build and only slightly taller than his mother. His eyes and his nose were also unmistakably his mother's. His thin beard barely obscured his dimpled chin, and his hands were thickened and weathered from his years of work as a stonemason. His cloak, and indeed all of his clothing, was fringed at its corners, in the manner of the most pious Jews. That day Yehoshua spoke very little, and from the distant look in his eyes, it seemed that his thoughts

were being directed to some far-off place. His brother Jacob, who then was a lively young man of fourteen, was at all times solicitous of his mother, attending to her every need.

We all enjoyed the ample supply of food that Miriam had brought, although Johanan, as was his usual habit, ate only very little. Afterward, he and Miriam conversed together for a long while. The others of us spent that evening with Yehoshua and Jacob, with the greatest part of our discussion devoted to Johanan's mission to bring redemption to the Jews of Galilee. From that, Yehoshua became much more engaged in conversation with us, and he asked us many questions about Johanan and about our travels in Galilee.

At dawn the following day, Miriam and her sons prepared for their return home. It was then that Johanan drew Yehoshua aside to speak with him:

"Come join us," Johanan said to him. "There is much we have to do, and I fear that there is only little time left to complete our mission. You can be a great help to our cause." To Johanan's considerable happiness, and mine as well, Yehoshua immediately agreed to go along with us. But when Yehoshua told his mother of his decision, Miriam tried to persuade him to reconsider.

"Please return home with your brother and me," she pleaded. But then, she seemed to sense that it was time for Yehoshua to find his own way in the world, and she recanted. She embraced Yehoshua tenderly, and then she gave him her blessing.

"Please take this warm wool blanket with you," she finally said to him, "and do make certain you get enough to eat." Then she and Jacob set out to return to their home in Nazareth, and the six of us proceeded on toward the Jordan River.

After we had traveled for some while, we stopped to collect grasshoppers and to gather chestnuts and wild olives for our midday meal. But before we recited the prayers and ate our food, Johanan, as was his usual practice, spoke to us from the holy writings.

"The Torah," he said, "tells us that those who lead lives of sinfulness will surely incur God's wrath, and it reminds us as well that God finds great favor with the righteous. Yet, so often we encounter evildoers who have gained great prosperity and who appear to have received all of God's blessings. And alas, we also see so many of the innocent whose days are filled with deprivation and suffering. Job was one such man.

"However, Job protested most vehemently that he was not deserving of God's punishment, and he complained bitterly that the terrible misfortune that had befallen him was entirely undeserved. I would have to say," Johanan continued, "that such words of irreverence and ingratitude, after all that God had given him, surely bespeak that Job was in fact not without sin."

"Did Job's unending reverence arise out of his love for God, or rather was it from fear?" the disciple Isaac asked Johanan.

"The answer to your question is difficult to discern," Johanan replied, "but I believe that Job was driven mainly by fear of God's wrath."

Then, most unexpectedly, Yehoshua rose from the place where he had been sitting.

"Master," he said, "I humbly beg to voice my disagreement with you regarding two of the things you have said."

We all were astonished to hear this newest member of our group take issue on matters of Scripture with our esteemed leader and teacher, but Johanan allowed him to continue.

"As concerns the question of whether Job's words could have bespoken irreverence and ingratitude toward the Almighty, the holy writings tell us, 'Job said nothing sinful.' From that, we must accept that Job was truly a righteous man in the eyes of the Lord. And was Job's reverence for God indeed driven by fear? We have his words from the Book of Job: 'Though He slay me, yet will I trust in Him.' Does that not surely demonstrate Job's unbounded love of God?

"I also want to ask," Yehoshua said, "that I be allowed to relate a parable that I learned from my father, Yosef ben Yakov. It was said that after causing Job to lose everything he possessed, his houses, his livestock, all of his wealth, and even his children, and moreover afflicting Job with horrible boils that covered his body, ha-satan also put Job's wife to the test. She had been obliged to work as a water-carrier, and when her master came to know that she did this work to keep her husband from starvation, he dismissed her. And so, lacking anything else, she cut off her hair to buy bread. Then ha-satan, disguised as the bread seller, said to her, 'All of this misery would not have befallen you had you not yourself been deserving *of it.' It was only then, in her great anguish, that Job's wife bade her husband to renounce God and die. But Job knew at once that ha-satan was the cause of his wife's suffering. Job then confronted ha-satan, telling him, "Away with your treachery; I will not be moved by the likes of you.' Ha-satan, defeated, withdrew, and Job remained forever devoted and faithful to God."*

From that, we first came to know of Yehoshua's amazing knowledge of the holy writings.

16

We arrived at the Jordan River later that day, at a place near the small town of Bet Evra. Johanan led us to a narrow stairway that had been cut into the high embankment of the river, and we descended onto a broad, sandy beach that ran along the water's edge. The late winter rains that year had been frequent and heavy, and the muddy waters of the Jordan streamed by us as a moiling torrent that splashed onto the shore.

A multitude of people, surely more than two hundred, had assembled along the riverbank to await Johanan's arrival. These were humble village folk of Galilee. But in one respect, they appeared to be different from the crowds of people I had previously seen who had come to hear Johanan speak. Most of them were waiting in silence, and from the somber expressions on their faces, it was clear that this was a momentous and solemn event for all of them.

When Johanan appeared, many rose to their feet out of reverence and respect for him. We five disciples remained behind, near the high embankment, as Johanan climbed onto a rocky mound near the river's edge. He raised his hands to speak, and with that, a hush fell over the crowd. All that could be heard were the churning and swirling of the river and the splash of a cormorant as it dove into the water in search of fish.

"Jews of Galilee," Johanan began, with deep passion showing in his voice and his gaze fixed on his listeners, "God's day of judgment will soon be upon us, and only little time remains." Then he spoke words of the prophet Malachi:

"'You shall come to see the difference between the righteous and the wicked, between those who have served God and those who have not served Him. For lo! That day is at hand, burning like an oven. All the arrogant and all the doers of evil shall be straw, and the day that is coming shall burn them to ashes and leave of them neither stock nor boughs.'

"Know this," he continued. "To enter God's kingdom you will have to be like a tree that bears good fruit. Even now, the ax is at the root, and every tree that does not bear good fruit will be cut down and destroyed. So, who will be worthy to enter God's kingdom?" he asked them. "It will be those with clean hands and pure hearts, who are faithful to God's law. And each one of you here today will surely be able to enter God's kingdom. But you must turn away from wickedness, follow God's path of righteousness, confess your sins, and vow they shall be no more. When you have done those things, come down to the river to be immersed, and then you will truly be pure before God and worthy to enter His kingdom."

Then, one of the men asked Johanan, "Is it so, as many are saying, that you are Elijah the prophet?"

Johanan answered him with other words of Malachi, saying, "'Lo, I will send the prophet Elijah to you before the coming of the awesome, fearful day of the Lord.'" Then Johanan added, "But I am not Elijah. I am merely a messenger." However, it was apparent to us that many of the people there believed the man they saw before them to be Elijah, who had returned to prepare the way for the great things that were about to happen.

Then, a farmer asked Johanan, "Are you the Messiah, who will drive the Roman idolaters out of our land, and who will bring peace to all of the world?"

To him, Johanan replied, "I am not the Messiah, but he surely will come before God's kingdom is established on earth, and you will see him. And indeed his first action will be just as you say. He will free our country and our holy city of Jerusalem from the tyranny of the Romans."

As Johanan spoke these last words, two men in the crowd took particular notice. We learned that the two of them were spies, sent by the Tetrarch Herod Antipas, who had been appointed by the Romans to rule Galilee. Herod, many were saying, was concerned about any who might incite rebellion against his regime, and he was suspicious that Johanan had been fomenting insurrection among the people.

After Johanan answered the questions asked of him, many came forward to immerse themselves in the river. A young man named Mattai, who had formerly been a tax collector, was the first of them. Johanan said to him, "Confess your sins so that you may repent of them."

And Mattai responded, "I acted dishonestly, and I took more in tax than was proper."

"And how did you make amends for these sins?" Johanan asked of him.

"I endeavored to find all of those whom I had wronged. I returned the money I took from them, and a fifth more besides."

"And did you also offer a sacrifice of atonement in the Temple, as the law requires?" Johanan asked. When Mattai affirmed he had made the sacrifice of a ram, Johanan held him by the hand as he immersed himself in the rapidly flowing river.

"Now you are truly pure before God, and worthy to enter His kingdom," Johanan said, speaking to him in a loud, clear voice so that everyone there could hear him.

Many others came forward in like fashion, and each of them confessed his sins and then immersed himself in the river, with Johanan holding him firmly by the hand against the perils of the turbulent water.

As all of this was happening, Yehoshua left the place where we disciples were waiting, and he too came to the river's edge.

"Are you prepared to confess your sins that you may repent of them?" Johanan asked him.

"I am," he said. "I raised my voice and I spoke angry words to my mother, distressing her and causing her to cry," he answered. "And from

*that, I surely failed to honor my mother in accordance with God's com-
mandments. Later, I made apology to her, and she forgave me. And on
the festival of Shavuot, I offered a sacrifice in the Temple to atone for my
transgression."*

Then, Johanan held Yehoshua's hand as he immersed himself in the
river.

When the sun finally fell low on the horizon, and the people there
began leaving to return to their homes, a man from Bet Evra invited all
of us to share a modest meal of lentils and bread with him and his family,
and he provided us shelter for the night.

Our host, a poor man, a cobbler, had little room in his tiny stone
abode, and when it was time for us to sleep, two of us, Yehoshua and I,
climbed up a narrow wooden ladder to bring our sleeping mats onto the
roof of the house. The weather was warm and clear, and we spent that
night under the bright stars that filled the sky. Yehoshua slept hardly at all,
and because there was so much he wanted to talk about, I too was obliged
to remain awake. What Yehoshua most wished to discuss was his immersion that day in the Jordan River.

"As I came out of the water," he said, "I felt myself filled with the spirit
of God. And since then, I have experienced a closeness to God far greater
than any I have ever felt before. I know now that the Lord will guide me
and protect me in everything that I do—that God is with me and that
His spirit is in me."

It was only much later that I came to understand the full import of
Yehoshua's words to me on the rooftop that night.

From Bet Evra, we continued on to other towns and villages in Galilee,
and wherever we went, Johanan delivered his message of atonement and
repentance and of the coming of the end of days. As we traveled together
from place to place, Yehoshua and I often spoke together, and the two of us
developed a close bond of friendship.

I related to Yehoshua how, as a young boy, I had first come to know
Johanan, and about the years he and I had spent together in Jerusalem.
Yehoshua, in turn, told me about his life and his family. But most of all,

he seemed anxious to speak about the time when he had distressed his mother and caused her to cry, as he had confessed before immersing himself in the Jordan River. It was very apparent to me that his memories of this event were continuing to cause him anguish and heartache:

"I must first tell you," he said, "that from time to time I find myself overcome by the most profound melancholy, and it often remains with me for a very long while. This happened to me most severely two years ago.

"My beloved father, who was a builder with stone, as he was working atop a wall, fell to the ground, striking his head. He never awoke from his coma, and by the next morning, he was dead. My brothers and my uncle buried my father before sunset that day, but I was so horrified by what had happened, I was unable to assist them with that obligation.

"When the period of mourning was over, I returned to my work, but I continued to be consumed by grief and melancholy. I eventually became thin and wasted for lack of eating. No one was able to console me. And then was when it happened. One day, when I was sitting alone, overcome by the worst of my anguish, my mother brought food to me, and she pleaded with me to eat. I sent her away, but she persisted, relentlessly, bringing me one thing after another in spite of my refusal of everything she had set before me. I finally became enraged with her endless entreaties. I admonished my dear mother, and in anger, I struck my fist against the table where I was sitting. My mother cried for a long time, in spite of my many apologies to her. I continue to hold myself blameworthy for the heartache and humiliation I caused her." I could see that he had tears in his eyes as he related the story to me.

One day a while later, as we were in the wilderness eating our evening meal, Nakkai, as was his usual habit, was speaking excitedly about one thing after another as he was swallowing mouthfuls of food. After he had stuffed several figs into his mouth, the food seemed to become lodged in his throat, and he was unable to breathe. He fell to the ground, and his face turned blue. He did not move, and it appeared that he was dead. Netzer, Nakkai's twin brother, frantically slapped at Nakkai's face, then he grasped him by the shoulders and shook him, but those attempts had no good effect.

Yehoshua pulled Netzer away from his brother. Then he raised Nakkai to a sitting position, brought his arms around Nakkai's back, and pressed *repeatedly below Nakkai's ribs. Nakkai coughed and expelled the figs. The blue color immediately vanished from his face, and he soon recovered and rose to his feet. We all were amazed at this miraculous cure.*

Johanan then said to Yehoshua, "You have a great gift of healing—you indeed are greatly blessed."

I asked Yehoshua how he had come to have such skill.

"I learned much," he said, "from the midwife and healer of our village, Hannah, the wife of Shlomo. I will always remember, when I was five years old, when she came to attend to my mother at the birth of my sister.

"The infant was strong and vigorous. But when Hannah returned on the third day, she found that blood was coming from the baby's navel. And later, she began bleeding from her nose and from her mouth. By the following morning, she had become pale and weakened. Hannah appeared very sad then. I heard her speak to my father, from a place where my mother could not hear her.

"'It is the bleeding affliction of babies,' she said, 'and she may die.'

"Then Hannah brought goat liver, which she prepared with oil to make a thin broth, and she fed small portions of it to my tiny sister, all that day and night. In the morning, the baby was no longer bleeding, but she appeared very weak, hardly moving her arms or legs. She was more pale than before, and Hannah told us that the infant's pulse was fast. Hannah fed her more of the broth, and my mother kept the baby at her breast. The next day, she had ceased to move at all, and her breathing had become rapid. My mother never stopped crying.

"But death did not come to my sister, and, after many days, she gradually regained her strength. It was then my father gave her the name Netanela, meaning a gift from God. Even as a young child, I was amazed at Hannah's wondrous healing, and I asked her many questions about it.

"Later, when I was in my ninth year, I observed another of Hannah's healings. It began as my father and I were making pilgrimage to Jerusalem for the Passover festival. Four families from Nazareth accompanied us on our trip, including Hannah and her husband. On the second day of our journey, we stopped near the town of Shunem, where the men raised our tents to stay for the night. The women had begun preparation for our evening meal when suddenly, Benjamin, the son of Lamech from our village,

appeared there. He had come to tell my father that Jacob, my younger brother, was gravely ill. So we returned with Hannah as quickly as we could to Nazareth.

"Hannah went immediately to see my baby brother, who then was but four months old. My mother had been frantic in her efforts to cool Jacob's fever, but she had been having little success. I could see that Jacob was restless, and his lips were parched and cracked. Hannah felt the soft part on the crown of Jacob's head, and she showed us that it was flat and also that his neck moved easily. But soon my little brother's arms and legs began to shake in violent fashion, and the gaze of his eyes turned upward. My mother became greatly distressed at this, and my father asked Hannah what was happening to Jacob.

"'It is what the Greeks call the sacred disease,' she said, 'but I have seen that when this happens to children with fever, it seldom causes them harm.' Hannah prepared water with honey and a small measure of salt, and she fed this to Jacob. Then, she showed my mother how to use cool, wet cloths and to swab him to slake his fever. Each day Hannah came to see Jacob, and he remained ill and distressed with fever. On the fourth day, Hannah told my parents, 'Soon his skin will turn red with rash, and his fever will be gone.' And indeed it happened just as she had said. Jacob's fever disappeared and he soon returned to good health. My parents rejoiced at his recovery. I was greatly fascinated by all that I had seen."

"As I became older," he said, "I sometimes accompanied Hannah when she visited the sick. We often talked together, and she taught me much about the art of healing."

We continued for nearly a year in our travels with Johanan, visiting the towns and villages of Galilee, and then making our return to the Jordan River. In the course of these journeys, several additional disciples joined us, so that in time our number increased to fourteen. One of the first of them was Mattai, the former tax collector, who earlier had come to the Jordan to confess his sins and to immerse himself in the river. Others of Johanan's new disciples included Boneh, a stonecutter from the village of Hammat, and Avraham ben Jonah, a fisherman from K'far Nahum,

who plied his trade in Lake Kinneret. Also among them were two brothers, Jacob and Jonathan, the sons of another fisherman named Zibhidi.

With the growing numbers of disciples, Johanan began to teach some of us to deliver his message about the coming of the end of days, and of the urgent need for atonement and repentance. By that means, it would be possible for us to carry the word to larger numbers of people. As I was the disciple he had known far longer than any of the others, I was the first of our group whom he selected. He explained to me for a long while how best to present his message.

When we arrived in the town of K'far Hahoresh, a large and enthusiastic crowd had assembled, as always happened when Johanan came to a town or village. But that time, it was I who rose to address the people. By then, I had heard Johanan's message on numerous occasions, and I was certain that I knew precisely what I needed to say. When it was time to begin, I mounted a high platform from which everyone could see me, and I raised my hands over my head. As I had expected, the crowd immediately fell silent.

"Listen carefully to what I have to say," I began. "Very soon, a horrible storm of fire will envelop the entire world. That will be the frightful beginning of the Day of the Lord, and the end of days will then ensue."

But the crowd did not respond as they did when Johanan had spoken to them. First, one man began to laugh, and then he started to talk loudly to another man who was standing next to him. Almost immediately, other people began conversing among themselves, not paying attention to me or to what I was saying. Finally, a tall man with a long white beard rose, shrugged his shoulders, extended his arms with the palms of his hands turned upward, and finally turned as if to leave.

Johanan, seeing all of this, stood up in my place on the platform. Once he began to speak, the crowd responded to him as they always had done, and having gotten their attention, he finished his speech in his usual fashion. Johanan never again asked me to speak, and of that I had no regret.

But over time, two members of our group proved to possess considerable skill in delivering Johanan's message. One of them was Mattai. The other, who had amazing abilities as a speaker, was Yehoshua. Whenever he addressed a crowd of people, everyone seemed enraptured by his every word. Yehoshua also spoke in parables on some occasions, telling stories that attracted the interest of his listeners. I will say more about that later.

In order to assure that his message reached as many of the Jews of Galilee as possible, Johanan directed small groups of us to go to different towns and villages. Each week, after the Sabbath had ended, he sent us off. Mattai was responsible for one group, Yehoshua another, and the third one he continued to lead himself. Then, before the start of the next Sabbath, we all assembled in the wilderness, at a place that Johanan had selected for us. And we continued in that fashion for many months.

On one of these trips, I accompanied Yehoshua to the town of Beit She'arim. When we first arrived, a man there made a most tearful entreaty to Yehoshua to come and see his small son, Menachem, who was gravely ill, indeed near death. The father explained that the boy's sister had been sick before him. The girl had burned with fever, and she often coughed; soon afterward, her eyes became reddened and also her skin. Then, after a few days, she was well again, but, after another week, Menachem became ill in similar fashion. In time, his fever and the redness of his eyes and his skin were gone, but he did not leave his bed. He made no movement at all, and he gave no answer when anyone spoke to him. The man thought his son to be dead. But Yehoshua showed me that the child's skin was warm and that he still breathed. Yehoshua took me aside.

"This boy is gravely ill," he said. "It is likely he will die, but it may be possible for him to recover."

Yehoshua showed the boy's mother all the things she needed to do to care for the child, and how to feed him small amounts of water and broth, both in the daytime and at night.

When we returned to Beit She'arim many weeks later, we learned that the boy soon afterward had begun to awaken, and that gradually his health returned. We all rejoiced with his family at Menachem's miraculous recovery.

On one Sabbath day when we were all together, the disciple Boneh asked Johanan, "Which is the greatest of the commandments in God's law?"

Johanan answered, "The most important of them is surely the Shema, the words of Moses from the Torah. It is this commandment that Hillel, the greatest of the Pharisees, always held most dear.

"'Hear, O Israel! The Lord is our God, the Lord alone. You shall love the Lord your God with all your heart and with all your soul and with

all your might. Take to heart these instructions with which I charge you this day. Impress them upon your children. Recite them when you stay at home and when you are away, when you lie down and when you rise up. Bind them as a sign on your hand and let them serve as a symbol on your forehead. Inscribe them on the doorposts of your house and on your gates.

"The other principle that Hillel and the others of the Pharisee sages most often quoted," Johanan said, "was this: 'Love your neighbor as yourself.'"

Johanan also taught us a prayer that we said together each day after we recited the Shema:

Blessed are you, Lord our God, King over all; May your name forever be holy, and your kingdom on earth come soon. Give to us each day the food we need. Remit us our debts, for we also forgive all who are indebted to us. And lead us not into a trial.

One day, we received terrible news. The messenger, Jacob, Yehoshua's brother, arrived at our campsite shortly before the start of the Sabbath. He told Yehoshua that their mother Miriam had taken ill, and that soon afterward she had died. Jacob and his younger brother Judah had buried her in Nazareth.

Yehoshua became overcome with remorse; he sat alone, with his head buried in his hands, unwilling to eat anything or to acknowledge our presence. Even after many days, Yehoshua showed no interest in the words of Johanan or any of the disciples. Finally, after a week had past, Johanan spoke to him.

"We all grieve with you in your time of sadness. Your mother was very dear to me as well. But now it is time to let the dead console the dead, and to continue with our work."

After that, Yehoshua soon overcame his melancholy.

17

One day, Johanan informed us that his teacher, Hillel the Babylonian, would soon reach the age of ninety years.

"I plan to go to Jerusalem for a short visit, to extend my good wishes to him," Johanan said. "Any of you who wish can make the trip with me."

Mattai, Avraham, and the two sons of Zibhidi preferred to remain there, to continue carrying Johanan's message of repentance and salvation to the people of Galilee. The others of us made the journey to Jerusalem. It had been more than three years since I had been in Jerusalem, and I was happy to return to the great city that had been my home for so long.

On our journey, Johanan spoke often about Hillel, and about the unbounded admiration and respect he held for the great Pharisee sage.

"Once at the end of a long day with our master," Johanan related to us, "Hillel told us he was going to perform a pious duty. One of his *disciples asked him what that duty would be. 'I'm going to take a bath,' our revered teacher answered.*

"'A bath?' the disciple asked him. 'Is that a pious duty?'

"'Have you not seen the man who is appointed to maintain the statues that the king has installed throughout the city?' Hillel asked, 'and the considerable care with which he cleans them? How much more then do I, created in God's image, have a duty to care for my own body?'"

"But why would Hillel need to take a bath?" Boneh asked Johanan. "Did you not tell us that your teacher immersed himself each day in rainwater in the mikva before he entered the precincts of the Temple?"

"Indeed he did immerse himself every day," Johanan said, "but these two are not the same, even though they might appear to be so. A bath is intended to cleanse the body, but immersion in rainwater, or in the moving water of a river, is done to purify the soul, for a holy purpose."

Johanan also informed us that Hillel no longer directed the academy he had founded—that responsibility had been assumed by his grandson, Gamaliel—but the great Pharisee sage was continuing to conduct public teachings in the Temple courtyard.

When we arrived in Jerusalem, we made our way directly to the Court of Gentiles in the Temple, and indeed Hillel was there, engaged in a discussion with a group of Jews who had assembled around him. That day, the great Pharisee was speaking to them about prayer. A young man asked Hillel, "How should the Shema be recited? It has been said that according to Shammai, all should recline when reciting the Shema in the evening, but in the morning we should be standing, for as it is written, 'You shall speak of them when you lie down and when you rise up.'"

This question brought a broad smile to the face of the great Pharisee.

"Has the great Shammai truly said such a thing?" he asked, shaking his head slowly, an incredulous frown darkening his face. "'When you lie down and when you rise up' refers simply to evening and to morning, that's all. I assumed that everyone understood the meaning of those words." And with that, he again displayed a bright smile. "Therefore, I must conclude that each may recite the Shema in his own way—one may stand, recline, walk, or even work while saying the Shema. What is important is that we never fail to recite it."

After Hillel ended his discussion, Johanan came forward to speak with him and to convey his greetings. Johanan then summoned all of us disciples to present us to the venerable Babylonian, and Hillel welcomed us and gave us his blessing.

That evening, the disciple Isaac took Johanan aside to speak with him. Isaac, usually a man of calm disposition, appeared to be in great distress; his breathing was rapid and shallow, and his face showed a pained expression.

"A rumor is now spreading in Jerusalem," he said to Johanan, gripping his master's arms with both his hands. "It concerns the tetrarch, Herod. He has evidently been told of the immersions you have been doing at the Jordan River, and of the great numbers of people who have been gathering there with you. It is being said that the tetrarch is fearful you are inciting the Jews to revolt against him and against the Romans. You may be in grave danger."

Johanan put his arm around Isaac's shoulders to calm him. "I'm grateful for all the concern you show me. But I don't feel there is any need for fear. After all, I'm only bringing people together to urge them to be obedient to God's commandments. The tetrarch himself should have more to fear than I do. He is one who defied God's law when he married the wife of his brother. Perhaps Herod will come with us to the Jordan River one day and turn away from his evil ways and become a righteous man."

After we had been in Jerusalem two or three days, Johanan met with us and told us he would soon be returning to Galilee. The other disciples began to make preparation to leave. But Yehoshua, who was enthralled with what he had seen of the teachings of Hillel, asked to be able to remain in Jerusalem for a while longer.

In the end, Yehoshua and I stayed there, with the intention of rejoining Johanan and the other disciples in Galilee three weeks later.

The following morning, Yehoshua and I returned to the great court of the Temple, where Hillel was giving a lesson about the law.

"It is God's commandment," the Babylonian said, "that 'You shall love your neighbor as yourself' and also 'Show loving kindness and compassion, every man to his brother.' Nothing in the law is more important than these words."

Then a young man—truly he was a boy of scarcely more than twelve years—asked the Pharisee sage, "How should we fulfill the commandment to love our neighbors?"

Hillel answered him, "The Book of Tobit tells us, 'Use discretion in all of your conduct; and what you hate, do to no one.' So if we truly love our neighbors, we must never do to them what is hateful to ourselves."

Then Yehoshua rose and asked of the Babylonian, "Would it not be better still to do to our neighbors as we would have them do to us?"

Hillel answered him, "Those are words of Aristotle and others of the Greeks. They surely carry good thoughts, but we cannot always be certain they can guide us properly in fulfilling God's commandments. If one is inclined toward gossip or shrewd dealing with his neighbor, or is of a quarrelsome nature, these words might give encouragement for such behaviors. Worse yet, how would sodomites and those who practice other abominations take such a precept? But if we speak, rather, of what is hateful to us, the meaning is always clear, and this will give no comfort to those with evil inclinations."

Then Yehoshua asked, "If we are to love our neighbors, should we not also love our enemies?"

"God's commandment," answered the Babylonian, "is to love our neighbors as ourselves. But when we speak of an enemy, we mean one we do not love and, more importantly, one who does not love us. If an enemy wishes us harm, or even to kill us, how then could we do as you suggest? For God has also told us, 'I have set before you life and death, blessings and curses. Choose life, so that you and your children may live.'

"So we cannot love an enemy as ourselves if that enemy seeks to destroy us. But we can treat even the worst of our enemies with mercy and justice, and so the commandment that we should act toward each other with loving-kindness can always be fulfilled. As the Proverbs of Solomon tell us, 'If your enemy be hungry, give him bread to eat; and if he is thirsty, give him water to drink.'"

But Yehoshua persisted, asking further of the Babylonian, "Even when an enemy seeks to do us harm, should we not say to him, as an act of loving-kindness, 'Strike me if you will, and do so again if that is your wish, but I will not strike you in return'?"

To this, the Babylonian replied, "If everyone would do as you have said, peace and mercy would fill the world. But such behavior is contrary to the ways of most men, and so who would abide by that counsel?"

Yehoshua and I remained in Jerusalem for two weeks more, and we went to the courtyard of the Temple each day whenever the great Hillel made his appearance there. Yehoshua asked many questions of the Pharisee sage, and we often discussed what we had learned from Hillel's teaching.

Then, one evening, as Yehoshua and I sat in the Temple courtyard awaiting the arrival of Hillel, two of Johanan's disciples, Netzer and Boneh, appeared there. From the look of sadness that showed on their faces, I knew that something terrible had happened.

"Johanan has been arrested!" Netzer said, as tears welled up in his eyes. "We were all together, on our way to the Jordan River, when a group of Herod's soldiers came. It was only Johanan they wanted. The rest of us they did not hinder. They put Johanan in chains and they took him to the fortress at Macherus, beyond the Dead Sea. The others of the disciples followed after Johanan, to remain close to him."

After receiving that terrible news, the four of us remained together in Jerusalem, in fear and dread of the fate of our beloved master. A week later, the other disciples came to us in Jerusalem. They had torn their clothing, an unmistakable sign that they were in mourning. And from the agony that showed on their faces, nothing needed to be said. Our worst fear had come to pass: Johanan had been put to death.

We mourned our grievous loss and attempted to console one another. I could scarcely imagine going on with my life without Johanan.

Finally, after the thirty days of mourning had passed, Isaac, who had been the first of Johanan's disciples, brought all of us together.

"It is time now to put our grief behind us," he said. "We must prepare to go forward and continue Johanan's work. And I believe that amongst us, there is only one who can serve as our leader, and that is Yehoshua."

I was delighted to hear Isaac's proposal, and I was happier still when the others agreed with Isaac—all of them, that is, except for one, and that was Yehoshua himself.

"I cannot now accept the formidable responsibility you wish to confer upon me," Yehoshua answered. "Let me take leave of all of you until tomorrow, and then I will tell you my decision."

Yehoshua departed, to a place outside of the walls of the city where he went for prayer and contemplation.

It was nearly nightfall the following day when he finally made his way back. His pace was slow, and he was bent forward, leaning heavily on his staff, with his gaze directed toward the ground. When he finally reached the place where we all were waiting, his expression was somber, and it appeared to me that in that one day he had aged noticeably.

"I will do as you ask of me," Yehoshua announced, and he appeared as though he were ready to take the burdens of the world onto his shoulders. We made preparations to depart from Jerusalem early the next morning.

18

The British Airways jetliner that brought Nathan and Chaim Elstein to Cairo landed shortly before midnight, and it was nearly 1:00 a.m. when they arrived at Amira Kahn's home. Amira welcomed them warmly, but Nathan was immediately struck by how much she appeared to have changed over the three months since he had last seen her. She had clearly lost weight, and her face showed a yellowish, waxy pallor. Her previously clear complexion was lined and furrowed. She needed a cane to walk, something Nathan had not seen before, and her gait was hesitant, with short, unsteady steps. She also seemed to be in pain.

Amira joined Nathan and Elstein for breakfast the next morning, and from the fatigue that showed on her face, Nathan surmised that she must not have gotten much sleep.

"My chef has prepared a traditional Egyptian breakfast, but he can make something else for you if it's not to your taste. If you like cereal, we have what's called bileela. It's made from wheat, and it's eaten with milk and sugar or honey." Both of the men sampled that first.

"Fuul medammis is the main breakfast food of most Egyptians," Amira said after a large bowl of fuul was placed on the table. Onion was a prominent element of its pungent aroma, with cumin and coriander also contributing to the inviting smell. "It's made from fava beans," Amira said, "and you'll find it to be a bit on the spicy side." Yogurt, pickled cucumbers, fresh dates and oranges, and strong, sweet coffee completed the meal. Nathan and Chaim Elstein enjoyed all of it, but Amira ate hardly anything.

Afterward, Amira seemed to have recovered some of her strength, and they began their discussion of the remarkable document that had brought the two scholars to Cairo.

"If our understanding about this is correct," Elstein said to Amira, "you have a truly ancient manuscript, and potentially an important one. The crucial question will be whether its pages contained text that faded away over the years. If so, it's possible that with the help of modern technology, such writing could be brought back to life."

"As I discussed with you last week," Nathan reminded Amira, "Mr. Samir Idriss, who's here in Cairo, is prepared to take the infrared pictures of your manuscript, starting tomorrow morning."

"Also," Elstein said to her, "I want to thank you again for your willingness to let us examine other documents from your collection. As Nathan may have told you, the best way nowadays for us to study old manuscripts is from high-quality digital copies. So, when Mr. Idriss is here, I'd like to have him photograph those as well. Nathan's pictures from his previous visit here weren't terribly clear."

"Of course," Amira answered. "And if you'd like, we could spend some time this morning so you can determine which of the documents would be of interest to you. Oh, and there's one other thing," she added. "I mentioned to my lawyer that you wanted to photograph some of the manuscripts. He told me it would be important to have a release agreement. It would certify that you wouldn't sell or publish any of the photographs without permission."

"That would be quite all right," Elstein replied. "It's standard."

"I'm glad that won't be a problem," Amira answered. "Here, this is the agreement he drew up," she said as she handed Elstein the paper.

"Uh, well, there's a problem with this, Mrs. Kahn. The whole thing is written in Arabic," Elstein said.

"Oh, my, I didn't pay any attention to that. Well, I'm sure my lawyer can prepare an English version. I'll check with him this afternoon."

The three of them spent the rest of the morning perusing Amira's extensive manuscript holdings.

"You have a truly extraordinary collection," Elstein said to Amira, "many beautiful and important Hebrew manuscripts. What's of special interest to us are the medieval works. Some of these must certainly have come from the Cairo *genizah*. And among them are several that are new to me. Really wonderful. I'm just delighted that you've given us the opportunity to see them."

After lunch, Elstein excused himself to make a telephone call, and Nathan sat alone with Amira.

"You've been very kind to spend all this time with us," he said, "and I...well...it seems that...that you may not be feeling so well."

"I'm sorry that you have to see me looking like this," Amira said. "I have rheumatoid arthritis, and it flares up rather badly two or three times a year. This time it was really awful. My doctor told me that at my age the disease should burn itself out, but so far it hasn't changed. He used to give me prednisone for my flare-ups, but that caused other problems. I would blow up like a blimp, and my diabetes would go out of control. With the medication I take now, I can avoid those complications, but it makes me sick, and I can hardly eat anything. I'm actually starting to feel better this morning. Oh, and I also wanted to tell you that my nephew David and his wife Leah will be joining us here for dinner this evening," Amira added.

"It will be wonderful to see him again," Nathan said.

Leah and David Kahn arrived early, in time for cocktails before dinner. In light of all that had happened since Nathan first met David on his previous trip to Cairo, he had come to feel a debt of gratitude to the young man for having brought him in contact with Amira and her remarkable manuscript collection. But he also felt a genuine and warm bond of friendship with David.

Leah, a slender young woman nearly as tall as her husband, wore a cobalt-blue dress that had as its only ornamentation a simple scrollwork design, embroidered in light blue along its hemline. Her necklace, as well as her earrings and bracelet, were of intricately filigreed silver, inlaid with polished amber, deep red coral, and, in her necklace, a single opal, all typical of traditional Jewish-Yemenite jewelry. Nathan assumed that she was Israeli, or at least from the Middle East, and her beautifully French-accented English came as a surprise to him.

"The two of us first met in New York—upholding what seems to be our family tradition of finding our spouses there," David explained.

"Were you in college together?" Nathan asked.

"Oh, no. Leah's family are also in the textile business, based in Marseilles. She was their company's representative in the United States. We met at an international trade conference."

Leah, it quickly became apparent, was well versed in politics, history, and the arts, and both Elstein and Nathan enjoyed an engaging conversation with her and David.

Amira's chef had prepared a sumptuous dinner, entirely vegetarian, respecting Elstein's eschewal of non-kosher meat. From Nathan's previous experiences with Amira's cuisine, he confidently anticipated an exotic and thoroughly gourmet experience, and the meal did not disappoint him. Amira again served her extraordinary Om Ali for dessert, and this time Nathan enjoyed its creamy goodness to the last spoonful.

Samir Idriss arrived early the next morning.

"We have quite a lot for you do," Elstein told him.

"I'm responsible for almost all of the document photography for the Egyptian Museum," Idriss replied, "so I'm quite used to large jobs."

Elstein seemed relieved after hearing that. "For the papyrus manuscript," he said, "we'll need a full set of infrared images of each page.

They should be done on film, both black and white and in color, and we'll also need high-resolution digital images. For the other documents, digital images alone will suffice."

After a careful examination of the documents to be photographed, Mr. Idriss made a few calculations.

"It won't be possible for me to finish all of these today," he said. "I'll do as much as I can now, and I should be able to complete the rest tomorrow morning."

However, that estimate turned out to be overly optimistic, and it was well into the afternoon the following day when his work was finally done.

Nathan and Elstein were relieved to be finished with the tedious task of preparing and handling the manuscript pages for the photography. As their final task, they collected additional samples from the papyrus manuscript, for radiocarbon dating and for analysis of the ink of the presumably forged Hebrew writing. Amira's attorney sent her an English version of the agreement, and after a short telephone conversation with his lawyer in Cambridge, Elstein signed the paper. He and Nathan looked forward to a restful evening before their flight home early the following morning. However, Amira, who had been a thoroughly gracious hostess, was suffering a recurrence of her arthritis pain.

"I hope you won't mind my not having dinner with you this evening," she told them. "David and Leah would like to see you again before you leave. If that's all right with you, they'll pick you up."

The Kahns brought Elstein and Nathan to a small French restaurant near Cairo's central business district.

"The chateaubriand here is always excellent," David told them. Nathan readily accepted the suggestion, but Chaim Elstein opted for the turbot.

At the end of the meal, they lingered over coffee.

"I trust you're aware of how grateful my aunt is for all that you've done for her," David said to Nathan. "She was becoming more and more withdrawn and depressed since my uncle died. But all the excitement about the manuscripts has rejuvenated her. It's such a pleasure to see her engaged in life again."

As a parting gift, and as a token of their appreciation and friendship, David and Leah gave the two men small paintings done on papyrus, reproductions of ancient temple scenes from the Egyptian museum.

Their flight from Cairo the next morning was delayed by nearly four hours, and it was late Friday afternoon by the time Nathan and Elstein finally touched down at Heathrow. Nathan could see that Elstein was tired from the long trip, but he knew that the director was happy to be back home before sundown and the start of the Sabbath.

Even before Nathan unlocked the door to his flat, the inviting aroma of baking challah bread wafted out from under the door to greet him. And once inside, the savory smell of roasting chicken added to his homecoming welcome. The table was set with Zippora's best tablecloth, candles, a small bouquet of bright yellow jonquils, and goblets for wine. Zippora was in the midst of slicing a tomato. Nathan was surprised to see that she was wearing a robe and slippers. She had done her hair into an attractive coif, and as he came near her, Nathan was taken by the sensual essence of her perfume.

"Mmm, smells wonderful," he said.

"Mother's very best recipe for Shabbat dinner," Zippora replied, dismissing the possibility that his comment referred to her perfume. "I missed you," she said as she turned give him a tender kiss.

"I missed you, too," he said, holding her in his arms for a long while.

"Nathan," she said, "would you come into the bedroom please? There's something I want you to see."

What Zippora showed him, dropping her robe onto the floor, was her slim, supple body in its full, unadorned beauty.

Nathan stood transfixed, unprepared for what he was seeing, but at the same time thoroughly enjoying the alluring sight before him.

"Lovely," Nathan finally responded, acknowledging the unusual welcome Zippora had contrived for him.

"Dinner won't be ready for a while," she said, "so maybe this would be a good opportunity to catch up for when you were away." She smiled and slowly unbuttoned his shirt.

A week after their return from Cairo, Elstein received a telephone call from Samir Idriss.

"I printed out the infrared photographs using a variety of different techniques," he said. "In spite of applying every method I know, there's no indication of a latent image on any of the pages. I'm sending you the prints and a set of CDs with the digital images."

Elstein conveyed the bad news to Nathan. "It doesn't look very promising. When we get the digital images, I'll ask Fergus Wylie to spend some time with them. He's really very resourceful."

A week later, Fergus intercepted Nathan as he was on his way to the director's office.

"I don't see anything on the photographs," Fergus explained. "I've also been searching around a bit on the Internet, and I can tell you that a lot of work is being done on image enhancement for this kind of analysis. So I'm not giving up just yet. There's a man in the U.S., an archivist at Arizona State, who's doing the most advanced work. He's written some software, and I'm going to try to download it."

One morning later that week, Fergus stopped by Nathan's office. "I've something to show you on my computer," he said. "When you have a few minutes, why don't you stop over?"

"I can come now," Nathan replied.

"Let me find one of the best areas," Fergus said, scrolling through a large file of images on his computer. "Here, what do you see?"

"Well, frankly, I don't see anything."

"Look, over here…and here, very faint to be sure, but there's definitely something."

"Okay, I suppose so. But certainly nothing that's readable."

"True enough. But this at least suggests that there may be latent images. Now we need to see if we can improve the resolution."

The following Monday, Fergus invited Nathan to come to his office again. "I've been tweaking these some more," Fergus said, "and now take a look."

"Well," Nathan noted, "the images are certainly stronger. I can see something on every page. Do you think the writing can be made legible?"

"No way to be sure, but it still may be possible to sharpen the resolution. I've been in contact with the fellow in Arizona by e-mail, and yesterday I talked with him by phone. He's really a nice chap. He suggested some other things I could try. He also sent me the newest version of his software. So let's see where that can take us."

On Wednesday afternoon, Fergus intercepted Nathan again.

"It's a good news and bad news story," Fergus reported. Come over and let me show you what I have."

The images showed distinctly better resolution than before, with occasional Hebrew letters that Nathan could readily decipher and, in a few places, what appeared to be entire words.

"There's no question now: this is a Hebrew text," Fergus said.

"But not one that's readable," Nathan said, shrugging his shoulders and slumping down in his chair. "Close maybe, but not close enough."

"I'll keep working with it."

"I'm not optimistic at all anymore," Nathan told Zippora that night. "I'm afraid this is going to be a very frustrating dead end."

"I think it's much too soon to draw that conclusion," Zippora replied. "Your friend Fergus can do amazing things. I certainly wouldn't give up now."

Fergus continued in his efforts to enhance the latent images, but he finally reported to Nathan that there was nothing further he could do.

It had been almost seven months since Nathan had arrived in Cambridge, and by any reasonable measure his work had progressed well. He was near to completing two major reports, and he was confident that both would be accepted for publication in well-respected scholarly journals. That would be an important addition to his curriculum vitae, and indeed a crucial one when he began his search for an academic appointment.

He had been coming more and more to envision Amira's magnificent old manuscript as the decisive factor that could give him an advantage over other well-qualified scholars in his field. He was certain that the discovery and analysis of an important ancient document would be the ticket to a faculty appointment at one of the first-rate universities. But now he had to face the reality that that tantalizing prospect might never materialize.

"Nathan, you've hardly eaten anything the last few days," Zippora said to him. "And you seem tired all the time. You obviously haven't been getting much sleep. I'm really getting worried about you. Perhaps we could spend a weekend in London for a change of scenery. I'm told that *Chicago* is playing at the Adelphi Theatre."

But Nathan would have none of that. He continued working on his two manuscripts, but making little progress.

One afternoon, almost a month later, Nathan received a telephone call from Chaim Elstein.

"Nathan," he said, "I've something to tell you. I'm at Oxford now, at a meeting. Over dinner yesterday, I talked with some people here about your problem of trying to visualize the latent images of that manuscript from Cairo. Did we ever discuss using multispectral analysis for that?"

"I don't know what that is."

"I should have thought of it, but frankly I didn't. It's a rather new technique. Some of my colleagues here just showed me an old Greek parchment that wasn't readable any other way, and they were able to bring out a remarkably clear image of its text. Really quite impressive, I must say. Perhaps that approach would be what you need. Also, they can do something here called x-ray fluorescence imaging, and with the availability of both of those techniques they seem to have a lot more to offer than I had been aware of."

It took Nathan a few moments to comprehend what Elstein had told him. "Well...okay," he said. "Uh...so...do you think they could do that with the digital images we have from the document?"

"No," Elstein replied, "I asked them that, and I was told they would need the original manuscript. In any case, the person in charge of that technology here offered to do it for us if we can bring the document to his laboratory."

Nathan hung up the telephone and sat for a long while, staring blankly at the bookcase across from his desk. *Another opportunity to get my hopes up and then more disappointment,* he thought. *And anyway, how can we get that manuscript here?* He slouched down in his chair, crumpled up a sheet of paper he had been writing on, and threw it toward the wastebasket, missing it by a wide margin. He stared at the ball of yellow paper on the floor, making no effort to pick it up. Soon afterward, Zippora returned to the office from a meeting with Sarah Jackson.

"It's tea time," she said in a cheery voice, but Nathan remained impassive. She positioned herself behind his chair, and reaching around it, she gave a tender squeeze to both of his arms. Then she drew her face close to his and kissed him on his cheek. "Shall we go?"

"Uh, sure, that would be fine," Nathan answered, in a slow monotone.

Nathan was silent as they walked toward the Tea Room. Finally, as they were sitting together, he said, "Dr. Elstein called me from Oxford. They have some new techniques there for bringing out latent images in old manuscripts. They're supposed to be very good. They said they would be willing to see what they could do with Amira Kahn's document."

"Why, that's marvelous," Zippora said. "Really wonderful news."

"Maybe so, but I don't want to get my hopes up."

"They would need the original manuscript?"

"That's what they said."

"Well, why don't you call the nice lady in Cairo and let her know the good news. Why not see what you can work out with her?"

"I suppose so. I don't know if this is good news or just another dead end."

Nathan telephoned Amira Kahn the next morning.

"I realize it may be difficult for you to send the document to us," he told Amira, "but if that could be done, it would give us a better chance to see if we can read it."

"Well, I'll see what I can do," she replied. Two days later, Amira returned Nathan's call. "There should be no problem with sending you the manuscript," she said. "And I've made the best of all possible arrangements to get it to you. As it turns out, my nephew David will be coming to London for a business meeting the week after next. He told me he'll be happy to bring the manuscript with him."

Nathan was encouraged to receive that news, but he found it very puzzling. How, he asked himself, was Amira able to arrange that so quickly, especially in light of all of the obstacles that Chaim Elstein had laid out concerning the transporting of rare documents? The next day, in a meeting with Thomas Gans, he got a very plausible answer to his question.

"Don't tell anybody I said so," Gans explained, "but Chaim, shall we say, might have overstated things a bit. You see, he really was most eager to see the Cairo lady's manuscript collection. And so he might have looked for some justification for visiting her. Going to Cairo to photograph the document could well have provided him the excuse he needed."

On the appointed day, Nathan went by train into London, where he met David Kahn. After a pleasant dinner together, Nathan took a late-night train back to Cambridge with Amira Kahn's document. Two days later, he brought the manuscript to Oxford University, and a week afterward, he returned to pick up the images of the text from the multispectral imaging.

As soon as he was seated on the train, Nathan tore open the first of the three thick envelopes containing the images of the manuscript pages. He held his breath as he examined the first pages. The results far exceeded his most optimistic expectations. But immediately, another potentially serious obstacle became evident to him. At the top of each of the manuscript's pages, one or two lines of clearly depicted Hebrew text were now, for the first time, vividly displayed. They could be read without difficulty, but the crudely overwritten lettering that had been added to the manuscript obscured much of the remainder of the text.

"Look how well this shows up now—it's absolutely amazing," Nathan said, as he presented the pictures to Chaim Elstein. The director was also obviously impressed by the clarity of the now-revealed text, but he shared Nathan's concern about the confounding overwriting. He summoned Thomas Gans and Fergus Wylie, and together they reviewed the new images.

"It's written in Aramaic," Dr. Gans said after examining the text. "Now that's interesting."

"All right, but the main question now is what can we do to deal with the overwriting?" Elstein asked. "It blocks out most of the original text."

"Is there some way to remove it?" Nathan asked.

"The chemical analysis showed that it's India ink or something close to it—fine carbon particles," Elstein replied. "Unfortunately, that would be impossible to remove from such fragile papyrus."

"Maybe the overwritten images could be suppressed with some help from the computer," Fergus suggested. "Let me see if I can work something out."

The following week, he explained to Nathan, "The approach I've been trying is to make scans of the overwriting, and then to let the computer subtract out that part of the image. Here's what happens," he said, bringing up a page of the manuscript on his computer. "This shows what's left after the overwriting is taken out. It's not terribly bad, and you might be able to figure out a good part of what's there, though that would take some guesswork and plenty of good luck." He showed Nathan another image on his computer screen. "Now, this is what I get by using an additional program that fills in some of the missing parts of the letters. To do that, first I scan in the sections of the text that are free of any overwriting. From that, the computer learns to recognize the normal forms of the letters and also the components of the letters. So, when it detects a fragment of a letter, it can usually fill in the parts that are missing, so as to give you the letter in its complete form.

"Well, that's not bad at all," Nathan said. "In fact, it may actually be possible to begin a serious effort at translating the text."

"Give me a little more time," Fergus proposed, "and let me see how far I can get with this."

On Thursday morning of that week, Fergus presented Nathan with a printout of the entire manuscript. For the next two hours, Nathan scanned through the text in a first effort to uncover the basic content of its message. Zippora looked at the manuscript with him. "Very clearly written Hebrew," she said, "but I can only make out a few of the words."

"It's in Hebrew characters," he said, "but it's Aramaic." After concentrating on the first page of the lengthy document, Nathan concluded that this was a long letter, written by a man in Jerusalem to his grandson in Alexandria.

That afternoon, Nathan met with Chaim Elstein and Thomas Gans again, to make a preliminary assessment of the manuscript.

"This is the writing of a very skilled scribe," Gans concluded. "The text is in semicursive Hebrew, and it was obviously done with great care. Another point—notice the different sizes of the letters in some parts of the text. That was typically seen prior to the Herodian period. But then in other sections you don't see that, which could well be an indication that this is from a somewhat later transition period."

"That's entirely consistent with the radiocarbon data," Elstein said. "Have you seen the results from the most recent study?" he asked Gans. "The data turned out not quite as clean as the first set, but still consistent. This time they came up with a somewhat wider time frame, between the first century BCE to the early third century CE."

"That's very decent confirmation," Gans replied.

"Nathan," Elstein said, "you've had some experience with Aramaic, haven't you?"

"Yes, in graduate school. That was a few years ago, but I did manage to get a reasonable grasp of the language."

"Tom Gans is the only person in our unit who has any real familiarity with Aramaic," Elstein said. "Edward Sasson at Oxford has worked quite a bit with Dead Sea texts in Aramaic, and I suppose he's the closest real authority on that language. I suggest, Nathan, that you ought to have a go at it yourself, see what you can come up with. Your two papers on the medieval Spanish poets are about ready to be sent off for publication, so you ought to be able to give this your full attention."

19

Exhilarated and filled with renewed energy, Nathan threw himself into his new undertaking. The manuscript posed formidable challenges, and some of its sections required many hours of analysis, sometimes to decipher the meaning of as little as a single word.

In spite of Fergus Wylie's triumph in resurrecting the text and freeing it from the confounding overwriting, the computer technology had its limitations. Ambiguities in the identification of individual letters in some of the words were the most vexing obstacles. And in spite of the effectiveness of the multispectral analysis technology, some sections of the manuscript's text came through poorly.

In the course of his work, Nathan made three trips to Oxford to meet with Professor Sasson, and with his generous help, and almost daily consultations with Thomas Gans, he was able to make steady progress with his translation.

Zippora provided Nathan with the most important support of all, and she also came to achieve considerable knowledge and competence in the Aramaic language. She was always close at hand to offer her ideas and her help when Nathan struggled with an obscure word or a confusing sentence, and she encouraged him whenever he became frustrated with the difficulty of his work.

But with his single-minded and unrelenting focus on his translation, Nathan increasingly withdrew from any other responsibilities he could possibly avoid. He soon abandoned his Thursday morning trips to the children's hospital in London, which had always been such a satisfying experience to him, and he even came to rely on Zippora to send occasional e-mail messages to his parents. These changes in Nathan's behavior were an increasing source of frustration to Zippora.

"That manuscript is two thousand years old," she said to him on one occasion. "If you'd take a break from it for a few days so we could just spend some time together, that wouldn't matter all that much. Couldn't we at least go into London for a weekend, maybe attend a play or a concert?"

"Uh, yeah," Nathan said, scarcely glancing up from his work. "By fall, it'll be time for me to start my search for a university faculty position. If I can make enough progress with this translation, especially if I can get a preliminary paper published, it'll give me a huge advantage. So I can't let up now."

"Well, okay, but let's at least go out for dinner," she said. "We haven't done that for a long while."

"Maybe later," he replied, "but not just now. The stakes are just too high."

"Your career plans seem to be all you care about lately." Zippora said, making no effort to hide her exasperation.

"Yeah," Nathan answered, making it clear that he had hardly been paying attention to what she was saying.

Zippora had been quite productive in her own research that year; one substantial report she had written had already been accepted for publication in a respected scholarly journal, and she was well along with a second research manuscript. She had submitted a request for an additional year of fellowship support from the Ginsberg Fund, and she was waiting for their answer.

A few days later, Zippora made an announcement:

"Nathan, I'm going to be leaving next week to spend some time with my family in Israel. I suspect you'll be perfectly happy here by yourself. And maybe you'll appreciate my not bothering you while you work on your translation."

"When will you come back?"

"I'm not sure. I'll have to see how things work out."

A week later, Nathan received a telephone call from Zippora.

"Hi, how's everything?"

"Uh, fine, I'm making decent progress with the manuscript, but it's still slow going. Not as much as I hoped to get done."

"Do you miss me?"

"Yeah, of course. The apartment's kind of a mess, but everything else is okay."

Nathan did miss Zippora. He missed her especially when he awoke in the morning alone. One time, while he was preparing a sandwich for lunch, he realized that he needed to call Zippora, but then he got engrossed again in his work and never followed through. The translation occupied all of his waking hours, and he allowed nothing to interfere or to distract him.

Three weeks later, Zippora returned to Cambridge, to find good news waiting for her.

"Nathan, they've extended my fellowship grant for another year."

"That's great," he said.

"Something else I have to tell you. I'm going to be moving back to the rooming house where I was before."

"Oh, no. Don't do that. Let's talk about it."

"It's too late, I already signed the lease. I'm going to move my things this afternoon. Nathan, I'm coming more and more to believe that your career is all you really care about."

"No—that's not true."

"Why don't you take a minute and think about it? Anyway, I'm moving out."

Nathan and Zippora continued to share their small office, but their relationship had cooled and their intimacy ended.

By the end of June, Nathan succeeded in completing a draft of several sections of Amira Kahn's manuscript. He was intrigued by the lengthy story that the letter revealed, even though several parts of its narration largely escaped his understanding.

20

In the months that followed, we continued to be despondent over our terrible loss of Johanan. But we were confident we knew what our former master would have wanted of us, and so we returned to Galilee. And as he had taught us, we again went together from town to town and village to village carrying his message of repentance and atonement, and of the coming of God's kingdom.

But as for Johanan's most fervent pursuit, that we did not continue. The memory that had been seared into the minds of so many of his disciples, of Johanan's arrest and his being put into chains just as they had arrived at the Jordan River, gave no heart to any of us to relive that horrible event. And so we never returned to the Jordan to perform immersions in the river as Johanan had done.

With Yehoshua as our leader, we soon began to see other changes. Yehoshua's abilities as a healer invariably attracted crowds of people whenever we entered a village or town, and at each place we went, he was pulled this way and that, most often by relatives of those who were sick or lame, imploring him to visit and to heal their ailing family members. And indeed, Yehoshua often was able to perform the most miraculous of cures. But even for those of the sick whom Yehoshua could not restore to health, he never failed to bring them a large measure of comfort and reassurance.

I well recall one of Yehoshua's healings in the town of Rakkath, where we came upon a young woman whose eyes were red from crying. She was so choked from her sobbing, we could scarcely understand her.

"My little brother," she said. "He is only three years old. He is bleeding, and no one can stop it. Can you help him?"

We went to see the boy. Blood was flowing from the child's nostrils, and the mat on which he lay was covered with blood. Yehoshua applied firm pressure to the boy's nose, continuing for some while, but when he removed his hand, the bleeding resumed. The child's sister, who observed this, again started to cry.

Yehoshua asked the boy's mother to cut several small pieces of cloth, and these he inserted forcibly into the child's nostrils. With that, his bleeding stopped. Then, Yehoshua looked carefully at the boy's skin and at the inside of his mouth.

"See," he said to the child's parents, "the small red spots on his face and his chest, and the bruises on his legs." Then Yehoshua carefully examined the boy's abdomen.

"Nothing else seems amiss," he said. "After three days, remove the pieces of cloth from his nose, and if there is no further bleeding, you will not need to replace them," he said. "Your son will soon regain his health."

After Yehoshua spoke to the people of the town that evening, we returned to see the child. He had had no further bleeding, and he already seemed to be recovering his strength. And when we returned to Rakkath several weeks later, we learned that the child had recovered fully. The boy's family prepared a festive meal for us in gratitude for Yehoshua's cure of their son.

In each village and hamlet we entered, it was always the same— Yehoshua first attended to the needs of the sick; afterward, he addressed the people there. In speaking to them, he always began by quoting passages from the Torah or others of the holy writings. Then he would repeat the words that Johanan had taught us: "Follow the path of righteousness and obey God's laws. Turn away from wickedness, and atone for your sins, so that you will be worthy to enter God's kingdom."

Increasingly, Yehoshua began to speak in parables, and I must tell you that these stories always attracted crowds of people. At first, Yehoshua followed the usual form of Pharisee parables: his stories were based on ordinary events that anyone could understand, and then, at the end, they delivered a clear moral lesson. In one parable, Yehoshua told of a good Samaritan, one whose people are despised by most Jews, and who themselves hate the Jews, but the man in this story nevertheless gave the most generous assistance to a Jew who had been beaten and robbed and left to die on the side of a road. Although it was hard for any of us to imagine a Samaritan being so charitable, the people of Galilee always found this story to be deeply moving.

But over time, it became increasingly difficult to comprehend the meaning of many of Yehoshua's parables.

"The Kingdom of God is like a certain woman who was carrying a jar full of meal. While she was walking along a road, still some distance from home, the handle of her jar broke and the meal emptied out behind her on the road. She did not realize it; she had noticed no accident. When she reached her house, she set the jar down and found it empty."

"The Kingdom of God is like treasure hidden in a field, which a man discovered and again hid, to keep it out of view. Then, without telling anyone of his discovery, he sold all that he had and bought that field."

"The Kingdom of God is like leavening which a woman took and sequestered in three measures of flour, until it was all leavened."

On one occasion, the disciple Mattai and I talked with Yehoshua about his parables.

"Johanan taught us," I said to Yehoshua, "that with the coming of God's kingdom, Jerusalem will be restored as our holy city, war and tyranny will be no more, and peace and brotherhood will fill the entire world. But what do these parables of yours really tell us about the Kingdom? What does it mean," I asked him, "that the Kingdom of God is like leavening for bread, or like a woman carrying a jar of meal?"

"We see that the people of Galilee are greatly attracted by your parables," Mattai told Yehoshua, "but none of us, your own disciples, can make any sense of many of them. We talk about them endlessly, but we can seldom discern what they mean."

Yehoshua laughed when he heard that. "If the people here find my parables to be of such great interest to them," he said, "and if my disciples discuss them amongst themselves, then my purpose for them is being fulfilled."

In all of his actions, Yehoshua was highly spirited and filled with boundless energy. And in common with our beloved teacher Johanan, Yehoshua appeared to need very little sleep. When I awakened during the night, I often found him deep in prayer and contemplation. On certain occasions, Yehoshua appeared to be downcast and in the throes of melancholy, and at such times he spoke only little; but invariably, he quickly recovered.

As we traveled with Yehoshua from village to village in Galilee, many more disciples came to be added to our group. Among the first of them was a man I had known many years earlier, from the time I was a young boy. He was one of those who had joined Amos ben Isaac in his ill-fated military campaign against the Romans. This was Simon, also known as Bariona, or zealot, and, true to his name, he was always armed, usually with a heavy iron sword. After the defeat of Amos' army, Simon had returned to his home village of Yodefat, and he was living there when we came to that village.

Another armed man who joined our group was known by the name Sikariot, because of the frightful dagger he always carried in his belt. This was Yehoshua's younger brother Judah, a tough and wiry young fellow. After the death of their mother, Judah had left Nazareth and gone to the city of Zabulon. There he had become part of a group of armed men who camped in the hills to the north of the town and made raids against the Romans and their sympathizers.

Yet another of the new disciples, Cheliel, was also a man of highly spirited temperament. His father was a Greek-speaking Jew, and Cheliel was the only one of the disciples who was able to speak that language. He also had a Greek name, Stephanos, which was the one he preferred. Some months later, Jacob, the other of Yehoshua's brothers, also joined us.

When we were in the village of K'far Nahum, Yehoshua gained yet another new disciple; this was Simon ben Jonah, an older man of stately bearing and serious demeanor. Simon's brother, Avraham, had been a disciple of Johanan, and he continued as a disciple of Yehoshua after Johanan's death. To distinguish this new Simon from Simon Bariona, Yehoshua referred to his new disciple Simon as ha-even meaning "the rock." It was perhaps because of Simon's firmness of purpose and his steadfastness that Yehoshua gave him that name.

On one occasion, when we were in the town of Sepphoris, Yehoshua was summoned to see a man named Pantera, who was an officer in the Roman army. This man, from the legion stationed at Cæsarea, was a brigadier of an archery cohort. He had been injured in battle by a spear more than a year before, causing a dreadful wound to his thigh. Because of his injury, Pantera was unable to walk, and he had been carried to Sepphoris on a litter so that Yehoshua could see him.

The officer was warm with fever. His wound had not healed, and a foul matter continued to seep out from it. His injured limb was covered with filthy bandages, and a great stench emanated from the wound. When we talked with the man, his manner was kindly, and he thanked Yehoshua abundantly for attending to him. But at one point, I took Yehoshua aside and I asked him, "Is it right for us to care for this man's wounds, inasmuch as he is a Roman soldier, one of those who have caused so much suffering to our country and to our people?"

"When a man is sick or injured," Yehoshua replied, "no matter from whence he comes, and even if he has caused great evil, we still must do whatever we can to relieve his pain and suffering."

Yehoshua removed Pantera's bandages, and washed his wound. Then, he probed deeply into the injured area with a long copper needle, which released much more foul matter. Then Yehoshua placed strips of linen into the wound, and covered it with a new dressing. He instructed Pantera that the covering needed to be removed each day and the wound washed and then wrapped with clean bandages.

We saw Pantera again several months later. His appearance by then had changed remarkably. He arrived that day on horseback, and when he dismounted, we could see that he could walk quite well. His wound had healed, his fever had disappeared, and his health and the function of his injured limb had been fully restored. I was amazed to see all that had happened.

"I am grateful to you, indeed overjoyed, for your healing of my wound," Pantera said to Yehoshua, and he gave him fifty silver denarii in payment.

Yehoshua replied, "I cleaned your wound, and I changed your bandages, but it was God who healed you."

Yehoshua gave the money to his brother, Judah, who served as the treasurer of our group. "Use some of this to buy food," Yehoshua said to him, "but most of it must be for the needy."

Increasingly, Yehoshua's concern and his preaching were about the poor, the downtrodden, and the dispossessed among the Jews of Galilee. He spoke often to the people about the need for charity and kindness to their fellow men, and he endeavored to raise the spirits of those who were destitute and had lost hope.

When Yehoshua addressed people in Galilee, he often began with the same quotation from the Torah: "Love your neighbor as yourself—treat your fellow man kindly and generously, just as God is kind and generous to you. And when you give to the poor, do so discreetly, so as not to bring shame on those who are in need of charity." Then, he repeated the words we had so often heard from Johanan: "If you own two cloaks, give one of them to someone who has none, and do the same with your food. And be humble and unassuming in your devotion to keeping God's ordinances and commandments." Yehoshua also often recited from the Psalms: "The meek shall inherit the earth, and delight in abundant happiness." And he quoted words of Hillel: "My humbling is my exaltation; my exaltation is my humbling."

In the towns and villages of Galilee where Yehoshua spoke, most who came to hear him were the desperately poor folk of that region. But on occasion, Yehoshua's audience included those who were more affluent, and sometimes there were men among them who had amassed considerable wealth. Whereas it had always been Johanan's practice to seek food and shelter from families of modest means in the places we visited, Yehoshua clearly preferred to dine with the rich. And among those from whom he accepted food and lodging were tax collectors, merchants of questionable scruples, and others whose wealth represented ill-gotten gains.

After accepting their hospitality, Yehoshua spoke to them thusly, "It will be hard for a wealthy person to enter God's kingdom—indeed it will be easier for a camel to pass through the eye of a needle than for a rich man to enter the Kingdom."

On one occasion, a merchant of considerable wealth asked Yehoshua what he needed to do to be righteous before God.

"First," Yehoshua said to him, "you must faithfully follow God's laws and commandments. Afterward, do this: sell all that you have, and give the money to the poor. Then you will be among the first to enter God's kingdom."

The man seemed dejected after hearing these words, and I doubt that he followed Yehoshua's counsel.

Some of the Jews in the towns and villages of Galilee began asking why our master was disposed to dining and consorting with tax collectors and the unscrupulous. When Yehoshua learned of this, he said to us, "It is the sick who need a doctor, not those who are healthy. And for my part, I call not on the righteous but rather on sinners."

Among those who came to hear Yehoshua speak, perhaps the wealthiest of all of them was a most remarkable woman. I had previously learned of her during the time I lived in Magdala with my sister and her children.

This woman, Mariamne was her name, lived in the country a short distance to the north of the town. Her house, in truth more a villa or a small palace, was build atop a hill with a sweeping view of the lush valley that lay beneath it, which, in the far distance, blended imperceptibly into the cobalt-blue waters of Lake Kinneret. Mariamne was known for her exceptional beauty, but equally so for her elegant bearing, her charm, and her intelligence. It was said that the sound of her voice, when she sang and accompanied herself on the lyre, was enough to melt the hearts of any who heard her. After she bathed each morning in her pool, servants anointed her skin with the finest scented oils, and then they combed and arranged the long red hair that flowed down over her shoulders. By midday, she was fully attired, always in the most exquisite fashion, in gowns of silk or other fine fabrics, and ready to receive those who would visit her.

Mariamne's considerable wealth was the beneficence of innumerable men who had come from near and far to seek her attention. Prosperous merchants, wealthy Greek travelers, important Roman military commanders, and even a Persian prince were among those who showered her with gold, pearls, and precious jewels.

One day when we were in Magdala, Mariamne appeared there in the crowd that had gathered in the town's marketplace to hear Yehoshua. We disciples, and, I could readily recognize, Yehoshua as well, were immediately taken by Mariamne's graceful bearing and her extraordinary beauty. After Yehoshua had finished speaking, Mariamne sent her servant to him, to invite us to dine with her and to stay at her home for the night.

The dinner she provided us was a sumptuous banquet, with the choicest of meats, fowl, and fish; the largest, sweetest, and most delicious fruits we had ever seen; and wine that was like an exquisite elixir. I had never experienced so wonderful a meal. And Mariamne was a most gracious hostess, sparing no effort to assure that we were comfortable and that all of our wishes were met. Though Mariamne was reputed to have wide-ranging interests and an extraordinary breadth of knowledge, our conversation that evening was devoted entirely to Yehoshua's message of the coming of God's kingdom on earth.

"As hard as it will be for a rich man to enter the Kingdom, it may be harder still for a rich woman," Yehoshua said to Mariamne. "You have amassed enormous wealth, but all of this will be of no good to you after the coming of God's kingdom. What you will need to do now is gather treasure in the Kingdom. And how can you do that? Sell your jewels and your finery; then take the money and distribute it to those who are in need. You will be forever blessed in the eyes of God."

And, surprisingly, Mariamne did just as Yehoshua advised her. Later, when we encountered her again in Magdala, we could see that she had given up her wealth; she was dressed in the most simple of clothing, and she had moved to a modest abode.

We accompanied Yehoshua for nearly two years, traveling from village to village, where our master spoke to the people, exhorting them to turn away from wickedness, to lead lives of righteousness, and to be obedient to God's laws. Yehoshua gained a reputation as a great and learned teacher among the Jews of Galilee, and there were many who came to regard him as a true prophet.

21

Myron Geller did not adjust easily to prison life. The reality of his incarceration was actually not terribly unsettling for him, and in some respects being in prison afforded him a measure of relief from the turmoil and anxiety that had dominated his life in exile. But there were other realities that did affect him greatly. For one, he found the food to be intolerable. In his frustration, he demanded that he be given kosher meals to accommodate his religious needs, and to his surprise, the prison authorities promptly acceded to his request. In all of the forty-nine years of his life, Myron had never before eaten a kosher meal, and he quickly discovered that the frozen packages of often heavy, tasteless food were even less to his liking than the usual prison fare.

Along with his kosher meals, Myron received an unexpected visitor: a part-time prison chaplain, a pleasant and cheerful man in his early forties, a Hasidic rabbi with a black beard, black suit, black hat, and curly black side curls.

"I will try to be available to you whenever you want," the rabbi said to him. "And if you need prayer books, *tefillin,* whatever, do let me know. Is there anything you'd like to talk about?"

"No, nothing," Myron replied. Afterward, he made it clear to the prison authorities that he had no wish to see the rabbi again. He also had them discontinue the kosher meals.

The prison, a low security federal correctional institution, was in the small West Texas town of Big Spring, halfway between Dallas and El Paso. The facility, developed from a former hotel, was on the grounds of what in past years had been the Webb Air Force Base. With the burgeoning population of federal inmates throughout the country, especially as a result of ever-increasing numbers of drug convictions, prison overcrowding had become the rule, and Big Spring was no exception. "Low security" meant that the inmates lived dormitory-style rather than in cells, and that they had considerable freedom of movement within the facility.

Drug trafficking, immigration offences, and extortion or fraud convictions were why most of the men were imprisoned there. Among its more notable inmates were David Duke, the former Ku Klux Klan leader and political figure; and two prominent Mafia members, Tony Vesuvio and Freddy "Big Fish" Milano, members of the Gambino crime family from New York. To be assigned to such a prison meant that an inmate had not been convicted of a violent crime, but Big Spring was no oasis of tranquility. The institution had had a long history of violent disturbances, the worst of them resulting in the deaths of several inmates, and with its ever-increasing inmate population, that risk increased proportionately.

At first, Myron kept mostly to himself, but in time he began to interact more with his fellow inmates. Once word got around the prison about the financial empire Myron had built through fraud, money laundering, and embezzlement, he acquired the status of a minor celebrity. Eventually, some of the better-off inmates, and a few prison staff members as well, began to consult him about their investments. And at one point, Myron was invited to present a lecture for his fellow inmates about the operation of the stock market. That was one of the best-attended lectures that year. Another of the inmates, Jose Cruz, had also been convicted of fraud and money laundering in his work as an investment advisor, and he and Myron occupied adjacent bunks in the room where they slept. The two of them often exchanged anecdotes about their escapades before the law caught up with them.

Myron's widowed mother kept in close contact with him by telephone and through letters, but for a long while Myron resisted her efforts to visit him. In time, that changed, and then, every few months, Rose Geller, sometimes together with Myron's older sister, made the long trip to Big Spring to see her son.

Myron's primary concern in the prison was to avoid the trouble-makers and to be on his best possible behavior at all times, in the hope that he could hasten his chance to be paroled. And although that goal was always foremost in his mind, it took Myron by surprise when the news finally came that he was eligible for a parole hearing.

"They told me that you appear before the board and answer whatever questions they ask you," he explained to his mother. "Then you keep your fingers crossed, and eventually they give you their decision."

"Shouldn't you have a lawyer to represent you at the hearing?" his mother asked.

"I don't think that's the way it's done, but I don't really know," he said.

Rose secured the services of a lawyer from Midland, Jimmy Baker, who had had a long history of working on behalf of the inmate population.

"I'll be able to prepare you, so you'll be ready with the right answers," he told Myron. And indeed he did provide his client a good deal of useful advice about how to comport himself at the hearing.

All of the documents presented to the parole board seemed favorable; Myron had never been involved in any trouble in the prison, he had done his work well, and in every respect he had been cooperative and well behaved. Moreover, Myron's Uncle Norman in Muncie had a position ready for him in his auto supply business. In answering the questions put to him by the board, Myron was quite certain that he had come across as optimistic, genuinely repentant for his past misdeeds, and posing no risk to society. But in spite of all that, the parole board did not recommend releasing him. However, from what they told Myron's lawyer, the next hearing, two years hence, might well bring Myron the news he was hoping for.

"Keep your nose clean for a couple more years, and you'll be out of here," Baker told him. "Meantime, I'll be available if there's anything else I can do to help you."

"Actually there is one thing you could do," Myron said, watching the attorney, to gauge his reaction. "Would you mind making a discreet inquiry for me? I have a personal bank account. Believe it or not, it's with the Vatican Bank. In Rome. Would you check with them to be sure that it's okay?"

"I hope you're not hiding money," the lawyer shot back. "If something like that turned up, you could plan on staying here for the rest of your life. And I could be disbarred."

"Nothing like that. It's just a small personal account."

The following morning, Jimmy Baker phoned the Vatican Bank and explained, "I'm calling on behalf of my client. He'd like to know the status of his account."

"We cannot divulge such information on the telephone. We would need to have written documentation showing that you are authorized to represent Mr. Geller," he was told.

"He only wants a status report," Baker answered. "I can fax you his power of attorney."

"Well, all right," the man answered, "hold on." After several minutes, his answer came: "There is no account here in the name of Myron Geller."

"Is it possible that the account is dormant? He hasn't used it in a long time."

"No."

"Are you sure? Did he have an account there in the past?"

"I have no information about former accounts, but he definitely has nothing here now."

When Baker called Myron to relate what he had learned, Myron was dumbstruck. Finally, he assigned an additional task to his lawyer.

"There's a priest in the Vatican, Carlo Delvecchio. At the Vatican Library. Would you see if you could get in touch with him? He should be able to tell you about my account with the Bank."

"Myron Geller?" the priest asked. "I can't imagine why he would have directed you to me. Did he have any connection with the Vatican Library? No, I'm quite sure I've never met your client. Did you say that he's in jail?"

"I don't believe I said that," Baker replied, "but I'm confident he'll be out soon."

"I'm truly sorry I can't be of help to you," the priest said, as he ended their conversation.

That evening, Myron picked up his lawyer's call on a pay phone in the prison.

"I got hold of Father Delvecchio," Baker reported. "Says he never heard of you. That's all there is."

With that news, Myron finally came to the realization that he had been skillfully swindled out of the sizeable fortune he had come to believe was waiting for him.

Myron slammed the receiver onto the wall phone, covered his eyes with his hand, and stood there facing the wall, shutting out the world that had destroyed his last glimmer of hope. He clenched his jaw until his molars ached, and then, like a tympanist executing a slow, thunderous crescendo, he hammered his fist against the wall, again and again. Finally, depleted, Myron slumped to the floor, where he remained motionless for a long while. Then, in a final act of desperation, he pulled himself to his feet and placed a collect call to his lawyer.

"Sorry I hung up on you. That bastard really screwed me. Look, will you do just one more thing? Check with my former banker, in Switzerland. I'll give you his number. He'll tell you about Carlo Delvecchio."

But that also led nowhere. The banker acknowledged he had handled Myron's account for many years, but he could muster no recollection, nor a record of any transaction from Myron's account involving the Italian priest.

Soon afterward, Father Delvecchio himself made a series of telephone calls, all from pay telephones located some distance from the

Vatican, using untraceable prepaid telephone cards. The first was to Naples, then two to Palermo, then one each to New York, Chicago, and finally, Abilene, Texas.

The following week, Rocco Conconi, an obese sixty-nine-year-old Chicagoan with a noticeably nervous manner and tobacco-stained fingers, flew into the Abilene airport. Two men met him there, and in the course of their brief encounter, Rocco handed them a small package carefully wrapped in silver foil. Two hours later, he boarded a connecting flight to Dallas/Fort Worth, and from there he returned to Chicago.

On a Tuesday two weeks later, shortly before noon, Myron made his way through the serving line for lunch. From there, he carried his tray to one of the long tables where the inmates ate their meals. Tony Vesuvio was among the last of the men to enter the chow room from the serving line.

As Tony moved forward, he collided with the inmate ahead of him, spilling a bowl of soup onto the other man's back, drenching him with the steaming hot liquid. The victim of the assault made a rapid about-face and unloaded the entire contents of his tray onto his attacker. In the melee that followed, all of the inmates, including Myron, were on their feet, shouting, laughing, and adding to the commotion. Order was restored quickly, and within minutes all of the men had quieted down and returned to their meal.

After lunch, the inmates lined up for mail call. Myron had some time left before he had to report for work in the prison's factory, and he stretched out on his bunk to look through the issue of Forbes Magazine that had come in the mail that day. After some minutes had passed, Myron got up and began pacing back and forth from one side of the cubicle to the other, fidgeting with a stack of books on the windowsill, sitting back on his bunk and then jumping to his feet only seconds later to resume his pacing. At first, Jose Cruz, sitting on the adjacent bunk, gave no notice to Myron's agitation.

"Are you okay?" he finally asked. "You look flushed." At that point, he could also see that Myron's hands showed an obvious tremor.

"I feel achy all over, and my stomach hurts. And also I'm kind of washed out." He laid back on his bunk and covered himself with a blanket.

"Alejandro," Jose called out to the guard, "Myron's sick."

"Wassamatter here, amigo?" Alejandro asked him. "You got a fever?" he asked as he put his hand on Myron's forehead. "Maybe a little bit warm. You wanna go see the doctor?"

"No, if I could just rest here awhile, I…I'm sure I'll be all right."

At one thirty, the other inmates left for their work assignments, but Myron stayed covered up on his bunk. The guard sat on a chair nearby and read his newspaper. Twenty minutes later, when he went to check on Myron's condition, he found him cold to the touch, and his lips had taken on a bluish tinge.

"C'mon, amigo, let's get you to the doctor," Alejandro said.

"Something's wrong," Myron said. "I can't move my legs."

"We need Dr. Ruiz *muy pronto*," Alejandro barked into his wireless intercom.

The doctor appeared at Myron's bunk minutes later.

"This guy's in bad shape," he said to his nurse after they had rushed Myron to the prison infirmary and begun administering oxygen. "Let's get an IV going, and then we need to get air transport to move him to the ICU in Lubbock."

Thirty minutes later, Myron was in the helicopter.

"We've got a bad one on the way in," the emergency transport technician reported to the telemetry physician at the hospital. "Flaccid paralysis of his legs, also weakness in his arms. His heart seems okay, only some tachycardia. His lungs are clear, but he has poor respiratory effort."

"How far away are you?"

"Pilot says ten minutes."

"You'd better intubate him now so we can get him onto a ventilator as soon as you get here."

"All right, we'll get an endotracheal tube in and we'll continue bagging him."

Minutes after his arrival, Myron was attached to a mechanical ventilator, and with that, the blueness of his lips receded.

"Phew," one of the intensive care unit nurses said to her colleague. "This guy smells like a dead mouse. He probably hasn't taken a shower in the last month." But Myron had showered that very morning. No one else at the hospital noticed, or at least commented on his unusual smell.

The senior resident in the intensive care unit quickly evaluated Myron and initiated treatment measures to stabilize his condition. A short while later, the director of the unit arrived, and the resident presented Myron's history to her.

"Rapidly ascending paralysis with impending respiratory failure. If it hadn't all progressed so quickly, I would say this is a classical presentation of Guillain-Barré syndrome."

"Yes, Guillain-Barré usually does progress more slowly than this, but it sometimes evolves over just a few hours, just like in this man," she said. "So what else should be in the differential diagnosis?"

"Well, disease of the spinal cord, perhaps a tumor," he said, "and systemic lupus, also HIV and *Campylobacter* infection."

"Yes," she said, "those are the important ones. There are also some oddball conditions that should be considered, such as tick fever and botulism.

"Botulism?" he asked.

"Yes, very rare in adults, of course, but we should send blood to test for that."

The director was then called to the telephone to speak with a surgeon about one of his patients in the ICU. The resident logged onto a computer terminal to check some laboratory results and to complete his progress notes for that afternoon. As he was finishing his last note, a nurse interrupted him.

"Mr. Geller's heart rate has fallen to the low fifties. I increased his IV fluid, but that didn't seem to do much."

When the resident arrived at his bedside, Myron's heart rate had dropped below forty, and within a minute, they could no longer detect any cardiac activity.

"Epinephrine," he yelled to the nurse, as he began manual compressions of Myron's chest. That had no apparent effect. In desperation, the resident attached Myron to a defibrillator and sent a jolt of electricity through his chest. Every resuscitative measure failed. Soon afterward, they pronounced him dead.

The autopsy was inconclusive, none of its findings pointing to a specific disease. The culture for *Campylobacter* was negative, and the blood test for botulinum toxin came back negative as well. The cause of his death was finally reported as "fulminant Guillain-Barré syndrome."

With botulinum poisoning excluded as the cause of Myron's illness, no thought was given to the possibility that he might have died from the effects of a different neurotoxin, one that imparted a characteristic mousy odor to its victims. And no one at all had paid heed to the fact that Freddy "Big Fish" Milano had been sitting at the table immediately behind Myron during the commotion at lunch on the day he became fatally ill, nor would anyone have had reason to imagine that Freddy might have put something in Myron's food.

22

Having completed his translation of a goodly portion of Amira Kahn's manuscript, Nathan took a week away from his work, joining with Fergus Wylie to prepare a preliminary report of their discovery. They entitled their article: "A First-Century Aramaic Letter Discovered in Alexandria."

In their report, they presented the findings from the radiocarbon dating measurements, and they described how the manuscript had been overwritten and the various steps they had taken to uncover its latent image. They also included a brief synopsis of the content of the letter's narrative, as well as an illustration of one of the pages of its Aramaic text.

Nathan submitted the article to the *International Journal of Biblical Research*, the same journal that two years earlier had published his paper on the Song of Songs.

Only three weeks later, Nathan was delighted to receive a reply from the editor:

Dear Dr. Tobin,

I am pleased to inform you that we are prepared to include your very interesting report in an upcoming issue of the *Journal*. A few minor modifications are indicated on the attached copy of your manuscript. If you have no objection to these changes, please contact our editorial office without delay, so that we can forward your report promptly to the publisher.

Yours truly,

Jerome Koblenz, PhD
Editor in Chief

With that, Nathan's fondest wish was about to be fulfilled. The publication of his report in such a prominent journal would assure him wide recognition for what would certainly be seen as a significant scholarly achievement. And more importantly, his ability to compete for a coveted tenure-track faculty position at a distinguished research university would be considerably strengthened.

Zippora was at her desk in their shared office when Nathan opened the envelope. He laid the letter on the desk in front of her.

"How's this for great news?" he asked her.

"Oh, yes, that's wonderful news all right," she replied with an unmistakably caustic tone to her voice. "So now you seem to be well on your way toward achieving the only thing you ever really cared about. Congratulations. I hope it brings you happiness."

Her biting rejoinder at first left Nathan speechless. Finally he replied, "Okay, I understand what you're saying. I know I treated you rather badly. You have every right to be upset with me."

"You obviously have no idea how I feel," she snapped back at him. "At one time, I believed that you really cared about me. Well, that was obviously a fantasy. You've made it very clear that all you really care about is yourself and your plans for your career."

"I do care about you," he said, "I care about you a lot, and I hope I can make it up to you."

"Don't bother," she said. And with that, she took the letter from her desk, folded it, and tossed it back to Nathan.

"Zippora," he said, "could we go to dinner so we can talk?"

"Save your money," she replied. "I'd rather have dinner by myself."

"Look, I said I was sorry," he protested.

"Is that what you said?" she asked. "I must have missed that. You know what? It's not quite that simple. You're an amazingly bright guy, and you can be very nice when you want to be. But I learned something else about you: you have all of the maturity of a two-year-old. I think it would be better if you call me after you've grown up—that is, if I'm still here. Then maybe I'll have dinner with you."

Stung by her rebuke, Nathan again fell silent. But, moments later, he resumed his pleading with her. Zippora, finally unburdened of the anger she had carried with her for three months, finally gave in and agreed to his request.

That evening Nathan picked up Zippora at her boarding house and took her to the Yellow Daisy, a restaurant in the Cambridge City Centre, near the River Cam, an establishment noted for its fine cuisine and its extensive wine list.

Paintings depicting views of the English countryside, interspersed with eighteenth- and nineteenth-century portraits, decorated the paneled walls of the restaurant's dining room. Wedgwood china, fine linens, crystal bowls of pink roses, and white-gloved serving staff all contributed to the elegant ambience of the place.

The waiter took their orders, and moments later, the sommelier presented Nathan with a leather-bound wine menu. His choice was a Bordeaux, a delicate and fruity Haut-Médoc.

Zippora ate very little, and took only a small sip of wine. After the verbal lashing she had unloosed against Nathan that afternoon, she had nothing more to say to him. He too was moved more to reflection than to conversation. The two of them were together, but mostly in silence, leaving Nathan quite alone in the celebration of his scholarly achievement.

He stopped at a flower shop the next day.

"I want something for somebody special," he told the shop-keeper.

"We just got a shipment of beautiful azaleas," she said.

"No," Nathan replied after looking at the white and pink potted plants, "that's not quite it."

"If you want flowers, you might consider long-stemmed red roses." Nathan shook his head, to convey that roses were not what he had in mind either.

"We have some lovely calla lilies," the florist suggested.

"They look a bit too formal," Nathan replied, after inspecting the elegant, pure-white flowers.

"Well then, if you don't mind spending a bit more, let me show you a gorgeous Phalaenopsis orchid," she said, directing his attention to the showy mass of deep lavender blossoms that covered the long, curved stem of the plant. "I can guarantee that your special person will be pleased to receive this."

He sent her the orchid, and on the card he wrote, "I hope you can find it in your heart to forgive me."

For the first time, Nathan gave serious consideration to the relationship he had had with Zippora and to the bitter invective she had leveled against him. Yes, he thought, this lovely and delightful young woman, who needed to produce a significant body of research in support of her own career plans, had spent so much of her time and energy to support him and his work. And yet he had ignored her and behaved in a way that was both reprehensible and inexcusable. He realized that Zippora did mean a great deal to him. He admired her, he had missed her since she moved out of his apartment, and he certainly did not want to lose her. Nathan also realized that he had never really loved a woman before, and that his feelings about Zippora were far deeper than anything he had experienced in the past.

He needed to make it clear to Zippora how much she meant to him, and to show her the attention she deserved. Perhaps, he thought, he and Zippora could reestablish their relationship. And he acknowledged that his immature, self-centered behavior needed to end.

Zippora, still unsettled by Nathan's thoughtlessness, remained wary and was slow to accept the sincerity of his apology. But over time, her anger and bitterness subsided, and their relationship, though primarily professional and collegial, gradually became friendlier.

Nathan resumed his work on the translation of Amira Kahn's manuscript, hoping he could bring it to completion by early that autumn.

23

One cool evening in early autumn, we made camp in a clearing near a stand of tall trees, about a half-day's journey from the town of K'far Nahum. All seemed well that night, although I could appreciate that Yehoshua slept very little, and what sleep he did have was even more fitful than usual.

When we assembled at daybreak for our morning prayers, I could see that something was terribly wrong. I first noticed Yehoshua's eyes—they were swollen and red—and I concluded from his appearance that he must have been crying. Yehoshua's hair was in disarray, his gait was so unsteady he was obliged to lean heavily on his walking staff to maintain his balance, and his hands, indeed all of his upper body, seemed to quiver. He was uncharacteristically agitated, and the pained expression he bore was a frightful sight to all of us. What he told us then was even more terrifying.

"There appeared to me a messenger during the night," he said, his voice tremulous and faltering. "It was an angel from God." Then he paused for a long while, and I could see tears welling up in his eyes.

"The vision came to me in a dream," Yehoshua continued. "The first time he appeared, I gave it little notice. But I again had the same dream the following night. Then, last night, the angel appeared for a third time, and he admonished me, harshly, to take heed of what he had to say. He spoke of great happenings that are about to transpire. He revealed to me that at Passover, this very year, the fearsome battle and the great day of God will begin. It will be then that the Roman idolaters will be driven out of our land and when God will establish His kingdom on earth."

We disciples were amazed at what Yehoshua had said, and none of us said anything for a very long time. It was Netzer who finally broke the silence. "How will this happen? How will the Romans be conquered?" he asked.

"The Messiah, the King of the Jews, will lead the battle against them, and God will assure that we are victorious," Yehoshua replied.

Again, a long while passed while we considered these words. Then, Nakkai asked Yehoshua, "When will the Messiah appear?"

Yehoshua did not answer Nakkai's question. Instead, he turned to his disciple Avraham. "Who do people say that I am?" Yehoshua asked him.

And Avraham answered, "There are those who say you are Johanan, our teacher, others say you are Elijah, and also some are saying you are Jeremiah or one of the prophets."

"And who do you say I am?" Yehoshua asked him.

Avraham paused again, and finally he answered, "When we, your disciples, speak amongst ourselves, some of us say that you surely must be the Messiah, our King." And after Avraham spoke those words, many of the others affirmed that indeed that was so.

Then Yehoshua replied to Avraham, and to all of us, "It is as you have said it, but for now, none of you must divulge a word of this to anyone."

After hearing that, I was overtaken with the most profound dread and foreboding. I had the greatest trepidation about where this would lead, and I was fearful of what might happen to Yehoshua. I covered myself with my cloak, so that my fellow disciples would not see the tears that were streaming down my face.

About a week later, very late one night, the piercing screech of an owl roused me from my deep slumber. Fully awake, I was surprised to see, off in the distance and clearly illuminated by moonlight, our master Yehoshua taking leave of our campsite, which was in the valley of a high mountain. Yehoshua was walking at a brisk pace, and I followed after him, out of curiosity but also from concern about his traveling alone in the wilderness at night. I was careful to maintain enough distance between us so that he would not be aware of my presence.

After some while, I saw Yehoshua climb down a muddy slope that led to the bank of a small but actively flowing river. Holding with both of his hands onto an exposed root of a willow tree, he immersed himself fully in the clear, rippling water. Afterward, Yehoshua made his way back to where the others of our group were still asleep.

At daybreak, Yehoshua led all of us disciples up a winding path along the side of the mountain. When we arrived at the place he had chosen, Yehoshua removed his outer garments and replaced them with a long robe woven from pure white thread. Then he prostrated himself on the ground and remained there for a long while in silent prayer.

Afterward, we all stood together in a circle, and Simon "the rock" recited from the Psalms of David:

"'I have installed My king on Zion, My holy mountain!

I have exalted one chosen out of the people.

I have found David, My servant; I anointed him with My sacred oil;

My hand shall be constantly with him, and My arm shall strengthen him.

No enemy shall oppress him, no vile man afflict him.

I will crush his adversaries before him.

I will appoint him firstborn, highest of the kings on earth.'"

All of us were deeply moved by these words. Then, Jacob and Judah, Yehoshua's brothers, unfolded a cloak of rich purple wool, and together they wrapped the garment around their brother's shoulders.

Afterward, Jacob, not the brother of our master, asked, "Have we no oil that our King and Messiah may be properly anointed?"

It was Yehoshua who answered his question. "We shall have the oil soon enough."

And then it was Avraham who said, "We must also have a crown for our king."

"You shall see my crown now," Yehoshua responded. *And with those words our master and Messiah began wrapping the leather straps of his tefillin around his left arm, his hand, and finally his fingers. As he did this, Yehoshua gave thanks, saying, "Blessed are you, Lord, King of the world, who has made us holy through His commandments."*

Then Yehoshua fastened the straps of the other of his tefillin onto his head, with its black leather box positioned above his forehead, and he prayed:

"Imbue me with your wisdom, supreme God;

From your understanding, grant me understanding;

Do great things for me out of your kindness;

And with your power, destroy my enemies and my adversaries."

Later, as all of us came down from the mountain, Yehoshua instructed us, "Tell no one of what has transpired here."

But then the disciple Isaac asked Yehoshua, "What of Elijah? Has it not been prophesied that he must first come to prepare the way?"

"I tell you," Yehoshua said, "Elijah has already appeared among us, and many of you have seen him."

From those words, we understood that he was referring to Johanan.

One day, a while later, Yehoshua accepted an invitation to us to dine at the home of a learned Pharisee named Simon. As our master sat reclining at the table, engaged in conversation with our host, a thin young girl entered the room. I am certain I had never seen her before. She carried an alabaster jar in her hands, and without speaking a word, she proceeded to the place where Yehoshua was sitting. She broke the jar, pouring the oil onto Yehoshua's head. Then she immediately departed. We were all amazed to see this. Netzer drew near to the others of us, and in a voice that was barely above a whisper, he said, "Now we can see that Yehoshua's prediction has been fulfilled. Our king has indeed been anointed."

I continued to be terrified over all that was happening, and the following day, I took Yehoshua aside to speak to him about my fear and foreboding. With great trepidation, I reminded him of the Pharisee Amos ben Isaac, who many years earlier had declared himself to be the Messiah, and who in spite of his great army, had met so tragic an end.

"Calm your fears—you have no cause for such worry," Yehoshua assured me. "Amos ben Isaac attempted to overcome the powerful Roman

army by force of arms, and inevitably, he failed. But this you need to understand: when the great battle begins, when that dreadful day of reckoning is finally upon us, we too will be soldiers, but God, through His great miracles, will be there to stay the hands of our enemies. Our victory will be assured. Of that, you need have no doubt."

But Yehoshua's confident words did little to dispel my unbounded apprehension.

24

The International Exposition, held in the baroque Piedmont city of Torino, attracted impressive media attention: Reuters News Agency, the Associated Press, and even Al Jazeera sent reporters, and CNN dispatched a TV crew to provide their viewing audience full coverage of the proceedings. Nearly 350 people, mostly Europeans but also a good many Americans, had registered in advance for the meeting, at which more than 100 lectures and symposia were to be presented by a distinguished panel of historians, archaeologists, chemists, physicists, and religious scholars.

The exposition had been organized to coincide with the quincentennial commemoration of Torino's Cathedral of St. John the Baptist, and accordingly, a strong representation of Church notables was in attendance, including members of the Roman Curia.

The conference was officially opened with brief but moving words of greeting from the honorable Umberto Pomodoro, President of the Republic of Italy, himself a Piedmont native. Afterward, Gianfranco Cardinal Coglieri, the Archbishop of Torino, welcomed the attendees. "It is a great joy for me that all of you are here for this exposition, devoted to what is surely the most beloved of all of the relics of our Lord Jesus Christ. Our precious shroud has had a long and fascinating history, and over these next few days, we will be hearing reports from foremost scholars and scientists whose work has expanded our knowledge about this great treasure."

A history session that soon followed began with a presentation by a distinguished Italian religious scholar, an emeritus professor from the University of Torino. In spite of the sweltering heat of that August day, the professor was meticulously dressed for the occasion in a woolen suit with vest, and a bright red cravat.

"The Shroud of Torino, the cherished icon that resides in this city," he began, his voice showing unmistakable emotion, "has been the centerpiece of my life's work, and I am greatly honored to address you today on this object of such profound reverence." He went on to describe the most notable features of the shroud: "Its fabric," he explained, "is composed of flax fibrils. And its weaving and sewing characteristics have been shown to be typical of fine linen textiles produced in the Middle East during the first century.

"The image emblazoned into the shroud," he continued, "is of course its greatest mystery. That image depicts, with amazing clarity, a tall, bearded man whose long hair is parted in the middle. The shroud also displays what certainly appear to be bloodstains: from puncture wounds in his forehead and scalp; from a wound on his side, extending into his chest; from wounds to both of his feet; and from a large wound in the one wrist that is visible in the image. In sum, all of this fits perfectly with what would be expected from a crucified man.

"During the fourteenth century," he added, "the Shroud was generally regarded to be a fraud, primarily because of its image of the wound corresponding to the man's wrist. From medieval iconography, and also from the description in the Latin Bible, it had been generally assumed then that at the crucifixion, the nails had been driven through Jesus' hands. But only quite recently, archaeological discoveries from Israel indicate convincingly that when the Romans crucified their victims, they indeed drove the nails through their wrists, which is entirely consonant with what the Shroud demonstrates!"

A symposium held the following morning dealt with scientific studies of the Shroud. One speaker presented an overview of the radiocarbon dating that had been done in the year 1988. He related how samples of linen taken from one corner of the Shroud had been analyzed independently by three highly regarded research groups. Their results, he explained, showed the fabric to date from between the years 1260 and 1390, indicating that the Shroud was of medieval origin. But then, later studies put all of that very much in doubt. One confounding issue was the recognition that over the years, the edges of the fabric had become heavily contaminated by bacteria, presumably from the hands of the innumerable people who had touched the shroud when it had been left on open display. Scientific evidence suggested that such bacteria could have resulted in significant errors in the radiocarbon dating analyses.

And what may have been more important still was the evidence, from subsequent analyses of its linen textile, showing that the portion of the fabric that had been taken for the radiocarbon dating studies may not have been a part of the original material at all. Rather, it appeared to be cloth of more recent origin that had been sewn onto the shroud in the course of repairing it. If that were so, it would nullify the radiocarbon dating results.

"So why don't they take new samples from what are clearly original sections of the shroud, and repeat the radiocarbon dating?" a man from the audience asked during the question-and-answer period.

"Recommendations have been made to do just that," the speaker replied, "but the Holy Father has not authorized any further analyses of the Shroud."

On the morning after the exposition had ended, Cardinal Coglieri received a guest in his office, a tall man dressed in a black suit with a Roman collar, an old friend from the Vatican.

"Franco," his visitor said, "it's always such a pleasure to see you. You look well—and haven't you lost some weight?"

"Thank you, Carlo," the cardinal replied, reaching across his desk to pat the hand of his dear friend. "I'm so glad you came. And by the way, I understand you are now Monsignor Delvecchio."

"An undeserved honor, I assure you," he said.

"I suspect not—such recognition is seldom undeserved," the cardinal answered. "So tell me, Carlo, did you enjoy our exposition?"

"Very much so," Delvecchio replied. "But I must say there was one thing that surprised me. In spite of the rather compelling scientific evidence to the contrary, it seemed that most of the people who were here believe firmly that the Shroud is a genuine relic of Jesus."

"I believe you're right," the cardinal said. "I have no doubt that the Shroud is a powerful symbol that binds large numbers of the faithful to their Church."

"I'm curious," Delvecchio added. "If you don't mind my asking, are you among those who hold to the view that the Shroud is an authentic relic?"

For a long while, the cardinal sat with his gaze directed at the floor, without replying to the question that had been asked of him. Then, after a long sigh, he gave his answer: "For many years, I did believe that the Shroud was a genuine relic of Jesus. But now I must confess to you that I did something terrible—disgraceful. I went against the express wishes of our Holy Father, and I will likely pay a large price for that.

"Out of my deep conviction that the Shroud was real, I wanted nothing more than to see that proven. And so, I contacted a scientist, a brilliant molecular biologist from an old aristocratic Italian family—a committed and true believer, I thought—and I offered to let him remove additional samples from the Shroud. He agreed he would submit the cloth fragments to very sensitive testing that would detect even the tiniest amounts of bacterial DNA, and he would treat the pieces of fabric by a special process that would remove surface contamination. I was very happy with what he proposed, and I had every confidence he would be able to show that the Shroud really dated from the first century. Well, he did all of those things. He was able to meet all of the conditions for a decisive radiocarbon analysis, and indeed there was excellent agreement among the six samples he finally analyzed. What he found," the cardinal said, with sadness and resignation apparent in his voice, "was that the Shroud dated from the thirteenth century.

"He gave me his solemn oath that he would tell no one, not even his wife, what his analyses showed. But now, in spite of what he promised, he tells me that he is considering publishing his findings. If he does that...I'm terribly fearful of what its consequences will be. For myself, having gone against the express order of the Pope, well, I can hope that the Holy Father would eventually find it in his heart to forgive me. But for the millions of believers for whom the Shroud holds such deep meaning and significance, unequivocal evidence that it's nothing more than a medieval forgery would be a tragedy. And frankly, it would make us all look like fools for having given so much attention to what is apparently little more than a clever piece of fakery."

Monsignor Delvecchio spent a few moments in thought, and then he asked the Cardinal, "Who is the man who did the radiocarbon analyses for you?"

"His name is Vincenzo Salerno," the cardinal replied. "He is the scion of one of Italy's most wealthy and influential families."

"I don't think I've ever heard of him before," the monsignor said, "but now...isn't there also a famous athlete by that name?"

"Indeed there is, and they are the very same man, "he said. "Dr. Salerno is an internationally recognized scientist and also a highly accomplished sailboat racer. He came close to winning a medal at the last Olympics, and I understand that he's training to compete there again next year."

"He is indeed a most talented man," Delvecchio commented.

Castello Salerno, with its massive stone walls and its distinctive bridge tower, had been built by the Normans in the eleventh century as a fortification against invasion from the sea. Perched high on an embankment overlooking the Tyrrhenian, the uppermost level of its tower provided a sweeping view of the coastline and a broad expanse of water. A more modern annex to this medieval landmark, extensively restored and upgraded during the 1970s, had been the residence of its namesake family for many generations.

Vincenzo awakened that morning well before dawn. He prepared himself a cup of espresso at his desk, and he immediately set to work on a lecture he was scheduled to give the following week. The window of his study looked out to the sea, but at that early hour there was only blackness, save for the occasional distant light of a passing ship. Shortly after daybreak, Vincenzo shared a light breakfast of brioches and fruit with his wife and his children, followed by two hours more at his desk.

A light drizzle had continued through most of the preceding cool autumn night, and though the rain had ended, a dense cloud cover continued to darken the sky. Gusts of wind out of the northwest pummeled the castle's seawall, producing great clouds of salty spray as each incoming wave crashed ashore. These were hardly ideal conditions for going onto the water, but Vincenzo had sailed under far worse. And in any case, having time that Saturday morning to practice his racing skills provided an opportunity he had no intention of passing up.

On his way down the stairway leading to the beach, Vincenzo, tall, muscular, and tanned, hoisted his daughter Teresa onto his shoulders. The curly-haired three-year-old squealed happily, bouncing up and down, patting her father's head with both her hands. Her brother Lorenzo, age nine, scurried down the stairs after them.

In the boathouse, a spacious stone structure with long, narrow windows and a high-pitched slate roof, Vincenzo selected a Laser dinghy from among the four that he kept there. He carefully examined the boat's hull and its rudder before pulling the vessel out to the water's edge. Within minutes, he finished rigging the boat. He donned his hat, his goggles, and his gloves, and finally he buckled himself into his life jacket before launching the Laser into the choppy water and jumping aboard. With a strong wind behind him, he set out on a rapid course toward the south, taking care to steer clear of the seawall. Moments later, he executed a skillful jibe and then tacked the boat into a more westward direction, causing it to move rapidly away from the coastline. His children, waving from the shore, were soon beyond his line of vision.

Their governess, appearing on the beachfront veranda with a tray of cookies and milk, distracted the children's attention. But had she not arrived quite so soon, the two of them might have noticed a sleek, black, narrow-beam racing vessel with two powerful engines that was moving rapidly in a southward direction.

Vincenzo, usually a very punctual man, had promised he would be back by one o'clock for dinner with his family. At one fifteen, after he failed to return home, his wife, Elisabetta, attempted to reach him on his cell phone, but there was no answer. By two, Elisabetta, after repeated unsuccessful attempts to contact her husband, notified the Italian *Guardia Costiera*. Two of their vessels promptly initiated a search of the waters in the area, and they continued their efforts until well past sunset that evening. They had no success in locating Vincenzo, nor could they find his boat.

The following morning, the gale having intensified to a full-scale storm with heavy rain, Vincenzo's bloated body washed ashore, fifteen kilometers south of the castle. A pathologist's examination later that day disclosed the presence of several bruises, on Vincenzo's head, chest, and right leg, but x-ray films of those areas revealed no evidence of bone fracture. There was no indication of his having had a stroke or a heart attack, and the only significant finding from the autopsy was that Vincenzo's lungs were filled with seawater, indicating that he had died from drowning. To those who had been close to him, that seemed surprising, as Vincenzo had always been a powerful swimmer. Stranger still, he had apparently not been wearing a life jacket when he drowned, and that seemed unimaginable to everyone who knew him, given the attention Vincenzo had always shown to water safety. Subsequent efforts to locate his boat continued to be unsuccessful.

A few days later, at his office adjacent to the Vatican Library, Monsignor Delvecchio received a package containing a small, leather-bound book. Its publication date was 1825, and its title and text were in Latin. According to the unsigned letter that accompanied the slim volume, it was a gift to the Library, from an anonymous donor.

The monsignor, after closing the door to his office, glanced at the book's cover and its face page. Then, after turning quickly to page twenty-three, he located a thin ribbon of paper that had been inserted close to the book's binding. "The Ebony Queen has returned successfully from her voyage," the note said. Delvecchio sent the book and its accompanying letter on to the acquisition librarian. He cut the note into multiple small pieces, taking care that none of the individual scraps carried any readable message. Later that day, he distributed the small pieces of paper among multiple trash receptacles.

Several months later, Monsignor Delvecchio placed a telephone call to Cardinal Coglieri.

"Franco," the monsignor said, "I hope you have been well."

"I have been well indeed," the cardinal answered. "I trust you heard the startling news about Vincenzo Salerno. Drowned in a boating accident! A tragedy, of course, but also…perhaps, in a sense… providential."

"Yes," the monsignor replied, "I did see something about that in the newspaper. Franco, there's also something I wanted to speak to you about. Our Library recently received a large bequest, more than a million dollars, from the estate of a wealthy American. The money was given specifically for the conservation and restoration of important old books and manuscripts. There's a lot more money there than we'll ever need, and it occurred to me that some of it could be used productively for work on your Shroud."

"That's very generous of you, Carlo, but I…I'm not quite sure what you have in mind."

"Well, from the exposition you had last summer, I came away with the understanding that the Shroud had deteriorated considerably, and that it's now in rather poor condition. So, I thought, why not have an expert conservator go over it—strengthen the weakened parts by cementing flax fibers behind them, attach a new cloth backing, that sort of thing. And also, you could seal it in an airtight enclosure under nitrogen, to impede further oxidative damage. We could let you have

fifty thousand euros without any trouble, which should be quite sufficient."

"You are exceedingly kind," the cardinal said.

"For an old friend, I'm happy to lend a hand," Monsignor
Delvecchio replied, "and I should point out to you that after a full
conservation has been completed, it will be nearly impossible to do
any further analyses of the Shroud. That should put an end to any
further speculation about its age."

"You are a true friend indeed," the cardinal said.

25

From my many years of living in Jerusalem, I had become well acquainted with the spectacle that unfolds in our holy city at the time of the Passover festival. Most apparent are the great masses of people who fill the streets and the marketplaces of the city all that week. Jews have always regarded the Passover celebration to be the most important and most joyous religious observance of the entire year, and of all of the annual festivals, this one invariably attracts the largest numbers of visitors. Jews from throughout Judea make their way to Jerusalem if they possibly can do so, and they are joined there by pilgrims arriving from many other countries.

Extensive plans need to be completed in the city well in advance of the festival, by the large numbers of priests and Levites who are needed to officiate and carry out the Temple rituals; by the vendors who fill endless rows of animal pens with the thousands of lambs and sheep that will be needed for the sacrifices; and by innkeepers, merchants, and almost everyone else who lives in the city, to accommodate the needs of the great mass of people who arrive for the celebration.

The Roman authorities also make careful preparation for this annual influx of pilgrims into the capital city. The coming together of such large numbers of Jews is always of concern to their occupation army, raising fear that the great gathering of people might give rise to acts of rebellion. To assure that order is maintained, it has long been the practice of the Roman procurator to take up residence in Jerusalem for the duration of the festival, so that he can oversee the security of the city. His generals also dispatch cohorts of soldiers from their base at Cæsarea, and they station these men at strategic points, especially near the Temple.

It was shortly before the start of the Passover festival that Yehoshua led us on our fateful journey from Galilee to Jerusalem. Toward the end of our trip, we spent the night in the town of Bethany, and before we departed from there, Yehoshua sent Netzer to purchase a donkey to take with us to Jerusalem. I wondered why we needed the animal when we were so close to our destination, and from Netzer's puzzled expression, he too seemed perplexed. But Yehoshua was deep in thought that morning, saying very little to any of us, and we knew that this was not a time to ask such questions of our master.

The final leg of our journey took us over the Mount of Olives and then across the Kidron Valley. Once the massive walls of the holy city came into sight, we had a magnificent view of the towers and arcades of the great Temple. The road leading into Jerusalem was filled with pilgrims, and when we finally arrived at the city gates, we encountered a crowd of people waiting there to enter. Their delay was caused by the stern-faced publicans at the customs station immediately inside the gate who were levying taxes on goods being brought for sale in the city. Several Roman guards were stationed there as well, to seek out and detain any potential troublemakers.

"Weapons?" one Roman soldier demanded of Yehoshua, after making a cursory inspection of our group. But our master, seeming oblivious to what was asked of him, remained silent. It was Judah who replied on our behalf:

"There are fifteen of us. We have three daggers and two swords."

That seemed to satisfy the Roman, and he allowed us to pass.

Once inside the gates, we faced a throng of jubilant people filling the broad street and struggling to make their way through the crowd.

"Follow behind me," Yehoshua said to us, "and stay close together lest we become separated from one another."

Our master climbed astride the donkey we had brought with us, and we all proceeded up the main avenue, in the direction of the Temple Mount. Although by then Yehoshua had gained quite a reputation throughout Galilee, in Jerusalem, there were only few who had come to know of him. Amidst the crowd, we seemed to pass quite unnoticed.

But at one point, when our forward movement had come almost to a halt, we saw a bearded man in a black robe make his way through the dense throng and approach close to where we were. I recognized this man as a prominent Pharisee, widely known for his extensive knowledge of the law.

At first, the man stood speechless, as he gazed at Yehoshua and then at the rest of us. Then, in a loud, clear voice, he recited words from the prophet Zechariah:

"'Rejoice greatly, Fair Zion; Raise a shout, Fair Jerusalem!

Lo, your king is coming to you. He is victorious, triumphant,

Yet humble, riding on an ass, on a donkey foaled by a she-ass.

He shall banish chariots from Ephraim and horses from Jerusalem;

The warrior's bow shall be banished. He shall call on the nations to surrender,

And his rule shall extend from sea to sea and from ocean to land's end.'"

This Pharisee then placed his hand on Yehoshua's shoulder, and in a much softer voice than before, he said to Yehoshua, "May God be with you in your great mission. I pray for your success." I could see that the man had tears in his eyes as he spoke. Then, he turned and disappeared into the crowd.

As we learned later, that Pharisee was not the only one who had taken notice of Yehoshua. Informers for the Romans also saw him, and they too understood the significance of his entry into the city, riding on a donkey as he did. They had sent word to the Roman procurator and to the High Priest, telling them that Yehoshua, and we his disciples, needed to be watched closely.

When we finally arrived at the Temple Mount, Yehoshua led us up the broad marble stairway that led into the Temple. As we approached the top of the stairs, Nakkai became overwhelmed with emotion.

"Look at the magnificence of all of this," he said, turning his head this way and that to take in all that was before him.

But then Yehoshua said something that surprised all of us. "Do you see these beautiful buildings?" he asked. "I tell you that every one of them will be thrown down. And for all of that to happen will take no more than three days—for when God's kingdom is established here, this temple will soon be gone. In its place will be a new temple, tenfold yet more grand than this. And God will establish his throne within it, and your Messiah will rule as King at His side."

We could not enter the courtyards of the Temple that day, because we had not immersed ourselves as is required of all Jews. But we lingered for some while on the stairway, which afforded us a clear view of much of this magnificent city, "the Jewel in God's Crown," as Jerusalem has often been called.

As we were leaving the Temple, we passed by several money changers who had set up their tables close to the wall of the Temple Mount. Amongst the vast gathering of pilgrims then in Jerusalem, goodly numbers of them had come from distant lands, and they all needed to exchange their foreign money to pay their Temple tithes and to purchase animals for sacrifice.

Taking notice of this, Yehoshua said to us, "I tell you that any who come into the house of the Lord should leave their wealth behind them. We should enter this holy place with clean hands, a pure heart, and an empty purse."

But then we saw that one of the money changers had begun to argue, in a loud voice and with considerable anger, with an Egyptian who had come there to transact business with him.

"These coins you bring to me have been shaved of some of their silver," the money changer said. "Get away with you, for you try to cheat me."

Then the Egyptian, and also one of his relatives who was there with him, shouted back at the money changer, "We are honest men—it's you who's a thief. You're offering us far less than our money is worth."

As the men continued to argue, people began gathering nearby, and soon there were sounds of shouting, jeering, and laughter. An old man standing on the stairway to the Temple waved his arms at the money changer and shouted loudly, "All of them are thieves." Two young boys, who had wrapped sackcloth about their heads, strutted about, making jest of the appearance and also of the foreign speech of the Egyptian men. That caused more laughter and commotion from amongst the growing crowd of bystanders.

Yehoshua witnessed the clamor and agitation taking place in the very shadow of God's holy Temple. I immediately could see our master's face redden, his hands become clenched until his fingers turned white, and his eyes blaze with fire.

Yehoshua rushed forward, and in his fury, he grasped the money changer's shoulder, violently thrusting him aside; then, with a forceful sweep of his arm, he upended the man's table, causing his coins to scatter and spill onto the ground. Never before had any of us seen our master in such a state of anger.

Fighting and disorder broke out among the people there, some of whom seized coins that had fallen from the money changer's table. Two men of the Temple Guard who were nearby observed what had happened, and they immediately came to restore order and disperse the crowd. A group of about a dozen Roman soldiers also arrived on the scene only moments later, but fortunately none of them had been aware of how the melee had started. Grabbing Yehoshua by the arm to pull him away, we managed to escape before we could be detained or arrested.

The following day, when the time came to prepare for the Passover celebration, Isaac asked our master, "Where should we make preparation for our Passover meal?"

"A Pharisee, a kind and generous man, has offered us the use of an upper room in his house," Yehoshua said, and he told Isaac how to find the place. Later that day, all of us went for our immersion in a mikva filled with rainwater, for our purification before entering the Temple.

Then, Yehoshua purchased a lamb from a seller of animals. Near the great stairway to the Temple, a priest examined the lamb, to be certain it was without blemish or disease, and afterward he placed a red mark upon the animal's head. Then we ascended to the entranceway of the Temple.

The vast Court of Gentiles was filled with a great crowd of people that day, more than I had ever remembered seeing there before. We made our *way into the Court of Israelites, where one of the Levites took our lamb and carried it into the Court of the Priests, near the parapet wall. The Levite confined the lamb, and Yehoshua put his hand on the animal's head. Our master then closed his eyes for a long while in silent prayer. Then he gave thanks to God for the great responsibility that had been entrusted to him. Yehoshua took the knife, and with one clean stroke sacrificed the animal. A priest collected the blood, and some of it he spilled onto the Temple altar. The skin and flesh of the lamb were prepared in accordance with the law, and we were given our portions. Avraham and I were responsible for roasting the meat for our Passover meal.*

We celebrated the festival together. To begin, Yehoshua stood, poured the wine, and recited the blessing, giving thanks to God. Then he raised his cup and spoke these words:

"God has chosen us from among all peoples, and He has exalted us among the nations and blessed us with His commandments. God has provided us this feast of the unleavened bread in remembrance of our exodus from Egypt. We give thanks to God who has given us life, preserved us, and brought us to this season."

We all drank of the wine. Then Yehoshua took the matzos, and he said the blessing, giving thanks to God for the unleavened bread. Then he said to us, "This is the bread of affliction, which our fathers ate in the land of Egypt. Let any who are hungry come here and eat of it, and let all who are in need come and celebrate the Passover with us."

Then he broke the matzos and distributed them to us, and we all ate of it. We partook, as well, of bitter herbs, to remind us of the hardship our ancestors had suffered as slaves in Egypt.

Then, Yehoshua recounted the story of how Moses our Teacher, aided by God's miracles, brought the Jews out of bondage from Egypt. Afterward, our master also spoke of the terrible oppression suffered by our fellow Jews at the hands of the Romans, and of how God would soon come to redeem us again. Then we ate the Passover meal together, and afterward we sang the psalms of the Hallel in praise of God. Finally, we again filled our cups, Yehoshua once more said the blessing, giving thanks to God, and we all drank of the wine to complete the Passover observance.

Then, Yehoshua rose to speak to us again. But first, he stood, with his eyes closed and his head bowed for a very long while. "I will not drink wine again until I drink it with you in God's kingdom," he said to us, slowly and without emotion.

We looked at one another in wonder over the meaning of those words. Then, Yehoshua moved away from the table and he gathered all of his disciples around him. Without saying a word, Yehoshua cast his gaze on our faces, one after another. It appeared as though he were awaiting an answer to some vexing question. Finally, he embraced each of us, as one would do with members of his family before departing on a long voyage.

What he said to us then will always remain fixed in my memory: "The fateful night has arrived when the prophecy of Zechariah is about to be fulfilled. The great battle will begin on the Mount of Olives, at the very place where David himself used to pray. We will be God's soldiers tonight, and God, through His miracles, will be with us to assure that we are victorious.

"So now," he said in a firm voice, "for any of you who lacks a sword, this is the time to sell whatever you have, even your cloak, to buy one."

Simon Bariona answered him, "Look master, we have two swords."

Yehoshua said nothing at first, but then he replied, "Two swords will be enough. For when the battle begins, God will provide whatever else we need."

I was terrified to hear all of this, and I felt as if my heart were about to burst within my chest.

26

"Come, we will all go out to the Mount of Olives," Yehoshua said to us. And when we arrived there, he directed us to an open, grassy area. "Remain here," he said to us. "Now we must all pray and remain alert for what is about to take place." Then Yehoshua went some distance away from us and kneeled down in prayer.

Some time later, when he returned to where he had left us, he discovered that the wine we had drunk that evening had taken its effect, and we had all fallen asleep. Yehoshua's voice bespoke anger, but also sadness as he aroused us.

"How can you sleep at such a time as this?" he asked. "All of you must pray now, to be truly worthy when your King leads you into battle. God's kingdom is now so close at hand!"

Then Yehoshua went back to the place where he had been, and he prayed there once more. But later when he returned to us, I confess that *we again had fallen asleep. As Yehoshua was waking us for the second time, there suddenly appeared a group of armed men approaching us in the dark. Mattai, seeing this, called out to all of us, shouting, "Roman soldiers—the great battle is beginning!"*

But Yehoshua, in a quiet voice, said, "No, these are men of the Temple Guard."

Simon, not having heard what Yehoshua had said, raised his sword and struck one of the men, injuring him and causing him to bleed from one of his ears.

Yehoshua bade Simon to stop his attack, saying in a voice filled with sadness, "This is not the great battle for which we have been preparing."

Then the captain of the Temple guards spoke. "The High Priest has sent us to arrest Yehoshua the Galilean, who is accused of inciting rebellion against the government."

Yehoshua had tears streaming down his face by then, and he appeared nearly overcome with grief, but he spoke out against the captain with anger in his voice. "You come out as against a thief, with clubs and swords, under cover of night, to take me? I have been here in Jerusalem in plain view, and yet you laid no hold on me until now."

Before I could fully appreciate what was happening, the Temple guards had taken our beloved master and bound his hands behind his back. Then they forced him to move on, in a rough and unkindly manner, as if they were handling a trussed animal. Yehoshua, his gaze turned downward, said nothing as they pushed him along. They took him directly to the house of the High Priest.

Yehoshua's captors had given no heed to the others of us, and when a few disciples followed, they made no effort to interfere. It tore at my heart to witness our master's humiliation and ill treatment at the hands of these men, but at least I was able to remain close to Yehoshua.

When they brought our master before the High Priest, Jacob, Isaac, and I were allowed to remain in the courtyard of the house, and from there we could hear the questions the High Priest asked of Yehoshua, although we could not see them.

"So, are you the one who claims to be the new Messiah, the mighty king who will lead the Jews into war against the Romans?" the High Priest asked him with disdain in his voice.

Yehoshua answered, in a firm, clear voice, "It is as you have said."

The High Priest, who, as I have told you was an ally of Rome, and made every effort to maintain peaceful relations with the Roman occupiers of our land, answered him angrily, "So where is your great army that will bring you victory against the Roman legions?"

In answer to this, Yehoshua replied, "God will assure that we are victorious."

Then the High Priest said to Yehoshua, "These preposterous ideas of yours can only lead to disaster and put us all in grave danger. Can you not understand this? The Romans will not tolerate any form of rebellion, and they invariably react with brutal reprisal. Do you want them to destroy our country and send us all into slavery? You surely must realize that none can overcome the might of the Roman military forces. And you have no army at all!"

Yehoshua gave no reply. After a few moments, the High Priest murmured something that I could not understand. Then he shouted to the Temple guards who had brought Yehoshua there, "Turn him over to the Romans."

At daybreak, several Roman soldiers came to take Yehoshua away, to their encampment outside of the city. Two other prisoners were already there in chains when they arrived with Yehoshua. An infantry soldier was assigned to guard the three captives.

The Romans would not, of course, allow us near, but by positioning ourselves in the shadow of the city wall, we were able to remain within sight and earshot of the place where Yehoshua was confined. We could see our master, prostrate on the ground, deep in prayer. The other prisoners with him had both fallen asleep.

Then we saw a guard cruelly grasp our Yehoshua's hair, forcing him into a standing position in spite of the heavy chains that restrained him. In a voice seething with contempt, the Roman lashed out at our master: "You wretched Jews cause more trouble than any of the others who are privileged to be part of our great Empire. In spite of our generosity toward you people, we receive in return only your hatred and ingratitude. Cæsar has ordered that we not interfere with your temple or your festivals, yet you Jews look upon us as if we were barbarians.

"Our subjects in other lands consider it a privilege to worship the Roman gods, but you people prefer to ridicule them, showing honor only

to your strange god that nobody can even see. You Jews behave as though you are superior to us, but I tell you that one day Rome will tire of your arrogance and we will destroy all of you."

Yehoshua said nothing in response. Then, in anger, the guard struck our master forcefully in the face, at the same time shouting at him, "Vile, despicable Jew."

The blow caused Yehoshua to fall to the ground, and undoubtedly he suffered considerable pain. Even from the distance, I could see that there was blood on Yehoshua's face, but he nevertheless did not utter a sound.

Then the Roman began to laugh, and he again spoke to Yehoshua in a derisive tone. "Ah, but I should not have shown you such disrespect, for I have been told that you are the King of the Jews, the mighty leader who will soon conquer Rome. But you hardly look like a king. Where are your royal robes? Did you forget to bring them from your palace?"

Then, that swinish guard spat upon our master and kicked him in his ribs. Later, a Roman captain came, and we heard the guard ask what decision had been made by the procurator as to the punishment for the three prisoners. The captain answered him, "Pontius Pilate is no longer in Jerusalem. He and his generals departed in haste last night to put down an uprising in Samaria."

"Then what is to be done with these men?" the guard asked him.

"Pilate would surely have had them flogged and then crucified," answered the captain, "so let that be their punishment."

I heard distinctly what the Roman captain had said, but something within me refused to connect his words to my dear master, who lay there in chains. But Isaac, who was standing next to me, immediately buried his face in his hands and began to sob uncontrollably.

Yehoshua and the other condemned men were taken to a place outside of the army encampment. We, Yehoshua's disciples, were some distance away, but we nevertheless witnessed the horrible events that followed.

The three captives were bound to wooden posts and then flogged mercilessly, in the usual ruthless Roman fashion, until their flesh was rent and their tormented bodies covered with blood. The other two men shrieked in pain, but Yehoshua made no sound. To each of us, it was as if every cruel blow inflicted on our master was also struck against ourselves, but in spite of that, we remained there, to be as close as we could to Yehoshua.

I scarcely can remember now the details of what happened next—the horror of it all left me so numb and confused, I could hardly comprehend the reality of it. The simple facts were these: the three men were dragged to a place nearby, where, in a most heartless fashion, they were nailed onto wooden crosses and left there, writhing in pain, to die a pitiless death.

Once the Romans' sadistic ritual was done, Jacob and Judah, our master's brothers, tried to come close to Yehoshua. But the soldiers there immediately drove them away. But then, two women, relatives of one of the other crucified men arrived, and I saw that the guards allowed them to remain nearby.

So, this is what I did: from a vendor of clothing nearby, I bought a large headscarf, a veil, and a woman's tunic. With these, I quickly dressed myself, and wearing this disguise, I was able to approach the place where Yehoshua was. The Roman guards there did not turn me away.

I came very close to the cross that held our beloved master, then I pulled aside the veil that covered my face. Yehoshua recognized me, and he addressed me by name. He no doubt could see the look of anguish on my face and the tears flowing from my eyes. Yehoshua spoke to me from there on the cross, and what he said amazed me:

"Cease your crying for, as you shall soon see, this will yet become a day of great rejoicing for us. The Passover has not yet ended, and I tell you that on this very day, God's kingdom will be established on earth. Before nightfall God will rule the world from his throne here in Jerusalem."

I stayed there for some while, making what attempt I could to comfort our master in his unbearable anguish. But I could not find words to express my profound sadness or the unbounded love I felt for this great prophet and teacher. Then I left and rejoined the other disciples, and I told them what Yehoshua had said to me as he hung from the cross.

As it happened, Yehoshua's sister Netanela was also in Jerusalem then with her husband. She learned the horrible news later that day and hurried to be with her brother. When she finally arrived there, Yehoshua was greatly weakened. She spoke to him, and after a time, he pronounced her name, to show that he recognized her. Then he said, "Sister, see what has become of your brother." And he added, "I am so thirsty." Later, he raised his head, directing his gaze toward the heavens, and he said, "My God, my God, why have you forsaken me?" And soon afterward, Yehoshua died.

When the Romans removed him from the cross, his brothers Jacob and Judah came and took Yehoshua away. They washed his body and they covered it with burial garments of linen. Before nightfall, they brought Yehoshua to a burial cave in the Kidron Valley, below the wall of the city.

We disciples remained together that night, benumbed and overwhelmed. We attempted as best we could to bring some measure of comfort to one another. The turn of events that day, ending with the suffering and death of the glorious man who had been our beloved master and teacher, seemed a horrible nightmare.

That night, the awful Day of Judgment and the coming of God's kingdom on earth, those overpowering visions that so dominated Yehoshua's thoughts, appeared to have been only the fanciful ideas of a brilliant and well-meaning man, who in the end was little more than a delusional dreamer. And the unspeakable pain and agony he suffered as a consequence of those beautiful dreams made our disillusionment all the more terrible. We had been abruptly returned to lives of oppression and hopelessness at the hands of the Romans, and it seemed then that that was to be our unalterable fate.

The following morning, after we had spent the night in a tearful attempt to find some shred of meaning in the events we had witnessed, three of my fellow disciples announced that they would be returning to Galilee as soon as the Sabbath ended. Jonathan and Jacob, the two sons of Zibhidi, planned to rejoin their family in K'far Nahum, and Boneh told us that he intended to go back to his home village of Hammat. Having no other thought in mind, in my continuing state of confusion and bewilderment, I also made the decision then to go back to Galilee, perhaps to stay again with my sister in Magdala. And so the four of us set out together.

27

On the first day of our journey back to the land of our birth, although we walked together, hardly a word was exchanged among the four of us. We each were deeply immersed in our memories of the momentous events from which Yehoshua, and indeed all of us, had suffered so greatly.

But later, we began to speak of our plans after our return to Galilee. Jonathan and Jacob expected to rejoin their father, to work once again as fishermen. Boneh, who had been a stonecutter, also intended to return to his trade. I at first had contemplated returning to being a scribe and notary in Magdala, but then Boneh proposed something else to me.

"Come with me to my village of Hammat," he said. "You will be able to stay with my family until you decide what you want to do."

When I accepted his invitation, Boneh was pleased. Neither of us wanted to be separated from one another, and by going to Hammat with

Boneh, I would be able to continue my close friendship with him. When we arrived at Hammat, the two of us bid a fond and sad farewell to our dear friends Jonathan and Jacob as they continued on their journey to K'far Nahum.

Boneh's parents were delighted at their son's return, and they prepared a wonderful feast, with roasted lamb and wine to celebrate that happy event. They welcomed me warmly, and they made room for me to stay with them in their modest dwelling.

Skilled stonecutters were very much in demand then in the nearby city of Tiberias, and Boneh soon found work there. And I was soon able to acquire a few clients who sought my services as a scribe. Hammat was a small, quiet place that afforded the peace and calm I very much needed. But the opportunity to spend time with Boneh, and for us to be able to comfort each other after the terrible events we had experienced, was most important of all.

I was gradually becoming settled into life in that small Galilee village when the most unexpected visitors suddenly made their appearance. It was a warm, pleasant evening. Boneh and I were sitting together after finishing our evening meal, recounting some of our experiences when we had traveled together with Yehoshua.

I looked up and before us stood three men. Two of them were Jonathan and Jacob, the sons of Zibhidi, with whom we had only recently traveled from Jerusalem. They had come back from K'far Nahum, and with them was another of Yehoshua's disciples, Mattai, who had remained in Jerusalem on the day we left there.

I had always known Mattai to be a thoughtful, serious man of even temperament. In the two years we had been together, I had never seen him as he appeared to us that evening in Hammat.

His eyes, strangely, were open widely, he held his arms stiffly and away from his body, and he was utterly unable to remain still as he spoke to us, pacing this way and that, in a most restless manner. Most surprising of all was how his face radiated with what unquestionably was intense happiness.

"I bring you the most wonderful news," he said, grabbing hold of both my arms, his gaze fixed on my face. "Our master, Yehoshua, he has risen from the dead!"

On first hearing this, I failed to comprehend what Mattai had said. Once I was able to grasp the meaning of his statement, I was dumfounded. I of course had been aware of the Pharisee belief that with the coming of the Messiah and the establishment of God's kingdom on earth, those of the righteous who had died would be resurrected from their graves. But never had I heard of anything such as this.

"How can that be?" Boneh asked, displaying an incredulous frown.

"Here is what happened," Mattai explained excitedly. "A few days after our master was so cruelly crucified, several of us of us went to Yehoshua's tomb to pray there. Afterward, I took leave of the others and made my way to the central marketplace of Jerusalem's lower city. That day, it was my responsibility to buy bread and olives for all of us for our midday meal. It was there that the most amazing thing happened to me. Some distance away, amongst a crowd of people, I saw Yehoshua! His face was turned toward me, and he must certainly have seen me, though he gave no sign of recognition.

"He was there!" Mattai continued. "There was no question about it—I surely can recognize our master when I see him! Of course, I made my way through the crowd as quickly as I could, but when I got to the place where Yehoshua had been standing, he was gone. I explained to the others what I had seen, but they all told me that I must have been mistaken. But now, listen to what else I have to tell you!

"That night I had a dream. It was as vivid and clear as day. Yehoshua appeared to me. He embraced me for a long while. Then our master spoke to me, saying, 'You saw me today, and you know that I am alive. I am whole, just as I was before—that is because God has resurrected me to life. The awesome day of the Lord is yet to come, but pay heed to what I say, for it will happen very soon. When that day arrives, I, as your Messiah and king, will lead you into the great battle against the occupiers of our holy city. But until I return, here is what I require of my beloved disciples: carry my message to all of Israel. Beseech the people to atone, to repent, to lead lives of charity and righteousness, and to be holy before God, before it is too late. And I tell you this also: my disciples must be the most perfect examples of righteousness for all to see. You must conscientiously obey the commandments of the Torah and do all that I have taught you.' And with that, my dream ended."

I reflected for a long while on what Mattai had told us. If only it were true, I thought, how wonderful that would be.

But Mattai had still more to say. "I went to tell the other disciples about my dream. When I arrived there, Simon, 'the rock,' was in the midst of relating an account of what had happened to him the preceding evening.

"'I was walking alone through the city, shortly after nightfall,' he told us. 'As I approached an intersection with another street, I heard, very distinctly, a familiar voice, although I could not quite hear what was being said. It was Yehoshua, and I can tell you that without any doubt! It was he! I proceeded quickly to turn the corner from whence the voice came, and for a fleeting moment I saw a shadow. And the form of that shadow was, I am certain, that of our master. But once I arrived there, he was nowhere to be found.'

"Others of the disciples have also told of having seen him," Mattai said, "and none of us now has any doubt of the truth of Yehoshua's resurrection. I implore you," he begged us, "come back to Jerusalem so that together we can do as our king and Messiah has instructed us."

At first, I rejected all of that—I recalled how the tragedy of Yehoshua's crucifixion had grown out of our master's dream, and so I had no faith then in anything coming from visions or wishful fantasies.

But the following day, Boneh made his decision: he would accompany the three others to Jerusalem. That left me with the choice of returning to the holy city with them, or going to Magdala where my sister lived.

In the end, it was the other disciples who most helped me decide. The five of us together there brought back memories of the wonderful camaraderie we had shared. And mainly because of that, I went back with them.

When I had departed from Jerusalem only weeks earlier, Yehoshua's disciples had been in mourning over the tragedy that had befallen our master. But on my return, I could see that the news of his resurrection had transformed them all. No longer were they grieving Yehoshua's death, indeed they seemed to be as happy as they had been when Yehoshua had been alive and was with us. It was also apparent to me that the disciples expected our risen master to be soon rejoining us.

Shortly after my arrival there, Simon called all of us together to answer an important question: which of us should serve as our leader until the time when Yehoshua would return? Isaac suggested that Mattai would be capable of guiding us, and several of the others agreed that he would indeed be a good choice. But then Avraham expressed a different idea:

"We all acknowledge that only Yehoshua, our King, can truly lead us," he said. "But until our Messiah rejoins us, would it not be more appropriate for a member of his own family to act in Yehoshua's stead? That is the usual practice when a king cannot fulfill his royal duties. And so I would propose that Jacob, the older of our master's two brothers, serve as our leader for the present time."

Everyone, including Mattai, accepted the wisdom of that recommendation, and Jacob agreed to assume the responsibility offered to him. As further events unfolded, Jacob proved to be an able leader. Among his first actions was to direct each of us to seek gainful employment, and we almost all succeeded in doing so within a short time. As for myself, I was able to reestablish my former profession, writing letters and preparing deeds, bills of sale, and other documents. From the wages we earned, there was more than enough to meet our modest expenses, and the rest we gave to the poor and the needy.

And so, the fourteen of us remained together. We prayed each morning and night, and we endeavored to lead lives of the utmost piety and righteousness, as Yehoshua had always done. We ate meat only from clean animals, and we strove to uphold all of the commandments of the Torah. We faithfully observed the Sabbath as a day of rest and for study in the synagogue, and we offered sacrifices in the Temple precisely as the Law directed.

In the evenings, in the courtyards of the Temple or elsewhere in the city, we spoke to any who would listen to us, carrying forth Yehoshua's message of repentance and righteousness before God. It soon became apparent to us that Simon, the one our master had named "the rock," was the most capable speaker among us, and it was he who most often spoke to the people. I well recall one evening when Simon addressed a large crowd in the outer courtyard of the Temple.

"Fellow Jews of Jerusalem," he began, "pay heed to what I say: the awesome day of God is now very close at hand, when the world as we know it will cease to be, and when God will reveal the glory of His kingdom to us. But know this," he thundered, "only those with clean hands *and a pure heart will be admitted into the Kingdom. Those who have pursued evil, who have not been faithful to God's laws, will be utterly destroyed. So what must you do? Cease your wickedness and atone for your sins before it is too late!"*

Simon often attracted sizeable audiences when he spoke, drawing many of his listeners from among Jerusalem's Pharisees. When he told of our master Yehoshua's many acts of charity and his kindness to the poor and the downtrodden, he always elicited a warm and compassionate response from the Pharisees in the crowd. And Simon's account of Yehoshua's tragic death on the cross never failed to evoke from them an outpouring of sympathy. But then, at the end of his address, when Simon spoke about Yehoshua as the risen Messiah, it appeared that hardly any of the people there gave serious attention to what he was saying. Some rolled their eyes, others laughed and made jest of Simon's words, and many of them rose from where they were sitting and immediately departed. It was only a long while afterward that any of the Jews began to show interest in what we had to say about Yehoshua's resurrection.

We were especially happy to see so many of the Pharisees among those who came to listen to us. We regarded ourselves as being Pharisees, and that was particularly so because Yehoshua had considered himself to be a Pharisee. Among the Jews of Jerusalem who took an interest in our movement, however, we came to be known as "Nazarenes," from the name of the village where our master was born, although many of us preferred something that Cheliel had suggested: "Ebionites," meaning poor men. In light of the modest lives that we led, I felt that to be particularly appropriate.

The Pharisees were not the only ones interested in what we had to say about our resurrected Messiah. There was one man in particular whose agents watched us with careful attention. That was the High Priest, who was always vigilant against any who would be a threat to the Roman rule over our land. And as we came to learn, any mention of a king of Israel, indeed even of the Kingdom of God, invariably raised the High Priest's suspicions.

I will explain more about the High Priest, to help you understand why he behaves as he does. First, I must tell you that the High Priest nowadays is appointed to his position by the Roman procurator, and he is subject to being dismissed and replaced whenever the Romans became displeased with him. So, to remain in the good graces of the Romans, the High Priest does everything possible to satisfy his masters. It is mainly because of this that most Jews hold him in such contempt.

But there are other reasons as well. The High Priests are drawn from a few very wealthy and aristocratic families whose interests always have had more in common with those of the Roman occupiers than of their Jewish countrymen. Moreover, the High Priests are Sadducees, a group that is bitterly opposed to the Pharisees. Part of their enmity is because of doctrinal differences—the Sadducees do not believe in the Oral Law, accepting only in the most rigid fashion the written commandments of the Torah. They do not believe in the resurrection of the dead; and they completely reject the coming of the Messiah.

Perhaps more important still is this: although the High Priests control the sacrifices and the other religious functions of the Temple, most of them have been abysmally lacking in their knowledge of the Torah and of the history and traditions of our people. They play no role in teaching or interpreting the scriptures to the people—all of that is in the hands of the Pharisees, who have the respect and admiration of most Jews. An often-quoted Pharisee saying is "a learned bastard takes precedence over an ignorant High Priest." And in the minds of most Jews in Jerusalem, those words are indeed true.

All of that should help explain the events that unfolded, some months later, after two of my fellow disciples, Simon and Jonathan, had spoken to a crowd of people in the courtyard of the Temple. Suddenly, a group of armed men of the Temple Guard appeared on the scene and seized the two of them. Their captain announced the charges against the men. "Simon ben Jonah and Jonathan ben Zibhidi, the High Priest has ordered your arrest for spreading lies and disturbing the peace."

Those words, so reminiscent of what we had heard that awful night when our master Yehoshua was arrested, struck me with fear and foreboding. The apprehension I felt became even more intense when we saw them take Simon and Jonathan to jail, and it remained with me the following day when they brought the two of them before a tribunal of the Sanhedrin. A member of the court, a Sadducee who was an advocate for the High Priest, was the first to speak when the indictment against them was read.

"These men have been heard on several occasions, in the precincts of the Temple, giving bizarre accounts of a so-called Messiah, who they say was crucified by the Romans. Further, they have repeatedly made the odd claim that their Messiah, after he was executed, was resurrected from the dead. Though it is difficult to ascertain the point of these utterances, it seems to many of us that they are of seditious intent. I am confident you will all agree that no good can come from spreading such lies. Their likely effect, if these men are allowed to continue, will be to incite unrest among the people."

But then another member of the tribunal, a Pharisee, arose to speak.

"I agree it is a strange story that these two have been telling," he said. "But unusual though it may be, I fail to see anything that is unlawful. Certainly there is nothing about it that could be considered seditious. And finally, why should we believe that any of this would provoke unrest among the people? The coming of the Messiah, who will bring peace and end all suffering in the world, has always been the dream and the hope of the Jewish people. If the man these people speak of is truly the Messiah, then we should all rejoice, and certainly not persecute them."

The discussion continued for some while, but in the end, the court, of which a majority of members were Pharisees, voted that Simon and Jonathan were not guilty of any crime, and the two of them were allowed to go free. I was surprised but delighted to hear their verdict. Then, together, we celebrated their release, and it was a joyful occasion for all of us.

Some months later, a similar scene took place, but this time its outcome was a tragic one. Yehoshua's disciple Cheliel, the one also known by his Greek name, Stephanos, was addressing a crowd one evening. His speech was an impassioned oration, in keeping with Stephanos's fiery temperament. He spoke of our resurrected Messiah, and he gave considerable emphasis to what would transpire when Yehoshua returned to us as our king:

"He will be at the head of the great army of God. He will restore Jerusalem as a holy city, and then God will establish his kingdom on earth with Jerusalem as its capital. It will be the start of the great messianic age, and all the world will then be at peace and tranquility, a time when swords can truly be beaten into plowshares and when none will need be afraid."

These words, of course, were no different from what Yehoshua, and Johanan before him, had spoken. And both of these great prophets had been put to death for saying such things.

Stephanos was arrested by the Temple Guard, under orders of the High Priest, and the following day he was brought before the full Sanhedrin, the highest court of the land. So that you will understand how his trial unfolded, I must tell you that the Sanhedrin, as well as its subordinate tribunals, operate under very strict regulations. It is required that the charges against the accused be clearly stated, and the trial can proceed only from that indictment. At least two eyewitnesses need to testify to the truth of the allegations, and lacking that, the person on trial must be immediately released. The defendant is allowed to bring witnesses on his behalf, and after everything is heard, the tribunal casts its vote. A majority of votes is required for conviction. And as its final action, the defendant must be informed of the court's verdict and of any punishment that has been decreed.

At the trial of Stephanos, an advocate for the High Priest presented his commentary concerning the charges that had been made: "Though there may be some who prefer otherwise, we are obliged to acknowledge that our nation has but one sovereign ruler, and that is Tiberius Cæsar. And I will remind you that by Cæsar's decree, the previous kingship of this country has been abolished. Therefore, any who would endeavor to impose a new king over us, either by force or through other means, is guilty of treason. And that most certainly is the offence committed by this man Stephanos."

But then, Gamaliel, the grandson of the great Hillel, and the most respected of all the Pharisees, rose to speak. He asked that Stephanos be taken outside, and then he addressed the Sanhedrin.

"Men of Israel, consider carefully what you intend to do with this man and with the others of his group. Some time ago, Amos ben Isaac claimed to be the Messiah, and thousands of men rallied to him. He was killed, all his followers were dispersed, and it all came to nothing. Prior to him, Judah the Galilean appeared and led a band of people in revolt. He too was killed and his followers were scattered. Now I advise you to leave this man, and all the others like him, alone! For if their purpose or activity is of human origin, it will surely fail. But if it is from God, you will not be able to stop them—you will only find yourself fighting against God."

These words brought us great comfort, especially coming from this greatest of all of the Pharisees, those whom Yehoshua always so much admired. But then the advocate for the High Priest spoke once again. "I ask that the court not pass judgment on this man until tomorrow. We have other witnesses who will be coming then to give testimony."

So Stephanos was kept in custody, to await the completion of his trial the following day. But then, very late that night, three men came to the jail where Stephanos was kept prisoner. They dragged him to a place outside the city and they killed him by stoning. No one could tell us who was responsible for this atrocity, but we believed they were henchmen of the High Priest. We mourned the loss of our dear friend for a long time.

The remainder of our group continued in close fellowship in Jerusalem, living as a brotherhood, breaking bread together and sharing all that we had with one another. We prayed each day for the imminent return of our king and Messiah, and we worked most earnestly to spread word of the coming of God's kingdom on earth. And we endeavored at all times to lead our lives in conformity with the commandments of the Torah.

But so as not to arouse the suspicions of the High Priest, who was ever vigilant to uncover any act of sedition against the Roman rulers of our country, we took extra care not to tell anyone that our Messiah was indeed our king, the one who, upon his return, would lead God's army to expel the Romans from our land. It was apparent to us, nevertheless, that the High Priest considered us, as well as the others of the Pharisees, as his enemies just as he had regarded Yehoshua and Johanan before him.

Our brotherhood continued in this fashion for more than ten years Then, most suddenly, I became reconnected with someone I had not seen for a very long time—a man whose bizarre ideas and unquenchable ambition would eventually upset and undermine our most cherished beliefs and memories of our beloved master.

28

The research report by Nathan and Fergus Wylie, in which they presented their preliminary account of the findings from Amira Kahn's manuscript, elicited considerable interest. Within weeks after the article was published, Nathan received a letter from an unidentified writer. The missive was written in pencil, entirely in block letters, on yellow lined paper. In place of a return address, the envelope bore a stick-on label depicting the Stars and Bars of the Confederacy; beneath the flag were the words "Proud to be from Dixie."

JEW BASTARD!

MAYBE YOU THINK YOU CAN GET AWAY WITH PUBLISHING YOUR STINKING CRAP

IN MAGAZINES THAT ONLY FANCY PROFES-
SORS AND OTHER PERVERTS READ AND
NOBODY WILL NOTICE. WELL FORGET
IT—WE KNOW ALL ABOUT YOU AND YOU
BETTER WATCH YOUR STEP FROM NOW
ON. YOUR BULLSHIT HAS BEEN POSTED ALL
OVER THE INTERNET SO THAT DESCENT
AND GOD-FEARING CHRISTIANS WILL
BE WARNED. SO LET ME ASK YOU THIS—
WHEN WILL YOU CHRISTKILLERS QUIT
WITH YOU'RE LIES AND INSULTS AGAINST
OUR LORD JESUS?
I HOPE YOU ROT IN HELL, AND I WOULD
SUGGEST, BY THE WAY, THAT YOU NEVER
COME ANYWHERE NEAR TUSCALOOSA.

Nathan at first felt a twinge of anxiety. After rereading the letter, he showed it to Zippora.

"Are you surprised?" she asked him. "I'm not."

Nathan finally filed the letter in a folder he labeled "Hate Mail," and over the following months, he added two similar letters.

But most of the responses he received were complimentary. Among the first was a note with congratulations from one of his former fellow graduate students at Johns Hopkins. And a month later, Nathan received a letter from Professor Norbert Yalow, of the University of Chicago's Oriental Institute:

Dear Dr. Tobin:

Your recent paper in the *International Journal of Biblical Research* is a wonderful contribution to Second Temple Era history. You are to be congratulated on this notable achievement, and we look forward to further reports of your findings.

On behalf of our Center for Middle Eastern Studies, I am pleased to extend to you an invitation to come to Chicago to present a seminar of your work for our faculty and graduate students.

Our departmental seminars are normally scheduled on Tuesday afternoons. The last Tuesday in October is still available, as well as the second and third weeks in November. If any of those dates will work out for you, that would be splendid.

Sincerely,

Norbert

He also received an e-mail from Professor Arnold McAllister, who had been his dissertation advisor in graduate school:

Dear Nathan,

I saw your paper in the *IJBR*. That's a terrific find and very nice work. You asked me to keep some feelers out for possible faculty positions, and I've got to tell you I haven't yet come across very much. There is a newly established professorship in Hebrew language and literature that they're recruiting for in Lawrence, Kansas. I don't know anything more, but if you're interested, I'm sure the University of Kansas will have information. Also—it's still a secret—one of our assistant profs will probably be leaving. He's close to accepting a position at Columbia; if he does, that will create an opening in this dept. I'll keep you posted.

Warm regards,

Arnold

Nathan's report also attracted the attention of a staff member of the research department of the Vatican Library. After reviewing it, the man passed the article on to the director of his department. The director read and then reread the report, and finally underlined several of its sections with a red pencil. Afterward, he wrote out two pages of notes that he attached to the report with a paper clip before placing it in a file folder.

Over the summer, Nathan had labored tirelessly to complete a first draft of his translation of Amira Kahn's manuscript, and that was finally behind him. Zippora had also been hard at work on her own research and on the completion of two major research reports she was preparing to submit for publication. Nathan and Zippora had resumed lunching together from time to time; however, their relationship continued to be cool and mainly professional.

Early that September, Zippora turned thirty.

"Let's go into the city for a day to celebrate your birthday," Nathan offered, partly in the hope that doing that might help rekindle their former relationship. "We could take in a matinee, and then have dinner." He was pleased when Zippora accepted his invitation. "You like musicals, don't you?" Nathan asked, as he perused the theater listings in the *Times*. "Well, there's *Phantom of the Opera*, and *Chicago* is still playing. Oh, and also they're doing *Fiddler on the Roof*."

At the last of those, Zippora wrinkled her nose in an exaggerated frown. "Either of the other two would be nice," she said. "Is there anything that especially appeals to you?"

"Well, I like Shakespeare. There's a production of *The Merchant of Venice* at the Globe. And the Gielgud Theatre is doing *Richard III*."

"I'm not really in the mood for the *Merchant of Venice*," Zippora said, "but nasty old King Richard might be interesting."

That Saturday, they boarded the train to London, to connect with the Underground that would take them to the West End theater district.

"You must be happy to be done with your translation," Zippora said, as their train pulled away from the Cambridge station.

"Well, yes, of course," Nathan said, "but there's still lots more to do. Now I'll need to work on a full journal article, with a detailed description of the manuscript's text. And I've got to give some serious attention to looking into available faculty positions for next year."

"I've begun doing a bit of that," Zippora said, "and just yesterday I got a very nice letter. An invitation to come to Ann Arbor to interview for a faculty appointment at the University of Michigan."

"Michigan?" Nathan said. "I always assumed you would be returning to Jerusalem next year. How come you're looking in the U.S.?"

"Well, I could go back to Israel. But as long as I have the opportunity, I thought I might see what else is available."

"Zippora, that comes as quite a surprise."

The century-old Gielgud Theater was scarcely half filled that afternoon, but the synergy between an exceptionally attentive audience and an inspired cast resulted in a fine and thoroughly impassioned performance. With the final "amen," the appreciative theatergoers gave the players an enthusiastic and extended ovation.

"That was really a bloody business," Nathan said as they left the theater.

"Yes," Zippora replied, "but isn't Richard a splendid villain? I think he's one of Shakespeare's most fascinating characters. Of course you have to remember that in his day, Richard was actually rather well regarded. Thomas More and Shakespeare took great pains to portray him as a despicable character, and they probably overdid it."

The two of them strolled through the theater district and selected a small trattoria near Piccadilly Circus. The restaurant was an inviting place with an oversized charcoal hearth for baking pizza. Mandolin music played quietly in the background. It was early for dinner, and most of the tables were still unoccupied.

"Could we have champagne?" Nathan asked the waiter.

"We have a nice Asti Spumante," the man replied. "I'm sure you'll like it." Moments later, he returned with the bubbly wine.

"Zippora," Nathan said, "here's to your birthday, and I hope it's a really happy one." And with that, he raised his wine glass, touched it against hers, and they both sipped the sweet-tasting Asti. "And," he added, "here's your gift to commemorate this occasion." He presented her with a small box, wrapped in foil paper and topped with a lavender bow. His present, which he had selected after examining the offerings of three different jewelers, was a rose gold bracelet, fashioned in a simple but elegant arabesque nouveau design with graceful, swirling lines that merged into a scroll-like pattern.

"It's beautiful," Zippora said. After attaching the bracelet's clasp on her wrist, she squeezed Nathan's hand and gave him an unmistakably affectionate kiss.

On the train ride back to Cambridge, Zippora snuggled closely to Nathan with her head against his shoulder, to his considerable satisfaction. And when he reached over and held her hand in his, she smiled contentedly.

Nathan waited impatiently for Monday to arrive so he could find out more about Zippora's intentions about a trip to the United States.

"So are you planning to visit Ann Arbor?" he finally asked her.

"They invited me for interviews and to present a research seminar," she said. "They want me to be there sometime in the next two or three months. They said they would try to be flexible. I haven't replied yet because there are still some other places I'd like to hear from. But I really can't wait too much longer."

"Well," Nathan said, "I'll be at the University of Chicago in late October or early November. If the dates work out, we might end up going just about the same time. Would you be interested in a traveling companion?"

"That would be lovely," Zippora said.

After several e-mail exchanges, the itinerary they arranged brought Zippora to Ann Arbor on November 12, with Nathan scheduled to speak at the University of Chicago the following Tuesday. The two of them then began preparations for the seminars they would be giving.

For the next weekend, Zippora invited Nathan for dinner at a cozy bistro, not far from the campus.

"Zippora," Nathan asked her, as he was spreading butter on a piece of thick-crusted French bread in the restaurant, "you told me that you were inquiring about faculty positions at some other universities. Which ones are they?"

"Well, one is Penn State," she replied. "They have a position in their Judaic Studies program that includes a faculty appointment in history. It's a similar arrangement to the one in Ann Arbor. The other, at UC Berkeley, is a position in medieval Jewish culture as well as history, exactly what I'm most interested in."

"Those all sound terrific," Nathan said. "My efforts have so far come up empty. There are some juicy rumors that could turn into something, but as of now, there's nothing that's all that attractive."

The evening was pleasantly warm, and as they walked slowly back toward the campus, Nathan took Zippora's hand in his.

"Nathan," she said, "I have my toothbrush in my purse."

"Your toothbrush?" he asked uncomprehendingly.

"Yes," she replied, "just in case you had any thought about having an overnight guest."

"Oh, I see," he replied, "you figure that's all you'll need for the night?" He smiled, and then he turned to face her, took both her hands in his, drew her close to him, and kissed her.

"Oh my God," he said, in a moment of sudden recollection, "the apartment's a terrible mess."

"Oh," Zippora teased, "in that case, maybe we should just forget it. Or, if you'd rather, I could wait in your living room while you tidy up."

"I promise you I'll have the place shipshape in no time at all," he replied.

That night, Nathan and Zippora resumed the intimacy they had enjoyed earlier that year. During the months they had been apart, while still sharing their small office, Nathan had come to recognize how precious Zippora was to him, and how terribly he had abused her affection and devotion. *If only she would give me another chance*, he had often thought, *I would show her the respect and the admiration she deserves*. Now that they were again together, he would have his chance to make good on that promise.

On a cool, overcast afternoon in early November, Nathan and Zippora flew out of Heathrow on their way to New York. From there, they boarded a connecting flight to the Detroit Metro Airport, only a short drive away from the University of Michigan campus.

"Someone from the Center for Judaic Studies will be coming to meet me in the baggage claim area and take me to the hotel," Zippora said.

"Well," he replied, "I'll take the airport bus to the hotel and you can call my room there once you're done for the evening."

"I'm only scheduled for one meeting tonight—dinner with the chairman of the history department," she said. "Tomorrow's the big day: breakfast with the director of Judaic Studies, then a tour, then my seminar at eleven, then lunch with some faculty, and finally dinner with the search committee."

"I brought along plenty of work to keep me busy while you're doing all that," Nathan said, "but don't be surprised if you see me in the conference room when you present your seminar tomorrow."

They arrived at the Detroit airport according to plan, and took their separate routes to the hotel where they were staying. After checking in, Nathan made his way down the street to a small Greek restaurant, a place where he was confident Zippora and her host would not be coming for dinner. Then he returned to his room to await her call.

"How was your meeting?" he asked when she telephoned him.

"It was lovely. The chairman is a woman, and she's really very nice. But I'm not sure I made a very good impression on her. I started to get drowsy during dinner from my jet lag. I hope she didn't notice. Anyway, my room is on the same floor as yours, and if you want to get here before I fall asleep, you'd better hurry."

Nathan arrived in Zippora's room minutes later, and as tired as they both were from their trip, they both were happy to continue the celebration of their recently reestablished intimacy.

The following morning, as Zippora set out for her interviews, Nathan retreated to the university's library. Then, well before eleven o'clock, he found his way to the seminar room where Zippora would be speaking, installing himself in a corner, in the last row of seats. Soon the room filled with faculty members, graduate students, and others, including two young women wearing Muslim headscarves. Finally, Zippora entered the room. A tall, bearded man wearing an embroidered *kippah* accompanied her. Moments later, the man rose, identified himself as the director of the Judaic Studies Program, and began his introduction.

"I am very pleased to welcome Dr. Zippora Bassat, who has most recently been working in England, at the University Library at Cambridge. She will present her research on the collection of documents from the famous Ben Ezra *genizah* in Egypt. Her talk is entitled 'Muslim-Jewish Relations in Medieval Cairo.'"

Zippora wore a navy blue suit and a white blouse with a frilly collar that she had bought specially for the occasion. Nathan was taken by her eloquence and composure, and how successfully she engaged her audience. He also came to appreciate how Zippora's beautiful, British-accented diction gave an air of authority to everything she said.

"During the medieval period," Zippora began, "Jews almost everywhere led a perilous existence. Both in Christian countries and in those under Muslim domination, Jewish people were subjected to discrimination, deprivation, humiliation, and to murderous pogroms. However, the animus and form of the anti-Jewish movements in the two cultures differed in very significant ways.

"In Christian Europe, particularly in the years following the crusades, theologically driven hatred led to systematic robbery and assaults against Jews, relentless persecution, and expulsion from individual towns, and eventually from entire countries. Wholesale slaughter of entire Jewish communities took place with tragic frequency. European Jews were not permitted to own land or to work in most occupations. They were forced to endure the most degrading segregation, and their lives were forever in jeopardy from the violent and unremitting hostility of their Christian neighbors.

"Whereas accusations of deicide animated much of the Christian hatred against Jews in Europe, Islam had no such scriptural basis for discrimination. Indeed, the Qur'an defines Jews, and also Christians, as being "people of the Book," a designation that accorded them special status as *dhimmis*—infidels, to be sure, but protected people who were allowed to live among Muslims and to practice their own religion, albeit with certain limitations. When there were Muslim excesses, such as the Almohad persecutions in Spain that in some instances led to massacres of Jews, it bears emphasis that Christians and other infidels generally were afforded quite equal treatment; 'Convert to Islam or die' was the choice they all were given.

"The primary focus of my research is on the social relations that existed between Muslims and Jews in medieval Cairo. And, as I shall emphasize, the wealth of information available from the extensive *genizah* document collection provides us a richly detailed portrait of life in that community.

"The picture that emerges is that of a vibrant and remarkably progressive society in which the Jewish and Muslim communities maintained their own distinct religious and communal institutions, but also one in which numerous interpersonal and business ties existed between the two groups.

"Many of the *genizah* documents, and I'll be showing you some of them, attest to thriving commercial relationships between Muslims and Jews. We know that Muslims provided capital for Jewish business ventures and vice versa. One eleventh-century letter describes a jointly run enterprise in which the Jewish partner attended to their business on Fridays and the Muslim one on Saturdays, allowing each of them to observe his own Sabbath.

"There are well-documented examples of Muslims visiting sick Jewish neighbors, and of Jewish physicians, the great Maimonides and his son Abraham among them, providing care and medical consultation to their Muslim neighbors.

"Here is a letter," she said, projecting an image of a yellowed page covered with Arabic writing, "from a Jew named Ezra ben Mordechai, who extends his good wishes to his friend Hasan ibn Mohammed on the occasion of Hasan's recent marriage. Other documents make it clear that Muslims and Jews sometimes shared meals in each other's homes.

"And perhaps most interesting of all are written accounts that speak of Muslims who participated in Jewish religious observances. The fragment of a letter, shown here, tells of a group of Muslims who had attended a reading of an Esther scroll on the Jewish festival of Purim. Another such interfaith observance involved groups of Jews and Muslims who journeyed together to pray at the tomb of the prophet Ezekiel."

Zippora then projected images of a series of *genizah* documents that illustrated other examples of community life in the Middle Ages. Finally, she provided an overview, concluding that in spite of the undeniable religious friction that existed between its religious communities, medieval Cairo was a remarkably open and tolerant society in which many Jews and Muslims lived and worked in a mutually supportive way.

After completing the lecture, Zippora responded to questions and comments from her audience. A few minutes into the discussion, a graduate student, a man in his late twenties whose English was noticeably accented, posed a question to Zippora: "Don't you think there's an obvious conclusion from what you told us? Haven't you shown very clearly that in Muslim countries, Jews can expect to receive kind and compassionate treatment?"

"In the twelfth century, in Cairo, they often did, though certainly not always," Zippora replied. "But in the present era, that obviously is not the case."

"Oh, so whose fault is that?" the young man demanded, with a hint of anger in his voice. "In recent years, Jews were welcomed and were treated very well in Muslim countries. But when the Zionist interlopers arrived in the Middle East, they destroyed the peace and tranquility of the entire region. They drove millions of Palestinians out of their homes, and since then, the whole area has been in turmoil."

"I would have to answer that your statements are only partially correct," Zippora replied, "and also, what you've said greatly oversimplifies a very complex situation."

"That's bullshit," the man shouted. "What's needed now is to get rid of the Zionist enemy—every man, woman, and child, and then to—"

At that point, Zippora, speaking firmly and loudly, directly into the microphone she held in her hand, overpowered the heckler. "You've made your point, and if you wish to discuss it further with me, I'll be available here afterward." Zippora then immediately took a question from another person in the audience, whereupon the irate graduate student returned to his seat.

It was nearly nine o'clock that night when Zippora finished her last meeting.

"That was a splendid lecture you gave," Nathan commented after stopping by her room. "And you handled that SOB in the audience very adroitly. I'll tell you this—if I were in charge here, I would have offered you a position on the spot."

Nathan and Zippora left for the airport the following morning. Their original intention had been to travel together to Chicago, where Nathan would be giving his seminar. But those plans had needed to be changed because in the meantime, Zippora had received another invitation, to interview at the University of California in Berkeley. So Nathan set off for Chicago and Zippora for San Francisco. They would reconnect in New York before returning to London.

The evening prior to his seminar, Nathan met for dinner with his host, Professor Norbert Yalow. Harold Auerbach, a distinguished scholar in Assyriology and chairman of the University of Chicago's Department of Near Eastern Languages, joined them. In the course of their conversation, a statement by Professor Auerbach particularly attracted Nathan's attention.

"You may be interested to know," he said, "that we will very likely have a new faculty position open in our department. I believe that your specialty, medieval Hebrew literature, might be a particularly good fit for our program. We expect to begin recruitment in the next few months."

It was still dark outside when Nathan awoke the following morning. A pot of coffee provided all he wanted for breakfast, and with a mug in hand, he went over his talk one final time. He was exhilarated to have this opportunity to present his work to the faculty at his alma mater, and he waited impatiently until it was time for him to leave for the lecture hall. His acute realization that his presentation would be attended by important members of the faculty, including members of the selection committee who would eventually be reviewing his application for a faculty appointment there, added a tinge of anxiety to his excitement.

He finally set out on the short walk up University Avenue to the Oriental Institute. A stiff north wind propelled him forward along the familiar, tree-lined campus street, bringing back pleasant memories of his undergraduate days. And the prospect that he might well be moving back to that great university, this time as a member of its faculty, invigorated him all the more.

The announcement of Nathan's lecture had generated considerable interest on the University of Chicago campus, so much so that his presentation had been moved to the Oriental Institute's auditorium from the smaller room where seminars were usually held. From the number of people who appeared there that morning, the decision proved to be a sound one. Nathan took note that among his sizeable audience were several clergymen.

"I am happy to welcome our speaker today," Professor Yalow began. "Dr. Nathan Tobin is a U of C alumnus. He completed his doctoral study at Johns Hopkins, and he is currently a visiting associate of the Cambridge University Library. Dr. Tobin will be presenting his work on a recently discovered first-century papyrus. His lecture is entitled 'The Alexandria Letter: A New Window into Early Events in the Foundation of Christianity.'"

Nathan began his talk by recounting how he had gotten access to the manuscript. Then he presented the results of the carbon dating analyses that established the age of the papyrus, as well as the various techniques he and his associates had applied to visualize its text. For the remainder of the hour, he discussed the content of the letter, emphasizing those parts that appeared to provide new insights into historical events of the period. Afterward, Nathan responded to questions from his audience.

"When do you think the letter was written?" a graduate student asked.

"From the events described in the text," Nathan replied, "it would appear to date from the time shortly before the great Jewish revolt—the uprising that ultimately led to the destruction of the Temple in Jerusalem by the Romans. And that, of course, would be just about the time when St. Paul presumably was writing his epistles."

"You said that the letter was written by a man named Todah, who describes himself as a disciple of Jesus," another questioner asked. "Are you suggesting that he was one of the twelve Apostles?"

"At times, I've wondered if he might have been the one who eventually came to be known as Thomas, the 'doubting' apostle," Nathan replied. "However, another Thomas, Dr. Thomas Gans, my colleague at the Cambridge Library, suggested something else that could possibly shed light on who Todah was. Dr. Gans showed me a rather obscure passage from the Talmud, from the section called 'Sanhedrin.' Let me read you its first line: 'Yeshu had five disciples—Mattai, Nakkai, Netzer, Buni, and Todah.' The Talmud, of course, was written hundreds of years after the time of Jesus, and I've been told that many questions have been raised about that passage and about what it means. For one, who the name 'Yeshu' refers to is not at all certain, as that was actually a rather common name. But I do think it's interesting that this passage makes mention of a disciple named Todah."

"Was Todah a Christian?" a student asked.

"From how he describes himself in the letter, Todah would more properly be described as a Jewish-Christian, one of the so-called Ebionites. They were the ones who made up the Jerusalem Church, which at first was composed primarily of the surviving disciples of Jesus. They were pious Jews who followed the laws of the Torah, but at the same time they believed in the resurrection of Jesus. From their description in the Acts of the Apostles of the New Testament, and also the writings of later Church fathers, Origen, Tertullian, Eusebius, and others, it seems clear that they strongly rejected Paul and his teachings. In fact, they seem to have considered Paul to be a scoundrel and an impostor. Anyhow, when Pauline Christianity eventually became dominant, the Ebionites were denounced as heretics and they were soon marginalized out of existence."

"You've said that Jesus' disciples considered Paul to be a villain, but doesn't Acts of the Apostles indicate that Paul and the disciples eventually came to an amicable understanding?" the same student asked.

"It does suggest that all right," Nathan replied, "but bear in mind that Luke, the putative author of Acts, was closely associated with Paul, and he presumably would have wanted to make it look as if they all were on good terms, even if they weren't."

A graduate student raised his hand.

"Did you tell us that his disciples regarded Jesus as being a Pharisee?" he asked.

"Yes, that was stated repeatedly in the letter," Nathan replied, smiling as several people in the audience frowned noticeably.

"How can that be?" the young man asked. "The Gospels make it very clear that Jesus hated the Pharisees. And we also know that the Pharisees were always plotting to kill him."

"Okay, let me start with your last point," Nathan said. "Why would the Pharisees, Jesus' fellow Jews, have wanted to kill him? Because he supposedly violated the Sabbath by healing the sick, or because he and his disciples didn't wash their hands before eating? That would seem awfully unlikely. Remember, the Gospels were written late in the first century, probably well after the destruction of the Temple. The Gospel writers were undoubtedly anxious to avoid the wrath of the Romans, and they made every effort to distance themselves from the Jews of Judea, who at that time were in open rebellion against Rome. So it was politically to their advantage to portray the Jews, including the Pharisees for whom Jesus held such great respect, as his scorned enemies. But then they went a lot further, casting Jesus' Jewish brethren as being the most vile and despicable of characters.

"There's no obvious explanation for why they went so far overboard in demonizing the Jews, not only in the Gospels but through much of the New Testament, but I suspect that Paul may have had a large role in that. Even the earliest of Paul's letters conveyed an intense anti-Jewish bias. In fact it was he, in 1 Thessalonians, who first accused the Jews of killing Jesus. And Paul's writings undoubtedly had a huge influence on the other New Testament writers who followed him.

"Now, about the Pharisees, the writer Josephus, who lived in the first century, described them as the dominant religious leaders of their day, viewed by most of the Jews with the greatest of respect and admiration. So what else can we say about them? They were pious and deeply devoted to the laws of the Torah; they were exceptionally knowledgeable about the scriptures; they were highly regarded religious teachers; and they were opposed to interpreting the laws in a rigid, uncompassionate way. In fact, the statement attributed to Jesus in the Gospel of Mark, 'The Sabbath was made for man, not the other way around,' was actually an old Pharisee saying. So far, Jesus looks an awful lot like a Pharisee, right?

"The Pharisees as a group did hold to certain beliefs that distinguished them, particularly from the Sadducees. They were fervent believers in the coming of the Messiah and in the idea that when God's kingdom is established, the dead would be resurrected from their graves. All of that fits perfectly with what is written about Jesus, and also, I would add, about John the Baptist, about the Zealots, and for that matter, about the disciples of Jesus who formed the Jerusalem Church—they all were Pharisees. Finally, I would point out that a considerable body of recent scholarly writing now strongly supports the idea that Jesus was indeed a Pharisee."

Then a man in the front row asked, "What about the Temple of Attis in the city of Tarsus that the letter describes? Are there other historical records that corroborate that?"

"There's nothing I'm aware of," Nathan replied. "However, there is a fascinating archaeological finding, a figurine that's in the Louvre Museum in Paris. The object clearly depicts the mystery god Attis. It was discovered in Tarsus, and they've dated it to the first or second century BCE."

"We have time for only one more question," Professor Yalow announced.

A graduate student, a young woman, rose from her chair. She hesitated before asking her question, and then she spoke slowly and deliberately, and so softly as to be barely audible.

"If what you have told us is true," she said, her voice tremulous, and with tears flowing down her cheeks, "it invalidates some of the most basic principles of Christianity. Then who could possibly believe the teachings of the Church? The effect of this would be to undermine and utterly destroy the Christian religion. Is that what you want?"

"Do you know what the likelihood is of that happening? Just about zero," Nathan replied. "Let's look at some relatively recent events that at first seemed to pose serious threats to Christian doctrine. One of those was the discovery of the Dead Sea scrolls, during the 1940s and '50s. Some of the scholars who studied those texts came to the conclusion that the Gospel stories had been directly based on preexisting Jewish sectarian traditions, and therefore, could not have been original. They went on to make confident predictions that their observations would shake the very foundations of Christianity, but of course nothing of the sort ever happened.

"And also, earlier in the twentieth century, after Albert Schweitzer and others began their analyses of the 'historical Jesus,' the very same fears were expressed. There were many then who believed that the historical and archaeological discoveries that were being made would contradict and therefore invalidate the Gospels.

"But even before all of that, the philosopher and theologian Kierkegaard put the whole issue into perspective when he asked, 'How can something of an historical nature be decisive for an eternal happiness?' And finally the Pope, I believe it was Pius XI, brought the matter to closure with his declaration that the Christ of faith is far more important than the Jesus of history.

"So, by any reasonable measure, the credibility of modern Christianity will be at no risk from what's in this letter. The manuscript's narrative certainly does lend support to the notion that religious principles and scripture inevitably evolve, often strikingly, as a new religion matures and develops. So, no one should be surprised when the actual events at the foundation of a religion differ significantly from what eventually becomes codified in the scriptural writings of that religion. Christianity would be no exception, and we do need to keep in mind that the New Testament is a religious text and not a historical record. And, of course, there's compelling evidence that a great deal of editing and reshaping of its text took place as early Christianity pulled away from Judaism and evolved into a separate religion."

After the question and answer period ended, Professor Yalow invited everyone to a reception in an adjoining room. There, amidst coffee and hors d'oeuvres, Nathan was happy to accept congratulations from well-wishers and to respond to additional questions. A half -hour later, the hors d'oeuvres having all been consumed, virtually everyone had drifted away. It was then that a tall, elderly man with pure white hair, a priest in a black suit and Roman collar, extended his hand to Nathan and presented his card: "Monsignor Carlo Delvecchio," it said, "Director of the Office of Research of the Vatican Library."

"That's a most interesting manuscript you have. I'd like to talk with you more about it. May I take you to lunch?"

"That won't work," Nathan replied. "I'm scheduled for lunch with some of the people from the Oriental Institute. But we could meet afterward. I'm leaving tomorrow on an early flight."

"Then why don't we have dinner together?" the priest asked. "If you like French cuisine, there's a place nearby that I rather like. It may be the only good restaurant in all of Hyde Park."

Nathan accepted the invitation.

"You're no doubt aware," Delvecchio said as they waited for their entrées to be served, "that over the years a good many documents such as yours have come to light. Many of them were condemned and rejected by the Church as heresy, and the document you described this morning could have fallen into that category. Of course, none of us likes to hear about writings that contradict the fundamental basis of our faith, but nowadays the Church fathers really don't bother with any of that. My own interest in your discovery, assuming it's genuine, is purely for its potential historical value."

"The data from the carbon dating analyses were very solid," Nathan replied, "and several features of the writing style also point to a first-century origin. So I think it's unlikely to be a fake."

"If you wouldn't mind," Delvecchio said as they were having coffee toward the end of their meal, "I'd like to visit you in Cambridge and have a look at your manuscript."

"Oh," Nathan said, "I thought I mentioned it in my talk—I no longer have the manuscript, only the digitized pages of the text. The original document belongs to an Egyptian woman, Mrs. Amira Kahn, who lives in Cairo. I've already sent it back to her."

"Do you think she would be willing to let us do some additional study of the manuscript?" he asked.

"I don't know, but I would certainly be willing to ask Mrs. Kahn."

The following day, Nathan flew to New York, from where he and Zippora left together to return to Cambridge.

Later that week, Nathan telephoned Amira Kahn in Cairo. He recounted his trip to Chicago, and he told her about the considerable interest in her manuscript. He also relayed the request from Monsignor Delvecchio to do his own study of the document.

"Do you know this man?" she asked. "Is he a reputable scholar?"

"He's the Director of Research of the Vatican Library, at least that's what he told me, but frankly he's not someone I'd heard of before."

"If you learn anything further, do let me know, but just now, I'm not inclined to give the manuscript to anyone else," Amira concluded.

Afterward, as he had promised, Nathan placed a call to Monsignor Delvecchio and informed the priest of Amira Kahn's decision.

29

In December, with the Michaelmas term at Cambridge coming to an end, Nathan and Zippora joined in the annual exodus from the university. They rode the Chunnel train from London to Paris, to take their first vacation together.

For the week, they rented a cozy apartment near the Place des Abbesses in Montmartre. In spite of the chilly weather, they spent much of their time strolling along the elegant boulevards and parks of the city. They also took long, leisurely tours through the Louvre, the Pompidou Center, and the magnificently restored seventeenth-century palace that housed the Museum of Jewish Art and History. And just as much, they enjoyed exploring the shops and sampling the cafés in their own neighborhood.

They slept until ten each morning, and they ended most evenings in extended conversations over wine or cappuccino in one of

Montmartre's many bistros. It was a carefree time for them, and their sole objective was to enjoy each other's company in that most romantic of places.

"Nathan," Zippora said to him one evening as they were sipping wine together, "could we talk about our relationship?"

"I'd like that," he replied, cautiously.

"Then tell me first," she asked, reaching across the table and taking his hands in hers, "how do you really feel about me?"

"Well," he began, choosing his words carefully, "I admire a lot of things about you—your intellect, your kindness, your warmth—and I think you're funny."

"Funny?" she said, while displaying an exaggerated frown.

"Witty, charming, lively, wonderful sense of humor, that's what I meant. And there's something else. You are without a doubt the most beautiful—the most elegant woman I have ever known."

Zippora smiled happily. "Do you love me, Nathan?" she whispered to him, squeezing both of his hands and drawing close to him.

Nathan had given considerable thought to that very question, and when Zippora asked it, he had no need to search for an answer.

"I love you more than I can find words to tell you," he said, with his eyes fixed on hers, "and I can't begin to tell you how happy I am that we're together again."

The expression on Zippora's face left him no doubt that this was what she had hoped to hear. But later that evening, the depth of Nathan's love and commitment to her were tested in a far more direct fashion, when they discovered that Nathan's condom had ripped apart.

"I wasn't planning on motherhood just yet," Zippora said, staring blankly. Nathan said nothing.

"There's nothing to do just now," she finally said. "My monthly visitor is due shortly, so we'll just have to wait and see."

The following week, in Cambridge, Zippora reported back to him, "I'm happy to tell you that there's nothing we need to worry about."

That news was a relief to both of them, but the incident provoked Nathan to wonder if Zippora was the woman he wanted to be the mother of his children. It was a question that continued to occupy his thoughts.

The months that followed were deeply satisfying for both of them. Zippora soon moved back to Nathan's apartment, and he spared no effort to give voice to his affection for her.

"I love you," he told her whenever the opportunity arose. He left her little *billets-doux,* in which he expressed his affection. They fell asleep each night in each other's arms, and every morning he embraced her tenderly before thanking her for bringing him so much happiness.

And for the first time, Nathan also began to assume some of the domestic responsibilities of their shared apartment. Zippora seemed surprised, and also slightly amused, to witness Nathan's energetic attention to washing and drying dishes, setting the dinner table, and other household chores. He also volunteered to assist with the cooking, but Zippora politely declined that offer.

The two of them were constantly together, but on those occasions when they were apart, Zippora was always in Nathan's thoughts. And Zippora returned his love wholeheartedly and happily.

Throughout that winter and spring, the young scholars were exceptionally productive in their work. The stress and anxiety that had overshadowed their first year at Cambridge had largely dissipated, and they were able to pursue their research and their writing with a minimum of worry.

During February, Zippora received word that both of the manuscripts she had submitted had been accepted for publication, and she lost no time in passing that information on to the universities where her applications for a faculty appointment were under consideration.

Nathan was completing an extensive research report describing his findings from the Alexandria letter. A British publishing house had shown interest in producing a book of the complete set of digital images of the letter, which would include Nathan's translation of each page of the manuscript. But Nathan needed to interrupt both of those projects, to make time for two visits to the United States.

The first of them, in late March, brought him to Johns Hopkins University to interview for a faculty position in Hebrew Language and Literature. His stay in Baltimore, a homecoming to his alma mater, provided him an opportunity to reconnect with many of his former teachers and colleagues. But most important, the interviewers were all encouraging, and Nathan left there feeling comfortably optimistic about his chances of being offered a faculty appointment.

His other destination on that trip was the University of Kansas. Although he had sent an application for the available faculty position there, Nathan had never had much enthusiasm about the opportunity, and had considered withdrawing his application. His visit to Lawrence, however, gave him a much different perspective. He found each of the faculty members of the Department of Religious Studies who interviewed him to be an accomplished scholar, and he was genuinely impressed by their enthusiasm and intellectual rigor. But he also sensed that something was missing: it was the all-too-familiar attitude, so pervasive at the topflight institutions—the need for the members of the academic elite to keep up their guard and remain ever vigilant lest someone else's intellectual brilliance outshine their own. Nathan saw nothing of that at Kansas, and its absence was striking to him.

And in contrast to the other research-oriented universities he had visited, Nathan also came to appreciate that the faculty there were all deeply committed to teaching, and all of them appeared to find the interaction with their students extremely fulfilling.

Nathan's other trip, the following month, brought him back to the University of Chicago, for formal interviews for the newly created position in their Department of Near Eastern Languages. Again, he received a warm welcome, and he left convinced that he was a strong contender for the appointment. Afterward, he took a flight to Boston, to interview for a position at Brandeis University's Department of Near Eastern and Judaic Studies. The seminar he gave there attracted a sizeable audience, and Nathan also considered that visit to be a successful one.

Before returning to Cambridge, Nathan stopped off in Cleveland, for a visit with his parents and his sister, who had come home for the weekend from medical school. It was a relaxing interlude for Nathan, and it provided him his first opportunity in a long while to put aside all thoughts about his work.

Nathan spoke with Zippora every day by phone, and he sent her at least one e-mail as well. It was usually Nathan who initiated their telephone conversations, but early one morning, just after six o'clock, Zippora phoned him at his parents' home in Cleveland. His mother wakened him to take the call.

"Zippora," he asked, "is everything all right?"

"Oh yes," she replied, "wonderful."

"Well, it's still early in the morning here," he said.

"I know, I'm sorry if I woke you up. But it's already noon here, and I just couldn't wait any longer to tell you. The University of Michigan—I just heard from them. They're offering me a tenure-track appointment!"

"That's fantastic," he said. "And you certainly deserve it. I assume you plan to accept their offer?"

"I'm going to wait a few days so I don't seem too eager, but yes, I will."

"Okay, well we really have some big-time celebrating to do when I get back there. I'm so happy for you—and I miss you and I love you."

And celebrate they did.

Over the next month, Nathan completed his research report on the Alexandria letter, and, with a high measure of confidence, he sent it off to the editor of a prestigious scholarly journal. He then turned his full attention to reviewing and revising his translation of the manuscript, in preparation for submitting it to the British publisher, who had offered him a contract with a £10, 000 advance.

The following week, late one afternoon, Nathan received a telephone call from Thomas Gans.

"I'm upstairs in the library," he said. "There's something here you need to see. And I'm afraid you won't like it."

What he had to show Nathan was the June issue of the *International Journal of Biblical Research*, which had arrived in the mail only hours earlier. Gans had left the journal open on the library table, to the title page of a brief research report: "A Reexamination of the Alexandria Letter."

What? Nathan asked himself after glancing at the title, *is this some kind of joke?* But then he examined the report more closely. Its authors were listed as Luigi Solaro, Enrico Poncelli, and Carlo Delvecchio, all from the Vatican Library. Scanning through the article, Nathan quickly grasped its main point: the Alexandria manuscript, it claimed, had been subjected to an independent radiocarbon analysis, which showed it to date from the nineteenth century. The unstated but obvious conclusion was that the Alexandria letter was a modern forgery. The report portrayed all of Nathan's hard work as meaningless, and perhaps even fraudulent.

Nathan could feel his heart pounding, and he experienced a tightness in his chest that made it difficult for him to breathe.

"Carlo Delvecchio," he said out loud, "that priest I met in Chicago." He grabbed the journal and bounded out of the library. By the time he reached his office, his face was flushed, and beads of perspiration had formed on his forehead. He felt dizzy, and he grasped the edge of his desk to steady himself. Finally, he collapsed into his chair.

Nathan quickly located the business card that Monsignor Delvecchio had given him. In his haste to get through to the Vatican Library, he misdialed the number, obliging him to start over again.

"The monsignor?" a melodic, Italian-accented voice replied. "He is unfortunately not available. When will he return? I really do not know."

"Well then, can I speak with Luigi Solaro or Enrico Poncelli?" Nathan shot back, his voice tremulous with anger.

"*Attenda, prego,*" she replied.

"This is Enrico. I—" But Nathan immediately cut him off.

"I'm Nathan Tobin," he said. "I'm calling you about your paper on the Alexandria letter."

"Dr. Tobin," he replied, "I'm happy to hear from you."

"Yeah, I'll bet you are," Nathan fumed. "Now what's this all about? Obviously your manuscript is not the same one I worked on, but your report claims that it is."

"I'm quite sure it is the same," the man replied in a calm, measured voice. "We've done multispectral analyses, just as you did, and the images look quite the same as yours."

"And the radiocarbon dating?" Nathan nearly shouted into the telephone.

"That part was all handled by the monsignor," he said. "I do know that he sent the samples to a very reputable laboratory in Germany."

"Where is Delvecchio?" Nathan demanded.

"The monsignor left here several weeks ago. He's gone to a monastery for a period of spiritual renewal. He does that from time to time. Nobody here seems to know where he is or when he'll be returning. It could be a very long time before he's back."

Nathan's next call was to Amira Kahn in Cairo.

"Mrs. Kahn," he said, "The strangest thing—some people in the Vatican are claiming that they did an independent analysis of your manuscript. I assume there's no truth to that, but I wanted to check with you."

"Why yes," she said, "it was some months ago—January, I believe."

"You let them have the document?" he asked her in disbelief. "But I thought you had decided not to do that."

"Yes, that's right, but after I got your letter, I saw no reason not to let them see it. They were very professional. They arranged for insurance, they sent a courier to pick up the manuscript—a nice young man named Enrico Poncelli—and they handled all the paperwork."

"You say I sent you a letter?" Nathan asked her. "But I never sent a letter to you."

"Give me a moment to find it. All right, here it is. Well, it's written on Cambridge University letterhead, and it was mailed from England. In fact, the cancellation on the envelope is from the Cambridge post office."

"Read it, would you please?" he asked her.

"All right…it's dated December 10 of last year. 'Dear Mrs. Kahn,' etc., etc. 'I have gotten more information about Monsignor Delvecchio. Since I last talked with you, I learned from several reliable sources that the monsignor is a highly respected scholar and a man of unquestioned integrity. I would therefore have no reluctance entrusting the manuscript to him, and indeed it might be worthwhile to have independent confirmation of our findings.' So, when they telephoned a couple of weeks later, I told them it would be all right."

"Oh, my God," Nathan exclaimed. "Did they return the manuscript to you?"

"Of course," she replied, "a few weeks later, their courier brought it back, all very nicely."

"I don't understand what's going on," Nathan said, in a tense, tremulous voice, "but I never sent you any such letter."

"But...now...if you didn't send it, then who did?"

Nathan sat at his desk, repeating in his mind the bizarre events that had transpired that day. The tightness in his chest was nearly suffocating, and a throbbing headache added to his misery. Zippora was working late in the library, and by the time she returned to their office, it was nearly seven o'clock.

They stopped at the Lebanese restaurant near their apartment, and over dinner Nathan recounted for her all that had happened. Being with Zippora calmed him, and his headache soon subsided. But his overwhelming anxiety continued unabated.

"It all seems terribly sinister," Zippora commented, "especially the letter that was sent to Mrs. Kahn."

"I damn well want to have a look at that letter," Nathan said. "At least they returned the manuscript to Amira Kahn. If those people are out to destroy my reputation, I wonder why they sent the document back to her."

What little sleep Nathan got that night was fitful and punctuated with dreams from which he awoke trembling and drenched with sweat. In the morning, he placed a call to the director of the Radiocarbon Laboratory of the Deutsches Archäologisches Institut in Berlin.

"An article by Carlo Delvecchio from the Vatican claims that your laboratory did a radiocarbon analysis of a manuscript. I'd like to know if you can confirm that."

"Ah, yes, I remember Monsignor Delvecchio—he speaks excellent German. Wait just a moment, please, and I'll find our report of that analysis. Now then, we received five samples of paper, each weighing between three and six milligrams. We ran all of the samples, by accelerator mass spectroscopy, and the agreement was quite good—they all came out to be between 120 and 180 years old."

"Can you tell me anything more about the samples? What did they look like? What sort of paper were they?"

"There's nothing I can really say. We run whatever people send us. And as I'm sure you know, the samples are completely combusted in the course of the analyses."

So he could have substituted paper from any manuscript they wanted, Nathan thought to himself, *and nobody would have known the difference.*

That afternoon, Nathan made a call to Jerome Koblenz, editor of the *International Journal of Biblical Research.* "Couldn't you have let me know you were going to publish that paper on the Alexandria letter?" he asked. "Evidently you don't realize it, but their whole report is a goddamn pack of lies!"

"Look" the editor replied, "You say one thing and these people say something else. One of you is obviously wrong. Are we supposed to turn down a report from the Vatican Library just because you don't like it?"

"So what the hell can I do now?" Nathan asked. "That report completely screws us—we'll have zero credibility from now on."

"Oh, for God's sake," Koblenz replied, "look, just get somebody else to do a radiocarbon dating from the manuscript. And this time also make sure you get solid documentation that it's the same document as before. If it turns out you were right, terrific. Send us another report, and we'll be happy to publish it."

Nathan phoned Amira Kahn again. "If you would be willing to lend me a few pages of the manuscript, I can arrange to have the carbon dating repeated. I'll also need an affidavit from you affirming the authenticity of the manuscript. With that, I should be able to straighten this whole thing out. There's a flight to Cairo the day after tomorrow, and if it's okay, I'd like to come then."

"That will be just fine, and it'll be nice to see you again," Amira said.

During dinner that night, Nathan told Zippora, "I wish I could go there tonight. I can't sleep, I can't get any work done. This is driving me crazy."

30

One day, Jacob, the brother of Yehoshua and the leader of our group, spoke to us about a man who was soon expected to arrive in Jerusalem.

"His name is Saul," Jacob said. "He is a Greek, a Jew from the north, who has taken great pains to impress upon me that he is a Pharisee and highly learned in the sacred scriptures."

I confess that I paid little heed to any of that, but what Jacob said next immediately captured my attention.

"This man was in the employ of the High Priest for many years, working tirelessly to identify and arrest any whom the High Priest suspected of bringing about unrest and rebellion. Foremost of those under his surveillance were the Pharisees, as well as us Nazarenes. Needless to say, Saul provoked fear in the hearts of many of us. But then, surprisingly, he ended his connection with the High Priest and apparently became an adherent of our own movement, although without having a connection with any of us. He has been traveling about from place to place, speaking most energetically about Yehoshua and about his resurrection. But strangely, he has been carrying his message not to Jews but rather to gentiles, and he claims he has brought many of them to our cause."

Could this be the Saul I had come to know so well many years earlier? I asked myself. But if so, how could he have become so strong a proponent of Yehoshua, whom I was quite certain he had never met? And as for his boasting of being a Pharisee, from what I knew of how much Saul hated the Pharisees, that claim seemed completely out of character. Perhaps, I concluded, this could have been someone else who also happened to be named Saul.

We had gradually begun to win adherents to our movement, especially from among the Pharisees. It was they who always had been so sympathetic to Yehoshua and to the cause for which our master was ultimately put to death. And in time, we also established our own Nazarene synagogue in Jerusalem where we all met each Sabbath to read from the Torah and from the other Holy Scriptures. We spoke often of Johanan and Yehoshua, and of their message of repentance and atonement and the coming of God's kingdom.

Two days later, Jacob summoned the twelve of us to meet with him and with our visitor from the north. Upon first seeing this man, there was little from his appearance to suggest that this was the Saul I had known. He was strikingly corpulent and in place of the fine clothing I had always come to associate with Saul, this man wore the simple cloak typical of a poor person. But when I observed how he held his head at a slight angle and how the corners of his mouth were turned slightly downward in a subtle expression of disdain, all of that persuaded me that my earlier supposition may have been correct. Then, when he spoke, his voice left no doubt; this indeed was Saul, the Jewish convert from Tarsus.

"Brothers," he said, with what seemed to be a mien of both pride and condescension, "I bring you most excellent news. My mission to the gentiles has won us thousands of souls who have come to accept the word of God."

"Have these men been circumcised? Are they proper Jewish converts?" Simon, "the rock," asked him.

"No," Saul replied.

"Then are they God-fearers who at least have accepted the God of Israel?" Simon asked.

"Not that either," he replied. "It is the resurrection they have accepted."

"That cannot be permitted," Simon said, so distraught as to appear on the verge of tears. "They must consent to circumcision and accept the obligation to obey the laws of Moses if they are to be brought into our fellowship. They must be Jews. And I will remind you of the words of Yehoshua: 'Do not go among the gentiles.'"

"But is there not but one God, Lord of both Jews and gentiles?" Saul asked in a quiet voice, seeming to be slightly amused. Then he quoted words of the prophet Isaiah: "I will make you a light for all the nations, that my salvation may reach the ends of the earth."

After the completion of a lengthy discussion, our leader, Jacob, announced his decision: "We should not make it difficult for gentiles who are turning to God," he said. "But there are certain of the commandments they must be obliged to accept. Among them are the laws in the Torah that God gave to Noah and to the gentiles. They must abstain from food used in the worship of idols; they may not eat meat unless its blood has been removed; they must eschew fornication; and they must not shed the blood of their fellow men."

We all agreed that this was a wise and just ruling. Saul gave his solemn pledge that these directives would be followed. But from his suppressed smile, I suspected that his promise might not have been sincere. Then, Jacob raised another, more serious, concern.

"Word has come to us that you have been encouraging the Jews who live in gentile lands to turn away from Moses—that you tell them not to circumcise their sons, nor to live according to our laws. How do you answer to this?"

"Most certainly not!" Saul replied. "I am a pious Jew, as much so as any of you here, and I would never do such things as that."

"Then this is what we will require of you," Jacob said to him, "and if it is as you tell us, this should not be a burden to you. Tomorrow morning, come with us and bring your tefillin to our synagogue, where we will pray together and read from the Torah. Then, immerse yourself in the mikva, as *we will do, so that we will be pure before we enter the Temple. Four men will be there who are completing their vows as nazirim. Pay their expenses so that they can have their heads shaved. Then everyone will know there is no truth in these reports about you, and that you are living in obedience to the law."*

"I will be very happy to do all you ask of me," Saul replied, "and I tell you those are all things I would have done even had you not required them."

The following morning he appeared at our synagogue and carried out everything that Jacob had demanded of him.

While we were walking up to the Temple Mount, so that Saul could fulfill the final part of his obligation, I had the opportunity to speak with him. He of course remembered me from the time we had spent together many years earlier.

"I had not been aware that you were a disciple of the one you call Yehoshua," he said. "I would like very much to hear your account of the time you were with him. I am staying in Jerusalem at the home of a man named Barnabas. If you are able, come there tonight, and there will be time for you to tell me about Yehoshua and the others of his disciples."

I readily agreed to Saul's request. But when I arrived that night to meet with him, it became clear to me that he had no real interest in hearing anything I had to say. Rather, he appeared most anxious to relate the transformation that had taken place in his own life.

As I sat there in the dimly lighted room across the table from Saul, my thoughts returned to the young Greek who, many years before, had come to Jerusalem with the fiercest determination to become a disciple of the great Pharisee Hillel. Even then, he had made it known to me that his ambition was to become a leader of the Pharisee movement. I so well recalled how, filled with unquenchable energy and determined to achieve mastery of the Torah and the other Holy Scriptures, he had carefully planned his course to become a great religious authority. And I also well remembered his profound disappointment and dejection when his efforts ultimately failed and he was not accepted into Hillel's academy. It was then that Saul's undying hatred against the Pharisees had begun. And afterward, he had joined forces with the High Priest, the Pharisees' most committed enemy.

Although Saul and I had seldom crossed paths during the succeeding years, I continued to be well aware of the anger and resentment he carried with him in his pursuits as a henchman of the High Priest. And I was also able to sense the unfulfilled longing that remained with him, the deep hunger to become a respected and powerful religious authority.

The Saul who sat across from me that night in Jerusalem was no longer a young man; his fleshy, jowled face had lost its youthful color; his hair was thin; and his supple, muscular limbs had turned bulky and stout. But his agitated energy, the fire that burned in his eyes, and the excitement and passion in his voice—all of that remained as intense as it ever had been. The story he related to me that night was clearly intended to win me over to the new, astounding creation of his fertile mind.

"You may have heard," he said, "that I was for a long time in the employ of the High Priest. It was my responsibility to seek out and arrest those who were inclined to foment unrest against the Roman authorities. In more recent years, much of my effort was directed against the Pharisees, including the members of your movement, especially those who preached the coming of a new king in Israel. The High Priest, you surely know, regarded the dissemination of any such ideas as being treasonable.

"Then, one day, the High Priest sent me to the city of Damascus, in the Kingdom of Nabatea. He directed me to capture two people there, sympathizers of the Nazarenes, men who had fled from Jerusalem. Since the High Priest had no authority to order arrests to be made in that country, he instructed me to do my work with special care, quickly and without attracting attention.

"It was on my way to Damascus that it happened." Saul said, and as he spoke these words, I could see his eyes turn glassy. Then he paused and he seemed disconnected from the place where we were. After a few moments, he resumed his story.

"I suddenly experienced a blinding flash of light," he said, "and I fell to the ground and needed to cover my eyes. That was when I heard the voice: 'Saul, Saul, why do you persecute me?' 'Who are you, Lord?' I asked. 'I am Isous of Nazareth,' he said to me, 'risen from the dead.' 'What should I do, Lord?' I asked him. And there, and again on many other subsequent occasions, he explained what he wanted of me."

"Isous?" I asked Saul, much surprised.

"Yes," he answered, "the one you knew as Yehoshua." Later, he explained to me that his proper name is Isous Christos, "the second word, in Greek, being the same as your word 'Messiah,' but it denotes much more than that—it means that he is God!"

"You are saying that Yehoshua was resurrected as a Greek god?" I asked him. I was more puzzled than angry at first hearing these things, but as Saul went on with his bizarre tale, I became increasingly distressed. I could no longer remain seated, and I stood, grasping the back of my chair to control my growing indignation.

"The Lord Isous directed me to establish his church among the pagans," he continued, "and he appointed me his apostle to the gentiles."

"What does that mean?" I asked him, for never before had I heard of the words "church" or "apostle." Saul informed me that those too were Greek words.

"So you are telling me that Yehoshua spoke to you in Greek?" I asked him. By then I am certain that Saul could recognize the agitation reflected in my voice. "I doubt that Yehoshua knew three words of Greek," I said to him.

"With God, everything is possible" was his sanctimonious reply.

And then I asked him, "Why do you speak of Yehoshua as Lord? There is only one Lord," I said, "and that is God."

"When the Lord Isous was here on earth," Saul continued, "those of you who were his disciples failed completely to recognize whose presence you were privileged to witness. Now I will make it clear for you: Isous Christos is God's only begotten son—He is the Son of God! Christos descended to earth, first to spread the word of his truth, then to suffer crucifixion, so that his death on the cross would bring redemption to all mankind. You were in the very presence of God, and you misunderstood the meaning of his magnificent sacrifice."

"So you have made him into a Greek god," I repeated bitterly, barely able to control myself. "I can assure you," I said, "that Yehoshua would have regarded all of that as blasphemy—indeed idolatry. Our anointed kings, even our great Messiah David, were not gods. Indeed our Teacher Moses, the prophet among all of the prophets, was a man, not a god."

"Ah, at last you are beginning to understand!" Saul replied, his face brightening into a broad smile. "It is only the Father and the Son whom we call God. And moreover, with the crucifixion of Isou Christou, the old covenant and the Torah have been annulled. Hear me when I tell you this: it is those who believe in the Son who will be saved. The curse of the Law no longer burdens us, and atonement for our sins will be made only for those who are in Christou in his crucifixion and resurrection."

I could scarcely keep my wits about me at hearing such things, but I managed to focus my thoughts sufficiently to protest what Saul had said about the Torah. "That is altogether contrary to what our master taught us: Yehoshua held the Law to be our greatest possession, our most precious gift from God."

"Now that the Christos has risen," Saul answered, "that no longer holds true."

In utter confusion and bewilderment over all of this, I asked Saul one final question: "Who has given you the authority to say such things?" His answer surprised me all the more.

"What I am telling you was not given to me by man, nor was it something I was taught. I received it directly through revelation from Isou Christou. God, who had set me apart from birth and called me through His grace, chose to reveal His Son to me and through me. And in Isou, I am the resurrection and the life, and those who believe in the Son, even though they may die, shall live."

Saul spoke these last words with the greatest of emotion, tearful and with a tremulous voice.

Saul departed from Jerusalem the following morning, and it was nearly two years before I heard anything more about his whereabouts and his activities. The source of that information was Benjamin, an upstanding and trustworthy man who had become a member of our movement and our brotherhood. Benjamin was a merchant who traveled frequently to other lands along the Mediterranean to purchase textiles and other goods to be sold in Jerusalem. What we came to learn from him after he returned home from one of his voyages distressed and angered us more than anything we had previously heard about Saul and his intrigues among the gentiles.

31

By two o'clock that morning, the oppressive heat of the summer day had finally given way to the rejuvenating coolness of night. The activity and noise were gone, leaving the normally bustling street empty of both traffic and people.

Four men, all in dark clothing, disembarked silently from a large van into the alleyway behind the mansion. Their leader, slim, with touches of middle age in his beard, wearing thick, rimless eyeglasses, scaled the wall surrounding the property with remarkable agility, taking care to remain clear of the photoelectric sensing device that protected the rear entranceway. Within minutes, he had severed the telephone lines to the building. Then, employing a laptop computer and a miniaturized electronic detection instrument from his backpack, he made a rapid analysis of the surveillance and alarm installation of the house, and in short order succeeded in disengaging the system.

Once it was safe to open the service gate that led into the garden, the men divided among themselves flashlights, rope, duct tape, plastic bags, a handgun outfitted with a silencer, and numerous eight-liter cans of gasoline. One of them carefully removed the glass pane from a basement window, and moments later he appeared at the open rear doorway to the house.

Their first objective was the servants' quarters, located behind the mansion's spacious kitchen. They quickly identified the adjacent bedrooms where the housekeeper and the chef were both asleep. Three of the men succeeded in entering the housekeeper's room without awakening her. Two of them simultaneously grabbed hold of the woman, immobilizing her in her bed, while the third forced a pillow firmly against her face. She struggled to free herself, but her assailants easily overpowered her. Within minutes, as her oxygen level diminished to a critical level, she lost consciousness, and shortly after that, her heart stopped beating. She died without there having been any sound to disturb the silence of the house.

The chef, their next victim, had also remained asleep when the three intruders arrived at his bedside. As two of the men fastened their grip on the young man's arms and legs, the other slapped duct tape over his mouth while thrusting the barrel of a revolver against his chest. They pulled him to a standing position.

"How many people are here in the house?" The terrified man held up four of his fingers. "Four? Including you?" The chef nodded in affirmation. "If you're lying to me, you won't leave here alive." The chef shook his head to confirm that he was telling the truth. Having gotten the information they wanted from him, one of the intruders slipped a thin cord around his neck and tightened it into a strangle hold. The other attackers forced him to the floor. The chef, a fit, muscular man, at first nearly managed to free himself from their grip, but his assailants, all of them skilled assassins, restrained him. Minutes later, as asphyxiation diminished the flow of oxygen to his brain, he erupted into a convulsion, with violent shaking of his arms and legs. That at first alarmed the intruders, who were fearful that the resulting noise might awaken the others in the house. After five more minutes, the chef's skin and lips turned deeply blue and, finally, his heartbeat stopped. But as the three of them were dragging the body back to his bed, they were interrupted by a voice from behind them.

"All of you stop! I have a gun, and I'll shoot if you move. Now, face against the wall." The voice was that of an older man in overalls, the groundskeeper, who was standing in the doorway with a shotgun pointed toward them. They did as he ordered. Then, holding his rifle cradled in his arms, he reached for a telephone to call the police, only to discover that the line was dead. Seconds later, two muffled shots could be heard, and the groundskeeper slumped to the ground. He had been unaware that a fourth intruder remained behind him. The two shots to his head killed him instantly.

The intruders then proceeded up the stairway to the bedroom of the old woman who was the owner of the house. Nearly deaf without her hearing aid, she had not heard any of the commotion that had taken place on the first floor of her home. The men burst into her room, wakening her immediately.

"What do you want?" she asked them in a calm voice. "Is it money?" The answer she got was a pillow jammed into her face. After less than a minute of suffocation, she felt crushing chest pain, due to the sudden occlusion of a coronary artery, followed by cardiogenic shock and a stoppage of the flow of blood to her brain. Moments later, she too was dead.

The four men filed back to the ground floor of the mansion.

"Gather up those things," the group's leader told his accomplices, pointing to the cabinets and shelves filled with precious objects. "Fill those bags—we have to make it look like a robbery. We need to work quickly."

Minutes later, the men began spilling their gasoline cans in each of the rooms on the building's ground floor. A cell phone exchange with their driver informed them that the way was clear for their escape. They made their exit as they had come in, through the rear entrance of the mansion. The leader of the group was the last to leave the building, setting a detonation device that would ignite ten minutes later.

By the time their van had crossed the bridge leading away from Zamalek Island, the house was already ablaze.

Nathan, exhausted and suffering from a lack of sleep, had dozed off during his flight. He awoke as the Boeing jet was making its descent into Cairo. It was a few minutes past midnight when his plane arrived at the gate. With his carry-on bag in hand, he made his way quickly through the passport check, planning to go from there to find a taxi that would take him to Amira's home. But as he left the customs office and entered the main waiting area of the airport, he was surprised to see a familiar face. It was Amira Kahn's nephew.

"David," he said, "how nice to see you."

"My aunt told me you would be arriving tonight, so I came to pick you up."

"You really didn't need to do that, but it's certainly very kind of you. How have you been?"

David did not answer. Finally, he said, "My car's parked right outside. Let me help you with your bag and we'll get going."

They traveled for some while in silence. Then David Kahn, without taking his eyes off of the road, finally spoke. "Nathan," he said, "something terrible has happened."

Nathan felt the muscles in his arms and shoulders tense. "What is it?" he asked. But the young man said nothing. For the remainder of the half-hour trip, neither of them spoke another word.

As David's Mercedes approached Amira's house, Nathan could see that the area was barricaded by a police cordon. After parking alongside the road, the two of them proceeded on foot toward the house. Nathan recognized the pungent smell of burnt wood and smoke the moment he got out of the car.

The house, he soon saw, had been reduced to blackened smoldering rubble. The roof had caved in, and one wall had collapsed. Nathan, stunned, stared blankly at the disaster scene that lay before him.

"It apparently started early in the morning," David said, shaking his head slowly. "By the time the fire department got here, the place was engulfed in flames. They told me no one survived: Amira, her cook and her maid, and also Ahmed, her gardener—their bodies were all charred almost beyond recognition. According to the fire chief, the situation is highly suspicious. Apart from how suddenly it started, there's evidence that Ahmed had been shot, two bullet wounds in his head. Some of the others might also have been killed, but they're not yet sure about that. They also found several gasoline cans in the house. Everything was destroyed, including my uncle's priceless manuscript collection."

Nathan stood there for a long while, gazing blankly at the disaster that lay before him. Finally, he asked David, "Do they have any idea who was responsible for this?"

"They thought at first that the fire might have been set as a cover-up for a robbery. But then they found a good many valuable gold and silver ritual objects that were in plain sight—things that would have been easy to take. So they're not sure if that's a likely explanation. They seem confident it's arson, and murder, but that's all they can say. The fire chief told me there will be an investigation, but in Cairo you can never count on anything coming from that."

Nathan spent the night at David Kahn's home, and the following morning, still dazed and benumbed, he hurried back to the airport to arrange for an early return flight to England.

He was shaken by the tragedy, his unrelenting anxiety supplanted by feelings of melancholy and hopelessness. He had come to Egypt to secure the precious papyrus pages that would have redeemed his reputation as a credible scholar, and now he was leaving empty-handed. Moreover, his dear friend Amira Kahn was dead, and it seemed likely that she had been murdered.

Nathan's five-hour flight gave him ample opportunity to reflect on the disastrous chain of events that had enveloped him that week. At the end, the Alexandria manuscript had been destroyed, and with it the sinister letter that had so effectively deceived Amira Kahn. It seemed all too clear that Carlo Delvecchio had plotted an elaborate scheme to discredit the manuscript. But was he also willing to resort to arson and murder to cover his tracks?

32

Nathan sat at the small wooden table in Chaim Elstein's office. For some reason, a great many books had been removed from the shelves and had been stacked in tall piles on the director's desk. Because of that, the room seemed to be smaller and felt much more confined than before. The director himself appeared disheveled, his thick gray hair uncombed, his shirt partly unbuttoned, and his necktie askew. He sat across from Nathan with his arms folded, and for a long while he said nothing. Then he rose from his chair, and leaning forward, his outstretched arms planted on the table, he brought his face so close that Nathan could feel the warmth of Elstein's breath.

"What you've done," the director said, speaking slowly and deliberately, "is to bring disgrace on yourself and discredit to our research unit and to this great university." And with those last words, spoken with such intensity as to leave Nathan's face speckled with saliva, the director supported his weight on his right hand and jabbed Nathan forcibly in the chest with the extended finger of his left.

"No, no," Nathan cried out. "That's just not so. I didn't do anything wrong. Please let me explain—"

But the director cut him off, slamming his fist onto the top of the table. "I'm not interested in hearing any more of your explanations. I want you out of here, today. I don't ever want to see you again."

"That's not right—it's not fair," Nathan said, choked with tears.

"Nathan," Zippora said, shaking him awake, "you've been screaming in your sleep."

"I'm trapped in a full-time nightmare," Nathan said to Zippora later that morning. "It torments me every night, and when I wake up in the morning it's still there. I spent a whole year working day and night on that manuscript. Now those bastards have destroyed everything, and while they were at it, they wiped out my credibility, probably forever."

In the days and weeks that followed, Nathan accomplished little. Much of the time, he sat at his desk staring blankly at the wall in front of him. On one occasion, as she entered their office, Zippora noticed that Nathan's eyes were red and swollen, and when she looked at him, he turned his face away from her.

"It's a lousy situation, I realize," Zippora said, "but I've been wondering if it's really as awful as you think. Who is this priest Delvecchio anyway? He's not a recognized scholar, and his connection with the Vatican Library can't mean all that much either. Your work is from Cambridge, and that carries real prestige. I doubt anybody will pay all that much attention to Mr. Delvecchio."

Nathan was not convinced, but he gradually managed to return to his work, preparing the pages of the Alexandria letter manuscript for the London book publisher. And he waited, more anxiously than before, to receive word from the universities where he had interviewed for a faculty position.

He received his first reply from Johns Hopkins. After careful consideration of Nathan's impressive academic credentials, they informed him, in the end they elected to offer the position to one of the other candidates. The message he got a short while later from Brandeis University was virtually identical to the one from Hopkins. Then, in early August, a similarly phrased rejection letter came from the University of Chicago. In desperation, Nathan placed a call to the chairman of the Department of Religious Studies at the University of Kansas.

"For various administrative reasons—I won't bore you with the details," the chairman told him, "we're not going to be able to fill that position for another six months or maybe even a year. If you're still interested, I'll be happy to keep you apprised of where we go with it."

Nathan also received word from the journal where he had sent his research report on the Alexandria letter. From the written comments by the referees who had reviewed his manuscript, it was apparent that no significant concern had been raised about the soundness of the report. Nevertheless, the editor, for no stated reason, made the decision not to accept it for publication. Nathan's book project came to a similar pass; he was informed that the publisher had decided to withdraw its offer.

Nathan had arrived at a dead end. Now he had no prospect for an academic position, and the fruits of his two years of work were rotting away on the vine. Monsignor Delvecchio's sinister schemes had discredited his research, and along the way, destroyed any future he might have had in his chosen career. Nathan's depression now consumed him. He ate almost nothing, his sleep was increasingly fitful, and for the first time, thoughts of ending his life entered the jumble of ideas that filled his clouded mind. Zippora attempted to console him, but to little effect.

September marked the end of the two young scholars' fellowship appointments at Cambridge. Professor Elstein and his wife had a party at their home for Nathan and Zippora, and all of the staff of the Taylor-Schechter Research Unit were there to wish them farewell. As a parting gift, each was given a book. Nathan's was a volume of medieval Hebrew poetry.

They departed the next day for their destinations in the United States: Zippora to begin her new faculty position at the University of Michigan, and Nathan to Cleveland, where, for the time being, he would be staying with his family. But before going to Ann Arbor, Zippora had accepted an invitation from Nathan's parents to spend a few days with their family.

"Tell me some more about your mother and father," Zippora said, as their flight took off from Heathrow.

"My dad's still chairman of the political science department at Cleveland Community College," Nathan replied. "After more than twenty-five years there, he continues to be enthusiastic about his work, though frankly I don't know why. I would imagine that teaching the same old thing year after year would be a terrible bore."

"And your mother?"

"She's in charge of the Hebrew program at B'nai Jacob. It's a large, conservative synagogue in a nearby suburb."

"Are your family members of that congregation?" she asked.

"My mother would have liked that, because she came from a more observant family. But my father, who never had any religious inclinations, insisted that they join a reform temple. And that's what they did. My mother was always unhappy about the quality of religious education at Temple Isaiah, so she gave my sister and me her own course of personal tutoring. Judy—she's three years older than I—hated Hebrew, and my mother nearly gave up in frustration. She started with me when I was only four, and for some reason, I really took to it. By the time I was in first grade, when the other kids in my class were just learning how to read and write English, I was already handling Hebrew rather well. And that was what gave me my start in Hebrew language and literature."

The Tobin family residence, a 1950s-era split-level, was the product of a large development that had spawned row upon row of moderately priced but featureless three-bedroom redbrick homes. But what distinguished theirs from the neighboring dwellings on their quiet street was Ellen Tobin's garden. Masses of blue and white asters were in full display along the entire front of the house, forming a finely sculpted backdrop for a contrasting border of purple and bronze chrysanthemums. Nathan had always admired his mother's floriculture, and for his homecoming Ellen seemed pleased that her showiest fall perennials were at their peak.

Arthur Tobin had been reading and smoking his pipe most of that afternoon, and the mellow, musty aroma of his Turkish-blend tobacco permeated the entire house. When Nathan and Zippora's taxi pulled up, Ellen rushed from the kitchen to open the door. She embraced her son, and then extended a warm welcome to Zippora. "It's so wonderful to meet you," she said. "We've heard so much about you."

Arthur added his greeting, but when Zippora accepted Arthur's handshake, she remained momentarily speechless. "Why, you and Nathan are practically twins," she finally said.

"I am, shall we say, the more weathered version," he replied smiling, "but yes, nobody seems to doubt that the two of us are related."

"Dinner will be ready shortly," Ellen announced. I'm cooking a brisket—it's Nathan's favorite."

"Let me take your bags up to Judy's room. It's all set up for you," Arthur said to Zippora.

After dinner, Ellen brought out the family picture album, providing Zippora an opportunity to see snapshots from Nathan's childhood, including a number of family portraits that were taken at the time of his bar mitzvah.

That night was the first time in a long while that Nathan slept without Zippora, and still in the throes of his depression, he felt very much alone.

After their relaxing visit with the Tobin family, Nathan borrowed his mother's car, and he and Zippora drove to Ann Arbor. They found a nicely furnished apartment, within easy reach of the campus, and they stayed there for two days before Nathan returned to Cleveland.

"Nathan," Ellen Tobin said to her son a few days later, "I'm reluctant to say this, but Zippora is really a lovely young woman, and your dad and I are so happy that you have each other."

"I'm glad you feel that way," Nathan replied, "but why the reluctance?"

"It's an old Jewish superstition—if your son or daughter becomes attached to someone you like very much, you shouldn't say anything, because that's a sure way to spoil it."

Nathan telephoned Zippora every night, and on weekends, he drove to Ann Arbor to be with her. While in Cleveland, he remained at home most of the time, mostly sitting in front of the television or reading magazines and newspapers. Occasionally, he looked through a collection of medieval Hebrew poems from the Cairo *genizah*, but he never could bring himself to give any significant attention to them. He became ever more dejected.

A short while later, Nathan began an extensive Internet search, using one of the computers at the public library to be sure that his parents were unaware of what he was doing. He discovered that he could easily purchase substantial quantities of diazepam and potassium cyanide from mail order companies. Then, the following day, he drove the nearly twenty miles to Lee's Range and Gun Shop.

"I'd like to find out about buying a pistol," he told the salesman.

"Are you looking for something for target practice?" the man asked.

"Well, no, you see, there've been a lot of break-ins in my neighborhood, and I…I want something for protection."

"Okay, if that's what you need, I recommend a .45 caliber. Take a look at this one—Springfield Armory. Very solid, and it holds fourteen rounds."

"It's awfully big and heavy," Nathan replied, after a cursory examination of the weapon.

"Well then, let me show you their ultra-compact model. You can see how much smaller it is, but it's still a .45. That one runs $775. If you want something smaller still, you might want to look at a revolver. Here's a nice one. It's a Smith & Wesson, a .38, and it comes with a really good laser sight. It goes for $569."

"Are the bullets included?" Nathan asked.

"No," the salesman said, "but I can give you a good price on ammunition."

In the end, Nathan decided that the gun option was impractical. He had already considered hanging, and carbon monoxide poisoning by running the car engine in the garage, but neither seemed sufficiently reliable. So he finally went to a nearby post office and paid the rent for a box with a PO number where small parcels could be sent. Then he placed his orders for the diazepam and the potassium cyanide. While he waited for the shipments to arrive, he began to compose his suicide notes, one for his parents and another for Zippora. He began by drafting the second paragraph, which he planned to include in both of the letters:

"My reputation as a scholar has been destroyed, irreparably and permanently, and it is quite clear that nothing I write or produce will ever be accepted for publication. It is also apparent that I will never be offered an academic position anywhere. So what kind of future can I possibly look forward to? None."

Within ten days, the shipments of the sedative drug and the cyanide had arrived, but by then Nathan had decided to put a temporary hold on his suicide plans. That decision had grown out of an offhand suggestion his mother had made to him after dinner one evening.

"I found out today that Temple Isaiah needs a Hebrew teacher for their sixth-grade class," Ellen Tobin said to him. "It's very part-time, only an hour on Sunday mornings and on Wednesdays after school. It wouldn't require any preparation on your part, and I wonder if maybe you'd enjoy it."

"Oh, for God's sake," Nathan exploded. "I didn't spend seven years in graduate school so I could teach the Hebrew alphabet to a bunch of snot-nosed kids." But after further reflection, he swallowed his pride and agreed to give it a try.

Beginning at four o'clock the following Wednesday, Nathan held his first Hebrew lesson for fifteen eleven- and twelve-year-old adolescents.

"So how did it go?" Ellen asked her son that evening.

"It came very near to being a complete disaster," Nathan replied with a touch of bitterness in his voice. "They're a nice bunch of kids, but they came there after a full day of school, and learning Hebrew was obviously the last thing in the world they wanted to do. None of them took it seriously, and most of them just goofed around. One boy sat in the back of the room with an electronic game, and there was nothing I could do to get him to stop. And if that weren't enough, the textbook they use is awful. I don't think it's going to work out."

"I see the same thing with my classes," Ellen said, "and it seems to get worse with each passing year. Sadly, that's what goes on in most Hebrew schools. Children nowadays are terribly overscheduled. They run from music lessons to soccer practice to rock climbing and who knows what else. Then on top of all that they have Hebrew. And it's a lot less fun than any of the other things they do. Let me make a suggestion. There's a man named Jerry Newman who teaches a class at Temple Isaiah, and they say he's very effective. He developed a unit on the Holocaust, and most of the children apparently pay close attention and take it very seriously. You ought to give him a call."

The following day, Nathan telephoned Mr. Newman.

"When I started teaching these kids, I had the same experience you're describing," he said. "By four o'clock, they've had enough for the day, so unless you can really grab their attention, you don't have a chance. Do you know how I teach the Holocaust? I use comic books. Are you familiar with *Maus* by Art Spiegelman? The Jews are depicted as mice and the Germans are cats. It's really powerful imagery, and the kids find it fascinating."

The following Sunday, Nathan appeared in his classroom carrying a stack of books and magazines.

"We're not going to use the regular textbook anymore," he said. Hearing that, several of the children applauded. "Instead," he continued, "I have a new book called *Og the Terrible*. It's a Hebrew comic book, and I think you'll like it. I've also got some other things we can work on. Have any of you read a book called *Chatul Taalul*? Nobody? Well, then, let me read you part of its English version: 'The sun did not shine. It was too wet to play. So we sat in the house all that cold, cold, wet day.'"

"*The Cat in the Hat*," one boy shouted, after which all of the others joined him in acknowledging their recognition of the well-known children's book.

"Yep," Nathan said, "and I also have some of the other Dr. Seuss books in Hebrew. Here's one," he said holding up a book, "that I think is particularly appropriate for Jews to read. It's called *Lo Ra-ev Velo Ohev*." A girl sitting near the front of the room, recognizing the picture on the book's cover, happily recited its opening line: "'I do not like green eggs and ham.'"

"And starting next week," Nathan continued, "we'll begin rehearsals for a play in Hebrew that we're going to put on for your parents. It's called *Kipah Adumah*, better known as *Red Riding Hood*."

In the weeks that followed, it became clear to Nathan that the children in his class were beginning to enjoy their Hebrew lessons, and most of them participated enthusiastically. This gave him a small measure of satisfaction, and it brought back to him memories of the happiness he had previously gotten from his participation in the reading program at the children's hospital. All of this helped Nathan emerge ever so slightly from the depths of his depression. He began to look forward to his teaching sessions, and he was increasingly impressed by the progress his students were making.

His Hebrew class and his relationship with Zippora served as two fragile threads that kept him tethered, ever so tentatively, to the world of the living. Nathan's mother also began urging him to see a psychotherapist.

"Why bother?" he asked her. "There's no mystery about why I feel so goddamn crappy, so why waste your money?"

But eventually his mother prevailed. The psychiatrist, a kindly, older woman, started him on a potent antidepressant. She also prescribed a second drug to help him sleep. Within two weeks, Nathan felt considerably calmer, and the nightmares that had tormented him each night had diminished. But he also experienced the drugs' side effects. They left him groggy and somnolent, and he was nauseated much of the time. Eating made the nausea worse, and he soon lost weight to the point that his face became gaunt and his clothes hung loosely on his thin frame.

33

Benjamin met with all of us one day to tell us what he had encountered during his recent visit to Antioch.

"I was in that city for five days," he said. "I happened by chance to hear the man called Saul, on two separate occasions when he spoke to groups of people there. The first time, he was addressing a small assemblage of Jews. He spoke to them in Aramaic. 'I am a Jew and well learned in the Law,' Saul said. 'First, let me clarify for you a common misunderstanding about the Torah. Did you believe that the Torah came to us from God? Absolutely not! The Torah, and I can tell you this with the utmost certainty, was given to us by angels, not by God. But the reason I am here today is to bring you wonderful news that will surely transform the lives of Jews everywhere.'

"Then he spoke to them about Isou, whom he referred to as the Son of God. 'From the Lord Isous' death on the cross and his resurrection,' he said, 'we Jews are now forever freed from the burden, indeed the curse, of the Torah. And because Christos has redeemed us, there need no longer be any sacrifice for sin.' But I will tell you, many of the Jews did not receive Saul's words at all gratefully, and one of the men became quite angry.

"'What you are telling us is outrageous,' the man said. 'The Torah is God's great gift to us—it is a blessing, surely not a burden. To refer to the Torah as a curse is blasphemy!' With that, the whole crowd became agitated, and Saul quickly departed.

"Later that week," Benjamin told us, "I again heard him address a much larger group of gentiles. On that occasion, he spoke in Greek, a language I understand quite well. To my surprise, he introduced himself not as Saul, but as Paulos, and he gave no indication of his being a Jew, although in his talk he boasted of having intimate knowledge of the holy writings of the Jews. Again, he spoke at length of Isou and his resurrection, but then what he said surprised me greatly: 'Isous redeemed us in order that the blessing God gave to Abraham might come to us gentiles.' Us gentiles? Is he a Jew or a gentile? I wondered.

"Then," Benjamin continued, "Paulos told us this: 'The Lord Isous Christos, during the last meal he had with his disciples, took bread, and, when he had given thanks, he broke it and said, "Take this and eat: it is my body." In the same manner, he took the cup and said: "This is the new covenant in my blood. Drink it in remembrance of me," and those were Isous' exact words!'"

"Idolatry! Blasphemy! There is no truth to any of that," I interjected. "Many of us were there on that fateful Passover night when Yehoshua was arrested," I said, "and we all know that our master never spoke of any such things, nor would he ever have done so."

But then, Benjamin told us still more. "Saul, or Paulos, then said to the gentiles: 'Isous Christos appeared on earth to redeem us and atone for us. And in establishing his new covenant, he abolished the old. Circumcision and the laws of the Torah, which for so long have tormented the Jews, now no longer hold sway. Our Lord and Savior has taken from us the burden of all our sins. Now, if only we believe in the Son, we will be saved.'

"At the end of his speech," Benjamin said to us, "Paulos told the gentiles of his warm and friendly relationship with Jacob, Simon, and the others of our group. And finally, he took up a collection of money that he told them was to provide support for our movement and our brotherhood in Jerusalem.

"Afterward, I spoke with this man Paulos," Benjamin said. "I asked him about the very different messages he had delivered to the Jews and to the gentiles there. His reply answered a question that had lingered in my mind.

"'To Jews,' he said, 'I become like a Jew, in order to win Jews. So to those under the law, I become as one under the law, even though as a gentile, I am not subject to the law. To those outside of the law, I become like one of them. In truth, I am not outside of God's law, but rather I am under the law of our Lord Isou Christou.'"

"This is all most disturbing," Jacob said, after hearing Benjamin's report. "Saul made a solemn commitment to us about his proselytizing among the gentiles, and it is apparent that he has shown bad faith in all of his promises."

We remained together until late that night, deep in discussion over the distressing news we had received. Finally, Jacob sent a letter to Saul, demanding that he return to Jerusalem to explain his actions. We waited for several months, and finally Saul arrived, in the company of three of his acolytes. Jacob then called us all together to meet with them.

Saul was as self-assured as ever, with a complacent smile radiating from his ample countenance. The men who had come with him appeared to be in a jovial mood.

"The news I have for you," Saul said to us, "far exceeds my most optimistic expectations. The last year has brought many thousands of converts to our movement, and now hundreds more each week are turning to God."

But when none of us responded to his triumphant declaration, Saul's smile turned to a scowl. Then it was Jacob who spoke. "From the reports we have received of your activities among the gentiles, you have not fulfilled the promises you made to us."

Saul gave no reply. Then others of us demanded answers from him.

"Is it true," Simon asked him, "that you were heard to say that on the night when our master Yehoshua was arrested, he said to his disciples, 'Eat my body and drink my blood?' Can this be so?"

"It is indeed," Saul said, "and that is precisely what transpired—it was all made known to me by a revelation from Christou."

"Lies, all lies," Isaac said, his voice choking and with tears in his eyes. "None of that happened as you say."

"Perhaps you were not paying attention to him," Saul retorted, "or else you simply forgot, but those were his very words."

"The very idea is outrageous," Mattai said. "The Law expressly forbids the drinking of blood, and Yehoshua would have been repelled by any such notion."

And I, too, spoke out. "Only pagans would engage in such rituals," I said. "Did you not participate in a ceremony of a very similar kind when you were a votary of the mysteries of Attis?" I asked Saul. "For Jews, to do that would be reprehensible—indeed blasphemous—and Yehoshua surely would have regarded it thusly. Even drinking wine as a symbolic substitute for blood would have been loathsome to him."

Hearing my question, Saul stopped abruptly, apparently surprised that I had remembered the account he had given me, many years earlier, of the time when he was a mystes of that barbaric Greek cult. But he quickly regained his composure, and he continued to cast aside every objection that was raised against him.

Finally, it was Judah, Yehoshua's younger brother, who spoke. "You say that Yehoshua is a god? I know as well as anyone that my brother was a prophet and a most remarkable and holy man, but a man is what he was, with the same fears and weaknesses that all of us have. That God resurrected him was surely a miracle, and although he is our Messiah, our anointed king, he is not a god. Also," Judah continued, "we are told you have been saying that Yehoshua's intention was to start a new religion and also to annul the Torah. So let me tell you this: my brother was always a pious Jew and a committed Pharisee. He regarded the Torah as the holiest of God's gifts to His people, and he surely would have considered abolishing the authority of the Torah to be the very worst form of blasphemy."

But to these and to yet other challenges we raised, Saul remained impassive and unyielding, rejecting each of our denouncements of the bizarre and utterly false drama he had invented. He was unwilling to be influenced by anything we had to say to him.

Saul and the men who accompanied him then took leave of us, but shortly afterward, he faced another confrontation: a group of Greek Jews, who had been visiting the Temple that morning, recognized Saul on the street.

"That is the man we saw in Ephesus," one of them shouted. "He is the one who spoke against our people and against God's Law."

The Jews, all of them incensed, seized Saul and began attacking him furiously. Fortunately for him, a group of Roman soldiers was nearby. They arrested Saul, thereby rescuing him from the angry crowd. We learned later what happened to Saul:

"This man incited a disturbance that resulted in fighting and commotion," one of the soldiers told their commander.

"Take him to the barracks and flog him, "the commander ordered, "then question him to determine why the people were so enraged by him."

But Saul immediately spoke out. "Civis Romanus sum," he said, grandiloquently articulating each Latin word. "And is it legal for you to flog a Roman citizen who has not even been found guilty?" he demanded.

"You claim to be a citizen of Rome?" the commander asked. "Show me the proof of that. Ah," he said, after reading the document Saul presented to him, "I see that you became a Roman citizen the same way I did, by handing over a substantial sum."

How, we later wondered, was Saul able to produce the money needed to buy him Roman citizenship? We finally concluded that the collections he had made from the gentiles, supposedly on behalf of our movement, had supplied him all that he needed.

The Roman commander then rescinded his order that Saul be flogged, but they kept him in custody. The following day, they turned him over to the Jewish court, to stand trial before a tribunal of the Sanhedrin. Three of the Greek Jews from Ephesus were brought there as witnesses.

Two indictments were brought against Saul: "This man has been heard teaching about a Messiah, who he claims is the Son of God. He is also accused of teaching that the laws of the Torah have been nullified."

All three of the witnesses testified to having heard Saul teach exactly as was specified in the first of the indictments. Several members of the court expressed the opinion that this was a serious matter, for which Saul should be punished. But the Pharisees, who were in the majority, rejected that.

"I do not pretend to understand this strange idea about a son of God," one of the Pharisees said, "but there is nothing about it that violates any law."

In the end, Saul was found not guilty of anything related to the first accusation against him. But there was still the second one to be decided, and that was far more serious, as it represented a charge of blasphemy.

One of the witnesses attested to having heard Saul teach that Jews were no longer obliged to follow the commandments of the Torah. But when the other witnesses were questioned, neither of them could state that they had actually heard Saul make such statements. Lacking a second witness to support the allegation against him, the charge had to be dropped, and Saul was therefore set free.

I do not believe that Saul ever returned to Jerusalem, and I have never seen him again. I know that he has continued going from place to place, preaching his new religion to the pagans. I more recently was told that he had gone to live in Rome, no doubt to be among the people whom he held in such high esteem.

I must tell you that in spite of this man's many distortions and deceptions, I am obliged to acknowledge how much he has accomplished, notwithstanding the enormous feeling of sadness it brings to my heart. More than anything else, he has succeeded in realizing his irrepressible ambition to become the powerful and influential leader of his own religious movement. He achieved that by cleverly devising events and ideas that had great appeal to pagan gentiles, skillfully adopting as the foundation of his new creation the tragic crucifixion of our beloved Yehoshua and his resurrection through God's great miracle. Saul—or rather I should say Paulos, which name he seems to be using again—then drew upon his experiences from a Greek mystery cult, including rituals such as eating the meat and drinking the blood of their sacrificed god.

And to gain adherents to his new movement, Saul also portrayed himself as a pious Jew and a Pharisee, although he certainly was neither. Indeed, this was a remarkable claim, in light of his unending hatred of the Pharisees ever since the time they rejected him from their academy. So why, you might wonder, has he pretended to be what he is not? Why was he willing to endure the enmity of so many Jews, including the members of our own movement here in Jerusalem, those of us who were Yehoshua's disciples? And why has he put his life in danger to do these things? I am confident I know the answer to these questions.

Our Jewish religion, and especially our Holy Scriptures, are widely known and greatly respected throughout much of the gentile world. By claiming that his pagan ideas have their basis in the holy writings of the Jews, and then purporting that his new religion is the fulfillment of our sacred Scriptures, Saul has been able to attract many unknowing gentiles to his movement. He has, moreover, promised his adherents a religion that offers them all of the blessings God bestowed upon the Jewish people, but without the duty to fulfill God's commandments. He tells his converts that they need only believe, and from that, everything will be done for them, and moreover, that they will be granted eternal life, even after they die.

In his proselytizing among the gentiles, Saul has claimed that his endeavors were a part of our Jerusalem Nazarene movement. And he collected money among his converts, supposedly for our benefit. But none of that was so, and from the very beginning, he showed only hostility and disdain for us. And, as his animosity for our movement grew over the last many years, he has increasingly fomented hatred and malevolence, not only against the Pharisees, for whom he held longstanding malice, but indeed against all Jews.

Most tragically, so much of what Saul has been saying about Yehoshua belies what our beloved master taught us. And Saul has also rejected the Torah, which Yehoshua always held to be the greatest gift God has given to us.

And, most disturbing to me, after our Yehoshua gave up his life in the great struggle to rid our land of its foreign occupiers and to restore Jerusalem as a holy city, Saul has worked tirelessly to bequeath Yehoshua's movement to the very Romans who were our master's most implacable enemies.

Yehoshua and Johanan before him were surely the greatest prophets of our time. And the lessons both of these revered teachers taught us were very much the same: atone, repent, turn to the path of righteousness, so that you will be worthy when God's kingdom is established in our holy city.

But Yehoshua also brought us much more. It has long been said that Hillel the Babylonian was the greatest Pharisee of them all. But I have now come to believe that even Hillel has been outdone, and I can say that it was surely Yehoshua who was the most praiseworthy of all of the Pharisees. My reasons are these:

Yehoshua taught and interpreted the Torah and the other Holy Scriptures as ably as any, and he deeply believed in the Oral Law and in the resurrection of the dead, as did all of the Pharisee sages. But whereas Hillel and the other great Pharisee masters taught us "Love your neighbor as yourself," it was Yehoshua among all of them who showed us the true meaning of that commandment from the Torah. It was only he who attended to the needs of the poor, the sick, the down of heart, and those who had lost all hope. And with that, he conveyed to us the fullest understanding of how to be truly righteous under the Law.

Now, all of us Nazarenes pray together, each morning and night, that our king and Messiah will soon be returned to us, and we pray for the coming of God's kingdom. We continue to study the Torah and to follow its commandments as Yehoshua taught us to do.

But when I am alone, when I awaken in the night, I am always overcome by the same worries. What concerns me most is that the oppression of our country by the Romans seems to worsen each day. Many of the Jewish people are on the verge of open rebellion, and if that comes to pass, its consequences will inevitably be tragic. How, I ask, could God allow this to happen? And, although I have never spoken a word of it to the others of our brotherhood, I truly am coming to despair of Yehoshua's return in the short time I might still have left in my life. It has been thirty-five years since our master was taken from us, and though he promised he would return soon, he has given no sign that it is about to happen. And because of that, many of the Pharisees who had previously joined our fellowship are beginning to drift away from our movement.

So I send this letter to you, my dear grandson, with sadness and great apprehension, but with my warmest affection.

Your grandfather,
Todah

34

One chilly morning in November, as Nathan sat in the living room of his parents' home perusing the Op-Ed page of the *Cleveland Plain Dealer*, his mother answered a phone call.

"It's for you," she said to her son, "from Italy. Somebody named Enrico Poncelli."

"What the hell does he want?" Nathan growled as he grabbed the telephone. "How did you get the phone number here?" he demanded.

"The people at the Cambridge Library gave it to me," Poncelli replied.

"Has Delvecchio come back?" he asked.

"No, and there still isn't any information about when the monsignor is expected. I was told it could be a very long time."

"So why are you calling me?"

"It's about the Alexandria letter," he answered.

"Haven't you caused me enough trouble already?" Nathan asked acidly.

"Look," Poncelli replied, "I understand why you're angry, but I want you to know that we're honest people. In spite of what you may think, we're not trying to misrepresent anything. Our findings from that manuscript don't agree with yours, so obviously one of us was wrong. We want to straighten this out just as much as you do, and I assure you that we'll cooperate in every way we can to make sure that happens. Let me tell you what Monsignor Delvecchio has always said to us: 'In your work, you should always seek the truth, no matter where it takes you.' He's not here to tell you that himself, but those words guide us in his absence."

"Very inspiring," Nathan said bitterly.

"Look, I'm calling to tell you something important, and—"

"Okay, so tell me," Nathan shot back impatiently.

"First I need to explain," Poncelli said, "that I'm not a very orderly person. My office is always cluttered with piles of paper—they cover the whole top of my desk. It's just the way I am. Anyway, a few days ago, I was searching through a stack of letters, and guess what I found? Evidently when we were gathering up the Alexandria manuscript, to take it back to Cairo, one of the pages inadvertently got buried amongst some other papers. And there it was! I had put it in a Mylar jacket, and it remained there all this time.

"Well, of course I tried to contact Mrs. Kahn in Egypt, to inform her that I would be sending her the page. That was when I learned the awful story of what happened to the poor woman—and that the Alexandria letter had been destroyed. What a terrible tragedy. I had met Mrs. Kahn when I went to Egypt to pick up the manuscript. She was such a kind and gracious woman."

"Did you say that you have one of the original pages from the manuscript?" Nathan shouted into the telephone.

"Yes," he replied, "and since I can't send it back to Mrs. Kahn, I decided it would be best to give it to you. I'm sure that if Monsignor Delvecchio were here, he would do the same thing. I can send you a scan of the page right now so you can see exactly which one it is. And of course I'll also be happy to give you a written statement attesting to its authenticity."

"Why are you willing to do all of that?" Nathan asked him, suspiciously.

"Look, I really want to know if the Alexandria letter is an ancient manuscript or not. If it isn't genuine, then we've all been wasting our time. But if it's real, then we have something extremely valuable. Frankly, I hope that you are the ones who got it right.

"Here's what I'd like to do if it's okay with you," Poncelli continued. "There's an excellent radiocarbon dating laboratory here in Italy, at the University of Lecce. It's in the South, not far from the town of Bari where my parents live. I'm planning to go there the day after tomorrow, to spend the weekend. I could take the document to the lab myself. And don't worry—I promise you I'll take very good care of it."

Nathan, barely able to comprehend what he had been hearing, accepted Poncelli's proposal without protest. Less than an hour later, a scanned image of the page appeared on his computer, and Nathan could immediately recognize the Hebrew overwriting that had obscured so much of the manuscript's original text.

Four weeks later, Enrico Poncelli called again: "I just got the results. It was a very thorough study—they used seven bits of papyrus from the page for the analyses. There was some minor variation, but all of the samples dated from either the first or the early second century! So you were right! That manuscript was a real treasure. Thank God we have the images so that the text has been preserved."

Tears welled up in Nathan's eyes, and he could barely speak.

"That's fabulous news," Nathan finally said. "Look, the editor of the *JBR* told me that if we could confirm our original radiocarbon dating of the manuscript, he would publish another article. If you'd send me a copy of the report from the radiocarbon dating laboratory, and your authentication letter, I'd like to submit something to them as soon as possible. Would that be all right?"

"Of course," Poncelli replied, "I'll do whatever I can to help."

"Would you like to be a coauthor with me?" Nathan asked him.

"Not necessary," he said. "If you want, you could mention my name, but there's no need for anything more. And by the way, congratulations."

Two days later, Nathan received a FedEx envelope from Poncelli, and in less than a week, he completed a brief communication, which he sent off to the editor of the journal along with the supporting documents.

Among the reports that appeared four months later, in the March issue of the *Journal of Biblical Research*, was Nathan's "Confirmation of the First-Century Origin of the Alexandria Letter." The article began with an overview of Nathan's previous publication, then gave a summary of the conflicting paper by Carlo Delvecchio and his collaborators, and finally presented the new radiocarbon dating findings that confirmed Nathan's original observations. At the end, Nathan had added an acknowledgement: "I am deeply grateful to Dr. Enrico Poncelli of the Vatican Library for providing me a page from the Alexandria manuscript. Without his generous help, it would not have been possible to obtain the confirmatory analysis."

Nathan sent a letter, with a reprint of his new report, to the British publisher who previously had expressed interest in producing the complete Alexandria manuscript and its translation as a book. Only weeks later, he received a new contract from them, stipulating the £10,000 advance they had previously promised him.

Most heartening of all, he soon received invitations from two distinguished institutions to present seminars on his work. One was from the Department of Religion of Princeton University, and the other from the History Department at Harvard.

Nathan was freed from his despair and hopelessness, and now it appeared that nothing would stand in the way of a successful academic career. He promptly discontinued the medications the psychiatrist had prescribed for him, and within a week, his somnolence and nausea abated. But Nathan's return to a tranquil emotional state evolved only gradually. The nightmares that tormented him were slow to recede, and he remained withdrawn and introspective for a long while, avoiding most social interaction and preferring to remain by himself much of the time.

In his solitude, he reflected on how his parents and Zippora had been such vital lifelines for him during the terrible months when he had felt he was sinking into a black hole. His musings also took him to the part-time job with his Hebrew class that had helped to sustain his sanity during the worst of his melancholy. And from that brief taste of being a teacher, he came to realize how successful he had been in connecting with his students, and the sense of fulfillment it had given him. So, as much as Nathan was committed to continuing his research, he also realized that teaching would figure importantly in his future academic life.

And those reflections brought him to think about the teaching careers to which both of his parents had also been so deeply committed. Nathan had never considered either his father or his mother to have done anything particularly worthy of admiration; indeed he had tended to denigrate his father's work as being trivial and largely inconsequential. He now began to see how wrong that assessment had been, and how much alike he and his father truly were.

But most of all, Nathan's thoughts returned to Carlo Delvecchio, who had been the cause of the grief he had endured. From every indication, the priest had engineered a heinous crime, involving deception and murder, all to discredit his findings from the Alexandria letter. *Was there some way Delvecchio could be brought to justice?* Nathan wondered. The key element of the whole repugnant plot, the phony letter that Nathan supposedly had sent to Amira from Cambridge, had been destroyed when that dear lady's house had burned, and that evidently had been a major objective of the entire despicable scheme. No, he reluctantly concluded, there seemed to be no way to make Delvecchio pay for the evil he had done.

And what had Enrico Poncelli's role been in all of that? He had been a coauthor of the damning journal article that tried to discredit him and the Alexandria letter, and moreover, he was the courier who picked up and returned the manuscript to Amira. From all of that, he would have believed that Poncelli had been an active coconspirator with Delvecchio. Yet his recent behavior, once he had discovered the page from the manuscript, showed him to be an honorable and very decent person. It appeared more likely, then, that Delvecchio had carried out his murderous scheme while keeping even his closest coworkers in the dark about what he had been doing.

35

In early April, Monsignor Delvecchio returned to the Vatican Library after his lengthy religious retreat. He immediately initiated a series of meetings with the members of his staff, to review the progress of their various projects during the time he was away.

But then, little more than a month later, the monsignor surprised everyone with his announcement that he would again soon be leaving for yet another period of seclusion, prayer, and contemplation. And, as had always been his practice, this would be at an undisclosed location and for an unstated period of time.

A short time later, Delvecchio placed a call to a banker in Naples, using a secure telephone line.

"I'll need euros and dollars, 100,000 of each," he said, "and an American Express business card—for that, use the Antonio Tamroni account. All of the cash can come from the Myron Geller fund—I assume there's still plenty left there. And also get me an Italian passport under "Antonio Tamroni," with my photograph on it. Leave it in the usual drop-off place and get the key and the locker number to me by tomorrow night."

Later that week, well before dawn, the driver of a small black Fiat picked up Monsignor Delvecchio at his apartment in Rome. The monsignor was dressed in dark slacks and a cotton pullover sweater, his outfit conveying no indication of his clerical profession. He carried with him a small bag containing a few personal effects. His destination was the busy central railroad terminal in Naples. Once inside the station, he made his way to a bank of storage lockers. He opened one of them and removed a leather attaché case. Leaving the building by a different exit, he boarded a taxicab that brought him a few kilometers north of the city, to a small harbor. There, a boat was waiting for him, a well-appointed yacht outfitted with powerful engines capable of propelling the vessel at high speed. A four-hour voyage brought him to a port in Sicily, to the east of Palermo, where a driver was waiting to take him the twenty kilometers inland to his final destination, a secluded villa high in the Madonie Mountains, near the Village of Caccamo.

The following morning, the monsignor was informed that a visitor had come.

"The man from Taranto is here. I searched him carefully, and he's ready whenever you want to see him."

"We'll meet outside," Monsignor Delvecchio replied.

The garden of the monsignor's villa was his treasured retreat, a place for contemplation and reflection. Built onto a gently sloping terrace along the side of the mountain, masses of roses, interspersed with tall, white lilies, the monsignor's favorites, dominated his meticulously manicured patch of paradise. His guest was directed to join him there.

"Here's where they live in Bari," Delvecchio said, handing him a slip of paper. "Memorize the address. And this is his photograph—make certain no one else sees it, and be sure to destroy it afterward. He'll be there starting the first weekend next month. Is there any other information you need?" the monsignor asked, as he handed the man a bundle of five-hundred-euro notes.

"Nothing," he replied, "it will all be taken care of."

Three weeks afterward, in the southern Italian city of Bari, an article appeared in the morning newspaper *La Gazzetta del Mezzogiorno*, describing a bloody crime scene:

Un Orribile Delitto

BARI - Lunedi' scorso quando Marco Poncelli non venne ad aprire la sua farmacia, uno dei suoi commessi chiamo' a telefono Casa Poncelli. Quando nessuno rispose, egli chiamo' la polizia. I due agenti che si recarono a Casa Poncelli si trovarono di fronte ad un massacro terrorizzante. Il signor Poncelli, di cinquantotto anni e sua mogli Cecilia, cinquantacinquenne, erano stati uccisi nel loro letto con pallottole in testa. Le due figlie, Gemma di quindici anni, Flora, di dodici ed il figlio venticinquenne Enrico erano stati uccisi in un modo simile. Il signor Poncelli era stato un farmacista in Bari per molti anni. Suo figlio Enrico invece era impiegato come assistente ricercatore alla Biblioteca del Vaticano.

La polizia indaga.

A Horrible Crime

BARI - On Monday, when Marco Poncelli failed to arrive to open his pharmacy, one of his employees called the Poncelli residence. When no one answered the telephone, the man contacted the police. The two officers who came to the family's home discovered a terrible massacre. Mr. Poncelli, 58, and his wife Cecilia, 55, were found in their bed, both of them with bullet wounds to their heads. Their two daughters, Gemma, 15, and Flora, 12, as well as their son Enrico, 25, had also been killed in similar fashion. Mr. Poncelli had been a pharmacist in Bari for many years. His son, Enrico, had been employed as a research assistant at the Vatican Library.

The police are investigating.

Two weeks later, Monsignor Delvecchio received another visitor, a man from Detroit. Their meeting was also held outdoors, as the two of them walked together along the narrow footpath that ran behind the villa, well out of reach of anyone who might overhear their conversation.

"It's a dark green Volvo station wagon, 1997, with Ohio plates," the man reported. "He goes there almost every weekend. He's always careful to lock it, and Volvos can be hard to break into, but he parks it behind the building where it's pretty much out of sight. There won't be any problem. Here's the license number and the address. The place is about a half mile away from the highway," he said, as he handed the monsignor a slip of paper.

"A Volvo," Delvecchio said. "That's just the information I need."

"What would you like us to do now?" the man asked him.

"Nothing more," Monsignor Delvecchio replied, before sending him off with a substantial payment for his services, all in one-hundred-dollar bills.

The monsignor's plan was to utilize the services of a man from New York, who in the past had proven himself highly effective in such assignments. The car at first would function normally, but once it had accelerated to highway speed, its brakes and the steering mechanism would fail, leaving the driver helpless to restrain or control it.

"Sergio," Delvecchio said to his trusted aide, "I want you to fly to New York on Tuesday morning next week. When you arrive there, call the telephone number that's written here—memorize it before you leave; I want nothing to be in writing. Ask for Guido, and arrange to meet him in a public place where you won't be overheard. Then tell him I'll be there the following day. I'll meet him at ten thirty in the morning, near the entrance of the Metropolitan Museum of Art, on Fifth Avenue, so I can give him his instructions. I will be carrying a maroon umbrella and a copy of *Newsweek* magazine. Tell him to bring a bouquet of yellow carnations so that I'll recognize him."

36

L ate on a steamy July afternoon, Nathan made the familiar drive from Cleveland to Ann Arbor. Arriving at his destination, he backed his mother's station wagon into a parking space behind Zippora's apartment building, grabbed the flowers he had brought, and bounded up the stairs to Zippora's apartment.

"Roses!" she said. "Mmm, how lovely."

Nathan kissed her and held her for a long while.

"I got some wonderful news today," Zippora said as she uncorked a bottle to pour Nathan a glass of his favorite sherry. "The grant I applied for—it's going to be funded. It's not a huge amount of money, but enough to hire a research assistant and to pay for some travel, and that's all I really need to get the project going. I'm really excited."

"That's terrific," Nathan replied. "Congratulations! I've also got some news. I found out about it three days ago, but I wanted to wait until I saw you to tell you. Evidently the people at Harvard liked the seminar I presented last month. They've offered me an assistant professorship in their Department of Near Eastern Languages and Civilizations. I'll be starting in September."

"Oh, Nathan, hooray," Zippora said. She wrapped her arms around his neck and kissed him. "Well deserved! I'm so happy for you."

"I only wish Boston were a lot closer to Ann Arbor," Nathan said. "I suppose we'll just have to put up with more commuting. One day we'll manage to be working in the same city—that is, if you're willing to go on with me like this."

"Well, no, actually, going on like this is not at all what I had in mind," Zippora replied, "and I think it's time for us to have a serious discussion about just that."

"Have you started seeing somebody else?" he asked her apprehensively. "I could hardly blame you if you were. I put you through a really miserable year, and you deserve better than that." Zippora could see that Nathan had tears in his eyes.

"No, there's nobody else. But there is something you need to be aware of," she said. "Do you recall the time my mother came to visit me, when we were in Cambridge? About two years ago?"

"Of course I do," he replied. "We spent a lovely evening together, and I really enjoyed meeting your mother."

"Um, yes," she said. "Well, then, you just might be interested to know something I told my mum during that visit. So listen carefully. I told her that you, Nathan Tobin, Ph.D., were the man I had picked out to be my husband. And can you guess what she said? 'An excellent choice. I approve.' Maybe you wondered why I took a job in the U.S. rather than going back to Israel? Well, I'll tell you—it was to keep an eye on you and make sure that you didn't get lured away by some other woman. So you see," she said, a smile brightening her face, "our future together has been pretty well settled for quite a long while, even though you didn't exactly know about it. So, now that you're going to be a gainfully employed professor, it seems to me it's about time for you to give up the life of a carefree bachelor. And you wouldn't want to disappoint my mother, would you?"

"I suppose we wouldn't want to disappoint my mother either," he said, holding Zippora close to him. "She seems to have the same idea."

"I'm glad we settled that so easily," she said, and she kissed him tenderly. "Oh," she added, "there's one more thing—and it's very important. Before we can even think about making wedding plans, you will need to get my father's approval. And for that, you'll have to go to Jerusalem."

"Do you think he would have any objection?"

"Well," she said, "it would help if you had a long beard and were very religious, but Mother will make sure that doesn't stand in the way. When we go there, I suggest that you bring a black hat, a black suit, *tzitzit*, and *tefillin*."

"*Tzitzit? Tefillin?*" he asked.

"You'll need to plan on doing a lot of praying with my father while you're there, and so you should come well prepared."

"That's a lot to ask," he teased.

"Maybe," she replied, "but think of what you'll be getting—me!"

Zippora and Nathan spent a joyful weekend together, welcoming the happy life that they confidently anticipated. Saturday morning, they strolled, hand in hand, through Ann Arbor's massive summer art fair. Then they shared a hot corned beef sandwich at Zingerman's Delicatessen, and in the afternoon they visited the conservatory and the nature trails of the botanical garden. That evening, they enjoyed a romantic, candlelight dinner. On Sunday, they slept very late, and after croissants and coffee, they spent the remainder of the morning reading the *New York Times*, stretched out on a bench at a nearby park. In the evening, after a quick dinner of take-out Chinese food at Zippora's apartment, Nathan prepared to return to Cleveland.

But as soon as he started the car's engine, a warning light on the dashboard caught his attention. It was one he had never noticed before: "Check Engine." He pulled the owner's manual out of the glove compartment, to find out what that warning meant. The manual advised him to drive the car as little possible before taking it in to be serviced, but it provided no other information. Nathan also began to wonder if the engine sounded quite right, but he decided that the low-pitched rumble he heard was only an indication that the muffler needed to be replaced. He realized that no repair shop would be open on a Sunday night, and since he knew that his mother needed the car the following morning, he felt he had no other choice but to drive on to Cleveland. But he resolved to keep within the speed limit. He stopped at a gas station near the entrance to the highway, and then, with a full tank, he set off on his 160-mile journey.

Although the "Check Engine" light remained on, Nathan's thoughts turned to recollections of the delightful weekend he had spent with Zippora, and then to their future together. Within minutes, he had accelerated to seventy-five miles per hour.

37

Monsignor Delvecchio spent most of the morning poring over his cherished collection of ancient Roman coins, and afterward he needed to hurry to complete the preparations for his trip. Later, just as his car arrived within sight of the airport, he reached into his pocket and realized that something was missing. He quickly telephoned his valet.

"It's a small silver coin, in a round plastic case—I may have dropped it somewhere. Please see if you can find it."

Moments later, his question was answered: "It's right here on the bureau in your bedroom. Do you want me to bring it to you?"

"Ah, I'm so relieved to know that you found it. No, just keep it in a safe place until I return."

The monsignor's chartered jet departed from the Catania-Fontanarossa Airport shortly before noon. Its flight plan took it on a broad arc to the north of Paris and then over southern Ireland on its way to New York.

The following morning, promptly at ten thirty, Guido Rossi appeared at the designated meeting place, bearing a bundle of bright yellow carnations. He repeatedly traversed the sidewalk at the base of the Metropolitan Museum's broad stairway, searching for a tall, older man carrying a maroon umbrella and a *Newsweek* magazine. But after a full hour without success, Guido returned home, anticipating that he would soon be receiving new instructions by telephone.

On Thursday that week, a brief notice appeared in the New York newspapers: A private charter flight from Catania, Sicily, bound for the Westchester County Airport, had failed to arrive at its destination. The aircraft had last made contact with the London air traffic control, and no problem had been reported. In addition to its two-man crew, only a single passenger was listed, a Mr. Antonio Tamroni, a businessman from Naples.

The Gulfstream jet, flying at an altitude of 38,000 feet, had traversed a placid ocean under a cloudless sky. As it reached a point nearly midway across the Atlantic, the captain switched on the plane's autopilot system and then engaged his second officer in a lively discussion about the upcoming elections in Sicily. Neither of them saw the streak of light flashing through the sky, and even if they had, there would have been too little time for them to have made any change in the aircraft's course. The twenty-three kilogram meteor, nearly the size of a basketball and fiery red from its rapid entry through the stratosphere, grazed the left side of the plane, producing a gaping tear in its fuselage. Only seconds later, the weakened left wing, together with its engine, ripped completely away, sending the jet spiraling uncontrollably downward. Then, as seawater displaced the air in its cabin, the aircraft began a gradual descent, eventually coming to rest on the ocean floor.

As with each of the missions Carlo Delvecchio had organized, this one had been planned with extraordinary care, giving meticulous attention to each detail and leaving nothing to chance. But as usual, in order to maintain total secrecy, the monsignor had not shared his intentions with anyone, nor had he left any paper trail. Consequently, his plan was never put into effect, and his intended victim remained entirely unaware and unharmed.

PRIMARY RESOURCES

Angus, Samuel. *The Mystery Religions and Christianity.* New Hyde Park, NY: University Books, 1966.

Charlesworth, James H. and Johns, Loren L., eds. *Hillel and Jesus; Comparisons of Two Major Religious Leaders.* Minneapolis: Fortress Press, 1997.

Crossan, John Dominic. *The Historical Jesus; The Life of a Mediterranean Peasant.* San Francisco: Harper, 1992.

Dukes, L. *Moses ben Esra aus Granada. Altona, Hamburg,* 1839.

Eisenman, Robert. *James the Brother of Jesus: The Key to Unlocking the Secrets of Early Christianity and the Dead Sea Scrolls.* New York: Viking Penguin, 1997.

Falk, Harvey. *Jesus the Pharisee: A New Look at the Jewishness of Jesus.* Eugene, Oregon: Wipf and Stock, 2003.

Funk, Robert W. et al. *The Parables of Jesus.* Sonoma, California: Polebridge Press, 1988.

Ginzberg, Louis. *Legends of the Jews.* Philadelphia: The Jewish Publication Society, 2003.

Holy Bible, New International Version. Grand Rapids, Michigan, Zondervan Publishing House, 1994.

Klausner, Joseph. *The Messianic Idea in Israel*. New York: Macmillan, 1955.

Maccoby, Hyam. *Revolution in Judaea; Jesus and the Jewish Resistance*. New York: Taplinger Publishing Co., 1980.

———. *Paul and Hellenism*. London: SCM Press, 1991.

———. *Judas Iscariot and the Myth of Jewish Evil*. New York: The Free Press, 1992.

———. *The Mythmaker; Paul and the Invention of Christianity*. New York: Barnes & Noble Books, 1998.

———. *Jesus the Pharisee*. London: SCM Press, 2003.

Meyer, Marvin W., ed. *The Ancient Mysteries; A Sourcebook of Sacred Texts*. Philadelphia: University of Pennsylvania Press, 1987.

Sanders, E. P. *Jesus and Judaism*. Philadelphia: Fortress Press, 1985.

———. *The Historical Figure of Jesus*. London: Penguin Books, 1993.

———. *Judaism; Practice & Belief, 63 BCE-66 CE*. London: SCM Press, 1998.

Tanakh. Philadelphia: The Jewish Publication Society, 1999.

Taylor, Joan E. *The Immerser: John the Baptist within Second Temple Judaism*. Grand Rapids, Michigan: William B. Eerdmans Publishing Co., 1997.

Williams, Paul L. *The Vatican Exposed. Money, Murder, and the Mafia*. Amherst, NY: Promethius Books, 2003.

"The Garden in Springtime" was freely adapted from verses by the twelfth-century Spanish poet Moses ibn Ezra.

ACKNOWLEDGMENTS

I am very grateful to those who read, critiqued, and edited my manuscript at various points in its development: Margaret Schmidt; Kent Carroll; Rabbi Elliot Gertel; Shirley Holbrook and the members of her Rodfei Zedek reading group; the team at Synergy Books; and especially my wife, Olga Weiss.

I received valuable help and counsel on Scripture and Talmud from Rabbi Gertel and Sinclair Kossoff.

Dan Sharon, Reference Librarian extraordinaire of the Spertus Institute of Jewish Studies, provided *Midrash* and myriad other source materials and spent untold hours searching out information for me.

I owe a special debt of gratitude to Dr. Robert Licht for introducing me to the writings of the incomparable exegete Hyam Maccoby.

I thank Dr. Rebecca Jefferson of the Taylor-Schechter Genizah Research Unit of the Cambridge University Library for providing the Dunash poem and related information.

I am grateful to Dr. Tony Scommegna for sharing his expertise as an Italian news editor.

Meira Faratci provided invaluable support with Hebrew and Aramaic translation.

A special word of thanks to the members of my Chicago writers group for their advice, repartee, and good fellowship.

And finally, to our children, our grandchildren, the many other members of our family, and all of the wonderful friends whose interest, enthusiasm, and encouragement sustained me in bringing this project to its completion.

Terracotta thymiaterion (incense burner) depicting the mystery god Attis; from the 1st-2nd centuries BCE, discovered in Tarsus, the birthplace of St. Paul.